We at Jove Books are thrilled by the enthusiastic critical acclaim that the Homespun Romances are receiving. We would like to thank you, the readers and fans of this wonderful series, for making it the success that it is. It is our pleasure to bring you the highest quality of romance writing in these breathtaking tales of love and family in the heartland of America.

And now, sit back and enjoy this delightful new Homespun Romance . . .

TENNESSEE WALTZ
by Trana Mae Simmons

Jove Titles by Trana Mae Simmons

TOWN SOCIAL
TENNESSEE WALTZ

Tennessee Waltz

Trana Mae Simmons

JOVE BOOKS, NEW YORK

TENNESSEE WALTZ

A Jove Book / published by arrangement with
the author

PRINTING HISTORY
Jove edition / June 1997

The Putnam Berkley World Wide Web site address is
http://www.berkley.com

ISBN: 0-515-12135-5

A JOVE BOOK®
Jove Books are published by The Berkley Publishing Group,
200 Madison Avenue, New York, New York 10016.
JOVE and the "J" design are trademarks
belonging to Jove Publications, Inc.

PRINTED IN THE UNITED STATES OF AMERICA

10 9 8 7 6 5 4 3 2 1

As with every book,
to my own hero, Barney.
Thanks for always being there
for me for all these years.
And happy thirtieth, babe!

To my sons:
Joe, with his lovely wife, Tammy,
who have given me
two wonderful grandchildren,
Brandon and Ransom.
And Kelly,
who will find a heroine someday
who takes over his heart
like Sarah does Wyn's.

I love all of you!

Prologue

"*S*HHHH! LISTEN, STEPHEN. Did you hear that?" Sarah pulled her escort to a halt and tilted her head. They'd lingered inside the opera house chatting with friends until they were among the stragglers leaving, and without the crowd noise, she clearly heard the sound when it came again.

"It's just a stray cat," Stephen said. "Come on. It's cold."

"It's not a cat," Sarah said. "It's a kitten. Look! Oh, the poor thing."

Dropping Stephen's arm, she hurried to the side of the building, where a tiny gray-and-white head peeped out from beneath a bush. Disregarding the damage that would result, she pulled her cape forward and knelt on the edge of it. The kitten meowed plaintively, then scuttled back under the bush when she reached for it.

"Sarah," Stephen called imperiously. "That thing will bite you, or at the very least scratch your hands right through your gloves. Forget it and come on!"

Peering through the dimness, Sarah ignored him. The

light from the opera house shone through the windows above the bush, penetrating through the dense branches, bare of leaves. She bent forward, her gloved hands landing in a slushy pile of snow.

"Here, kitty," she called. "Come here, you poor thing."

From the back of the bush, the kitten meowed again. There was something else back there, too, and Sarah gasped when what she'd at first taken for a bundle of rags moved. Oh, God, it looked like a small child lying there.

"Stephen! Come here!"

When he didn't appear immediately, she glanced over her shoulder to see him talking to another man and paying not the slightest bit of attention to her. He did that a lot, she recalled, assuming she would obey his commands without question. His carriage rolled to a stop behind him, the clops of the horses' hooves and sound of the wheels on the cobblestone street drowning out her words when she called to him again. Chewing on her lip, she debated barely five seconds. Then she dove beneath the bush, struggling through the dense branches toward the prone figure beyond the kitten.

She touched the figure and realized she had been right— a live child lay inside those rags. Or at least the child was alive right now, since it moved in response to her touch and moaned pitifully. Sarah took a second to brush some matted hair from the child's forehead, making a guess that it was female by the delicate features she uncovered. She quickly ran her hands over the slight body, checking for any noticeable injuries. Protruding ribs and a hollow stomach spoke of malnourishment, but she didn't seem to have any broken bones. She shivered uncontrollably, then opened her eyes slightly.

"Mama?" she asked on more of a sigh than an actual utterance.

"No, darling," Sarah murmured in reply. "But I'll take care of you."

"S . . . so hungry," the child slurred. She dropped into unconsciousness again, and a lump choked Sarah's throat.

Grasping the tiny shoulders, she crawled backward, tugging the little girl along while the kitten followed. Free of the bushes, she gathered the child into her arms, rose, and studied the bedraggled figure in the better light.

The child's eyes in the dirt-encrusted face remained closed, and it was impossible to determine the color of the matted curls covering her head. Sarah couldn't repress a shudder as she imagined what filth she also held in her arms. On top of that, the smell almost made her gag.

"What in God's name are you doing, Sarah?" Stephen said from behind her. "The carriage is waiting."

"Stephen!" Ignoring the smell and dirt, she gathered the child closer, wrapping her cape around it. "This little girl was under the bushes. She can't be more than five or six, and she's unconscious and shivering horribly. We need to get her to a hospital!"

Stephen glared down his nose at Sarah and her burden, his face wrinkling into a sneer. Hurriedly, he pulled a handkerchief from his breast pocket and held it to his nose. "Not in my carriage, you won't. Take that . . . that foul thing inside and leave it with the opera house staff. Have them call the authorities."

The child stirred in her arms and the kitten meowed at her feet, then rubbed against her ankle. Sarah stared at Stephen in horror. She'd known he was self-centered, but she evidently hadn't realized the depth of his callousness.

"You're more worried about your carriage than a child on the verge of death?" she asked, grasping the child even tighter. "Then call a livery carriage. I'll take care of this myself!"

"Don't be silly, Sarah—"

"I'm not being silly! I'm being human and concerned for another human being—a child, at that!" She pushed past him and went to the curb, where a doorman from the opera house directed carriage traffic picking up the few remaining gowned and jeweled opera attendees.

"I need a conveyance," she ordered the doorman. She knew Stephen well enough to realize he was standing there fuming at her defiance and probably humiliated if any of his friends happened to be watching. Her disregard of his dictate surprised even her, but she had a more pressing worry at the moment. The child groaned again, and a hacking cough erupted from her chest.

"Please call one of the rental hacks," she commanded the doorman when he hesitated and glanced behind her, presumably at Stephen.

"Ma'am?" he questioned. "But you arrived in—"

"Did you hear me?" she spat. "Get me a conveyance! Now!"

The doorman turned away and reached for the whistle hanging around his neck just as Stephen's hand fell on her arm. "Get in my carriage," he said through gritted teeth. "I'll not have the gossip tomorrow being that I left you here and you had to get home on your own."

"I don't understand you at all, Stephen," she said, shaking her head. "I personally could care less that New York City society thought I had more compassion for a child than I did for their gossiping ways!" Turning from him, she hurried over to his carriage and climbed in without waiting for his footman's assistance. When Stephen started to enter, she blocked the doorway.

"Don't forget the kitten," she said.

"What? Now listen here, Sarah. I only agreed to take that child in here! I'm not—"

"Either get the kitten or I'll get back out," she said in exasperation. "It might belong to this little girl."

He glared at her for a long moment, his jaw tightening. Finally he huffed in frustration and backed from the carriage door. A moment later, as she settled on the cushioned seat, he climbed in with the kitten in his hand. Shoving it at her, he sat down opposite her.

"I told my driver, Hans, to go to the hospital. Is that what you want?"

"No," she said. "Tell him to go directly to my house. I think that will be better. We might be at the hospital for hours before anyone could look at this child, and I can send for Dr. Jones from home."

The light from a streetlamp shone on him as he tightened his lips, but Stephen shifted over to the side window and raised it. Sticking his head out, he delivered the revised destination to his driver and leaned back.

"This isn't the way I expected the evening to end," he said, petulance plain in his tone of voice. "We've only been engaged two days and here we are fighting."

Sarah cuddled the tiny child closer to her breasts. The kitten clawed its way up her arm and onto her shoulder, sniffing at the child and mewling in a low tone. Sarah let the tiny animal stay, although her scalp tightened at the thought of fleas. The kitten's ragged fur was far from clean, its weight barely discernible, testifying to its undernourished state also.

The bundle of bones and dirty cloth in her arms stirred again, and she mentally urged Hans to hurry. The child's breath feathered in and out, fostering a slight hope, although her breathing had a slight rasp to it. She hadn't coughed again, which Sarah took to be a good sign.

"We'll talk about this later, Stephen," she said. "Right now I'm more concerned about this child's health than I am your hurt feelings."

Though she had tried to conceal her disgust at his selfish actions, Stephen evidently comprehended her displeasure. He immediately changed his tactics.

"Of course," he said soothingly. "It's just that I'm terribly disappointed at our evening being interrupted this way, darling. As soon as you turn that child over to your servants, we'll talk. I really do want us to discuss setting our wedding date."

The carriage wheel bounced over a rut, and Sarah gripped the child tighter. The change in Stephen's attitude made her recall the conversation she'd overheard during the break in the opera performance earlier that evening. A petulant blonde had evidently just been informed of her betrothal to Stephen, and the haughty sniff from the other side of the large plant had drawn Sarah's attention.

"I suppose Sarah has a large enough dowry to satisfy Stephen VanderDyke," the blond woman Sarah had recognized as the newest belle of the season, Petula Hardesty, had said with a smirk. "I'll admit, I wouldn't have minded

having Stephen in my bed for a while, but I wouldn't fancy
knowing that a year or so down the road he would have
probably run through my entire dowry. Even Stephen will
be hard put to make a dent in the Channing fortune, though.
And we all know that every bit of that money will soon be
at Sarah's disposal, when her father dies. From what I hear
of the old man's health, that could be very soon."

Distracted, instead of listening to the performance during
the entire second half of the opera, Sarah had pondered what
she'd heard. She'd known all along that Stephen only
wanted her for her money, but then, her father had warned
her ever since she was old enough to understand the spoken
word that she would have to buy herself a husband. Her
father hadn't even bothered to hide his own lack of
sympathy for Sarah's plainness or his jealousy of his friends
who had more comely daughters.

The reality of her father's words had sunk in even deeper
when she watched her friends being courted and getting
married, without even one of the men Sarah found herself
attracted to showing an interest in her. Instead, she always
sensed a tolerance of her homeliness beneath the veneer of
the men who did come calling—and a deep concern as to
her future financial state. If she overlooked that, her father
made sure he passed their not-so-subtle inquiries on to her.

She'd managed to sidestep the few proposals she did
receive, even getting her father's cooperation in that. It
seemed he was in no hurry to pay out the large dowry it
would take to secure her a husband. But by the time she had
reached the almost unmarriageable age of twenty-five, her
desire for her own home and children had been soul-
wrenching. Wouldn't everyone in New York City society be
surprised if they knew she had only pretended to be
infatuated with Stephen, having finally decided to secure
herself a husband?

Why did her heart ache so horribly, then, at the thought
that society was well aware the Channing fortune had been
Stephen's aim all along? The child stirred in her arms,
moaning softly and reminding her of why she had to have a
husband. A husband was necessary to have children. She

yearned for children of her own—children who would give
her the love she had been denied all her life.

When she had decided to look seriously for a husband,
handsomeness had been the top priority in her list of
characteristics. Stephen definitely fit that requirement. She
never wanted to bring children into the world who were
plain and nondescript like herself. Stephen's seed would,
she hoped, dominate, and the children he fathered would be
beautiful and loved by all. They'd never spend their
childhoods being hidden away, or worse, having their
plainness excused over and over again by their parents.

Perhaps if her mother had lived, things would have been
different, but Sarah didn't even have a slight memory of her.
Her mother had died in childbirth, as her father always
reminded her when he deigned to talk about the beautiful
woman in the portrait beside his, which hung in the
mansion's art gallery.

Stephen's carriage stopped in front of Channing Place,
and Sarah barely restrained herself until her fiancé alit first.
He turned to assist her, withdrawing his arm with a look of
aversion on his face when she tried to pass the child to him.
Awkwardly, Sarah climbed down unassisted, sweeping by
Stephen and up the walkway. She heard him mutter a
halfhearted apology, which she disregarded as the insincere
statement she knew it was.

Not waiting for her butler, she pushed the door open,
calling for her housekeeper. The kitten raced past her,
skidding on the marble floor until it regained its balance.
The heartrending meow it emitted corresponded with Sarah's
concern for the pitiful child.

1

*A*TTUNED TO THE chill still lingering in the late morning air, Wyn MacIntyre pushed his pa's wheelchair onto the porch along the storefront. Stopping the chair by the split-log railing, he draped an afghan over the older man's lap. As expected, Dan MacIntyre gave a resigned sigh.

"You know what Dr. MacKenzie said, Pa," Wyn said. "You've got poor circulation in your—"

"—Legs, since I can't move them," Dan finished in an irritated voice. "I know, son. But blast it all, it still makes me feel like a dodderin' old woman to sit out here with that colored piece of wool over my lap."

"I know, Pa," Wyn sympathized. "But look at it this way. If you come down ailing, it'll be one more burden on poor Sissy. Proud as she is about taking care of her family, that sister of mine would sooner hoist up her skirts and dance a jig all the way down the middle of the trail to Razor Gully than let anyone else take care of you. And with her fixing to present you with your second grandchild any day, we don't need to be adding to her work."

Wyn adjusted the afghan his mother had made as he went on, "I know how much you like looking at the mountains, and it's rare that we have a spell as warm as this in March. So you enjoy the chance to get outside, Pa, but be sensible about it, all right?"

"I suppose I'm of an age where I *have* to be sensible," Dan muttered in a resentful rather than sensible voice. "Look, you leave the rest of that bookwork alone today, so I'll have somethin' to do tomorrow. That accident didn't hurt my brain none, just my legs."

Nodding agreeably, Wyn gazed out over the panorama before him for a moment, wishing he could sit down for a while and enjoy the view he loved every bit as much as his pa. His mother, dead now for over two years, had taught all her children to appreciate her beloved mountains. She always moved any chores she could do out there to the front porch, in order to savor the vista around their store. They had spent many evenings with her on the porch, helping her shell peas or husk corn for supper.

The MacIntyre General Store sat in a high mountain valley a ways up the side of Sawback Mountain. The settlement had been named for the mountain, assuming a town would grow up around it.

Instead, when the railroad had finally reached into the mountains it missed Sawback Mountain by ten miles. Razor Gully got the railroad and the resulting growth.

Wyn admitted Razor Gully had some pretty scenery, but it couldn't compare to Sawback Mountain. As far as he could see, mountain peaks stretched into the distance, covered by a smoky blue tinge that gave the Great Smoky Mountains their name. This time of year snow covered the mountainsides, deeper on the high peaks. Most of it this far down on the mountain had melted to slush in the unusual warmth of the past couple days, although the ground remained frozen beneath it.

Across the dirt road and down a ways, Widow Tuttle's boardinghouse still survived as part of the original settlement of Sawback Mountain, although it had needed a coat of paint for years. Somehow they'd also managed to keep the schoolhouse opposite the boardinghouse operating and hold church services in the same building whenever Reverend Jackson managed to get to them on a Sunday. However, he had a sneaking suspicion that Prudence Elliot, the current school-teacher, wouldn't agree to return next year, even though the men had built her a small cabin of her own so she wouldn't have to board with the various families scattered hither and yon throughout the beautiful mountains. With no children of her own, Widow Tuttle saw no need to offer free board to a schoolteacher. They could have squeezed Miss Elliot into their living quarters over the store, but Wyn doubted very much this teacher would accept that.

Wyn had to concede that the MacIntyre children were part of Miss Elliot's discontent. Not his other two sisters, of course. The holy terror twins, six-year-old Luke and Jute, were a large part of the reason the teacher probably wouldn't return. He sighed in annoyance at the thought of having to undertake the job of once more assisting his pa in trying to entice a capable teacher to Sawback Mountain.

"Son," he heard his pa say, "someone's coming up the trail. It ain't mail day, neither, and we ain't due no supplies this week."

Not that he didn't believe his father, but Wyn had to resist rubbing his eyes when he saw the wagon himself. It sure enough was Jeeter's wagon, pulled by the wizened freight-er's mules. Jeeter only had two hitched up rather than the usual team of six it took to carry a wagonload of supplies up the mountainside to the MacIntyre General Store. The simple reason was that the mules only had the wagon to pull with the small load of the two passengers sitting beside Jeeter.

Wrapped in a light gray cape and wearing a stylish bonnet completely covering her hair, the woman on one side of the seat sat tall and straight. Between her and Jeeter sat a small child. As the wagon drew closer, he saw the child had a remarkable resemblance to his youngest sister, Pris.

"Mairi," Dan said in a tortured voice. "Wyn, something's happened to my brother Cal and your aunt Selene. That's your cousin on the wagon—their daughter, Mairi."

A dim roaring filled Wyn's ears and his chest froze, making it impossible to draw a breath. Uncle Cal and Aunt Selene. The seer and healer, Leery, had been right when she visited the store last summer. He'd urged Leery to keep her dire prediction of the death angel visiting the MacIntyre family again from the rest of the family, but he had believed Leery. He'd never known her to be wrong.

How would his father bear it? Cal had been Dan's favorite brother—and his last living one.

"Go help Jeeter set 'em down," Dan ordered, and Wyn shook himself back to reality.

After a quick glance at his pa's white, strained face, Wyn descended the porch steps as the wagon pulled to a stop. There was no avoiding the coming pain. It would have to be borne, and no one could blame the plain woman on the wagon seat, who obviously brought the message. He read her concern for the devastating news she carried in her deep, brown eyes.

"Cousin Wyn!" Mairi scrambled across Jeeter's legs and flung herself at Wyn. He caught her, and she wrapped her arms around his neck and buried her face on his shoulder. "Cousin Wyn," she said around a sob. "Ma and Papa—! Miss Sarah says they's in heaven. But I miss 'em so much!"

Blinking back his own tears, Wyn laid his cheek against Mairi's soft, blond curls. "It's all right, sweetheart," he murmured. "We'll take care of you now. You'll have a home with us, just like you were your uncle Dan's own little girl."

Glancing up, he met the compassionate eyes of the woman. Mairi had called her Sarah. He'd already noticed her plainness, except for her unusual eyes, and it was apparent from her smooth, well-cared-for skin and expensive garments that she came from a monied background. His primary thought right then, however, was to thank her for caring for Mairi and bringing the child home.

"Would you like to get down, ma'am?" he asked. "We can offer you some hot tea or coffee."

When she smiled, it made a person forget all about her plainness. The smile came from her entire face—the velvet brown eyes to her firm but rather large lips.

"I would thoroughly enjoy some tea." She waited for
Jeeter to scramble down, then placed her hand in his when
he offered to assist her. Gathering her skirts, she stepped
from the wagon with a grace born of quality. Wyn had never
once seen one of his three sisters manage to dismount a
wagon without either a wobble or a flash of ankle. The
woman called Sarah did it as though it were nothing
unusual—which it apparently wasn't for her, although
probably her descents were usually from a fancy carriage.

Shifting Mairi so he could reach out his hand, he said,
"I'm Wyn MacIntyre, Mairi's cousin."

"Sarah Channing," she replied, grasping his hand lightly,
then smoothly disengaging the grip. "I found Mairi in New
York City. She was very ill, but she's regained her health
now—at least, her physical health."

Wyn nodded, immediately understanding Sarah's infer-
ence that Mairi was still coping with the pain of her parents'
deaths. Mairi had been an only child, though his aunt
Selene, like plenty of other mountain women, had lost
several unborn babies. His uncle Cal had taken Selene and
Mairi to New York City a year and a half ago, giving up his
poor farm on the mountainside in disgust. His uncle had had
such high hopes.

"What happened to my aunt and uncle?" Wyn asked in a
low voice, trying to get an emotional handle on things in
order to help his pa better bear his grief.

"I believe it was typhoid—" Sarah began, but Dan called
from the porch.

"Bring 'em up here, son. Holdin' off ain't gonna make
whatever it is I have to hear any easier."

Wyn noticed Sarah straighten her shoulders and realized
his pa's words had made the woman gird herself even more.
Compassion for her stabbed him, as well as admiration for
her bravery. He instinctively reached out and laid a comforting hand on her shoulder, but she hastily stumbled back
from his touch, not meeting his eyes or even acknowledging
her reaction. Recalling the way she had dropped his hand as
soon as politely possible when he welcomed her, he decided

she was a person unused to physical contact with other
human beings.

Too bad, because there were times when another pair of
arms made the burden of some of life's unforeseen adver-
sities somewhat easier to bear. Mairi hadn't loosened her
hold on him for even a second.

Restraining his urge to take her arm courteously, Wyn
nodded at the porch, and said, "My pa. His brother was
Mairi's pa." He moved back a step, and Sarah lifted her
skirts, walking up the steps to meet Dan. Carrying Mairi, he
followed.

Dan held out a hand. "Dan MacIntyre. I heard you
introduce yourself to my son, Miss Channing." Wyn noticed
that Miss Channing allowed his pa only the same brief
handhold of greeting. "Excuse me for not risin'," Dan
continued. "As you can see, I'm confined. Please have a seat
yourself, unless you'd rather step inside."

"This is fine," Sarah said. She sat down in a cane-back
rocker next to Dan, clasping her hands firmly in her lap,
spine rigid. The chair didn't even dare to rock, Wyn
observed.

"I'm very sorry to have to bring you this news, Mr.
MacIntyre," she said to Dan. "Mairi's mother and father are
indeed . . . gone. From what I understand, they caught
typhoid in the last epidemic in the part of the city where the
immigrants are crowded together. I checked the records at
the orphanage Mairi came from. I also took her to their
graves before we left, and ordered a monument put up."

Tears streamed down Dan's face. "That's right nice of
you, Miss Channing. You just let make know how much that
there marker was, and we'll pay for it."

Sarah waved a hand negligently. "That's absolutely not
necessary, Mr. MacIntyre."

Dan stiffened, but Sarah appeared not to notice that she
had smacked his pride down. She seemed extremely ill at
ease with the emotionalism of this situation, but Wyn sensed
she would carry through with it. Otherwise she could have
easily delivered Mairi to someone in Razor Gully and
returned to her safe haven in New York.

Dan wasn't about to allow his pride to stay trampled. "You don't seem to understand, Miss Channing. It *is* necessary. *I* will pay for the markers on my brother and sister-in-law's graves."

Sarah studied him for a moment, then nodded. Just then Jeeter called from beside the wagon, "Miz Channer there said she was a-wantin' to stay for a day 'er so, Dan, so's we brought her bag with us. An' we got that there cat in its cage. You want I should set 'em down, too?"

"He has mistaken my name ever since I hired him yesterday," Sarah said with a tolerant smile. "And I very much *would* like to put off having to say good-bye to Mairi just yet. Jeeter said there was a boardinghouse here."

"Widow Tuttle's," Wyn explained, pointing to the house she had passed on her way to the store. "You'll have no problem getting a room with her this time of year." Raising his voice, he told Jeeter to take the bags over to the boardinghouse, and inform Widow Tuttle that Miss Channing would be along shortly.

"I'm a-gonna head on back soon's I do that," Jeeter called in return. "It's warm as a baby's bottom right now, but I feels a storm a-comin'. We's a-gonna have snow up to the porch rails by mornin'."

The freighter climbed back on the wagon, but Sarah leaped to her feet before he drove off.

"Oh! Leave Gray Boy!" she cried to Jeeter. "Mairi will want him near."

Before Wyn could ask her who Gray Boy was, Sarah hurried down the steps. He started to ask Mairi, then realized she was asleep on his shoulder, her breath soft against his neck. Murmuring to his pa that he would be right back, he carried Mairi into the store and deposited her on the bed in Dan's room off the back of the storeroom.

They'd built the bedroom for Dan almost two years ago, when it became apparent he would never walk again. Dan had insisted he didn't want Wyn struggling up and down the steps to their living quarters over the store with him in the wheelchair.

He met Sarah just outside the bedroom door. "Your father

told me where you'd probably taken Mairi," Sarah said in her cultured voice. "I brought Gray Boy to her. The kitten and she are inseparable, and Gray Boy will be the first thing she looks for when she wakes. He stayed with her through her entire recovery, and in fact, the kitten led me to Mairi."

Wyn took the basket from her and returned to the room. When he set the basket beside Mairi and unlatched it, a beautiful, half-grown gray-and-white kitten scampered out. It blinked at him and meowed once before it strolled over and curled up on the pillow beside Mairi's head. He turned back to Sarah, halting when he saw the look on her face.

She stared at Mairi with so much love Wyn could feel it crowding the room. His defenses came up immediately. If this woman thought she could offer a home to Mairi because his aunt and uncle had died, she'd soon find out different. Mountain people cared for their own. All the money she could offer them would never buy Mairi.

Sarah started, glancing at Wyn, her expression changing in a heartbeat when she saw his face. He tried to smooth the glower he knew was there away, but he could see the fright in her eyes.

"Please," Sarah whispered, amazing him when she continued and he realized she was practically reading his mind. "It's not what you think. I *have* fallen in love with Mairi, but the sole reason I wish to stay here for a day or so is to have just a little more time with her. I know she belongs with her family. I could have kept her in New York and never even notified you I had her, if I'd wanted to keep her for myself."

"I suppose," Wyn admitted. "But when we didn't hear from my aunt and uncle, one of us would have eventually gone to see what had happened. And we'd have checked the orphanages for Mairi."

"She'd run away," Sarah said. "I found her near death. I . . . look, can we go back out on the porch, so I can tell your father the story at the same time? There's no sense having to repeat it."

Wyn gestured for her to precede him, following her back through the store, past the shelves of goods and barrels of different items. This time of year the shelves were rather

barren, since the winter snows made it impossible at times
for Jeeter to deliver their orders. They anticipated that in the
fall, stocking up prior to winter. And they already had orders
mailed off to restock next month, when they could expect a
clear enough trail after spring broke for Jeeter to make it
through with a large load.

A new scent niggled at his nose, and he realized he'd been
smelling it ever since she arrived. It intermingled with the
smells of pickles and salt pork, leather and dried apples, but
he picked it out anyway. He guessed she probably used
some lotion to make her skin so soft, and the light, floral
scent suited her. Few of the mountain women used a scent,
but those who did pretty much stuck with what they made
from dried rose petals. This was different, almost like a
mixture of flowers.

Back on the porch, Sarah walked steadily over to Dan and
took her seat in the rocker again. His pa had recovered
somewhat, although his cheeks were still wet and his eyes
red rimmed. Wyn supposed his own grief would fill him and
overflow soon, but he had to control himself right now.
Mairi needed him, as did his pa.

Sissy would return any minute from cleaning the schoolteacher's house, and in a couple hours, the other children
would be out of school. They would all have to be told of
the new deaths in the family and Mairi's presence explained.
With Sissy's husband, Robert, off looking for a job in the
West Virginia mines, Wyn would have to make sure Sissy
didn't upset herself and harm her unborn babe.

For a second, his responsibilities weighed on him, but he
knew plenty of mountain men his own age—twenty-two—
who had responsibilities just as heavy. He forced his attention
to Sarah when she finally spoke.

"I found Mairi beneath some bushes as I was leaving the
opera one night almost two months ago," Sarah said. "The
kitten led me to her—or perhaps an angel guided the kitten
to me so I'd find her. She was cold, sick, and starving, and
I took her home with me. It was two weeks before she was
well enough to talk, since we almost lost her a couple of
times. At first I'd thought she was only around five or six,

because she was so tiny. But when she could talk, she told me that she was eight. After that, she told me all about her family here in Sawback Mountain, but she was very reluctant to tell me about the orphanage. It was only after she began to trust me, and knew I wouldn't send her back to that home, that she gave me the rest of the information."

Sarah shifted in her chair, gripping her hands in her lap once again. "That orphanage will take proper care of the children it houses in the future," she said in a grim voice. "It has new management, and my attorney has orders to make regular reports to me."

For a moment she remained quiet, sadly shaking her head as though in remembrance. Then she took hold of herself. "I verified that Cal and Selene MacIntyre, Mairi's parents, were indeed deceased. I even talked to the doctor who signed the death certificates and learned they'd both been casualties of the typhoid epidemic last fall. I asked Mairi what she wanted to do, and she was adamant about returning here.

"I'll admit," she said, staring into Dan's face in a straightforward manner, "I offered to let her stay with me, although I did tell her I'd inform you of what had happened. When she objected, I never tried to talk her out of it; I agreed to bring her here. We would have come sooner, but my father died three weeks ago. As soon as I was able, we got packed. We left four days ago."

Wyn and Dan both murmured condolences to Sarah on her father's loss, which she accepted with a calm look. Then, tears gathering again in his eyes, Wyn walked over to the porch railing and stared across the cove. The mists and clouds on the mountain peaks were already darker, and he had no doubt Jeeter's prediction of snow would prove true. He'd never known the freighter to be wrong.

His uncle Cal had loved these mountains, as had his aunt Selene. It had broken both their hearts to leave, but their hardscrabble piece of land had quit producing even the bare necessities. Cal had been unyielding in his determination never to get involved in the moonshining other mountain men did to make a living. Cal wouldn't even drink the corn liquor the stills hidden deep in the mountains produced.

The mists covering the mountain peaks blurred in Wyn's vision, and he wiped his eyes with the back of his hand. He couldn't afford to let go right now. The chill was deepening, and he should get his pa inside.

As he turned, Sarah rose to her feet. "I'll go on to the boardinghouse," she said quietly. "May I come back later this afternoon to see Mairi again?"

"We'd be proud if you'd come to supper," Dan spoke up. "You can meet the rest of my family then. We'll all be wantin' to thank you for takin' care of our Mairi. We eat at six, but you come on over early. You can visit with Mairi afore supper."

"Thank you," Sarah said in a heartfelt voice. "May I please make one other request of you, Mr. MacIntyre?"

"Wishin' you'd call me Dan," he said. "And yeah, you can ask. I can't promise I'll say yes, but you can ask."

"Thank you," Sarah repeated. "And I'm Sarah. What I want to ask is this. I didn't ask Jeeter to leave Mairi's bag, because . . . well, because I realized after what you said about the grave markers that I might be overstepping again. But I did buy her a new wardrobe and she picked out presents for each of her cousins. I paid for them, but I really wish you'd let Mairi give them to her cousins. She put a lot of thought into the choices she made."

"I'll send Wyn over to Mandy Tuttle's to get the bag after a while," Dan conceded, and Sarah released a sigh Wyn took to be relief.

"Thank you, Dan," Sarah said once again.

She nodded at Wyn, then picked up her skirts and descended the steps in that royal walk she had. He thought about offering to escort her to the boardinghouse, but it was only a few hundred yards away. The mountain women walked miles each day. But then, Sarah Channing was a far cry from a mountain woman.

"You know," Dan mused, "I think I sorta like her."

"You're just grateful to her for taking care of Mairi," Wyn

replied. "You haven't known her long enough to make a decision about whether or not you like her."

"Nope, I do believe you're wrong this time, son. She's right, you know. She could've just kept Mairi for her own. Mebbe even used all that there money she 'pears to have to fight us when we tried to get her back. Lots of women would've figgered Mairi was better off in a rich household than livin' here in the mountains. Lots of women would've looked down their noses at the thought of even comin' here to Sawback Mountain. That there Sarah just asked our little Mairi what she wanted to do, then packed her bags and came on soon as she could. Yep, I do like her."

"Well, you can bet your bottom dollar she'll be ready to get out of here in a couple days," Wyn sneered.

"You know, son, you can't judge all city women by the one you got tied up with. I mean—"

"I don't want to talk about Rose, Pa. I've told you that before. Now, you want to come on in? It's starting to cool off."

"Think I'd rather you just bring my jacket out here for me," Dan replied. "I'd sorta like to sit here and remember Cal for a while." He nodded toward the small cabin behind the schoolhouse on their right. "There comes Sissy. You mind a-tellin' her, Wyn? I promise I'll help you tell the rest of 'em when they get in from school. I oughtta be up to repeatin' the story by then."

"I'll do that, Pa." He patted Dan on his shoulder, then stepped inside the store and grabbed his pa's jacket from a peg. After handing the jacket to Dan, he went to meet Sissy, who had her two-year-old, Bobbie, toddling after her. Despite her advanced pregnancy, Sissy carried a bucket with her cleaning supplies in it, and Wyn reached to take it from her as soon as they met.

A moment later, Sissy sobbed in his arms, and Wyn glanced over at Widow Tuttle's. Sarah stood on the porch watching him, and somehow he could sense her concerned gaze. Telling himself he was only remembering her unusual, expressive eyes, he lifted a courteous hand to her, then led Sissy toward the store.

His pa could like her all he wanted, and he admitted that he really didn't *dislike* the woman. She was as different from the mountain women as night from day, though. She stood out like a Christmas tree in July in these surroundings, where he was used to women with tired eyes and weary shoulders.

He'd always enjoyed snowstorms in the mountains. For one thing, they gave him an opportunity to relax and catch up on his reading, when he could keep his brothers and sisters out of his hair. But right now he wished this coming storm was over with, since it would keep Sarah Channing from leaving for possibly a week. He didn't exactly understand why he felt threatened by her, especially since there were qualities about her that he admired. He'd just keep his distance until he saw that straight back and perfectly styled hair riding down the mountains in Jeeter's wagon.

Too, he couldn't forget the hunger in Sarah's eyes when she gazed at Mairi. Despite her assurance that she only wanted to delay her good-bye to Mairi for a day or two, he would cautiously keep an eye on her. He knew pretty much what Sarah could offer Mairi, and he could only hope that the child's deeply instilled mountain pride would mean more to her than the material things Sarah could give her.

His pa had a huge dose of mountain pride himself, and a loyalty to family unsurpassed by any other man Wyn knew. His pa would wrap Mairi in his love and loyalty, and it would wound his spirit mightily if his niece turned her back on her family and opted for the life of a rich girl.

2

$\mathcal{S}$ARAH IMMEDIATELY LIKED Widow Tuttle, who said to call her Mandy. Round, chubby, and talkative, Mandy made no bones about being extremely happy to have Sarah's company. Within a very few minutes, she had Sarah settled in a large, airy room with a cherrywood bed and armoire, and beautiful handwoven rag rugs on the polished pine floor. Over cups of tea, she avidly listened to Sarah's story of finding Mairi and filled Sarah in on the MacIntyre family history. However, Sarah noticed Mandy avoided explaining how Dan had ended up in the wheelchair. She would have followed up with the history of every mountain family in the area if Sarah hadn't suggested they leave some points of conversation for future teatimes, since she intended to stay for a few days.

"Good thing that's your intention anyway," Mandy responded. "Jeeter said there's a storm on the way, so there won't be any travel in or out of here for a few days."

"Jeeter told the same thing to the MacIntyres. Is Jeeter always right about his weather predictions?"

"Never known him to be wrong," Mandy said. "They say the male children don't usually inherit the power, but Leery never had any girl children, so maybe some of her sight got passed on to Jeeter. Jeeter's her son, you know."

"Well, no, I didn't know," Sarah reminded Mandy. "Um . . . who is Leery?"

"Leery?" Mandy frowned briefly, appearing to concentrate on her words. "Well, Leery's a lot of things," she said at last. "She's a healer, and she was all we had before Doc MacKenzie came around. She's still the only midwife most mountain women will have, though Leery seems to know when she needs to bring the doc in with her for a bad case. Like maybe the babe's gonna have the cord wrapped around its neck or start out breech and be hard to turn or something. She's got the sight, just like her mother and grandmother and great-grandmother had before her. Leery can't call it up at will, but when she has a vision, she passes it on to whoever needs to know."

"I don't much believe in stuff like predicting the future," Sarah admitted. "But I do know that a lot of the remedies that have come down through time do work. I had a nanny once who gave me sage tea with lemon for a sore throat, and mullein tea for a cough and stuffy nose. Of course, my father would have had an apoplectic fit if he'd known about that."

"Some believe, some don't," Mandy said with a tolerant shrug. "Oh, sounds like someone's knocking."

Curious, Sarah followed Mandy. They found Wyn at the door.

"Come in," Mandy offered.

"No, I'll only be a minute." He turned to Sarah. "Mairi woke. And she would rather wait until you come over to pass out her presents to her cousins. Thought I'd better let you know, so you didn't think I'd forgotten about picking them up. I'll come over at five and carry them for you."

His tone was polite, but for some reason Sarah bristled just a tad. He hadn't asked her if five would be agreeable to her but had only told her of a decision already made.

"Pa said for you to come on over, too, Mandy," Wyn continued. "And he'd plan on you bringing the cornbread, if you'd leave the onions out this time."

"Very well," Mandy agreed. "Need I bring enough for Prudence?"

"I imagine. She finds out we got a visitor, she'll probably invite herself to supper instead of cooking on her own."

He started to leave, but Mandy touched his arm. "Have you made any plans for the wake?" she asked in a quiet voice.

Sarah watched the pain fill Wyn's deep blue, expressive eyes—the same pain she'd noticed when he approached the wagon even before he had known the sad message she brought. As tall as she was, Sarah only had to tilt her head back a little to see his gaze. His broad shoulders slumped inside the worn though neatly patched tan workshirt he wore.

"I guess soon as we can get word out after this storm is over," he said, his voice roughened. He swiped at a blond curl of hair that had fallen across his forehead. "Say, a couple days after the storm."

Mandy nodded, and Wyn bobbed his head briefly at both of them, then turned and left. His rangy stride ate up the distance between the boardinghouse and general store, covering the area in a third of the time it had taken Sarah to walk over there. She'd barely had time to become chilled before he turned for one last glance at them and then entered the store.

"He looks so much like Dan at that age," Mandy murmured. "Maria would have been very proud of him."

When Sarah glanced quizzically at her, Mandy motioned her back inside and closed the door. "Maria was my best friend," Mandy explained as they walked back to the kitchen. "Dan's wife. She and Dan were coming back from Razor Gully with a load of supplies for the store. They used to go themselves when the supplies arrived, rather than paying Jeeter to deliver them."

Mandy chuckled tolerantly. "Sometimes I teased Maria about using the trips to get away from that brood of children she and Dan had. She always winked, but she never once let on to her children that she needed a little time away from them."

Motioning Sarah to a chair, Mandy began gathering up cornbread makings as she spoke. "Something spooked Dan's horses. Jeeter always uses mules on his freight wagon, because he says they don't spook as easy as horses, but Dan's never owned a mule that I know of. Anyway, Dan heard a mountain cat howl a few minutes earlier, and he thinks it might have crept up on the wagon. He didn't see it, but the horses smelled it."

"The wagon must have wrecked," Sarah said, her heart filling with sympathy.

"Yes. Maria . . . Maria was killed—her neck broken. Dan hurt his back and hasn't walked since the accident two years ago. Wyn came home to take care of everyone."

Not wanting Mandy to think she was inappropriately interested in the handsome man across the way, Sarah changed the subject. "I do appreciate being asked over to the MacIntyres' for dinner. . . ."

"Supper," Mandy corrected. "I know you call the evening meal 'dinner' back where you come from, but here we call it 'supper.' "

"Uh . . . supper, then. What I was getting at, though, was that this is one of the strangest invitations I've ever heard, especially when Mr. MacIntyre actually told you what to bring with you."

Mandy laughed gaily. "Oh, I already knew what Dan would want me to bring. He just mentioned leaving out the onions—even though that's the way he likes my cornbread—because Sissy gets an upset stomach, her being with child and all. And you'll find out, if you stay around long enough, mountain men don't *ask* womenfolk. They tell them what's expected and presume that's the way it will be. And in the mountains, sometimes there's a reason for it."

Sarah thinned her lips in displeasure, thinking it was just as well she wouldn't be staying around very long. For twenty-five years she had kowtowed to men—first her father and then her fiancé. She'd had a taste of defiance in her relationship with Stephen the past couple months, due entirely to her deep affection for Mairi and her desire to see the little girl safe and cared for again. Surprising her,

Stephen had backed down in his insistence that she turn Mairi over to the authorities and get on with their wedding plans. Even knowing that Stephen didn't want to take a chance on losing her money if she broke their engagement didn't lessen her enjoyment of having the upper hand with him.

To pacify him, she had at least set their wedding date for the coming June. Then her father had passed away, and the restraints and chains had dropped from her like fall leaves as she discussed her future with her father's attorney. Despite her deep, abiding desire for children, she wasn't in one bit of a hurry to marry Stephen and return to the constraint of having a man in control of her life again.

Wyn MacIntyre's attitude of assuming that Mandy would follow his and his father's dictates without question chafed her. And, to be truthful, she had another, larger problem with Wyn, which bothered her even more. She'd felt those same feelings around him as when she would become infatuated with one of the more handsome, eligible men during the season in New York City. Her wallflower status left her yearning for just one man to become truly sappy over her. But it had never happened.

Mandy's voice broke into her thoughts. "Would you hand me the sugar, please?"

According to Mandy's parlor clock, Wyn arrived on the dot of five. Sarah glanced at the clock the moment she heard a knock, then set aside the embroidery she'd brought with her to while away the time on the train. She debated for a few seconds whether or not to keep him waiting, but decided Mandy would come after her if she tried that. By the time she got to the front door, he already had the satchel containing Mairi's things on his shoulder. Still, he managed to help her into her cloak after assisting Mandy into hers. As soon as Mandy retrieved the black iron kettle of cornbread from the small table in the entranceway, he motioned them out the door.

Already the sun had dropped behind the mountaintops, and a sliver of moon shone, though faded in the lingering twilight. Here and there stars winked into sight, their light visible, then not, as the clouds scuttled across the sky. A few snowflakes wafted lazily to earth on feathery flights while the three of them walked toward the store.

"No wind yet tonight," Mandy observed. "At least we'll probably get back home before it starts drifting."

"I'll make sure you get home all right, Mandy," Wyn promised.

He ushered them up the steps and held the door for them. Mandy led the way through the store, with Sarah glancing overhead at the sounds pounding down on them. Wyn didn't appear to notice, since he followed them through the dim interior with surefooted steps, carrying the satchel on his shoulder.

Mandy paused at a stairwell in the rear of the store, turning slightly toward Wyn.

"Go on up," Wyn said without her even having to speak. "I took Pa up an hour ago."

Nodding, Mandy picked up her skirts and climbed the stairs. Sarah and then Wyn followed her up. The noise grew louder with every step. On a wide landing at the top of the stairwell, Mandy reached for the doorknob, then murmured to Sarah before she turned it, "Better prepare yourself."

She opened the door to pandemonium. A huge, sprawling room lay on the other side of the door. Two red-haired whirlwinds immediately caught sight of them and headed toward them at full speed, small legs churning and whoops of welcoming joy rising above the clatter of their booted footsteps. Somewhere another child began to cry, probably scared witless at the increased clamor.

A woman who looked on the verge of giving birth smiled at them from the stove, then pulled the spoon out of a large pot she was stirring and laid it aside. Placing a fist in the small of her back, she wobbled toward the crying little boy, who was curled up in a child-size rocking chair by a huge stone fireplace. Sarah gasped in disbelief when the woman actually bent down and picked up the child to cuddle him close, but at least the child's shrieks quieted somewhat.

A blond girl in her teens sat on a stool in one corner of the room, strumming some sort of instrument that looked like a small, flat harp. The song she was playing had a minor melody, and her out-of-tune voice singing the words loud enough so at least *she* could hear them didn't help one bit.

On the other side of the fireplace, Dan sat in his wheelchair, talking to a girl who seemed to be about Mairi's age. Mairi sat on his lap, and Gray Boy curled under the wheelchair. Dan and the girls appeared oblivious to the noise around them, as did Wyn when he dropped the satchel and grabbed the two redheaded terrors by the backs of their shirts to prevent them from crawling up Mandy's skirts. Pulling them off Mandy, he held them at arm's length, their legs windmilling as they shouted their displeasure.

"Mr. MacIntyre!" another voice demanded, and Sarah swept around in a whirl of cloak and skirts to see yet another woman approaching, this one about her own age. The dangerous glint in the woman's eyes foreboded more bedlam in an already overburdened atmosphere.

Wyn dropped the twins, who took their revenge on him by each tackling one of his muscular thighs, and the woman's strident voice matched the whine of her spoken words.

"Mr. MacIntyre," she said. "I warned you the last time." She stopped in front of Wyn, and the twins ducked behind his legs, still pummeling him and chanting gibes at each other. The woman propped one fist on her hip, then raised her other hand and shook a finger at Wyn.

"I've told your father, but he thinks I'm just making threats again," she said. "However, this time I mean it. I am *not* crying wolf! When the mail wagon comes up the mountain again, I'm going back down with it!"

"What happened this time, Miss Elliot?" Wyn asked, making a sudden swipe for the twins. The mirror images obviously had anticipated just such a move, and they danced out of range, giggling wildly at Wyn's miss.

"What happened? What happened!?" Miss Elliot's voice rose higher with each word. "Besides Polly Cravet having her pigtail dipped into an inkwell and getting black ink smeared all over the brand-new dress her mother had made her? Then there was the tack that Billy Peters sat on."

Wyn started to say something, but she held up her hand in warning. "I'm not done. I sat them in the corner both times, with the dunce caps on their heads. I'll also have you know that this is the first school I've taught where I've needed *two* dunce caps! Plus, I have always thought that a teacher who couldn't control her class without physical punishment wasn't much of a teacher. However, your two hooligan brothers have just about changed my mind."

Sarah glanced down at the two hooligans, surprised to see them not a bit frightened or embarrassed that their teacher was tattling on their disobedience. Indeed, they appeared to be validating the teacher's complaints with their continued out-of-control behavior.

"Anyway," Miss Elliot continued, "the next thing I knew, there was a *snake* crawling around the room. Now, I am educated enough to know that snakes hibernate in the winter, so this had to be a pet snake. I assume you know without me having to put it into words where this snake came from, don't you, Mr. MacIntyre?"

"Swishy," Wyn said. "I suppose it had to be him. Where is he now?"

"He better be in Luke's lunch pail," Miss Elliot said in a huff.

One of the redheads raced off to the side of the room and returned, carrying a covered tin pail. The other twin whooped and danced around him as his brother started to open the pail.

"Oh, my." Sarah spoke very quietly, a mock shiver in her voice. It may have been the softness contrasting with the bedlam in the room. A wave of silence swept across the atmosphere, and she bent down near the twin holding the tin pail with the lid hanging half off. "I do not care for snakes," she said. "I'd prefer that you not open that pail if there is indeed a snake in it, whether or not it has the cute name of Swishy."

"Yes, ma'am," the little boy whispered, dropping the lid

back into place and giving her a wink. His mirror image beside him gazed at Sarah in open-mouthed awe.

"Now," Sarah continued. "I assume you are Luke, since it's your lunch pail that contains Swishy." When he glanced up at her briefly and nodded, she pursed her lips and turned her gaze to the other child. Placing a fingertip beneath his chin, she closed his mouth. "And you are?" she asked.

"Jute. Uh . . . ma'am," he hurriedly added before she could frown at his lack of manners. "And I'd be honored to take you round and tell you everybody else's name, if you figure you'd like me to do that."

"I would," Sarah confirmed. "But first I wonder if both you and your brother could remove those boots in the house. They're extremely noisy, and it's warm enough in here for you not to need them, don't you think?"

"Yes, ma'am," they echoed each other. Plopping down, they started unlacing their footwear. Luke's elbow hit the lunch pail he'd dropped beside him when he sat, and it clattered across the floor, the lid flying loose. His eyes widened in horror when a small green snake slithered free, and he threw the teacher a terrified look.

"I'll . . . I'll get him, ma'am," he said. But he had one boot half off and couldn't seem to decide whether to jerk it free or pull it back on. The snake raised its head a tad and swiveled it around, then dropped back to the floor and started crawling.

Gray Boy flew out from under Dan's wheelchair, back arched and hissing as loud as a den full of snakes. The schoolteacher let out a scream, and Sarah heard Wyn stifle a chuckle beside her. She glanced sideways at him, a haughtiness stealing over her when she saw his grin of delight. He didn't make a move toward the snake and cat.

"You know," she mused in a voice she considered barely loud enough for him to hear, "I do believe the MacIntyre men are all cut from the same mold."

Giving a sniff, she walked across the floor. Swishy, evidently used to people, paused and turned his head to look at her. After swiping Gray Boy aside, Sarah reached out and placed her index finger and thumb on each side of the snake's head. Lifting him to dangle in the air, she raised her eyebrows at Luke.

Jute scrambled to his feet first. Swiping up the tin pail, he raced over to Sarah and held it out. She gratefully realized he had removed the boots and his steps were almost silent in his stocking feet. Delicately, she held Swishy over the pail and laid him inside.

"The lid," she reminded Jute, who stared wildly around until he saw it lying behind Luke. A second later, Swishy was safely penned up.

"Now," Sarah said, dusting her hands together. "Please introduce me around, Jute."

Taking her hand, Jute said. "Yes, ma'am, I will. But you ain't tol' me yet just who you be."

"Forgive me. I'm Sarah Channing. I'm the lady who brought your cousin Mairi back to Sawback Mountain."

"Gee!" Jute's eyes widened in awe. "Then you must be one of the nicest ladies on earth. We's mighty glad to have Mairi home."

"I'm very glad that you are glad, Jute. Now, the introductions?"

Jute gripped her hand tightly as he led her over to the teenaged girl in the corner. "This is my sister Carrie," he said. "She's purty nice, but she's more interested in finding someone to hitch up with right now, since she's been fourteen for nigh unto six months."

Carrie nodded and smiled shyly at Sarah.

"Carrie," Sarah responded, wondering what "hitch up" meant. She couldn't imagine this slender girl pulling a buggy or a plow. "I'll bet you could really help your sister cook, given her advanced state of being with child. Couldn't you? I would think playing the whatever-it-is you have there would be something we would all enjoy after we eat."

Surprise filled Carrie's eyes, but she stood up at once. "This is a dulcimer," she said, indicating the instrument in her hand. "And I guess I really oughtta be helping Sissy."

She hurried across the room, and Sarah heard a faint grunt behind her. Slipping a look, she saw that Wyn had followed and thought perhaps she saw a measure of respect on his face. Jute pulled on her hand again, however, and led her over to Dan.

"Guess you already knows my pa and Mairi," Jute said, and Sarah acknowledged that with a nod. "This here's my other sister, Pris. She's eight, and her and Mairi is both of the same age."

"Pris," Sarah said. "And hello again, Mairi. You know, I'll bet Pris would like you to show her how we set the table at my house, Mairi. Whatever's cooking over there smells almost ready, and I don't see a plate or piece of silverware on the table."

"Yes, ma'am," Mairi said with a wide grin. She slid from Dan's lap, then threw her arms around Sarah's waist. After a brief hug, she took Pris's hand and the two girls crossed the room.

Dan slowly bobbed his head up and down. "Nice work, Sarah," he said.

"Thank you, Dan."

Jute took her over to the stove next, and Wyn's footsteps continued to follow. She even caught a hint of some masculine odor that she realized had been tugging at her senses for quite a while. It smelled like the cold air from outside had followed them in here, tinged with a hint of bayberry. Then she told herself it had to be the candles burning around the room, adding to the lantern light.

"This here's Sissy," Jute said, breaking into her thoughts.

Sissy turned, with the little boy on her hip. Sarah cast a worried glance at Carrie, and the teenager reached out quickly to relieve Sissy of the little boy. Sissy's brows went up in astonishment, then she smiled widely at Sarah.

"Pleased to meet you, Miss Channing," she said. She glanced at Carrie holding her son. "Very, very pleased to meet you. My son's name is Bobbie."

"And she's gonna have another one," Jute said in an awestruck voice. He tentatively reached out a grubby finger and touched Sissy's extended stomach. At a movement beneath her apron, he jerked his hand back, then clapped both hands together. "Ain't that just sumpthin'?"

"It most surely is, Jute," Sarah told him with a sincere

smile, although the heat of a blush covered her cheeks at the child's candor. When Sissy reached for her hand to lay it across her stomach, Sarah resisted, but only for a second. She'd never been this close to such an imminent birth, and she honestly admitted a desire to feel the babe move. All of her friends disappeared from the social scene as soon as their rounded stomachs couldn't be hidden by the folds of whatever fashion carried the season. The next time she saw them, they usually had their figures back.

Sissy held Sarah's hand flat against her rounded stomach, and Sarah felt a ripple of movement. Then something struck against her palm, and Sarah gasped. Her eyes flew to Sissy's, and the serenity in the other woman's eyes curled all the way down to Sarah's own stomach. Her stomach, or perhaps it was that place a little lower, felt very empty.

She heard that little chuckle beside her again, and Sarah's face heated anew. Wyn reached around her and laid his large, work-roughened hand on Sissy's mounded stomach, right beside hers. For a long, tender instant, Sarah gazed at the three hands lying on the mound sheltering what would one day be a living, breathing baby, then a child, then an adult. But try as she might, she couldn't fight off the embarrassment. Jerking her hand free, she stepped back.

"Um . . . when . . . when is your confinement?" she asked Sissy.

"Confinement?" Sissy asked. "Oh, you mean when am I due to birth this one? Well, it was last week, but as you can see, no one told the babe about that."

For some reason, Sarah's mouth went dry. She had absolutely no tie to this birth. Why should she be worried about being in the vicinity of an overdue babe?

"And I sort of think I've got maybe another week yet," Sissy went on. "Think we might have miscalculated. Babes usually calm down when they're gettin' ready to get born, and this one's still keeping me up nights. Robert should be back by the time the storm's over, so I'm hopin' the birthin' waits for him."

"Robert?" Sarah asked.

"My husband. He went up to West Virginie a couple

weeks ago, 'cause he heard the mines was a-hiring. I ain't heard back from him, and he'd have sent me a letter if he got the job. But since I haven't got a letter, I figure he's on his way back."

While she had heard and understood everything Sissy said, Sarah continued staring at Sissy's stomach. Wyn's large hand still lay there, and his index finger stroked back and forth. Sissy tolerated the touch without a trace of embarrassment.

"Hey!" Wyn said. "Bet that's his head."

"Her!" Sissy said in a mock stern voice, as though this were a continuing argument. "Leery promised me it was a girl this time."

"Well, if Leery says girl, it's probably a girl," Wyn responded. He finally removed his hand and took Sarah's arm. "Lute didn't introduce you to Miss Elliot."

"Do you think I could remove my cloak first?" Sarah asked.

Wyn dropped her arm rather quickly, and as she started to turn around for him to assist her, her gaze caught on his, and she noticed a puzzled look in the blue eyes. He lowered his eyes to his palm, then to her arm.

"Did a burr or something on my cloak stick your palm?" she questioned, vocalizing the only conclusion that came to mind from his action.

Wyn stared back into her face, slowly shaking his head. "No, nothing like that," he said quietly.

He was so close his breath fanned across her cheek, raising a cascade of goose bumps, which skittered down her shoulder. She'd been this close—even closer—to Stephen without her body reacting in this way. Jerking her gaze free, she unclasped the button on her cloak. From the corner of her eye, she saw Wyn take hold of the cloak using only his forefinger and thumb. Still, the back of one hand brushed her chin, and he pulled the cloak free in a rush.

Deciding she could introduce herself to the schoolteacher, Sarah strode across the room while Wyn hung up the cloak.

3

*L*EAVING *M*ANDY *AND* Miss Elliot in the corner of the room, where they were leafing through the Montgomery Ward catalog, Wyn carried a chair from the table over beside Dan. Settling into it, he crossed his arms and frowned at the unusual atmosphere in the room. "Ordered chaos" came to mind, followed quickly by a remembrance of his mother.

His mother had somehow kept order and managed to get the multitude of chores that filled each day accomplished without yelling or becoming perturbed at the high spirits of her children. Since his return, Wyn now realized, the loving discipline had been missing, with the children becoming more and more out of control. He and his pa had evidently assumed Sissy would manage her brothers and sisters, forgetting Sissy had her own family to worry about. He supposed he really couldn't blame Prudence Elliot for resigning.

Neither the schoolteacher nor his sister had ever managed the rowdy twins as easily as Sarah. Part of that probably came from Sarah's handling Swishy the snake so well. Her dislike of the snake was plain, but she had shown no sign of fear. If she had, Luke and Jute would have used the snake to tease her unmercifully.

Dan took his pipe from his shirt pocket, then called, "Sarah. Do you mind the smoke?"

"I appreciate the smell of a good tobacco," Sarah replied, then turned back to directing the children.

Since the table was now set, she sent the twins and the two younger girls to the basin of water in a corner, telling the girls to be sure all four sets of hands were clean for the meal. When Bobbie began whimpering in Carrie's arms and Sissy automatically reached for him, Sarah shook her head.

"Find him something to play with," she ordered Carrie. "You can entertain him while your sister and I get the food on the table."

Carrie headed for her dulcimer, which she'd left in the corner of the room. When she picked it up, Sarah called, "Something soft and soothing would be appropriate, Carrie."

"I never heard you ask permission to smoke in your own house, Pa," Wyn said rather disgruntledly.

Dan answered with a shrug that told Wyn absolutely nothing, then drew on his pipe again. The scent of the vanilla-flavored tobacco drifted to Wyn's nose, intermingled with the smell of fresh-baked bread and venison stew. With a fire going in both the fireplace and the stove, the loft area was adequately warmed. After supper, he'd open the doors on the bedrooms lining the far wall, taking some of the chill off the rooms before the family crawled into bed.

He continued to frown as Sarah ignored another ritual Wyn had come to expect of the evenings. Instead of filling the plates at the stove, she and Sissy carried two large bowls of stew to the table, placing ladles in them. Now there would be the added strain of worrying about the twins dropping the bowls as they were passed around the table, Wyn silently fumed. Sarah had no idea what was the easiest way to manage meals for this large family. She was used to servants at the beck and call of each guest seated in a high-back chair.

"I believe I'll go to the table myself tonight," Dan mused,

glancing at Wyn. "That is, if you don't mind putting me back in my wheelchair."

"'Course not, Pa," Wyn replied. "But are you sure you want to suffer through the turmoil we usually have? You've preferred your meals on a tray here by the fireplace recently."

An enigmatic smile crawled over Dan's face. "I've missed having meals with my entire family gathered at the table, son. And I doubt the turmoil will be nearly as bad tonight."

And it wasn't, Wyn realized a while later, although for some reason he still couldn't shake his annoyance at the altered routine. Sissy announced the meal ready about the time Wyn got his father transferred to his wheelchair. Wyn watched his family and guests file to the table as he pushed his pa up to it.

Prudence Elliot, as always when she ate with them, ignored the others as she took a seat across from one of the large bowls of stew. Mandy helped Carrie put Bobbie in the high chair and the two of them settled on either side of the child. Waving away Sissy's thanks, Mandy began feeding Bobbie, leaving Sissy to enjoy at least this one meal.

The twins scrambled to the same chair, each trying to shove the other one away. Sarah just stood there looking at them, not saying a word, and their struggles turned feeble. Finally they both glanced sheepishly at Sarah. To Wyn's absolute amazement, since he had no idea the twins had ever seen such a thing, they both pulled out a chair for Sarah. They stood behind it until she settled herself, then climbed into the chairs on either side of her.

As soon as his sisters and Mairi took their places, Wyn sat down across from his father, Sarah and the twins. Immediately Jute grabbed for a piece of cornbread on the stack in front of him. Sarah's calm voice halted his hand an inch from its target.

"Jute, whose night is it to say the blessing?"

The twin glanced up at her in awe. "How'd you start being able to tell me 'n Luke apart so quick?"

Sarah actually winked at him, a characteristic Wyn hadn't associated with the woman so far.

"That's my secret for now," Sarah said. "Now, the blessing?"

"Sayin' the blessin's a man's job," Jute said. "I'll do it."

"Nah, I'm five minutes older'n you," Luke said. "I'll say it." He ducked his head, and clasped his hands, while the rest of the people at the table followed suit. "Good food, good meat. Good Lord, let's eat!"

Wyn felt a blush stain his cheeks at the irreverent blessing, and a string of feminine giggles swept around the table amid the various-toned amens. Some of the prayer endings were uttered in resigned voices, Prudence Elliot's being the most resigned. Wyn glanced uneasily at Sarah, seeing her studying Luke with an unreadable look. When Sarah lifted her gaze to his, he defensively prepared himself for a lecture. But the crash of the milk pitcher on the floor forestalled whatever she had been ready to say.

"Damn it—" Wyn jumped from his seat.

"Supper table's not the place to swear," Dan reminded him in a stern voice.

"Well, gosh darn it, Pa!" Wyn retorted. "That's why we started filling plates and glasses over at the sink and stove, then carrying them to the table. The young ones didn't break so much stuff that way as when we had to pass around stuff at the table."

"If children aren't allowed to handle things, and taught the proper way," Sarah said, rising to her feet, "they will never learn how. I'll clean up the mess Jute made, with his help."

"You're a guest," Wyn said. "Sit back down and I'll take care of it."

He hurried across the room for the mop, broom, and dustpan, returning to find Sarah on her hands and knees, a surprisingly perky and firm rear sticking up at him as she reached beneath the table. Pulling back, she smiled in satisfaction at the large piece of clay pitcher in her hand. She handed it to Jute, admonishing him to be careful it didn't cut him, and the twin raced over to the trash can beside the sink.

In the meantime, the rest of the people at the table continued passing around the various dishes, and Dan assisted Luke with the bowls passing through his hands. Each dish came to rest in front of Wyn's unoccupied chair.

Feeling a tug, Wyn looked into Sarah's face. She'd risen and was indicating for him to let her have the mop. He loosened his fingers.

Within another minute, Wyn found himself back in his chair, filling his own plate and passing the bowls across to Sarah. The meal continued without further mishap, and with an easy give-and-take of conversation. He actually found himself listening to what each child had to say about how they'd passed the day, rather than refereeing whose turn it was to talk. But when the meal was over, he couldn't seem to recall more than the calm presence across from him in what had been a tumultuous time of day for many of the preceding months.

His stomach calm and full rather than tense and upset, he clasped his hands on it and leaned back in his chair, dropping his chin onto his chest. Lord, it felt good to relax. The murmurs around him faded into a drone and his entire body slackened.

The blizzard raged for two days, and Sarah passed the time visiting with Mandy and working on her embroidery. Periodically, she walked to the parlor windows and wiped away the frost on the windowpanes to peer out at the blowing snow and trees whipping in the wind. At times she couldn't even see the schoolhouse across the dirt road, let alone the general store catty-corner up the way.

On the morning of the third day, however, a brilliant blue sky hung over the beautiful panorama outside the window. Powder-puff drifts piled willy-nilly in the picture-perfect scene, and pointed teeth poked up from where huge pines rested under their snow blankets.

Sarah had missed Mairi, but she might as well get used to that. She would be leaving in a couple days—as soon as

Jeeter could make it back up the mountain—and her only contact with Mairi would be in the letters the little girl had promised to write. She could hope that Dan would allow Mairi to visit her in New York City once in a while, but she hadn't broached that request with Mairi's uncle yet.

Probably the schoolteacher would accompany her down the mountain when she left. Prudence Elliot had made it clear when she cornered Sarah at the MacIntyres' the other night that she couldn't wait to get back to civilization. Who would teach the children then?

The twins were so lively and bright, she couldn't imagine them not enjoying learning, if their energy could be properly channeled. Having spent hours with Mairi in the bedroom while she recovered, Sarah already knew the child eagerly soaked up knowledge like a flower turning its face to the sun. Mairi had begun reading fairy tales along with Sarah before they left New York City.

She didn't know Pris or Carrie well yet, but she'd listened to their chatter after dinner, or supper, as Mandy called it. She'd actually heard the two girls discussing one of the classics, and Dan had answered her puzzled look by nodding at a wall of shelves beside the fireplace. So many books stuffed it, several were haphazardly lying on top of the upright spines of others.

Dropping the curtain back into place over the window, Sarah turned around into the parlor. Mandy had gone to the kitchen for tea a few minutes ago, and the fire was dying. She crossed to the log basket and picked up another piece of wood, tossing it onto the fire.

A blue flame flared from the new wood, and Sarah stopped resisting the thoughts of the other MacIntyre family member hovering at the edge of her mind—the one with piercing blue eyes. She could still see him, slumped in his chair, a slight snore issuing from his nostrils. She remembered the love and tolerance of the rest of the family when they realized Wyn had dropped off to sleep. The din of noise ceased and everyone tried to allow Wyn his nap.

Never having been around a large family, Sarah was amazed at the almost visible feelings among them. Had she fallen asleep at the dinner table back home, her father would have gruffly awakened her and ordered her to her room until she remembered her manners. To the elder Channing, appearances were everything.

When Wyn woke, he seemed to take his family's solicitude in stride, unembarrassed at drifting off. Sissy even heaved herself to her feet and brought him a piece of the blackberry pie he'd missed at dessert, for which he thanked her with a warm, loving look.

A pounding on the front door made Sarah jerk around, her hand at her throat. Before she could move, she heard the door slam open and thud against the wall, then Wyn's voice shout Mandy's name.

"Where are you? Mandy!" he called as Sarah hurried to the parlor door. Wyn tromped into the house and slammed the door behind him, his gait an odd cadence.

"It's Sissy, Mandy!" he yelled. "It's her time, and it'll take me forever to get Leery back here in this snow!"

He glanced over at Sarah, and she had to bite back a laugh. His hair was rumpled and his shirt tucked only half in his pants, as though he'd just gotten dressed. He didn't even have on a coat, and his eyes were so harried Sarah would have thought it was his wife giving birth, rather than his sister.

"Mandy's in the kitchen, fixing some tea," she told Wyn in what she hoped was a soothing voice. "I'll go get her—"

"I'll go!"

Wyn bolted away, his feet again making that odd clumping cadence. She saw the reason this time. He wore only one boot, and his sock hung precariously on the other foot, flopping at the end of his toes and leaving a wet smear on the shining hall floor. She bit the inside of her cheek to still her laughter and followed him. He had to be freezing, after running over to the boardinghouse in only one boot and without a coat, but he didn't slow down one bit.

Mandy met him at the kitchen door, already holding a small black satchel. "I heard you hollering, Wyn," she said. "Have you tried to get hold of Doc MacKenzie?"

"You know Sissy wants Leery, but I'll go after Doc as

soon as you get over there, Mandy." Wyn grabbed the older woman's arm and started dragging her down the hallway toward the front door. "Hurry! Her water's already broke and she's having pains."

"I'd hope so," Mandy murmured, then tossed Sarah a tolerant glance, handing her the black satchel as she passed. "Medical supplies," she murmured. Then she pulled away from Wyn, and propped her hands on her hips.

For a moment, Wyn didn't seem to notice he wasn't holding Mandy any longer, and he barreled on toward the door. He flung it open and started through before awareness evidently hit him. Swiveling around, he raced back to Mandy, reaching for her again.

But Mandy stuck her face into his and shouted, "Wyn! Settle down!"

Wyn jerked back as though Mandy had struck him, and Sarah choked on her laughter. She'd heard stories of how her friends' husbands acted during the births of their offspring, but she'd never been around a man who was actually a part of a birth. Wyn's wild-eyed stare grew worse, if anything, and he held out his hands to Mandy in a pleading manner.

"You've gotta come *on,* Mandy! She's having the baby!"

"It took Sissy sixteen hours to birth Bobbie," Mandy said in a placid voice. "I figure we've got a few minutes yet before this babe starts to crown."

"Crown?" Wyn repeated with a gulp that bobbed his Adam's apple up and down. "Mandy, you gotta get over there and check Sissy. Carrie has no idea what to do!"

"Sissy does," Mandy assured him with a pat on the arm. "Now, you settle down and help Sarah and me on with our cloaks."

"Me?" Sarah said around a croak of fear. "Uh . . . I have no idea what happens at a birthing. I'd probably be more trouble than help."

"You can help with the children, dear," Mandy said.

"Yeah, you can help with the children, dear," Wyn echoed distractedly. He stared around for a moment, then said, "Oh, yeah. Cloaks."

Plunging to the hall closet, he threw the door open and grabbed two cloaks from inside. Throwing one over his arm, he frantically flapped the other one at Mandy until she shook her head and turned around to allow him to place it over her shoulders. Before Sarah could protest again, he stuffed her into the other cloak and shoved her and Mandy out the door.

When a sudden wind whipped around her ankles, she realized Wyn had given her Mandy's cloak, and vice versa. However, a muscled arm suddenly clasped around her waist left her no alternative but to plow through the snow beside Wyn, down the path his feet had cleared on his way over to the boardinghouse. Wyn pushed Mandy ahead of him, and once she thought he was going to stop and bodily pick up the smaller woman. Finally they clumped onto the porch and through the door to the store.

Dan sat in his wheelchair beside the front counter, serenely smoking his pipe, and Wyn didn't even acknowledge him. He shoved both of the women away from him, then turned.

"I'm going after Doc and Leery. . . ."

Mandy swiveled and grabbed the back of Wyn's collar. "Wyn MacIntyre," she ordered. "You put on your other boot and get a warm coat and hat! And get yourself a pair of dry socks."

Why stared at his feet as though just now realizing what had been carrying him around. Dan calmly reached onto the counter and threw a pair of socks at Wyn, who caught the movement and instinctively grabbed them out of the air. Without ceremony, he plopped down on the floor and removed his wet sock, then pulled off his boot.

"Your other boot's over there beneath your coat and hat on the coatrack," Dan said. "And I sent all the kids on to school, 'cept for Carrie. Figgered she was old enough to help by at least taking care of Bobbie."

"Oh," Sarah said in relief. "Then you won't need me."

"'Course I will," Mandy admonished. "Come on."

"Where the heck are you going, Wyn?" Dan yelled.

Sarah turned to see Wyn half in, half out the front door, a puzzled look on his face as he stared at his father.

"After Doc and Leery," Wyn said. "I told you that."

Dan sighed and shook his head. "Go out the back way and get one of the horses, Wyn. No need to walk all that way."

"Horses?" Wyn asked.

"Yes, horses," Dan said with a chuckle. "We've got six of them out back in the barn. Remember?"

"Oh, yeah."

Sarah barely managed to step back from Wyn's plunging flight. Mandy wasn't so lucky, and she yelped, leaning back against a pickle barrel and lifting her left foot.

"Darn it," Mandy muttered. "He stepped on my toe."

The two women looked at each other and burst out laughing. When their hilarity finally subsided to snickers, Mandy walked over to Dan, who had a wide grin on his face.

Patting him on the shoulder, she asked, "Do we have everything we need upstairs? Or do I need to take anything from down here?"

"I think it's all ready," Dan said. "Everything Sissy and I could remember, anyway. We even put the knife under the bed."

"Good," Mandy said with a nod. "Leery will look for that first thing. We'll check on you now and then, to see if you need anything before Wyn gets back."

"I'll be fine," Dan assured her.

Mandy led the way towards the back stairwell.

"Knife?" Sarah asked in an undertone as they climbed the stairs.

"It's to cut the pain," Mandy said. "Don't know as it helps, but it doesn't hurt. It's one of Leery's requirements, and it's a belief here in the mountains."

Inside the huge loft area, Mandy guided Sarah over to one of the bedrooms at the right side of the room. The door was open, and feminine voices sounded inside. Sarah looked in to find Sissy propped up in bed, with Carrie standing there holding Bobbie. Taking the black satchel from Sarah, Mandy walked to the head of the bed.

The next few hours passed slowly, and Mandy even allowed Sissy up to pace around a few times. A tall, spare man arrived after the first hour, who was introduced to Sarah as Doc MacKenzie. He examined Sissy while the women stood by, announcing that she was doing well and informing them that he would be down in the store with Dan if he was needed.

"*If* he's needed?" Sarah asked Mandy after the doctor left the room.

"Leery will handle everything unless there's a problem," Mandy informed her. "That's the way Sissy wants it. Leery and Doc work pretty well together, and the reason they do is that they let their patients decide who's their main doctor. The other one is available if needed. There's no jealousy between Doc and Leery."

"I see," Sarah said.

Two hours later, Leery arrived. At first Sarah thought one of the children had returned from school, but the tiny bird-like woman continued to remove her outer wrappings and lay them on a nearby chair until she stood revealed. Her face was as wrinkled as a dried apple, her hair a mixture of gray and white streaks. She wore a snow white apron over a neatly pressed, blue gingham dress, and her deep-set, light blue eyes seemed to be able to pierce straight into a person's mind, past any attempt to conceal feelings.

Rather than heading directly to Sissy, Leery stood silently studying Sarah for a long moment after they were introduced. Giving a nod she evidently didn't feel a need to explain, Leery finally shooed everyone out of the room.

"Go get a cup of coffee," she ordered in a surprisingly firm voice for someone Sarah decided was possibly very ancient. "And Carrie, put that child down for a nap. It's going to be a while yet."

"How does she know that without even examining Sissy?" Sarah asked Mandy as the door closed.

"She knows," Mandy replied, reminding Sarah that her landlady had informed her of the belief in the mountains that Leery had second sight.

Sarah also recalled that Leery had predicted a girl for

Sissy this time, deciding to keep that in mind while still not thinking it would prove anything. After all, the mountain midwife had a fifty-fifty chance of being right.

But the little girl was born just before sundown, with very little fuss and bother. Sissy had a few very hard pains, and she grabbed the headboard and bit her bottom lip. Very soon, Leery held up a tiny, wet figure, with legs and arms waving and a howl that filled the room and intermingled with Leery's announcement of the babe's being a girl child.

Leery laid the baby on Sissy's stomach and took the knife Sarah had waiting. After cutting the cord and separating the baby from its mother, she placed her in the blanket Mandy held in her hands. Sarah followed Mandy over to the washbasin in the corner of the room.

"Won't Sissy want to hold the babe immediately?" Sarah questioned.

"She needs to expel the afterbirth first," Mandy informed her. "That will give us time to clean the babe up."

Sarah grimaced, glad Leery hadn't asked her to stand by for that procedure. But she was also extremely proud of herself for keeping vigil all day and doing her part in the birthing, while Mandy handled feeding the family. Now Sarah busied herself helping bathe the baby, her eyes filling with tears and her heart swelling as she touched the tiny person. When it instinctively wrapped miniature fingers around her thumb, she choked back a sob.

"Beautiful, isn't she?" Mandy asked in an understanding voice.

"Precious," Sarah admitted. "I want a dozen of them."

"One at a time, I hope," Mandy teased, handing the clean baby to Sarah and nodding for her to take it over to Sissy.

After Sissy had duly admired her baby and counted all her toes and fingers, Leery sighed reluctantly and informed them it was time to allow the men into the room.

"Then," she continued sternly, "you will rest, Sissy. Your Robert will be home within a week."

"Thank you for telling me that, Leery," Sissy said.

Sarah stood back in a corner while Mandy called down the stairwell to announce the birth and allow the rest of the family upstairs once again. Carrie brought Bobbie in first to meet his new sister, although the youngster didn't appear impressed. Mairi and Pris each held a hand of one of the twins when they came into the room, but the restraint wasn't necessary. Luke and Jute were suitably awed, and didn't begin arguing about who would take the little girl fishing first until after they left the room.

Wyn and Dan came last, and Sarah assumed this was because Wyn had to get his father up the stairs in the wheelchair. Dan accepted the baby from Mandy first, snuggling her in his arm and tracing a gentle finger around her face.

"Welcome, new little grandbabe," he whispered before handing the newborn to Wyn.

At first Wyn shook his head and backed away, but Leery gave him an admonishing look. He hesitantly reached out, cupping his hands beneath the babe's head and bottom.

"I always forget how tiny they are," he murmured. "And it always scares the bejesus out of me the first time I hold a new one."

Tears dimmed Sarah's eyes again as she watched him, his huge hands cradling the tiny bundle. She found herself wondering if Stephen would hold their first child with so much reverence, so much tender concern and pride. Placing a hand on her stomach, she soothed the emptiness there, all at once becoming aware that Wyn had turned his head to look at her. She heard Sissy's voice saying something, but couldn't seem to focus on the words.

When she realized everyone in the room was looking at her, she gave a start. "I'm sorry," she said. "I didn't hear what Sissy said."

"She asked if you minded if she called the babe Sarah Maria," Wyn said. "Maria was my mother's name."

Her brimful eyes spilled over, and Sarah could only nod, since her throat was far too choked to allow a word past. Very carefully, Wyn walked over to her and handed Sarah her namesake. She cuddled the baby close.

"Hello, Sarah," she whispered.

*　　　*　　　*

Hours later, Sarah wiped the last plate and put it away in the cupboard. She'd sent Mandy on home a half hour before, assuring her she would be right along. Carrie, with Pris and Mairi's help, had done an admirable job of getting Bobbie, the twins, and themselves to bed, and Sarah sank down in one of the rocking chairs in front of the fireplace for just a second.

The quiet around her would have been utterly impossible to imagine earlier, with the cacophony of the noisy family ringing from the rafters. When she'd taken a plate in to Sissy, she asked her if she would like her door closed, to barricade the noise somewhat. Sissy had shaken her head, saying the baby might as well get used to the noise, since she would be living in it.

Now only the crackle of the fire in the grate sounded, and a faint rustle as one of the children turned over on a mattress. Baby Sarah whimpered, but only for a second. Hearing a tiny slurping noise, Sarah knew her namesake was nursing. It was so peaceful she felt her eyelids droop—until a crash from downstairs brought her to her feet.

4

CHEWING HER BOTTOM lip in deliberation, Sarah took her cloak from the peg beside the landing and peered down the dark stairwell leading to the first floor. She heard a snicker, then a chuckle, then murmured voices. After that came what sounded like a hiccup, and more snickers. It didn't sound like burglars, so she donned her cloak and silently crept down the stairs, the tiredness seeping into her bones made her long for her bed over at Mandy's boardinghouse.

Someone had left a lantern burning, hanging on a ceiling hook, so she could see well enough to wend her way through the goods in the store. The noises were coming from Dan's room, off the back of the storage area. She could only make out a few words.

"Here's . . . new grandpa."

". . . uncle again. And one for Robert."

Glass clinked, and Sarah decided the men must be celebrating the birth of the baby. Smiling tolerantly, she felt certain it was safe enough to stick her head into Dan's room and let them know she was leaving. She continued on, intending to knock on Dan's door, but found it standing wide open.

Dan, Wyn, and Doc MacKenzie sat in front of the fireplace in Dan's room, holding glass fruit jars with a clear liquid in them. Even from the doorway she could smell the aroma from the jars, but she couldn't identify it. The fruit jars didn't surprise her that much, since the family also used them to drink from upstairs. But the only liquor she had ever seen was brown in color. This didn't look like white wine, either, or the ale or beer her father drank.

"Yep," Dan said, then drew the back of his hand across his mouth. "One of the best batches Ro—"

He caught sight of Sarah and fell silent, but only for a second. "Sarah," he said, bringing the other two men's attention to her. "Are you on your way back to your room? I want to thank you kindly for your help today."

His words were slightly slurred, and Sarah smiled in understanding. "I'm glad I could help," she replied. "I see you're toasting your new granddaughter. I may be partial, since she shares my name, but I think baby Sarah's very deserving of having her birth celebrated. Might I join you in a toast?"

The men's eyes widened, and a rather guilty expression filled Wyn's face.

"Oh, I don't imbibe that much," Sarah assured them. "Only a sherry now and then. But I see this is a man's time, so I'm sorry I interrupted you."

"No, no." Dan motioned to her with his free hand. "That's all right. Come on in and set a spell with us. You're right. Sh . . . Sarah's your namesake, and you oughtta toast her with us."

"Pa—" Wyn began.

"Pour her a glass, Wyn," Dan ordered. "She's a lady and ladies don't drink out of fruit jars."

"Well," Sarah denied as she sat in the chair Wyn vacated and motioned her into, "I drank ice tea from a fruit jar at the table tonight. And I have to admit that it tasted wonderful from the jar. There was something different about it—a taste that you don't get when you drink from crystal."

Dan choked on a laugh, then drew the palm of his hand across his mouth as though to silence himself. A soft snore met her ears, and Sarah saw Doc MacKenzie slumped in his chair, chin on his chest. Wyn quickly grabbed the fruit jar Doc held when it threatened to fall from his hand and, shaking his head, placed the jar on the fireplace mantle. Then he handed Sarah a small glass of the clear liquid.

"Thank you," she murmured, and Wyn started to say something, but clamped his mouth shut.

Sarah held up the small glass. "I'd like to propose a toast to Sarah . . . oh, it just dawned on me. Since Sissy is married, I guess her last name isn't MacIntyre."

"It's Frugel," Wyn informed her.

"Then here's to Sarah Frugel, a precious, beautiful baby." Sarah held her glass steady until both Wyn and Doc clicked their jars against it, with Dan having to lean forward somewhat in his chair to accomplish the task. Dan weaved just a bit, and Wyn placed a hand on his shoulder to push him back. Then they both lifted their jars to their mouths.

The innocuous-looking liquid fooled Sarah. It looked like water, and she drank it with that thought in mind. To Wyn's credit, he moved toward her as though realizing she was going to take way too large of a drink. But he was too late, and a generous swallow slid down Sarah's throat.

It almost came back up and she choked violently on the fiery liquid—the complete opposite of the sweet sherry she was used to. Tears filled her eyes, then flowed down her cheeks. She opened her mouth, having trouble breathing. Surging from the chair, she stared around wildly, waving her hand in front of her mouth and searching for a water bucket for a drink of real water.

Any second she expected to hear the men laughing their fool heads off at her, but instead Wyn slipped an arm around her waist, speaking in a soothing voice.

"Easy, Sarah. You drank too much. Let it set a minute, and you'll be fine."

It couldn't have been his voice that did the trick, but it seemed that way. The fieriness diminished, replaced by a spreading warmth. Wyn took a handkerchief from his back pocket and wiped her cheeks, and she leaned back in his arm.

"Ohhhhh," she breathed. "Oh, my, that was . . . what was that?"

"Just liquor. If you're ready to go, I'll walk you over to the boardinghouse."

For some reason Sarah's mouth curved into a smile and a giggle erupted from her throat. "But I haven't finished my drink."

"I'll bring it with me, and you can finish it in your room. Pa needs to get into bed now, and I don't think he'd feel comfortable doing that with a lady in the room."

"'Course," Sarah said with a regal nod. "'Night, Dan." She glanced at Doc MacKenzie, the sight of him sending her into renewed giggles. "'Night, Doc."

Wyn gave a half chuckle, half sigh, and led her from the room, through the store and out the front door. The cold air outside didn't faze her. Instead, she took a deep breath and gazed overhead. The path had been shoveled at some point that day, and she had no problem walking beside Wyn while studying the sky.

"Isn't it beautiful?" she asked. "And I'd be willing to bet it's absolutely gorgeous in these mountains in the spring-time."

"It is," he agreed. "There's mountain laurel, rhododen-dron, azaleas, and meadows filled with wildflowers and sweet clover. There's not a more beautiful place on earth than the mountains in the spring."

"I'll have to come back during the spring and see Mairi," Sarah said with an emphatic nod.

When Wyn halted, she glanced around to find herself at the boardinghouse porch steps. She lifted her foot for the first one, but her toe caught on the edge of it. When she stumbled, Wyn caught her to keep her from tumbling into the snow. She heard a small plop, which was probably her glass of liquor falling when Wyn dropped it to catch her.

"Whoops," she said with a smile, then realized she was looking straight into Wyn's eyes, her lips so close to his that her breath fanned across his face when she spoke. She froze, feeling as though a cocoon were closing around her, encasing only her and this broad-shouldered mountain man in its circle.

She expected him to draw back any second, but instead he continued to gaze into her eyes, his arm taut around her to keep her from falling. Even after regaining balance, her legs threatened to spill her into the snow.

"Sarah," he whispered. Then he kissed her.

There was no preliminary caress of his lips. He took her mouth fully, as though he expected any moment for her to flee and he wanted to take everything he could before she pushed him away. He buried one hand in her hair, holding her firmly enough that she would have had to struggle to get him to release her quite a bit more than she was able to manage at the moment. The instant that thought crossed her mind, she knew the last thing she wanted him to do was release her.

Stephen's kisses were obligatory, as had been any of the other kisses her potential suitors gave her. This kiss came out of the blue from a man who had absolutely no reason to kiss her—unless he actually wanted to. From a man who was as handsome as those men whose attention she had yearned for in years past. From a man she now admitted she had wanted to kiss from the very first moment she saw him.

The tip of his tongue licked at her lips, and she instinctively parted them. The thrill shooting through her when his tongue entered her mouth caused her nipples to peak into hard points. He swept his tongue around her mouth, and the sensation crawled downward, starting an ache between her legs.

He seemed to know what to do about that ache, because he lowered one arm and encircled her hips, pulling her against his lower body. That brought her to her senses, and she frantically pushed against him, stumbling backward and landing on the step when he released her.

Staring up at him, she stuttered, "Oh! Oh, I . . ."

Wyn ran his fingers through his hair before he stuck his hands in his pockets, his shoulders slumping. "I . . . look, Sarah, I apologize. I guess it was the liquor. I'm sorry."

She frowned at him as she rose. Maybe the liquor also gave her the courage to say what she did, but she didn't regret it even for an instant.

"I'm not sorry," she murmured. "Not one bit."

She turned and climbed the steps, opening the door and sweeping through it without pause. As soon as she closed it, she cautiously pulled back the curtain over the window to peer outside. Wyn was still standing in the same place. He hadn't moved even an inch. And his eyes were glued to the door.

Suddenly his shoulders straightened and he pulled his hands from his pocket. She thought it looked as though his lips pursed, perhaps to whistle. Her own lips pursed in response, and she once again felt his kiss. When he turned and sauntered back down the path, she watched him until he disappeared back into the store.

The next morning, she woke with her cheeks flushed from embarrassment and a slight headache. She had been dreaming about a broad-shouldered, blue-eyed mountain man, and even in her dream she had known she was betraying her fiancé. She was betrothed to Stephen, and she had allowed another man to kiss her.

Land sakes, she had not only allowed it, she had participated wholly in it and gloried in the participation!

Her headache could be either a result of her imbibing the liquor last night or her restless night of betraying dreams. Whichever, she concluded she deserved it and would just have to suffer, instead of lying in bed and coddling herself. Sissy would need some help today, and Sarah intended to be there to lend a hand.

By the time she rose, washed, and dressed, her headache had disappeared. As she descended the stairs, she smelled breakfast cooking. She took a slight sniff at first, wondering if her stomach would rebel, as she had heard happened sometimes to people after they overindulged. But the odors wafted through her senses deliciously, and her mouth watered.

She walked in to find the MacIntyre children gathered around Mandy's kitchen table, and their older brother standing behind the twins. Wyn's gaze came to her unerringly, and her breath caught in her throat. His expression was unreadable, and she desperately wished she *could* read it. He nodded good morning to her, but he didn't speak.

"Sarah," Mandy called from the stove. "Good morning. I'm glad you're up, because I was afraid the children's chatter would wake you. I'm fixing them breakfast over here this morning, since I'm more familiar with my own kitchen. Sit down, sit down. I'll have you something ready in just a minute."

Sarah tore her gaze from Wyn and walked over to the stove. "Nonsense. I can't sit down while you've got all this to do. Let me help."

"Oh, but you're a paying guest," Mandy said in a flustered voice. "I can't ask you to serve yourself or work here."

"Mandy, it didn't bother me at all yesterday to help out when Sissy was birthing the baby. And I'd feel very guilty sitting here and letting you wait on me with all these hungry children needing to be fed. Now, what can I do?"

"Well, can you fix three plates for Wyn to take over to the store? Or better yet, just wrap a stack of flapjacks and ham, then stick them in the picnic basket over there on the shelf. Wyn can get plates over at his place. And I made two pots of coffee. Give Wyn one of those to take over to Dan."

"I made coffee this morning," Wyn said from right beside Sarah. "And I can load the food into the picnic basket myself, if it's ready. I think those young'uns would shut up some if they had flapjacks to stick in their mouths."

Sarah stared up into his smiling face, wishing that smile was for her instead of the thought of the children quieting down. But she instantly admonished herself, remembering her contrition that morning when she recalled kissing one man while betrothed to another one.

She moved away from him and picked up one of the stacks of flapjacks Mandy had piled high on a plate. Carrying it over to the table, she started placing flapjacks on the children's plates. By the time she had them all laid out, Wyn had left. Mandy sat down, reaching for Carrie's hand, and the rest of the children took hands, circling the table.

Mandy bowed her head and said grace, and as soon as the last person had uttered "Amen," Jute gave a shout.

"Flapjacks! Boy, them's my favorite! Thanks, Miz Tuttle!"

A mannerly bedlam settled in, and finally the children were all fed and headed off to school. Mandy assured Sarah that Prudence Elliot would conduct classes that day, since the mountain people would send their children in. Only on days when a blizzard made traveling much too hazardous would the mountain people permit the teacher to close down the school.

As soon as the last child scampered out the door with a lunch pail in his hand, Mandy fell into a chair and sighed tiredly.

"I'm too old for this," she told Sarah, as Sarah headed for the stove to pour them each another cup of coffee and enjoy the quiet. "Raising children is for younger women."

Sarah smiled and placed Mandy's coffee in front of her. "I don't understand why you also had to pack everyone a lunch. The children are right next door to home, and they could just as easily come back for their lunch."

Mandy shook her head. Reaching for her coffee cup, she said, "All the other children eat lunch at school. The MacIntyre children wouldn't want to stand out and be different. Besides, it gives Dan, Wyn, and Sissy some peace and quiet."

"I understand. I suppose Prudence will be leaving soon. When I looked outside, I saw the snow already melting. I imagine Jeeter will be able to get back up here by tomorrow."

"Prudence will probably tell the children to inform their parents that she's leaving when they go home today," Mandy conceded. Then she tilted her head and looked at Sarah.

Sarah instantly interpreted the gleam in Mandy's eyes and jumped to her feet. "Oh, no, you don't, Mandy! I can't stay here and teach. I need to get back to New York."

"Why?" Mandy asked. "You said your father had passed on. Is there someone else waiting for you?"

Sarah was reluctant to talk about Stephen for some reason. But why? Land sakes, Mandy would never meet her fiancé. She couldn't imagine Stephen in these mountains. Stephen had probably never walked on anything except cobblestones, pavement, or carpet in his entire life. Heaven forbid that he traipse across a dirt road. She'd even seen him ride his horse across a courtyard and dismount, rather than risk dirtying his boots in front of a stable door. The various grooms always made the trek back to the stable with his mount.

"Yes, I lost Father," Sarah admitted. "But despite that, my life is back in New York. I . . . well, there's a few things yet to settle on Father's estate, and . . . uh . . ."

Her voice trailed off when Mandy shrugged and stood. "I see. And I apologize if you thought I was trying to push you into something. It's just that I care so much for Dan's children and know how important an education is to a child having a good future. Sissy got lucky with Robert and married for love. She'll never want for a thing as long as it's within Robert's power to give it to her and their children."

She sighed and shook her head. "Carrie is already looking around for a man, although Maria was adamantly opposed to the mountain tradition that a girl of fourteen is of marriageable age. But Pris and Mairi are smart—they could easily be something more than some man's wife."

"Mandy," Sarah said helplessly.

"It's all right, dear. Truly, it is. What will be, will be, as Leery says. It's just that there are only six more weeks of school scheduled for this year. By the middle of April, the children are needed at home to help plant. We'll never find anyone for just that short amount of time. I guess Dan just needs to begin looking for someone to start next fall, after harvest."

She had no business even considering what Mandy was talking about, Sarah chastised herself. If anything, the kiss she'd shared with Wyn last night should tell her that she needed to get out of here immediately and content herself with her plans to marry Stephen. She would soon have children of her own to care for, probably at least one within a year of her marriage.

In a year, baby Sarah might be walking, she thought. *And*

Mairi will probably forget what the woman who rescued her even looks like, unless I can get back here for a visit or two.

And Wyn MacIntyre would probably be married himself, with a start of his own brood of babies. Surely as soon as the snow melted, there would be a trail of single mountain women visiting the store as often as possible.

"I wish I could teach," she became aware of Mandy saying. "But I didn't go beyond third grade myself. I can read and write and cipher, but just enough to get by on. Of course, I've read a lot over the years, so I suppose I'm a little beyond when I had to leave school and help care for my younger brothers and sisters. Still, it's not enough to teach with."

"I can't stay, Mandy. I *can't*."

She rose and hurried over to the sink. Grabbing one of Mandy's aprons from a hook beside the cabinets, she donned it and plunged her hands into the dishwater. She'd never had to wash dishes at home, but she'd done pretty well last night when she had her first lesson.

She scrubbed a plate, set it in the rinse pan, and picked up another one. No, she'd never washed dishes back home, but she hadn't minded it one bit last night. Not with the sounds of everyone cuddling and cooing to her namesake, before Sissy lovingly but sternly told them baby Sarah needed to sleep. She'd helped wash hands and faces, also, and prepared two grubby little boys for bed. They had demanded that she kiss them good night, their arms clinging to her when she did.

The rowdy, rambunctious, loving MacIntyre family was a complete contradiction to what she had known all her life. But she had to admit that it was exactly what she would want her own family to be like, if she could choose.

She became aware of her surroundings again with a start. She had been staring out Mandy's kitchen window and dreamily circling the dishrag around and around on the same plate. Sneaking a guilty look over her shoulder, she sighed gratefully when she didn't see Mandy. Her landlady must have returned to her room to make her bed.

Turning again, she gazed at the magnificent view out the

window. Far away, snowcapped mountains stretched before her, disappearing in the distance without end. On one side of Mandy's yard were several huge, bare trees, one with a set of swing ropes hanging from a large limb. She could imagine children laughing and shouting in that large back-yard in the summer, but she didn't recall Mandy saying she'd had any children of her own.

She would bet that Wyn would enjoy swinging his children high into bright sunshiny air in the summer.

For heaven's sake! She thinned her lips and wrenched her gaze away from the swings, digging back into the dishes. She'd only met the man two days ago, kissed him once, and was already building a future with him in her mind! How stupid! Plenty of men kissed plenty of women without there being wedding bells in the future for them!

And her own wedding bells were going to ring for her and a different man.

A stab of sorrow cut into her heart. Probably, too, Wyn only had a fancy for a little dalliance with the city woman who would be leaving quickly and wouldn't threaten his bachelorhood.

Seemed as though he would have picked a prettier woman than her to dally with, she mused. A man as handsome as Wyn should have his pick of the beauties and not have to settle for wallflowers like her.

5

FROM BEHIND THE counter, Wyn stared out the window, watching Sarah approach. Instead of coming into the store, though, she turned and walked down the pathway he had shoveled to the schoolhouse. Something tugged at him, urging him to follow her, but he resisted.

He'd do well to steer clear of Miss Sarah Channing until she put her tall, slender frame on Jeeter's wagon seat and left. Even the additional white lightning he'd drunk last night after he walked her home and foolishly kissed her hadn't given him a good night's sleep. Her face had wavered through his dreams, and once he actually woke up with his pillow clasped in his arms, his face buried in it. The morning light had brought further confirmation that he never should have kissed her. He'd enjoyed it way too much, and they were worlds apart.

But hell! What really bothered him was her kissing him back. He kept trying to blame her response on the white lightning she'd drunk, but that didn't work at all. He found himself thinking about setting up his own still—brewing his own moonshine—carrying a bottle around with him so he could get her to take a sip whenever he caught her alone.

Yep, it was a good thing the warming day was melting the snow. If Jeeter didn't show up tomorrow morning, he'd take Sarah and Prudence down to Razor Gully himself!

He picked up his coffee cup and took a long swallow, nearly gagging on it when he realized it was cold. Telling himself he only needed to dump the coffee, he walked out onto the porch and over to the railing. He flung the coffee into the snow, barely registering the brown surface stains before he shifted his gaze to the schoolhouse.

She'd evidently gone inside. Whatever her purpose over there, it didn't take long to accomplish, because she came out again as he watched. Her movements appeared rather careful—until she closed the door. Then she straightened to her full height and stared at the door for a full minute. Suddenly she turned and headed back down the path to the store.

She saw him before Wyn could escape inside and hesitated slightly. Then she came on again, sweeping up the steps and stopping several feet from him.

"Mandy told me that Dan was head of the school board," she said without a preliminary greeting. "Where is he?"

"In his room doing books. And calling what we have here in Sawback Mountain a school board is stretching it a tad. Pa and a couple other men meet whenever there's a need to hire a new teacher, and the other two men bring Pa the money they collect from the various families each fall for the teacher's salary. But that's about the extent of their organization."

"Thank you."

Before Wyn could surge forward and hold the door for her, Sarah opened it and went through. He pulled back his hand quickly and sucked on the tips of his fingers, which had gotten caught between the screen door and doorjamb when the door slammed behind her.

What could be so darned important Sarah needed to talk to his pa? Maybe her brief peek inside the schoolhouse had made her decide the school wasn't good enough for Mairi. She'd definitely developed a soft spot for his niece, if the wardrobe Mairi had unpacked last night was any indication of Sarah's feelings.

Determined to protect his pa, Wyn hurried after her. At the bedroom door, he saw Dan leaning back in his wheel-chair, a serious look on his face and his bookkeeping pen tapping against his chin. He flicked a glance at Wyn, but made no other sign he was aware of his presence, keeping his concentration on Sarah.

Sarah stood before him, talking in a low but ardent voice, and Wyn walked a quiet couple of steps closer. Just inside the bedroom door he stopped, straining to hear what she was saying. From his position he could also see Sarah in the bureau mirror behind his pa, although the angle protected him from Sarah's view.

". . . suppose it's because she considers this her last day, but she might as well dismiss the children and send them home for all they will learn today," Sarah said with a huff of indignation. "It's total pandemonium, and she's just sitting there reading a book!"

"To tell you the truth, Sarah," Dan said, "I wasn't gonna offer Prudence Elliot a contract for next year anyway. I ain't never made no effort to gussy up my talk like I probably could, since the men and women who buy stuff from me would think I was putin' on airs. But I had a full slate of school years myself, and I've tested my young'uns off and on. They ain't learnin' near as fast as they oughtta be. Given how hard it is to get teachers to come here, I figgered leastwise they was a-learnin' somethin', which was better than nothin'. And I've got a passel of books for my young'uns to read on their own."

"Do all the other families have books to supplement the lack of education they're getting in school?" Sarah demanded.

"No, they don't, though I've let it be known anyone is welcome to borrow any I've got. They're real respectful of books, though, and I imagine they're afraid somethin' would happen to a borrowed book and they couldn't replace it for me."

"There should be no need to supplement the children's

education. Reading for pleasure or for seeking further knowledge on a child's own is different. I surely hope you don't intend to give that woman a reference!"

Sarah shook her head, and a tress of brownish-blond hair loosened from her careful chignon. She lifted a hand to push it back into place, her movement straining the loose bodice material on her gown across her breast. When the tress stubbornly refused to stay in place, she lifted her other hand behind her head to help tame it.

Wyn's mouth went dry. Last night when he'd kissed her, there had been his heavy jacket and her cloak between them. Still, he'd managed an adequate feel of her rounded hips. She didn't wear one of those "enhancers" so popular with the women he'd seen during his time in Washington, D.C., which made those ruffles and bows wobble so enticingly on their backsides. Now he realized she'd also hidden a completely adequate set of breasts under her loose-fitting garments. With her height, he'd be willing to bet those legs went on endlessly, too.

He took a hesitant, unwilling step forward, and she glanced up at the mirror. She dropped her arms so fast they whooshed through the air. Those soft, chocolate eyes met his, the expressions in them changing so quickly his brain barely had time to register each one—from concern, probably as to her discussion with his pa, to a hot flash of awareness, then to humiliation that she'd let the awareness show, and on to a haughty attempt to wipe her face free of any emotion.

To distract himself from the stab of response in his groin, Wyn concentrated on what he'd decided her purpose in visiting the schoolhouse had been.

"So," he said as nonchalantly as he could as he walked on into the room. The safest place for him to talk to her seemed to be behind his pa, just in case he couldn't control what happened between his legs. Dan's wheelchair would block her view. He moved over that way.

The problem was, then he could see his pa's bed reflected in the mirror behind Sarah. In the slightly wavy surface, it appeared it would only take a slight shove to send her tumbling back onto the wedding ring quilt his mother's relatives had presented her on the day she married.

He took a steadying breath. "I don't want to make assumptions here, but if you're going to malign our attempts to give the area young'uns an education—"

"Attempts is right," Sarah said, waving a hand in obviously checked anger. "That woman is robbing you instead of earning her salary."

"I suppose it's Mairi you're worried about," Wyn said.

"Wyn!" Dan cautioned.

"Mairi?" Sarah's brow furrowed, then wrinkled deeper when she narrowed her eyes and glared at him. "Are you insinuating that I'd try to talk Dan into letting me take Mairi back with me because she would get a better education that way?"

"Would you?" Wyn shot back at her.

"No! It's not only Mairi who's being rooked out of proper schooling! Why, in the short time I've been here, I've seen that both Jute and Luke have extremely sharp minds. I'd be willing to bet that the reason she has so much trouble with the twins is that she's not keeping them challenged. They're probably willing and able to learn a lot faster, if she'd just spend the necessary time with them!"

Not understanding at all why he defended Prudence Elliot, since he didn't much care for the woman himself, Wyn said, "She's got fifteen young'uns over there, with hardly more than three of them each at the same level of learning. She can't spend every minute of her class days with Jute and Luke."

The color flared higher in her cheeks, and her eyes sparkled with gold dust when she slapped her palms on her hips. Her motion smoothed down the skirt material to outline that hidden shapeliness.

Maybe that was why he antagonized her, a corner of his mind said. She was a completely different woman when she forgot and stepped outside that haughty, cool exterior, which preceded her like a shield from the days of knights and ladies. She was the woman she'd been last night, with a swallow of moonshine in that flat belly.

"Teachers are trained how to handle a room full of varying levels of children," she spat. "It's just plain laziness when a teacher doesn't properly handle her children."

"I suppose you could do better."

"I darned sure could!"

"Then I'm glad that's settled," Dan put in. "Mairi will be glad you're not leaving yet, Sarah."

"What?" Sarah's head snapped around and she stared at Dan in puzzlement. Wyn could have sworn he saw his pa wipe a satisfied gleam from his face and replace it with a questioning look.

"I hope the salary we can afford is adequate," Dan continued in a musing voice. "We really can't pay any more than what we're giving Miss Elliot."

"I'm not . . . I didn't . . . I don't think you understand, Dan," Sarah sputtered.

"Of course I do," Dan replied. "You've just agreed to teach the young'uns for the rest of the school year."

"No!" Wyn and Sarah both yelled in unison.

Suddenly Sarah turned her attention back to Wyn. "Why not?" she asked, glaring at him once more.

"Hey!" Wyn threw out his hands. "You said no, too! Besides, our children need to know a little more than pretty needlework and what the season's fashions are."

Sarah advanced on him, sidestepping Dan's chair. Wyn thought he heard his pa chuckle, but he kept his eyes warily trained on Sarah as Dan grabbed his wheel rims and rolled himself out of the way, continuing on out the bedroom door.

The mattress hitting Wyn in the back of the knees told him that he'd unconsciously retreated from Sarah, and he chastised himself for his apprehension. Hell, she was just a woman. A tall, extremely pretty woman, but a woman still. He cautiously held his ground. It was either that or end up flat on his back on the bed, staring up at her. If he did that, he was going to take her with him!

He imagined having her lying on top of him on that bed, and his groin throbbed again. There was no wheelchair to shield his reaction from her this time. Luckily, she seemed focused on his face, the gold dust in her eyes shimmering as though it would erupt into sparks any moment.

"I could teach those children better than Prudence Elliot if I had laryngitis the entire term!" she fumed.

"Could not," Wyn sneered childishly.

"Could too!" Sarah leaned close to him, her nose almost touching his.

Then he kissed her.

He didn't even become aware of what he was doing until he realized his hands were buried in that bountiful gold-brown hair, which was a shade or two lighter than her eyes when she got excited. But the awareness hit him like a fist in the stomach as soon as his lips touched hers. She gasped, drawing in his breath with her own, and he fit his mouth to her welcome.

And welcome him she did, for at least a good, long— extremely short—ten seconds. Then she worked her hands in between their bodies, pushing against them and trying to say something, but his lips kept her words smothered. Finally she twisted her head free.

"I can't!"

"Can't what, Sarah?" Wyn whispered. "Can't kiss me again or can't stay here?"

"Neither." An anguished look filled her eyes. "I'm betrothed."

Wyn jerked with the news, but he said, "You don't love him. You couldn't, and kiss me that way."

"It doesn't matter," she said in an astonished voice. "It's a fact and I can't change it."

He tightened his fingers in her hair and slowly pulled her to him again. After an initial second of resistance, she complied, tilting her head to let him fit his lips to hers again. She lifted her arms, placing one around his neck and threading the fingers of her other hand in his hair. With a sigh, she settled against him for a long, delicious moment.

Then, reluctantly, she pulled back. "There. I wanted to see if it was my imagination, but it's not. You're temptation itself, Wyn MacIntyre, but it's a temptation I need to resist. If I'd found you sooner, it might be different. But it's too late now. And besides, I'm not interested in a few days of experimentation with you."

"Experimentation? What the hell's that supposed to mean?"

She gave one of those haughty sniffs he was starting to hate. "I don't appreciate your using profanity around me, either."

For her being such a tall woman, he was able to move her rather easily. He lifted her by the waist and whirled her around, pushing her onto the bed before she could regain her balance. The springs squeaked loudly, and she landed with her arms propped behind her to keep from falling flat on her back. He allowed her that much dignity, but stood over her, daring her to try to rise back to her feet.

"I want to know what you meant by my experimenting with you! You're the one who kissed me a few minutes ago to see if it was your imagination or not. That sounds a hell of a lot more like experimenting than what I was doing— kissing you because it felt damned good to me and because I thought you were enjoying it, too!"

"M-men like you don't k-kiss women like me for pleasure," Sarah sputtered.

"Men like me? What's that supposed to mean?"

She turned her head sideways to avoid his gaze and chewed on her bottom lip. Wyn continued to stare steadily at her, vowing to himself not to say another word until she explained her asinine statement. The silence stretched out, broken only by the ticking of an old clock Dan had on his fireplace mantel and an ember popping in the grate.

At one point she shifted on the bed, and the mattress springs protested the movement with a loud squeal. A hot blush covered her cheeks. Wyn chuckled, biting back the urge to make a comment on the noise.

Finally she sat upright, pushing him back a step when her nose almost ended up in his belly button. Since he didn't particularly want her eyes on that portion of his body, he pulled one of the chairs close to the bed and sat. Crossing his arms, he leaned back and silently waited for her to speak.

She cut him a glance, and her blush heightened. "All right!" she finally fumed. "I'll tell you what I meant, but then you've got to agree to answer a question or two for me!"

"Agreed," Wyn said with a nod.

She took a deep breath, her shoulders rising and falling with the movement. Gazing everywhere in the room except at Wyn, she said, "Men who are handsome like you don't need to kiss homely women like me. They can have their choice of the pretty women to kiss. So I don't understand at all why you kissed me."

Wyn's mouth dropped in astonishment. "Homely? You consider yourself *homely*?"

"I prefer the word 'plain.' And I'm well aware that I'll never be considered anything other than that. I've had enough people confirm my plainness to me over the years, including my own father."

Wyn shook his head in disgust. "Your father must have been half-blind and the rest of them vicious in their jealousy. And you evidently haven't looked into a mirror lately. You're about as homely as a dew-sprinkled bush of mountain laurel flowers with the sun shining on it."

Sarah managed to get to her feet before he could stop her. "I don't know what your game is, Wyn, but I'm not interested. I'm going up to see if Sissy needs any help with baby Sarah. Later today, I'll get packed in case Jeeter makes it up the mountain tomorrow."

Wyn remained in his chair. "You said you had a couple questions for me," he reminded her.

"I've . . . lost interest in the answers."

She left the room, and Wyn stared at the empty doorway for a long time. He didn't understand his own reaction to her, so it was just as well she didn't pursue her questions. He hated to think of her going through the rest of her life, though, thinking she was homely—plain.

Hell, and thinking he was handsome! He knew darned well that his nose was a little crooked from that time he fell out of the apple tree. And more than once his sisters had teased him about how wide his mouth was. He'd even felt hesitant when he'd kissed Rose sometimes, since his mouth had completely swallowed hers, with lots of lip left over.

Funny, it fit perfectly fine over Sarah Channing's mouth.

He got to his feet and turned to the fireplace. Picking up the poker, he jabbed at the logs, sending sparks up the chimney.

There was definitely no future for him and Sarah Channing. He knew that beyond a shadow of a doubt, after having once made the mistake of thinking he and a woman not from his mountains could make a life together. He was relieved Sarah hadn't asked her questions, because he had an idea what they might have been. She probably wanted him to admit he was just enjoying a brief flirtation with her, knowing she would be leaving fairly quickly.

And he was, wasn't he? Shoot, he'd kissed the girls at the barn raisings and husking bees right along with the rest of the fellows. The girls had kissed their share of fellows, too, until they decided which one they wanted to take up with.

Even after his split with Rose, he knew he would find another woman someday. It hurt like hell for a while, but looking back on it, some of the hurt came from his shame at misjudging the woman he'd allowed into his heart. Still, he had sense enough to know all women weren't like Rose. He just needed to get back out there and try again. He fully intended to spend his old age with a couple dozen grandchildren tugging at his white beard!

Bet those long, slender fingers of Sarah's would thread through a full beard quite nicely!

Rather than continue straight up the stairs to check on Sissy—the intent she had indicated to Wyn—Sarah sat down halfway up the stairs. Bending forward, she propped her elbows on her knees and clapped all ten fingers across her lips. Staring through the dimness, she tried to see Dan's bedroom door, but it was too far away. She stayed quiet as a mouse, straining to hear Wyn leave the room, so she could scamper on up the stairs if necessary. But she heard no movement.

Adamantly she ordered her thoughts to steer away from

what had happened in the last few minutes, but they disobediently focused on exactly what she was trying to avoid thinking about. Over and over again she relived the feeling of being in Wyn's arms, of his kisses.

She'd never, *ever* felt like that in Stephen's arms, and definitely not when he kissed her. Had she made a horrible mistake by finally deciding to buy herself a husband? Could she have possibly found a man who would make her feel more like Wyn did, if she'd only waited a while longer?

No doubt about it, she'd settled for Stephen instead of having the opportunity to chose him from among an entire pool of candidates, as had most of the other single females she knew. She overlooked Stephen's moodiness at times, and his supercilious attitude. Overlooked catching him staring at other women, too, accepting the fact that a man with normal urges wouldn't be satisfied with a plain woman on his arm. That their relationship was an agreement, not a love match.

Oh, there was definitely no future for her and Wyn, either. She didn't fit into his world at all, and she couldn't imagine him giving up his life here to come to New York. Within a minute after meeting him, she'd known how strong his ties were to his family.

As she rose to her feet, her shoulders slumped in acceptance. It was nothing but a little frustration. They were a man and woman of an age to eye each other and be curious enough to take advantage of the opportunities to explore each other's response. She couldn't really blame Wyn for that. Land sakes, she'd done her own little bit of experimentation.

And his telling her that she wasn't plain, wasn't homely, was just part of the game. A short game that would be over very soon, but a game all the same.

Something tipped over in the storeroom, and Sarah paused as she started up the stairs. It was probably Gray Boy, since she'd seen the cat prowling around earlier. She started to call him, then changed her mind. If he was after a mouse, Dan would appreciate the cat getting rid of it.

6

"*W*HEW!" MAIRI WIPED her brow and carefully stepped out from behind a barrel of flour as Miss Sarah climbed on up the stairs. She probably shouldn't have hidden, but she'd done it anyway. And after she did, she didn't know how to come out without making Cousin Wyn and Miss Sarah mad at her for hiding in the first place. They'd think she'd been spying on them for sure, and make her explain why she wasn't in school.

But Miss Elliot wasn't even teaching at all today. Since it was Mairi's first day back in the mountain school, she'd been excited about showing all her friends how much she had learned from Miss Sarah. After over two hours of Miss Elliot only stirring herself to glare and pick up her ruler when the children got too loud, Mairi had had enough. As soon as Miss Elliot turned a page and buried her face in the book again, Mairi slipped into the cloakroom at the rear of the school, then on outside.

Uncle Dan hadn't seemed surprised to see her at the store a few minutes ago. She told him she was worried about Miss Sarah leaving without saying good-bye. That wasn't a real lie, since she really had forgotten to ask for Miss Sarah's promise not to do that, although she'd been intending to ever since they arrived in Sawback Mountain. It was just that there was so much else to do—so many things to talk to her cousin Pris about, since they hadn't seen each other in close to two years. Why, they barely remembered each other.

Uncle Dan told her that Miss Sarah was in his room talking to Cousin Wyn. He also said for her to go on back there if she wanted. And she did want to, so she went. But at the bedroom door, she stopped so quick that Gray Boy ran his nose right into the back of her leg.

She'd grabbed the kitten up.

"Shhhhh, Gray Boy," she whispered very, very quietly. "Look. Look at that."

Pointing Gray Boy's head in the same direction she was looking, they both watched Cousin Wyn kiss Miss Sarah like Mairi had seen her mama and papa kiss each other when they thought nobody was a-watching. And an idea leaped straight into Mairi's mind, all full blown and ready to go without her having to chew on it at all before it made sense.

Wouldn't it be great if Cousin Wyn and Miss Sarah got married? Then Miss Sarah could stay here in the mountains with them, and Mairi could see her anytime she wanted to! More than once her mother said it was her duty to follow her papa wherever he went, 'cause the Bible said something about whither thy husband went, a wife went, too. And one thing Mairi knew for sure was that her mother meant what she said. Mama went with Papa without once crying over it.

That seemed to be the way of things, too. When older sisters of her friends got hitched up with a feller, they mostly always moved into the house everyone helped the feller build before the wedding. Mairi had gotten real fond of Miss Sarah—sort of really loved her—and would miss her a lot if she left. So, she thought logically, if Cousin Wyn and Miss Sarah got married, Miss Sarah would stay in the mountains with her husband.

She knew about Cousin Wyn's girlfriend in Washington, D.C., from her cousin Pris, and that Cousin Wyn had left her

back there. Rose, she remembered her name was—Cousin
Wyn left Rose when she refused to come to the mountains
to live. Cousin Wyn would never live anywhere but the
mountains for very long, Pris said. He told them how much
he missed the mountains while he was gone.

Mairi didn't blame Cousin Wyn at all. Miss Sarah's house
was about the fanciest thing she could imagine. When she'd
told Pris about it, her cousin said it was probably even
fancier than some of those houses in Uncle Dan's books that
Carrie read aloud to Pris. Yet Mairi would choose to live in
Uncle Dan's happy house here in the mountains over that
sad, beautiful house Miss Sarah called Channing Place
anytime.

Although she knew it wasn't true, she could almost
believe she hadn't even breathed for real until she came
back to the mountains. Even Mama and Papa had been
ready to give up trying to live in that terrible city and come
home. But they got sick instead.

She didn't understand much of what Cousin Wyn and
Miss Sarah talked about after their kissing was over and
done with. For one thing, she wasn't sure how soon one of
them would come out of the room and catch her there, so
she'd ducked behind the flour barrel. She couldn't hear a
whole lot from there.

She felt just a tiny bit guilty and knew what she was
doing wasn't exactly proper.

"But how can I start puttin' my plan to work if I don't get
some idea first whether or not it's the right thing to do?" she
whispered to Gray Boy. "After all, I wouldn't want Cousin
Wyn and Miss Sarah to get married up to each other 'lessen
they was really in love. So I gotta listen and see what they're
a-sayin', don't I?"

Gray Boy only blinked his eyes at her, purring loudly as
she stroked his back.

Turning her attention back to the goings-on in Uncle
Dan's room, Mairi heard Cousin Wyn say something about
Miss Sarah and those pretty mountain laurel flowers Mairi
loved to pick. And Miss Sarah said at one point Cousin Wyn
was handsome, so that meant she was taken by him. Carrie

said that was the first step toward a feller and a gal getting together—them eyeing each other and being pleased with what they saw. Carrie oughtta know, since she was old enough to be looking for a feller of her own.

Mairi had met that there Stephen feller who hung around Miss Sarah back in New York, but she didn't think much of him. Fact is, she'd never even gotten close enough to him to see if there was anything at all about him to even like. He kept his distance from her, sort of wrinkling up his nose when he did forget and look at her. For the most part, though, he pretended like she wasn't even there.

Cousin Wyn would be a much better husband for Miss Sarah, far as Mairi was concerned.

After all her heavy thinking, Mairi cuddled Gray Boy in her arms and wandered toward the front of the store again. She didn't bother glancing in Uncle Dan's room to see what Cousin Wyn was doing, since it was really Miss Sarah she'd come to talk to. And now she'd have to wait a while. If she went up there to talk to Miss Sarah, she didn't think Cousin Sissy would be as easy on her for playing hooky as her Uncle Dan had been. Pris said Sissy took it real serious about being the one to mother them now that their real mama, Mairi's aunt Marie, was dead.

Finding her uncle Dan busy talking to a customer who had traveled through the snow to the store, Mairi went on out to the porch. Hitched to a sled, the customer's mule was tied to a post beside the steps. There was a wooden box built on the sled to carry whatever the customer bought home with him.

About the same time Mairi came out the door, someone else walked around the side of the porch toward the steps.

"Miz Leery!" Mairi called excitedly.

Every child in the mountains loved Miz Leery, Mairi included. When Mairi had roamed the blackberry patches or traveled around searching for mushrooms after a spring rain with her MacIntyre cousins, they'd always stopped by Leery's cabin if they came close. Miz Leery kept molasses cookies and striped candy on hand for them, and the children shared their berries and mushrooms with her.

With Sissy birthing the baby, Mairi hadn't had much time yesterday to say more than howdy to Miz Leery. The woman the older folks called the mountain healer had, however, hugged her tightly and told her that her mama and papa missed her but still loved her. She believed Miz Leery. Everyone on the mountain knew Miz Leery could see things the rest of them couldn't, and that Miz Leery could even talk to people after they died sometimes. It wasn't scary at all, 'cause Miz Leery said it wasn't.

"Why, howdy, little Mairi," Leery said. "How's baby Sarah and her mama today?"

"Fine, Miz Leery," Mairi said. "Sissy's a-stayin' in bed like you told her to, and Miss Sarah went up there a while ago to check on her."

Leery nodded her gray-haired head and peered closely at Mairi. "You 'pear to have somethin' on your mind, child. You want to talk to me about it? If you do, spit it on out, now, hear?"

Mairi screwed up her mouth and furrowed her brow in concentration. After a good long reflection that must have lasted at least a full half minute, she nodded her head.

"I needs your help, Miz Leery. I needs me a love potion."

Leery cocked her head and studied Mairi without laughing, as Mairi had been a tad afraid she might.

"Ain't you a mite young to be a-thinkin' 'bout trying to get some rascal to follow you 'round with moo eyes, child?" Miz Leery asked. "I'd think you'd wanna wait at least another year or two for that."

"Oh, it's not for me, Miz Leery. Can you keep a secret?"

"Kept bunches of them over the years, honey. Bunches and bunches of them."

"Then listen . . ."

Sarah folded another petticoat and placed it in her satchel. After Leery had arrived to check on Sissy and baby Sarah, the old woman had announced that her son, Jeeter, would be coming up the mountain that afternoon instead of tomorrow. She said the snow wasn't nearly as deep on down the mountain between Sawback Mountain and Razor Gully, and it was Jeeter's birthday today. He'd want to see his mother on this day and get the present she had for him.

Just in case the woman was right, Sarah immediately went to her room to begin packing.

Land sakes, it hadn't seemed nearly as much work to pack for the trip here, she grumbled to herself as the next petticoat she picked up from the dresser drawer slipped from her fingers and fell. She grabbed it from the floor and started folding it again. Well, she'd had her maid, Rachelle, to do most of the packing for the other trip, she admitted. Rachelle had even packed Mairi's bags, and had wanted to come with Sarah.

And although Rachelle had been invaluable in helping care for Mairi when she was so ill, Sarah had left her maid behind. She didn't know how she herself would be accepted in what might be a backwoods town, let alone how they would treat her if she brought a maid with her. Mairi's awe of her luxurious surroundings at first had told Sarah that mountain women probably had only heard of having maids in books.

The petticoat slithered to one side in the lopsided pile of clothing in the satchel, and Sarah gave up, shoving it into a corner. Rachelle would wash and iron everything anyway, whether or not the clothing had been worn.

She heard loud shouts from outside and walked over to her window. The schoolhouse door was open and children burst through it, whooping in glee. Someone had evidently also told Prudence Elliot that Jeeter would arrive today, and the schoolteacher had dismissed school to do her own packing. From her vantage point on the second floor of the boardinghouse, Sarah could see Prudence hurrying out the back door of the schoolhouse and down the path to her own small cabin.

Some of the older children disappeared around the back of the store to Dan's stable, where Sarah knew they had left the mules they'd ridden to school that morning. In fact, she'd stood in this same spot this morning, watching them arrive. She'd wondered how they would travel through the snow, smiling to herself when she saw sometimes three children on the back of one bony mule.

She leaned her head against the cold glass, her breath frosting the pane. Children who made such a huge effort to get to school in the heavy drifts ought to have a teacher who was committed to giving them the best education she could. Some of those children had probably started out while it was still dark in order to be there when the doors opened and classes began.

Sarah pulled away from the window. "No!" she sternly told herself. "I can't do it. It's out of the question!"

She strode over to the bureau again and snatched up a handful of wool stockings from the next drawer. Tossing them at the satchel on the bed, she grabbed the rest of the stockings and carried them to the satchel. She shoved everything into another corner, then stared down at the bag, remembering the quick glimpse of the children she'd allowed herself at the school a while ago.

If she'd stayed any longer, she would have been in tears—both from her anger at Prudence Elliot for ignoring the children and the choking sensation in her throat as she stared at the children's boots lining the cloakroom floor. Some of the boots had twine wrapped around the toes to hold them together. And there didn't appear to be a large enough number of boots there for all the children in the classroom.

The older children were in the last row, and she could smell that they needed a bath. She supposed it was hard to heat water to bathe in the wintertime up here. The girl who sat beside Carrie would have had a beautiful head of blue-black hair—had it been clean.

On her way back out the door, she'd noticed the ragged jackets and coats hanging on the hooks above the tattered boots. Now she sat down on the bed, leaning her face in her hands.

"Damn that Prudence Elliot!" She jerked her head up, surprised at the curse word. Ladies never, never cursed. That had been drilled into her as soon as she understood what exactly manners were.

"Damn her!" she repeated in a louder voice, this time nodding her head in pleasure at the sound of the curse word and continuing to the room at large. "How on earth could she sit there and harden her heart against that bunch of children, who were crying out to learn what she could teach them?"

She jumped to her feet and began pacing the room, waving her hands around in a very satisfying accompaniment to her anger and wishing Prudence Elliot were in the room to hear her.

"An education can make a huge difference in those children's lives! It can open the entire world to them. It can give them the choice of whether they will be happy staying in the mountains or whether they could manage in the rest of the world if they chose that! And that Elliot woman has their future right in her hands and she's been wasting it!"

With urgent movements, Sarah went to the closet and pulled out her dresses. Without worrying about creases, she shoved them into the portmanteau beside her satchel. She had a time getting both pieces of luggage latched, but finally she managed it. Then she began dragging them both toward the door.

"I'm going to find someone to come here and finish out the school term," she told herself sternly as she pulled the bags toward the top of the stairs. "No one in Sawback Mountain needs to know that I'll also be giving the teacher double her salary here myself, so those children can get an education."

She managed to get her luggage out onto the boarding-house porch before her strength gave out. Then, as Leery predicted, she saw Jeeter's wagon coming up the trail. Leery had said that she and Jeeter would visit for a while before he started back down to Razor Gully, and for sure Jeeter would want to see baby Sarah. Sarah left her bags on the porch and went to find Mandy to say good-bye.

A little over an hour later, Wyn carried Prudence Elliot's bags out and loaded them beside Sarah's in the back of Jeeter's wagon. Sarah had already said good-bye to her namesake and Sissy, and now she started around the gathering of MacIntyres, hugging them one by one, her eyes tearing more and more after each hug, and especially when she held Mairi. Mairi, however, didn't tear up so much as pay extremely close attention to her, once in a while glancing at Wyn, also.

After she got her most vigorous hugs from the twins, one in each arm, she waved at Mandy, Dan, and Leery on the porch. Leery was engaged in a final conversation with her son, Jeeter, and she supposed Jeeter would be there in a minute to drive the wagon down the mountain. Sarah turned away. She could say good-bye to Wyn when he assisted her into the wagon.

When Prudence Elliot walked out of the schoolhouse and headed for the wagon, Sarah paused and waited for the woman. She gasped at Prudence's rudeness when the former schoolteacher completely ignored the gathering of MacIntyres and climbed onto the seat. Instead of telling anyone good-bye, Prudence stared straight ahead, her back rigid.

"'Bye, Miss Elliot," the twins called.

"Harumph!" Prudence responded.

Both Luke and Jute looked up at Sarah in bewilderment, and a tear formed in the corner of Jute's eye.

"What'd we do to her, Miss Sarah?" he asked with a tremulous sniff.

"You did absolutely nothing, Jute," Sarah assured him in a controlled voice, holding her fury in check. "You did nothing other than be the wonderful little boy you are."

Then she turned from him so he couldn't see her face, dropping her hold on her anger. But from his position, she realized Wyn could see her, and he took a surprised step back. She didn't pause to explain herself to him, knowing he would find out in an instant what she was so furious about.

Stomping over to the side of the wagon, she glared up at Prudence, wishing it were true that a person's eyes could shoot sparks when she was angry, instead of it being just something she'd read in a book once. She'd singe that woman's cloak if she could!

"You witch!" she spat viciously. In deference to the little

pitchers with big ears within hearing distance, she barely refrained from making the word a more vicious one.

Prudence swiveled to face her, and her jaw dropped. "Why . . . why . . . you . . ." she sputtered.

Sarah plopped her hands on her hips. "You have absolutely no business being around children, and I'm going to see that you never hold another teaching position in your life! So you better look for something else to do after you leave here!"

"How dare you?" Prudence huffed, although Sarah could see the fear in her eyes. She knew Sarah wasn't bluffing and that she could follow through on her threat. No, her promise!

"How long have you been here?" Sarah demanded.

Evidently Prudence didn't feel that offering any defense would make Sarah change her mind, since she faced to the front again and remained silent. Wyn stepped up beside Sarah.

"She's been here since last fall—a little over five months."

"Thank you," Sarah said, keeping her glare fixed on Prudence. "That means she's wasted five months of these children's lives. And she's been drawing a salary from these people and not doing her job!"

"Well," Wyn said in a musing voice, "Pa said they were learning a little bit."

"'Pa said'?" Sarah whirled on him. "Your own brothers and sisters were wasting time at that school. Did you ever stir yourself to find out whether or not they were being taught properly? Did you care about what was happening to your brothers and sisters?"

First anger flashed in Wyn's face, then resentment. He abruptly turned away and left her. Shame immediately filled her, since she'd seen Wyn's love for the children from the first moment they arrived and Mairi threw herself into Wyn's arms. Torn between going after him and apologizing for her cruel taunts and continuing her lambasting of Prudence Elliot, she heard Prudence give a sniff behind her.

"There's no sense even trying to teach these people,"

Prudence said when Sarah faced her again. "They always come back here and squander their lives." She nodded in the direction Wyn had taken. "He had a chance. He did a favor for Senator Collingsworth and got offered a job in Washington, D.C., as the senator's aid! He was even betrothed to the senator's daughter, Rose. Do you think he took advantage of the opportunity? No, he gave up everything and came running back to these godforsaken mountains."

The news that Wyn had once been betrothed—and to a senator's daughter—pricked Sarah's anger. It leaked out of her like air from a balloon, leaving her deflated. For one thing, she knew Rose Collingsworth. Father had many times hosted important government officials at his parties, courting their favor to amass an even larger fortune.

Just this past year, Rose had been in New York City over the Christmas season. Tiny, brunette, and with vivid blue eyes, she had made Sarah feel as awkward as the giraffe she'd seen at Washington's National Zoological Park the previous year, when her father had been invited to tour the soon-to-be-open park. Rose had clung to the arm of her new husband, Petula Hardesty's brother, the heir to the Hardesty fortune.

Jeeter walked up and held out his hand to Sarah. "Gots to get goin', Miss Channer. Don't wants to get caught on the road too late. I'll be helping you up now."

With a defeated sigh, Sarah took Jeeter's hand. One of a string of governesses had long ago helped her master the art of smoothly climbing in and out of buggies, and wagons weren't that different. But she didn't want to hurt the little man's feelings by ignoring his assistance. Prudence scooted over on the seat to give her some room, and Sarah settled on the space left for her.

Tears misting her eyes, she swiveled to get one last look at the family that had come to mean so much to her.

Having decided she could both help her sister Sissy and get experience for when she had her own babies, Carrie held Bobbie in her arms. Cuddling the toddler's cheek against her own, Carrie picked up Bobbie's arm and helped him wave at Sarah. Pris and Mairi stood beside Carrie, arms around each other's waists. Mairi glanced over her shoulder at the porch, a somewhat questioning look on her face, and Sarah looked up in time to see the old mountain woman give Mairi a nod. Mairi gazed back at Sarah and smiled, lifting a hand to wave.

"'Bye, Miss Sarah!" Luke and Jute shouted, then turned and raced away. They'd been begging to go sledding ever since they got out of school, so Sarah assumed they were heading for their sleds.

She looked at the porch again, and received a lift of an arm from Mandy and Leery. Dan took his pipe out of his mouth, but before he said anything her eyes slid from Dan to follow the direction Wyn had taken. She saw him headed back toward her, an unreadable expression on his face.

He came on over to the wagon. "Didn't want you to leave with us having harsh words between us," he said. "I thank you for what you did for Mairi and for your help with the birthing and all."

Too choked to speak, Sarah could only nod at him. The wagon swayed, and Jeeter climbed into the seat on the other side of Prudence. Sarah heard the brake squeal when Jeeter released it and closed her eyes, waiting for the wagon to jerk into movement.

"Sarah!" Dan called.

Her eyes flew open, and she stared at Dan.

"You change your mind, you just let me know," he said. "I doubt anybody else will bite on the offer of only a few weeks' worth of work here in Sawback Mountain. Nobody worth nothin', that is."

Prudence shifted on the seat and gave a smothered harumph. "A fool's born every moment," she muttered. "But I'm through being a fool."

Sarah gritted her teeth and stared ahead of her. Jeeter picked up the reins and flapped them over his mules' backs.

"Hie on thar!" he shouted. "You lazy critters get a-movin', now! We got miles to go!"

"Stop!" Sarah reached across Prudence and grabbed the reins. Jeeter leaned forward so he could see her, and Sarah repeated her command more softly.

"Stop. I'm not going this time."

A crooked grin split Jeeter's mouth, and he muttered, "Didn't think so. But Ma said you had to choose yourself."

Rather than anger her, the twinkle in Jeeter's eyes warmed Sarah's heart. She winked at the little man, then said, "I'll have a couple letters for you to send out for me on your next trip. Do you know when it will be?"

"Oh, probably 'bout a week," he replied. "Need some he'p a-gettin' down?"

"I'm fine," Sarah said with a huge smile. "Finer than I've been in a long while."

She turned and started to climb from the wagon, but froze in the face of Wyn's stern gaze.

"What do you think you're doing?" he demanded.

"I'm applying for a job as schoolteacher," she said, tilting her nose up at him. "I would appreciate it if you'd remove yourself from my pathway, so I can go speak to your father about it."

"Look, Sarah, you don't have to feel guilty. We'll take care of the children's educations."

"Guilty? Wyn MacIntyre, guilt has absolutely *not* been one of the feelings I've been having since I arrived here. I've had more soul satisfaction in the past few days than I've had in my entire life!"

"What about your *betrothed*?" Wyn said, seeming to cover up a sneer.

Sarah shrugged, then opened the reticule on her arm, pulled out a pencil, and tore off a piece of paper from the notepad every lady carried. She scribbled a few words and handed the paper across Prudence to Jeeter, following it with a coin she dug from her reticule.

"Please ask the telegraph operator in Razor Gully to send that wire to my attorney," she said. "His name is there. He'll notify everyone who needs to know that I've been delayed, so they won't worry about me."

"Mr. Charles Caruthers," Jeeter said, surprising Sarah when he read the words. He gave her a wink similar to the one she'd given him. "Been a-readin' for years. How'dcha think I'd know who to deliver the mail to?"

Sarah shook her head in admonishment at herself for her erroneous assumption about the little man. "Thank you for taking care of the wire for me," she said.

Then, ignoring Wyn's glare, she climbed down from the wagon without his assistance. As she walked to the rear of it, the wagon swayed again as Jeeter clambered over the seat into the bed. Picking up her satchel and portmanteau, he dropped them over the side. After a sly grin and a brief glance at the porch where Leery stood, he took his seat again and "hied" the mules once more.

Giggling conspiratorially, Mairi and Pris rushed forward, each of them trying to take the luggage from Sarah.

"We'll take them back over to Miz Tuttle's for you," Mairi insisted.

"It's too heavy for you," Sarah said.

Wyn stepped forward. "If you're taking the schoolteacher job, you'll be staying in the cabin behind the schoolhouse. It's part of the salary." He picked up the bags, one in each hand, and carried them over to the porch. "Pa?"

"Reckon you might's well take 'em to the cabin, son. Me and Sarah will have us a talk, then you can show her round the schoolhouse and—"

"Me?" Wyn broke in. "I'm not part of your school board!"

Sarah moved a step closer, carefully watching Dan's face. He rolled his eyes heavenward, and she saw Wyn's face tighten in reaction to his pa's annoyance.

"I s'pose I could ask you to push me over there in my chair so's I could show Sarah where everythin' is," Dan said. "If that's the way you want it. But the snow's still sorta deep for that, even on the pathway."

"Hell, it'll be easier for me to show her myself," Wyn said with a grunt. Hoisting the satchel to one shoulder and adjusting his grip on her portmanteau, he stomped away.

7

THE FIRST WEEK flew by so quickly, it was the day before Jeeter was due again before Sarah knew it. The weather continued to warm up, the snow melting and disappearing. This afternoon she'd even opened the windows on the schoolhouse and slipped over to her tiny cabin to do the same there. The mountain breeze would cool things off soon, but when she'd dismissed the children a minute ago, it was still a beautiful day.

The other mountain children ran for their mules to go home, while Carrie, Pris, and Mairi headed over to their own house to do homework and help Sissy. Their older sister had finally left her bed the day before, insisting she would prepare her family's meals herself from now on. And Sissy was terribly anxious for Jeeter to come back, since she fully expected her husband, Robert, to be with him, as Leery had predicted.

The twins had taken to hanging around with Sarah after school, and with Dan's permission, she often helped them with their homework over at her own cabin. Today they were sweeping the schoolroom, cleaning the blackboard, and tidying up before they went to her cabin.

Standing at the door and watching the children scatter, Sarah allowed herself a few minutes of reflection while Jute and Luke worked. It had been amazingly easy for her to figure out how to do her job. She hadn't attended public schools herself, but it made sense that since she was the lone teacher in a roomful of different-aged children, she had to set up different teaching levels. Then she needed to keep each group occupied somehow while her attention was on another one.

Lesson plans done the previous evening took care of that, and she'd even begun allowing Carrie and her friend, Patty, to help with some of the younger children. It had amazed her how much pride Carrie and Patty took in their own knowledge when they had a chance to pass it on to others.

She shook her head in disgust. Prudence Elliot didn't have any idea how much self-satisfaction she was missing out on by not doing her job properly with these children. The wide-eyed awe when a child managed to read an entire sentence in a book—and understand the meaning of the sentence—tugged at Sarah's heart. Just today, Jute had looked at her, red hair flopping over his forehead and his eyes wide with delight.

"Now I know what the word 'twin' looks like. Allus knowed that's what me and Luke was, but now I can write it down if I want to."

Those two little boys were becoming awfully dear to her heart—almost as dear as Mairi. And not once had they pulled a trick on her this past week. They'd been too busy devouring their readers and writing on their slates.

Suddenly she shook her head in disgust. She wasn't standing there watching the children scatter and head home. They were all out of sight, except for the last mule carrying Patty and her young sister, Edwina, which was disappearing around the bend in the mountain trail. She was watching for a blond head and broad shoulders.

Yesterday, a day nearly as warm as today, Wyn had been waiting on the front porch with Dan when the children came home. After showing her around a week ago, she'd only seen him at supper each evening, since she continued to assist Mandy in feeding the MacIntyre children while Sissy remained in bed. But today Sissy would take over her own family, and Sarah assumed she would be expected to fix a lonely supper in her own cabin. That didn't appeal to her at all since she'd become accustomed to the friendly company at meals after her arrival at Sawback Mountain.

The door on the general store opened and her breath caught in her throat. Chastising herself didn't make her feet carry her back into the schoolhouse at all. Only when she saw Dan push himself out the door did she wave at him and turn away.

Back inside, she watched Luke put away the broom and dustpan and Jute scrub at the blackboard with a sponge. She'd opened the windows today, drawing more than one child's eyes longingly to the outdoors.

"Tell me," she said to Jute, who was the more vocal twin. "Do you think all you children could behave well if we went walking in the woods tomorrow? I'd like to teach everyone what happens when the seasons change."

Jute gave her a strange look, then turned his attention back to his job without answering her. Sarah frowned and looked over at Luke, who didn't meet her eyes.

"All right, you two," Sarah said. "What's wrong with me taking my class for a walk in the woods?"

The silence stretched out for a while, but Jute finally put his sponge down. Ducking his head and toeing at the pine floor, he cleared his throat. "Well, it ain't—"

"Isn't," Sarah corrected him.

"Yes, ma'am. It *isn't* the walkin'. It's the teachin'."

"The teaching?" Sarah asked in astonishment.

"Yes, ma'am," Jute repeated.

Sarah waited expectantly, but the boy didn't go on. "Jute," she finally prodded, "tell me what's wrong with my wanting to teach about the seasons and what happens in the woods when they change."

Surprisingly, Jute shot a pleading look at his twin, and Luke answered her. "It's that you's a city woman, Miss Sarah. I reckon we knows lots more about what happens in the woods when it turns from winter to spring than you do. 'Spect we do."

"Hmm," Sarah said, lowing her eyelids to hide the twinkle she thought might be in her eyes. "Let me ask you something, Luke. Do you think we have winter in the city?"

"Yes, ma'am," he replied immediately. "Figger they have winter everywhere."

She nodded at him. "And do you figure we have spring in the city?"

"Yes, ma'am." Luke's blue eyes gleamed. "But we gots dirt and mud under our snow when it melts, not them there cobblestone streets like Pa reads about in them books. Reckon them shoes o' yours ain't . . . aren't real proper for walking much in dirt and mud. Takes you a while to clean them when you been outside during recess and lunch, you know."

"You're very observant, Luke," she admitted.

"Ob . . . observant?"

"It means that you pay attention and remember what's happening around you. That's a very good trait to have. So how about this. Our walk will focus on the differences in spring in the country and spring in the city. And I *do* have a pair of boots I brought with me, which I can wear instead of my shoes."

Both twins contemplated the idea, then nodded. Jute took back over the conversation.

"That sounds like fun to me, Miss Sarah. And learning's lots easier when it's fun, like you make it. Ol' Prune Face—" He clapped a hand over his mouth in horror.

Laughter bubbled in Sarah's throat, but she held it back. Obviously the children had done a play on Prudence's first name. But it wouldn't do to encourage their disrespect.

"Shows some imagination, which is also a good trait, isn't it?" a voice said behind her.

She swiveled into the laughter shining from Wyn's blue eyes, although he appeared to be trying to keep the rest of his face stern. Ever one to take advantage of a situation, Jute scampered forward and began dancing around Wyn.

"Miss Sarah's gonna take us into the woods tomorrow,

Wyn! We won't have to sit in them ol' hard seats all day. We can have some real fun and learn stuff, too."

"Sounds like a fine idea to me," Wyn agreed. "Now, are you done here? I need you to check Miss Sarah's woodbox and carry over some wood from our pile if she needs it."

"As a matter of fact," Sarah said, "I do need some more wood. And a little coffee, too, if I could buy some. I believe that's the only thing low in the supplies Prune . . . uh . . . Prudence left behind."

"I'll send coffee when the twins come over for you to help them with their homework. Pa would like to see you now if you've got a minute."

He turned and left before she could answer him, escaping her presence as quickly as he had ever since he'd shown her around the schoolhouse and cabin. He almost ran back to the store and disappeared inside. So much for his seeming attraction to her. She knew beyond a doubt now that he had only been dallying with her—testing his own allure with a willing female who would be gone before anything serious could develop.

Then, when she'd decided to stay around, he ran like . . . like . . . well, as Dan would probably say, like a hound with a scalded tail! Only problem was, there weren't too many places for him to hide, with her living practically in his lap.

Sighing in disappointment, she turned to inspect the schoolroom, then dismissed the twins. She followed them more slowly to the store, smiling at Dan when she approached.

"Wyn said you wished to see me," she said.

Dan removed his pipe from his mouth. "Yep. Couple things. Have a sit down."

Sarah obediently sat in a chair across from him.

"Reckon you remember me mentioning having a wake for my brother and his wife," Dan said, a look of sorrow on his face. Sarah nodded in response.

"It's only right, 'cause most of the people round here knew them," Dan continued. "Figgered I'd do it the day after tomorrow, since Leery said Robert was a-comin' back tomorrow. Just thought I'd let you know that it would be a good time for you to meet all the young'uns' mas and pas. And you'll probably be a-gettin' invites to come see them. It would be right nice if you could have some idear of how you want to take care of that when they ask you, since it's sorta an expected thing for a new teacher to visit each family. 'Spect I could talk Wyn into taking you round, maybe one family every other day or so."

"I really appreciate your telling me this, Dan. It wouldn't have occurred to me that I'd be considered rude if I didn't visit each of the families. But perhaps I could just go home with one family of children each evening and come back with them in the morning."

"Some of them cabins won't be fit for you to spend the night in," Dan told her. "'Specially this near spring, when they been shut up without baths all winter. I feel you got a right to know that, and also that it'd be considered right prideful on your part if they caught you a-sniffin' and coverin' your nose when you was there. They's a-gonna expect you to eat what they have for you, too, which won't be much more than tater soup and cornbread. But we'll bring over a plate of whatever we have those nights for you and leave it on your stove."

"Thank you, Dan," she said, rising to her feet. "I appreciate your help. I truly wouldn't want to hurt anyone's feelings by inadvertently snubbing them."

"Know you wouldn't do it on purpose, Sarah." He stuck his pipe back in his mouth, then pulled it out and stared at the cold bowl. "Dang. I forgot to get me a new pack of tobacco afore I came out here."

"I'll go ask Wyn for you."

"Mighty nice of you to offer, Sarah. I'd be appreciating it, if you don't mind."

"Of course not."

When she entered the store, Wyn was stepping behind the counter, but she caught a whiff of the light bay rum scent he used just inside the door. Surely he hadn't been eavesdropping on her and Dan, had he? Of course not. His scent probably permeated the store, since he spent so much time there.

"Your father needs some tobacco," she said as she approached the counter. "And I might as well get my coffee while I'm here. Would you prefer I pay for it now or have you put it on a tab and take it out of my salary?"

"Your food is part of your salary," Wyn said, avoiding her gaze and scanning the shelves as though he weren't completely aware of where each item sat. "There's no need to pay for your coffee."

Instead of responding, she studied him. He finally took a can of tobacco from the shelf, then ripped off a piece of brown paper from a roll beneath the bottom shelf. After he scooped some tobacco onto the paper, he rolled it and handed it to her without looking at her. Then he walked over to a bag of coffee beans and scooped some into a grinder. A moment later, the smell of fresh-ground coffee covered up the bay rum scent.

"Thank you," she said as she took the smaller bag he placed the ground coffee in. She heard him sigh in relief as she started to move away and gritted her teeth in irritation, which flared almost immediately into indignation.

Whirling on him, she said, "Don't you think it's about time we got this out in the open? You act like you expect me to jump on you every time we get within two feet of each other! I assure you, I'm well aware that you only kissed me for the fun of it! I'm not expecting a marriage proposal from you, especially since I'm already betrothed."

Wyn had the grace to blush, but he held her gaze steadily. "You underestimate yourself, Sarah. At times I wonder who shredded your self-esteem so badly."

"Being honest with oneself is not necessarily a lack of esteem. And from what Dan just told me about what's expected of me, it appears I'm going to have to depend on you to escort me to visit the area families. Those journeys would, I'm sure, be much more pleasant for both of us if we could just forget those kisses and carry on polite conversation to pass the time. Otherwise, they will be long, unpleasantly silent trips."

"Can you forget them, Sarah?" he almost whispered.

She drew in a breath and held it. A thread seemed to stretch from Wyn to her, winding around her chest and slowly, every so slowly, drawing tight. She stared at him helplessly, unable to break the contact.

Her eyes dropped to his lips. "I'm . . . I must," she finally managed to say.

"Then have it your way," the lips said. "Is there anything else I can do for you right now?"

"No. No, I need to get home and write some letters. Can I leave them here at the store, in case I'm out with the children when Jeeter comes tomorrow?"

"That will be fine."

"Thank you."

The thread loosened at last and she hurried back out to Dan. Barely pausing long enough to give him the tobacco, she hastened down the steps and toward her cabin. As she went in the door, she recalled her last comments to Wyn.

Home. She'd said she needed to get home. Funny, she'd never called that large twenty-room mansion in New York City home. It had always been Channing Place in her mind.

She stared around the tiny one-room cabin. It held everything she needed in that small space. In New York, sometimes all twenty rooms seemed crowded with things.

She had a small stove in the far right corner, which provided both a cooking facility and enough heat for the well-insulated cabin. She hadn't tried to do much more than make coffee on it and really didn't intend to. For a nominal charge, Mandy had cheerfully agreed to provide meals for her when Sissy got back on her feet, and she intended to take her meals over there beginning this evening. However, she did like her coffee first thing in the morning, and that meant preparing it herself rather than waking to a tray delivered by a maid.

She'd figured out how to make her own bed, enjoying seeing the tidiness of the brightly colored quilt tucked neatly around the mattress on the bed in the other corner. And she'd found some dustcloths on one of the shelves holding her cooking supplies. They worked to polish the small end table by the little settee and the surface of the writing desk in the near corner. If she needed any further room, she could always go back to the schoolhouse and use that larger desk. Dan had said Sissy would do the cleaning when she got back on her feet, but in the meantime, keeping the cabin neat gave Sarah a warm feeling of satisfaction.

The pine floor shone with wax, and she always carefully removed her shoes as soon as she got inside the door. Her first evening alone, she had been appalled to see her muddy footprints marring the waxed surface and the handmade rag rugs scattered on the floor. A Channing Place housemaid would have cleaned up after her before, but she'd learned yet another skill—how to use a broom and mop.

Now she sat on a stool normally kept over by the shelves and used her buttonhook to take off her shoes. After wriggling her toes in pleasure for a moment—she wouldn't have thought to go barefoot anywhere at Channing Place except her own bedroom—she went over to her writing desk. She might have time to write one letter before Luke and Jute showed up, and she could do the others after they left. She would write a letter to Stephen first and get that out of the way.

As she pulled her desk chair out, she wondered why she considered writing to Stephen a chore rather than a pleasure. After all, he was the man she would be spending the rest of her life with. But when she attempted to call up Stephen's face, his blond hair and blue eyes, Wyn's features appeared in her mind instead. In comparison, they were much more rugged than Stephen's less angular countenance. Guilt filled her immediately over her unfair parallel.

She put pen to paper and wrote "Dearest Stephen" rather than "Dear Stephen" as she had been considering beginning her letter.

"Shhhhh," Jute whispered.

All the children halted and respected his request for silence. Sarah felt her heart swell with pride as though the boy were her own son. He was going to be such a leader when he grew up. All morning during their walk in the woods, he had counteracted her recitation of the differences in what they were finding here in the mountains from a city with additional things she hadn't thought of.

He'd mentioned the muddy paths again, and she reminded him there were bridle paths in the city, which definitely didn't have bricks on them. So then he pointed out rocks on the trail, which she had to admit would have been removed on a city bridle path, to avoid injuring the horses' hooves.

The birds in the trees back in the city were sparrows and wrens. Here Jute pointed out blue jays and crows, and identified the calls of a mockingbird and red-winged blackbird, which he claimed was a harbinger of an earlier spring than usual. Blackbirds didn't usually show up until in April, he assured them.

The other children joined in the lesson, their eyes bright with excitement when they were able to point out a significant difference to Sarah. Pris spotted the deer first, but it bounded away the moment she pointed it out to everyone else. Sarah had to admit it was the first deer she had seen outside of picture books.

She'd thought she'd already noticed the clear, crisp air here as compared to the usually smoggy air in the city, which resulted from the many factories. But the farther they walked into the woods, the crisper the air became. She found herself wishing she could gather it in her hands and wash her face and hair in it. Surely she would miss the clean air when she went back to New York.

After a few seconds of silence, Jute dropped to his hands and knees and started crawling toward the top of a small rise ahead of them.

"Jute!" she whispered loudly. "Your knees are getting soaked on this damp ground!"

He waved a negligent hand behind him, then peered over the rise. Jumping to his feet with a whoop, he disappeared over the top.

Luke started after his brother, and some instinct made Sarah grab the back of his shirt. Shoving him at Carrie, she ordered her and Patty to keep the other children there.

Gathering her skirts, she raced up the rise. A hundred feet or so on the other side, she saw Jute with his arm inside a dead tree stump.

"Come back here!" she demanded.

"All right, Miss Sarah," he called submissively. And unfortunately for Sarah, he complied. But, dangling from one hand, he also carried the striped kitten he pulled from the tree stump. The kitten's mother poked her head out of the stump and snarled at him.

"Oh, my God!" Sarah screamed. Even a city girl knew what a skunk was!

"Drop that baby!" she yelled at Jute.

Jute glanced behind him and saw the mother skunk leave the tree stump and start after him. Giving a yell, he tucked the baby close to his chest and pumped his legs, heading straight for Sarah.

She screamed and froze, trying to decide whether to wait for Jute and grab him up or save herself. There wasn't nearly enough time to decide, because Jute was making a beeline for her, and he raced around behind her. The mother skunk followed—for one turn around Sarah's skirt.

Sarah risked a glance behind her and saw Carrie looking at her in horror.

"Get the children away from here!" she yelled. Carrie immediately turned away to obey, but not before Sarah thought she saw a grin spread over her face. A second later, the group of children was screaming with feigned fright and racing back down the path they'd just come up.

Jute rounded her skirt again, then skidded to a stop. It was too late. The mother skunk was already on her front feet, her tail over her back. The mist filled the air, stinging Sarah's eyes into desperate tears and causing Jute to drop the kitten to rub frantically at his own eyes. Her vision quickly clouding, Sarah could barely see the skunk grab her kitten in her mouth and carry it back toward the stump.

She groped for Jute's arm and found it, then stumbled down the pathway. Surprisingly, she didn't hear Jute crying. She felt like giving in to that emotion herself, but held it in check. If she gave in to one emotion, she might just give in to another one tugging at her—the urge to stop and pull Jute across her lap and spank that little rear of his! She didn't believe in physical punishment for children, though. And to think, she'd been so proud of him a few minutes ago—even wishing he were her son!

Finally she sank to the ground and grabbed a handful of petticoat from beneath her dress hem. Ripping it loose, she split it in two by feel and gave half to Jute. She scrubbed at her eyes, then waved the cloth beneath her nose.

"What on earth possessed you, Jute?" she demanded. "I would think a boy as smart as you would have enough sense not to take a baby skunk from its mother!"

"I . . . I figgered I could outrun it," Jute admitted, wrinkling his nose and giving a sniff. "Pa said he had a skunk for a pet when he was little, and that iffen you got 'em early enough, when they was babies, they didn't stink."

Sarah rolled her eyes and shook her head. "Well, you surely *weren't* able to outrun it! And now look at the fine mess you've gotten us both into!"

"I's sorry, Miss Sarah. Really I is. But I knowed that there skunk had her babies in that same stump last spring. I didn't find them till they was way too big for me to get one for a pet that year, though. I thought since we was already here this early this year, I'd just see iffen them baby skunks was already born."

He glanced at her rather hopefully. "Bet you don't have baby skunks on your bridle paths in the big city."

Her chuckle caught Sarah by surprise. She closed her eyes to shut out the sight of that carrot-colored head and those freckles speckled across the rosy cheeks beneath those bright blue eyes. The little scamp had just gotten her sprayed by a skunk, and he should be disciplined, not forgiven.

"I didn't mean it to happen like this, Miss Sarah," Jute said in a soft voice. "I's ready for you to punish me however you sees fit. Me and Luke hid the dunce caps ol' Pr—uh . . . Miss Elliot used to use. But I can show you where they's at."

With an extreme effort, Sarah choked back her laughter and rose to her feet. "Well, young man," she said, "I'll think about a fitting punishment while we walk back. I do realize that you didn't mean for anything bad to happen, but it did. Perhaps the memory of that might be sufficient punishment for you. What do you think?"

Jute rose to his feet and started down the path beside her. "You mean," he asked in wonder, "you'd let me help you decide whether I needed a lickin' along with havin' to carry this skunk smell round for days on end?"

"There will be no lickings," Sarah began, then stopped and stared down at him in dread. "What do you mean, carry this smell around for *days on end*? Can't we just take a bath when we get back and get rid of this odor?"

Jute solemnly shook his head in denial. "Uh-uh. Skunk smell hangs round forever. We's even gonna gave to bury our clothes, from what Pa told me."

"Your pa actually told you what would happen if a skunk sprayed you, along with telling you that he had a baby skunk for a pet? And you still went ahead and tried to steal one of those babies from its mother?"

"Sounds sorta dumb when you put it that way, don't it?"

"Dumb?" Sarah's voice rose in a squeak. "Do you have any idea how many days this smell hangs around?"

Jute shrugged his shoulders.

"But I'm meeting all the mountain families tomorrow at the wake!" Sarah cried. "And I have to go out and visit them! Oh, Jute!"

She took Jute's arm again and started down the trail, the bright day dimming for her. Instead of hearing an almost human-sounding "thief, thief" in the blue jay's call, its voice reverberated like a discordant squawk when the bird burst from a pine tree and swept through the woods, warning the other animals of their presence.

And, of course, she couldn't enjoy the clear mountain air! Instead, acrid skunk odor wafted around her, no matter how fast she quickened her pace to try to outdistance it. If Jute were right, her entire little cabin would probably soak up the odor and she'd never get rid of it!

Wyn alternately hurried his steps on the trail and slowed them. The excited passel of children had somehow managed to get the tale of their teacher's run-in with a skunk across, along with the fact that his baby brother, Jute, had instigated the encounter. In turn he stifled laughter and chewed over concern, although he couldn't decide whether his concern should be for his brother's physical safety or Sarah's likely injured dignity.

Skunks in the wild were normally early evening or nocturnal creatures, but leave it to Jute to know where there was a den. The twin had taken to the woods as soon as he could walk, and at times he appeared to know more about the animals than the animals knew themselves.

Finally he saw Sarah and Jute coming down the trail. Sarah's gold-brown hair hung in ragged tresses instead of her usual careful coif, but other than that, she looked all right. Well, except that now that she was closer, he could see her petticoat hem dragging the ground on one side of her dress skirt.

Jute, on the other hand, had muddy patches on his denim trousers and dark smears on his light blue shirt. One denim shoulder strap hung halfway down his arm.

Then the breeze shifted.

Wyn gagged. He hated skunk smell. Hell, he could smell skunk cabbage in the woods a mile away. That, not the arrival of the returning ducks and geese, always told him spring was close. In some years as early as February the skunk cabbage would flower, the terrible odor overriding the usually pleasant, pungent woodsy aromas. When flowering, skunk cabbage even heated up to where it melted the snow around it in order to spread its smell and attract pollinating insects.

Jute saw him and tried to jerk his hand free from Sarah's. "Wyn!" his little brother called.

Thankfully, Wyn saw Sarah maintain her hold on Jute.

"Uh . . ." Wyn halted and held out a cautioning hand. "Uh . . . you don't need to come any closer!"

Sarah pulled Jute to a stop, but snarled back at him, "What are we supposed to do? Stay out here in the woods with the baby skunks and their mamas until the smell goes away? Jute tells me that could take weeks!"

"It's too early in the season for baby skunks," Wyn tried to tell them.

"Tell that to that mother skunk!" Sarah started forward again. "We're coming down to take a bath! You're in our way!"

Her warning was plain, and Wyn backed up, stumbling over a rock in the trail. Barely catching himself before he fell, he ducked off the trail a ways and let Sarah and Jute pass. At least they would be downwind from him as he followed them. But he let them get quite a distance in front of him before he stepped back onto the trail.

"You'll have to use tomato juice," he called.

Sarah stopped again to look back at him, and Wyn immediately halted also. No way was he going to get any closer. One night in his teens he'd been out coon hunting with a friend, and they'd encountered a skunk. Even though they escaped the spray, they'd smelled it when the skunk warned them off. Wyn had lost his supper and never lived down the embarrassment.

"Tomato juice?" Sarah asked. "What on earth are you talking about?"

"It helps get rid of the smell," Wyn told her. "Nothing can get rid of it completely, but tomato juice helps. Mandy will know what to do, I'm sure."

"Mandy? It wasn't Mandy's relative who stirred up this mess. It shouldn't be Mandy's house that has to get smelled up while we try to wash this stuff off us."

"But we've got a baby at the store," Wyn pleaded, proud of himself when the quick retort flashed into his mind. "I don't know as having that smell there would be good for baby Sarah." And it darned sure wouldn't be good for him!

Sarah sniffed, and then her face got white. Wyn barely managed to hold back his laughter when he realized she'd been attempting a sniff of scorn for his excuse, but had forgotten about the smell and gotten a nose full of skunk scent. Then guilt stabbed him, and he lost the urge to laugh. He even took a step toward the pair, but the wind shifted once more.

"Aaggghhh!" He tore off into the woods again. He made it

to a fallen tree trunk to lean on while his stomach emptied.

When the dry heaves started, he heard Jute's voice say matter-of-factly, "Wyn don't take to skunk smell very good. I heard Danny Boy Peters a-tellin' 'bout how Wyn puked for ten minutes once when they run across a skunk when they was out coon huntin'. We might's well go on. Wyn'll probably be there a while."

They were gone when Wyn managed to stumble back to the trail. He figured his face was probably as white as Sarah's had been, but he had to get back down to the store.

8

THE MOUNTAIN FAMILIES began arriving soon after daybreak, on another clear, beautiful day. The first arrivals helped Wyn move sawhorses and boards from the storeroom and set up tables in the front of the store. From the boarding-house porch, Sarah watched them work, summoning her courage as she had tried to do most of a restless night. She had moved among the cream of the elite in New York society with complete ease, her background giving her equal footing with them. Here she would be judged on her ability to teach the mountain people's children—not her breeding or dowry.

Skirts flying, Mairi raced down the porch steps of the store and headed for the boardinghouse. Sarah watched her with an ache in her throat. No matter how hard she tried to distance herself from Mairi, she found it impossible. She was fair in the classroom, of course. She stifled the urge to praise Mairi to the rafters when the young girl proved herself a very apt student with a quick mind. Instead, she contented herself with a "Very good, Mairi," while her heart swelled in pride. It would be hard on Mairi if the other children accused her of being the teacher's pet.

To be honest, she was starting to feel a tiny bit of pride in almost all of the children. The first day she taught they'd been wary of her, probably because of their treatment by Prudence Elliot. But by the end of even that first day, she'd overheard Patty telling Carrie that she'd actually enjoyed school.

It had taken Carrie a little bit longer to decide the fun of learning was just as important as having Lonnie Fraiser smile back at her. Carrie had done her own turnaround, however, a couple days later when she realized Lonnie truly was enjoying their discussion on the differences in life in the South before and after the War Between the States. At first, Carrie appeared only to want to impress Lonnie with her knowledge, then she'd started to become interested herself.

Mairi rushed up to her, carrying a cloth-covered basket. "Hope you haven't finished eatin', Miss Sarah! I baked some muffins yesterday evening, and I saved back a couple for you and Wyn, since you didn't neither one get any last night."

"How thoughtful of you, Mairi. Can you come in and sit with me while I have another cup of coffee and enjoy my muffin?"

"Sure." She skipped over to the door and held it open for Sarah. "I already helped do the breakfast dishes at our house. Carrie fixed breakfast for us, 'cause Sissy and Robert are still in bed."

As they walked toward the kitchen, Mairi continued, "Can you figure it out? All these folks are coming today, and we'll have all sorts of friends to play with, all day long instead of just at recess. And they're still lollygagging in bed. Guess they're probably making over baby Sarah. Robert, he was right proud of baby Sarah when he saw her."

"I didn't get a chance to meet Robert last night," Sarah said, looking around the kitchen for Mandy. But the older woman wasn't in sight. "I'm looking forward to it today."

"Hope you don't mind me saying this, Miss Sarah." Mairi wrinkled her nose a tad. "I think you oughtta take another bath in that tomato juice before you come over to meet all the folks."

"Oh, dear!" Sarah sniffed, but couldn't smell herself. "I put on some rose water this morning. I was hoping it would cover up the scent."

Mairi shrugged. "Just smells like a skunk's got into a rosebush."

Although she forced a chuckle at Mairi's comment, Sarah's eyes teared. That wasn't like her in any way. She usually handled a dig at herself with complete aplomb. Lord knew she'd had plenty of practice covering up her feelings with her father. It must be the strain of meeting the parents with so little sleep, she decided.

She tried casually to wipe off the tear that escaped, but Mairi's face creased in remorse. "I'm sorry, Miss Sarah. I shouldn't have said that, but I thought you might want to know." She set the basket on the table and shoved it across to Sarah. "Here. One of my muffins will make you feel better. Please eat it. I'll get you a cup of coffee from the stove."

Sarah blinked her tears back and sat, pulling the tea towel from the basket. The muffins did look delicious, with what might be blueberries in them. Stomach tense with worry, she'd eaten hardly any breakfast. As Mairi set a cup of coffee in front of her, Sarah picked up a muffin.

"Sissy had some blueberries left from what she'd canned last summer," Mairi said as she settled in the chair across the table. Propping her chin on her palm, she watched Sarah very closely, it seemed, while she took a bite of muffin. "I been practicing how to cook, since I'm getting of an age where it's time I learned."

"Well, these are delicious," Sarah assured her.

Mairi's face creased in a smile. "Then you be sure and eat every bite, so I'll know you really mean it."

"There seems to be some other taste here — something besides blueberries."

"No!" Mairi's eyes widened and she stared around the kitchen instead of meeting Sarah's gaze. "I mean . . .

uh . . . well, you know. Sometimes cooks don't want to tell their recipes. It can be like a family secret recipe."

The back door off the kitchen opened, and Mandy walked in, with Wyn following her.

"Hello, Mairi," Mandy greeted. "Oh, muffins. You've been practicing baking again."

"Yes, Miz Tuttle. Uh . . . I'm sure you're probably too full from breakfast to have one. But I bet Wyn's got room for a muffin. He left before Carrie got the mush done this morning."

Wyn shook his head, slowly backing toward the door. His nose twitched.

"I thought you were out on the porch," he said, his words aimed at Sarah. "I came over to see if Mandy had any more canned tomatoes from last summer. Jute's still a little rank this morning."

"As I am, I guess! Something like a skunk in a rosebush?" Sarah shoved her chair back and stood, leaning on the table to brace herself as she prepared to tell him exactly what she thought of his rudeness.

But he disappeared out the door. Her breath whooshed out in anger, and she looked over at Mandy to see the older woman with a hand over her mouth, eyes twinkling above her fingers.

Catching another movement out of the corner of her eye, she twisted her head in time to see Mairi sidling out of the kitchen, her muffin basket in hand.

"I'm gonna take Wyn his muffin," the little girl said. Without another word of apology, she scurried down the hallway.

Sarah sighed in defeat and looked at Mandy again. "*Do* you have any more tomato juice? I can take it over to my cabin and send for Jute, so we can both take another bath."

"No need," Mandy said. "I do have some more jars of juice in the basement, and I've also got a large tub in the room off the kitchen here. It'll be warm in that room, and we can fill the tub from the reservoir on my stove. After you soak in the tomato juice first."

"But the smell . . ."

"This house is larger than your cabin and the bathing room's got windows I can open. Go on in there while I get the tomato juice. You can tell me what dress you want, and I'll get it for you when I go over to bring Jute here. The one you have on has probably already soaked up the odor, but it shouldn't be as bad as the dress we had to bury from yesterday. This one will probably come clean, if we soak it long enough."

Giving in, Sarah started toward the room Mandy indicated, leaving her muffin half-eaten on the table.

"And Sarah," Mandy said. "Don't mind Wyn. He doesn't handle skunk smell very well, from what I hear."

"Yes. I've heard that, too." With a huge effort, Sarah kept the snarl from her voice.

Sarah could tell there was at least a touch of odor still clinging to her as she met the mountain families. But they were too polite to say anything, unlike Wyn MacIntyre's rudeness that morning. Or perhaps some of them had had a run-in with a skunk a time or two. Whatever the case, they were all very nice to her, only wrinkling their noses briefly, then catching themselves and stopping.

She kept a few names straight by pairing them with their children, but many of the families didn't have children in her school. They all appeared to be either lifelong friends or relatives, though. Mairi appointed herself Sarah's escort, and Pris tagged along after them.

Mairi gloried in her own importance when she told and retold the tale of Sarah finding her in New York City. Her voice got a tad hoarse when she spoke of her parents, but she visibly brightened when she told of Sarah's loving care.

The families continued to arrive all morning, as the day warmed even beyond the previous day's temperatures. Sarah stopped midsentence when she noticed a garishly painted red, white, and blue wagon coming down the trail. A butterscotch-colored mule wearing a straw hat covered with red poppies pulled the wagon. In the back of the wagon was a rocking chair with someone sitting in it, although

Sarah couldn't tell if she knew the chair's occupant or not, since the rear of the chair faced forward.

A respectful pall of silence filtered through the crowd of people, and each creak of a wagon wheel badly in need of oil made Sarah wince until the wagon pulled up to a space that appeared to have been left for it at the front of the store. Indeed, the other wagons and even a couple buggies were all parked at the sides of the road stretching up and down the mountain. The butterscotch-colored mule, without apparent guidance from the small, gnarly faced man on the wagon seat, walked straight into the open space and stopped.

Dan rolled his wheelchair over to the edge of the porch. "Howdy, Tater," he said. "Glad you and your mama could come."

The little man nodded and stood. Reins dangling from knotted-knuckled fingers, he stretched his back as though to relieve the strain from riding with his elbows on his knees.

"Mama wouldn't miss comin' h'yar lessen it be that she was havin' her own wake," Tater said. "She figgers to pay her respects to Cal and Selene, and welcome the new little one God give ye to take one of them's place."

Sarah stared at Tater in astonishment. He looked like he had to be at least a hundred years old himself, although she supposed the hard life in the mountains could have aged his body beyond his years. Then she looked at the back of the wagon, wondering how old Tater's mama was.

She didn't have long to wait.

"Wyn," Dan called. He turned partially around in his chair. "Where on earth is he? He was right here a minute ago."

Sarah saw Wyn over on the edge of the porch, where he had moved when she approached Dan. As he walked over in response to Dan's summons, he eyed her warily where she stood at the bottom of the steps.

"Oh, there you are," Dan said. "Get a couple men to help you move Granny Clayborne's chair up here beside me, son. Then tell Sissy that Granny's here, will you? She'll want to bring baby Sarah down and get Granny's blessing."

"Sure, Pa."

Rather than climb down the steps, Wyn launched himself over the railing on the far side of the wagon. The entire crowd of people had gathered around the wagon, so he didn't need to ask for help. Lonnie Fraiser and Patty's father, Jason, jumped up onto the wagon bed.

Curious as to how the rocking chair stayed in the wagon instead of sliding around, Sarah stepped closer. Wooden props had been nailed in the wagon bed, just wide enough apart for the rockers to slide into, with one board laid crosswise in front of the chair. Jason and Lonnie lifted the rocker free and scooted it to the edge of the wagon, where Wyn waited. He picked up the tiny figure in the chair and carried her around the wagon, while Lonnie brought the chair.

Wyn hesitated when he saw Sarah, then drew in a breath and swiftly passed her by. She caught a glimpse of a barely wrinkled face and bright blue eyes on the elderly woman in his arms. The eyes pierced straight back into her own gaze in the brief second they made contact. She quickly decided to follow Lonnie, since it was apparent Granny Clayborne was a very important personage on this mountain.

As soon as Lonnie sat the chair down, Wyn shoved the young man aside and settled Granny in it. Then he headed into the store, and Sarah heard him finally release his breath. She narrowed her eyes, torn between greeting Granny and going after him to shove her smelly fragrance right under his nose.

"Don't worry 'bout him, child," a warm, full, feminine voice said. "He'll come round."

Brows lifting in surprise, Sarah turned to Granny Clayborne. The old woman chuckled at her, then waited until Tater wrapped a brilliant multicolored blanket around her lap and pulled her scarlet shawl back up on her shoulders.

"No need to tell me that Tater looks older'n me," Granny said. "I been told that plenty of times. I tell Tater I've lived a purer life than him, but that ain't really true. Couldn't ask for a better son. He's outlived two wives who were two of the best women God ever put on earth, and it's just him and

me now. The young'uns done scattered all over—in and out
of the mountains."

She reached beneath the blanket and pulled out a small
woven bag, digging inside until she came up with a corncob
pipe. Dan immediately handed over his own tobacco pouch.

"Thankee, Dan," she said. After she filled her pipe, Tater
lit it for her, then headed out into the crowd of people.
Granny rocked back and forth for a few puffs, then pointed
the pipestem at Sarah.

"You're the new teacher."

"Yes, ma'am," Sarah said respectfully.

"Good 'un, too, from what I hear."

"Thank you. I do believe I'm enjoying teaching more
than anything I've ever done in my life." Knowing she was
staring at the blanket and shawl, and afraid Granny would
think her rude, she added, "Could I ask you about your
blanket and shawl? I've never seen anything more beautiful
in my life. Did someone you know make them for you?"

"Made 'em myself when I could use my hands good
enough. Here, feel the wool."

Sarah reached out and touched the shawl, finding it as
soft as the best cashmere. Granny guided her hand to the
blanket, which was just as fine.

"The colors have stayed so brilliant," Sarah said.

"You mean for them bein' so old, since I musta made
them so long ago, me bein' nigh onto a hundred?"

When Sarah flushed, Granny patted her hand. "There,
there, child, don't go on so. I like to tease. I do love my
bright colors. Always have. And I ain't the only one on the
mountain that can do work like this. I writ down my recipes
for the dyes, and my grandchildren and nieces all have
them. The material's a mix of sheep and goat fleece, of a
type my man brought over from Scotland with him. A few
of the families raise 'em for the fleece and we drink the goat
milk. Makes mighty fine cheese, too."

"I would love to buy a couple of the blankets, and even
a shawl, if anyone had any for sale," Sarah said.

"Reckon we can find someone who does."

Granny rocked again, peacefully puffing on her pipe.

Seeing the old woman's attention turn elsewhere, Sarah took it as a dismissal and left the porch. She wandered over to the table where food was being set out, only to be told the women had everything under control. Her former escort, Mairi, seemed to have found something more important to do, and she didn't see Mandy anywhere. Not feeling comfortable joining any of the conversing groups, since she had only just met most of the people, she decided to investigate the sounds of children's laughter around the side of the store.

She walked down a well-worn path, glancing up at the side of the building at one point. She'd been able to see the side and rear of the store from her little cabin, but had never actually been on the porch off the back storage room or in the stables where Dan kept his horses. There must also be a cow there, she realized, since milk had regularly appeared at the meals she shared with the MacIntyres. Perhaps Dan kept even more than one cow, since there always seemed to be plenty of milk for the entire family, as well as butter and cheese.

Thinking to explore the barn, where the noise from the children now seemed centered, she didn't at first notice the two people on the back porch. A man's raised voice finally caused her to halt beside a large newly leafing bush, which hid her from view. She only caught the last of the man's words, something about whoever he was talking to not understanding. The woman who answered him was Sissy.

"You have two children now, Robert! It was bad enough when it was just you and me. What on earth will I tell Bobbie and Sarah if you're not around to watch them grow up?"

"You knew what I did when we got married," the man Sarah decided must be Sissy's husband, Robert, answered. "This store won't support all of us, and I don't expect it to. It's my duty to take care of you and the young'uns, not your pa's! I tried every danged mine I could get to, and none of them were a-hiring. 'Sides, I do something like that, I might not be around either to watch my young'uns grow up. There's plenty of men not that much older than I am a-settin' on porches and coughing up their insides from Black Lung!"

"I didn't want you to go look for work in the mines, Robert. You know that. I love you, and I want you to grow old with me. There's got to be something else you can do."

"What? I ain't cut out to be no farmer. I hated every minute I had to hoe weeds on my daddy's place while I grew up—hated every danged kernel of corn I had to shell off of every corncob. If I have to do that, it'll kill me real slow. There's only one thing that I enjoy doin', and I do it danged well! But there ain't much call out there in the rest of the world for that."

"Oh, Robert. I'm scared."

Sarah heard movement and peeked around the bush to see Sissy in Robert's arms. He cupped the back of her head with his large palm and bent over her, his eyes closed and a pained look on his face. He was a nice-looking man, Sarah admitted, dark where Sissy was blond—dark where Sissy's brother Wyn was fair like her. Sarah shook her head at herself when she realized she was comparing Robert to Wyn.

The storage room door opened, and Sarah recognized Wyn's voice.

"Granny Clayborne's waiting to see you two," he said. "I've got baby Sarah here for you. She was sleeping and didn't wake when I picked her up."

Sissy stepped from Robert's arms and took her baby. She hurried through the door, but Robert paused a moment.

"I don't know what to do, Wyn. She ain't changed her mind, and I hate like hell to keep hurtin' her. But I can't sit around and let you and Dan take care of *my* family. I might just as well head on out and forget I've got a wife and young'uns if I can't take care of them myself."

Wyn laid a comforting arm on Robert's shoulder. "You'll do what you have to do. Most of the men here appreciate you, and even some of the women. Leery's said her remedies work even better when she gets the one ingredient she needs for them from you instead of Cabbage Carter. 'Course, old Cabbage don't appreciate losing Leery as a customer, but Leery's only good for a quart or two now and then."

"Yeah." Robert sighed deeply. "Well, I better go pay my respects to Granny."

Wyn dropped his arm, and Robert left the porch. Sticking his hands in his pockets Wyn walked over to the porch railing. Sarah tried to leave silently, but when she took a step back, a stick snapped loudly beneath her heel. Frowning, Wyn leaned past the railing until she realized he could see her.

9

*T*HINKING WYN WOULD immediately withdraw, Sarah remained quiet. But he continued to stare at her, his face closed to any emotion she could detect at that distance. Finally she picked up her skirts and started forward.

"I was going out to the barn to look for—"

Wyn vaulted over the porch railing, a drop of at least eight feet, and landed in front of her with barely a sound. Sarah gasped and laid a hand on her breast. Land sakes, for such a muscular man he moved awfully gracefully. She literally felt a stab of apprehension at his emotion-laden eyes, now clearly visible. The blue was darkened to an actual thunderstorm color, and she sensed a warning as clear as the one preceding a summer lightning display.

She tilted her chin defiantly, and repeated, "I was going out to the barn to look for the *children*. And I'd appreciate it if you didn't come close enough to get a whiff of my odor and get sick on me! Though I can't smell it myself, I'm assuming from the actions of the people I've met today that there's still a trace of it. And even a trace seems to be too much for you."

His mouth twitched and the color of his eyes lightened.

He took a step backward. "You shouldn't be eavesdropping."

"I know. I didn't mean to. I . . . heard a strange voice along with Sissy's and stopped. I should have called out. I realize that now."

Slipping his thumbs into his belt, Wyn continued to study her. His action drew her gaze downward, where his fingers curled in a relaxed manner near the point his thighs joined. Only recently had her married friend, Eve, explained the hows and wherefores of the marriage act to her. Learning of Sarah's betrothal, Eve had taken pity on her motherless state and passed on both the lore her own mother had given her and the actuality of the process.

Funny, though. After her extremely enlightening chat with Eve, she hadn't had even a touch of desire to examine surreptitiously Stephen's manly attribute, as she was trying to avoid doing with Wyn right now. Eve had said that men were made diversely from each other down there, and those variations could make a huge difference in how a woman enjoyed the *Act*. With Stephen, she had thought probably to have to tolerate what sounded like an extremely uncomfortable *Act* in order to fulfill her desire for children. With Wyn, that one little word "enjoy" seemed to take on a great deal more importance.

Wyn's trousers twitched right before her eyes, the way his lips had a minute ago. A horrible blush spread over Sarah's face—she could feel the heat like a summer brush fire—and she curled her fingers in her dress bodice. On either side of her hand, her nipples puckered into hard pill balls. Some darned little imp seemed to be sitting on her shoulder, though, holding her head in place so she couldn't jerk her eyes free. It wasn't until Wyn took a step forward that she wrenched her eyes free to look at the ground.

"Th-there's a patch of violets!" she said with a gasp. "Aren't they pretty?" Disregarding the potential stain to her dress, she knelt and reached beside the bush to pick one of the small, purple blooms.

She placed the violet to her nose, inhaling the light scent. When she started to rise again, Wyn held out his hand to her.

Since he was standing right beside her, it would be extremely rude to ignore his offer of assistance. Besides, the alternative, given her awkward position, was to sit on her rear and scoot away from him before she attempted to get to her feet.

She did the polite thing and took his hand. Rising, she quirked a brow and held the violet out. He took it, inhaling the scent, and she felt the tickle on her own nose, as though she still held the flower.

"Johnny-jump-ups," he said. "That's what we call them here. Not violets."

"They're the same flower. With the same odor."

"Truthfully," Wyn said after a second and in a low voice, "there's not enough hint of the encounter you had yesterday left to bother me or anyone else. I think the people you're meeting have just heard about it and are trying to see if they smell anything without hurting your feelings."

"Mandy used vinegar and even some lemon along with the tomatoes this morning. But if it worked to get rid of the smell, why have you been keeping as far away from me as you can today?"

"Hell, Sarah, that's not because of any skunk odor." He gave a start as though he'd only just realized what he'd said, then quickly changed the subject. "You're heading in the right direction if you want to find the young'uns. There's a couple litters of baby kittens in the barn, and I imagine some of them are making their picks already, before the litters get all spoken for. One of the hounds—Lady—is fixing to whelp any day, too, so there might be a few men out there checking her over. 'Course Pa don't get out to hunt anymore, but he still breeds the best coonhounds on the mountain."

Changing the subject suited her fine, and Sarah came up with the first thing that popped into her mind not having to do with the reason Wyn kept sidestepping her.

"What were Robert and Sissy arguing about, Wyn?" she asked instead of heading to the barn. Her cheeks had cooled while he slowly rambled on about kittens and coon dogs, but her knees still felt a little too wobbly to try to walk yet.

He shook his head. "I don't want to be discourteous, Sarah, but some things are private. Sissy thought she was having a personal conversation with Robert. I figure if Sissy wants you to know what they were talking about, she'll tell you herself."

With barely a break for a breath, he continued, "The services for the wake will begin in another half hour, then we'll eat. If you want to see the barn, you should go on now."

At that moment, a crowd of youngsters exploded from the barn door. Sarah watched them over Wyn's shoulder until he turned also to see where they were headed. The twins led a group of children, with even a couple of considerably older boys tagging along. They rounded the barn and their voices and shouts grew dimmer.

"Land sake," Sarah said. "That was Jute at the head of that group. I hope he's not taking them out to see that skunk's den."

"It still amazes me that you can tell Jute from Luke," Wyn admitted. "And even at a distance like that. It took me until they were a year old to be able to tell them apart, and I saw them every day."

Then his voice grew sterner. "But don't worry about Jute heading back up to that skunk den. He knows better. More than likely, he's checking the compost heap to see if the worms are stirring up where he can get to them yet. I heard Jimmie Jack Carlson tell him the bass were biting in the stream over by the Carlson cabin."

"Oh, I love fresh fish. I wonder if Jute would take me with him when he goes."

"We've got a rule around here you might want to consider before you go offering to help catch fish."

A huge smile spread over Wyn's face, and Sarah paid more attention to it than she did his next sentence. Suddenly what he'd said clicked in her brain.

"You catch, you clean?" she repeated. "You mean you expect women to clean fish if they catch them?"

"Mairi, Pris, and Carrie all know how to clean fish. Sissy, too, although Robert does that for her now. I heard tell my ma could slice off fillets with the best of them, but she turned that over to me after I got old enough to handle a knife. So the only way women in our family get out of cleaning their own fish is if they use their feminine wiles on a man and talk him into doing it for them."

"I guess that leaves me out then," Sarah mused unthinkingly.

The thunderstorm color returned to Wyn's eyes. "What the hell's that supposed to mean?"

"Uh . . . I'm going on out to the barn now." Sarah walked around him, but Wyn took her arm and fell into step behind her.

"You didn't answer me, Sarah. Damn it, you're betrothed to some man, so you should be well aware what sort of rewards feminine wiles bring a woman."

Sarah sighed, wondering how long he would keep his mannerly hold on her arm. She didn't need to answer him. As he'd mentioned about Sissy a moment ago, some things were private, and it hurt her deeply to discuss her homeliness. Her father had mentally pounded her lack of beauty into her from the time she could reason, and she'd come to accept it as a fact.

She couldn't change the looks she was born with. Although her gawkiness had filled out some, she still stared down on all her female friends, as she'd done all her life. She'd never be one of those dainty blondes so popular with the male species, or even a wild, fiery redhead. All she could do was keep herself neat and clean, as well as take care with the clothing she chose.

Now, instead of belaboring the looks she could not alter, she concentrated on how well Wyn's steps matched hers. They were both tall and, among other things, Stephen had decried her long stride. He insisted women should take dainty, tiny steps. Trying to do that only made Sarah feel as awkward as the newborn colt she'd seen once in her father's stables.

Releasing a breath with a measure of frustration in the sound, Wyn said, "You've got a wonderfully smooth walk,

Sarah. Do they teach things like that in finishing schools, or does it come naturally to you?"

Sarah halted in surprise. "Were you reading my mind?"

"No," Wyn said with a chuckle, which sparked in his eyes as a twinkle. "Why? Were you thinking, too, of how easy it was to walk together?"

"I . . . I think I hear Mairi's voice. I didn't see her with the other children, did you?"

His fingers tightened on her arm and she felt every tiny quiver of her response. The murmur of Mairi's voice faded into the background, along with her awareness of the barn door looming beside them and the faint wheeze of a mule's hee-haw. His hold on her arm changed more into a caress than a polite gesture, and Wyn raised his free arm. She stood helpless as he ran a gentle fingertip ever so slowly down her cheek, across her jawbone to the middle of her chin, and then down her neck.

When he traced a back-and-forth pattern a few inches wide just beneath her dress collar, her eyes sluggishly drooped. She instinctively grabbed his waist to steady her legs.

"Don't close your eyes," Wyn growled in a barely discernible voice. "They're beautiful. Like pools of deep brown velvet."

She flushed at the compliment, her head dropping to avoid letting him see the misery she knew had to be filling her face. She'd started to think of him as a friend, but she couldn't tolerate teasing gibes about her looks, even from a friend. She got enough of those from other people.

He tucked his index finger beneath her chin and brought her head back up. "What?" he asked. "Would you rather I compare them to that bright, pretty brown Granny uses to trim some of her blankets?"

"I'd prefer you didn't tease me about them at all." Sarah forced herself back from his hold. "I know how plain I am. I've had enough mocking of my looks over the years to last me a lifetime."

"I don't understand what you mean by mocking, unless you're jeering at me instead." Wyn shrugged his shoulders.

"You're betrothed. I'm sure you had plenty of suitors before that, and evidently one man found you attractive enough to propose to. And you found him attractive enough in return to accept his proposal."

"So what are you trying to do?" Sarah said angrily. "Dally with someone already spoken for? Or seeing if you're missing something that Stephen saw beneath all my plainness? For your information, I'm the one who chose Stephen, not the other way around. It's amazing what money will buy, even for a homely woman!"

With a sob, she gathered her skirts and raced away toward her tiny cabin.

Stunned, Wyn stared after her until she disappeared through the cabin door. With her long stride, she was gone before he could take a second breath. He moved a step after her, then paused. What on earth was she talking about? But having seen her temper before, he didn't feel like taking a chance on following her right then and demanding an explanation. He'd wait until she cooled down a little bit.

He started toward the back porch, but when he came to the steps, he stopped again. He didn't feel like being sociable to all the neighbors with his mind in a turmoil over what Sarah had said. Wandering back to the barn, he reached down and pulled a blade of new grass, then leaned against the wall beside the door. Sticking the stem in his mouth and propping one booted foot behind him against the barn wall, he turned to gaze at the little cabin once more.

Did she really think she was plain? Lord God above, didn't the woman ever look in a mirror? Sure, she was tall, but that meant she fit into a man's arms like a proper armful. A man wasn't squeezing air half the time with a woman like Sarah in his hold.

He hadn't been teasing her about those beautiful brown eyes, either. A man could fall into them if he didn't watch out, like a shooting star streaking across the vast night sky and disappearing, never to be seen again. It would almost be worth it to determine if the velvetyness were as soft and soothing as it looked. He'd gotten hard in an instant when those eyes touched his crotch, faster even than when he was a randy sixteen-year-old lusting after the Widow Silverton.

Yet when Sarah got angry or excited, the gold-dust sparks in her brown eyes danced and sparkled. They reminded him of the sparklers he ordered for the younger children's enjoyment on the Fourth of July.

Her features weren't dainty. Hell, dainty features would be awkward on her. What she had fit in good proportion—a straight nose and high cheekbones. A mouth wide enough to fill that space above her firm chin and fit just right over a man's mouth—his mouth.

She wasn't anything like Rose, and at one point he'd thought Rose about the prettiest thing that God ever put on earth for a man's enjoyment. Pretty is as pretty does, though, he remembered his ma saying more than once when she was talking about one of the young mountain women she'd caught him watching. Even before Rose had refused to return to Sawback Mountain with him, he'd realized their relationship had been a mistake. Rose was all surface, with none of Sarah Channing's deep caring for others.

And, damn! He'd already decided her legs would put those fragile limbs Rose tottered around on to shame. Sarah's legs would be a fine sight for a man with the right to see them. Hadn't that damned fiancé of hers told her how beautiful she was? If he hadn't, and from her comments Wyn was pretty damned sure he hadn't, why should that jackass be the one to live with her all her life?

That brought him back to the truth of one of Sarah's other comments, however. She had been right about her already being spoken for. He'd had his hands on another man's property, whether it had been Sarah's decision or not to become betrothed.

He didn't feel a bit guilty about kissing her for some reason, and the reason became clear as soon as he admitted his lack of guilt. If that jackass Stephen didn't appreciate Sarah, he knew of one man who did.

Not that he had any intentions of getting serious with a woman like Sarah Channing, he reminded himself. She would go back to her nice, rich life as soon as she had her fling here in the mountains. Right now she fancied herself on one of her do-good missions in life, which people with plenty of money felt obligated to accomplish now and then—although it seemed Sarah had a little deeper feelings about what she was doing than some of the do-good political wives he'd met in Washington. Most of them had done charitable works to enhance their husband's careers and their own status among the other wives.

But look at what she'd said about the orphanage where Mairi had ended up—that her attorney was overseeing the new management of the place. Sure as shooting some of her own money was being used for the maintenance and management.

Perhaps he could repay Sarah's kindness to Mairi and the other children who were in that orphanage through no fault of their own, by helping her overcome her erroneous thoughts about being homely. Perhaps . . .

He heard the giggle first, then concentrated on making out the words of the conversation.

"I thought for sure Wyn was gonna kiss her, Miz Leery." Mairi's voice, Wyn decided.

Confirming his guess, Wyn's niece and the old mountain healer walked out of the barn. With the door shoved back at an angle and Wyn standing in the lee of it, they didn't catch sight of him.

"Probably he would have," Leery told Mairi. "But you said Sarah didn't eat all her muffin. And she's the one who broke it off and ran away."

"I didn't see her half of muffin on the table until after she'd taken her bath and left Miz Tuttle's house. By then, it was sorta dried up, and I didn't figure Miss Sarah would eat it if I took it to her."

"Well, the love potion won't do any good iffen you don't get enough of it in their bellies. Although it looks to me like your uncle Wyn got plenty of it in that belly of his."

"Yeah, he ate both of the muffins I gave him. Can you make me up some more potion, Miz Leery?"

"We'll talk about it, gal. Come on. Let's go visit with some of the folks for now."

Wyn stood stunned against the side of the barn. What the

hell was Mairi doing, consorting with Leery and feeding him and Sarah a love potion? Hell, he'd seen those darned potions work before, and he didn't care at all for the thought of one of them rolling around right now in his own belly. And it was evidently aimed at getting him and Miss Sarah Channing together!

It was one thing to think about making Sarah aware of her own attractiveness; it was quite another one to take a chance on being caught in the web of her attractiveness himself and spend the rest of his life mooning over her. He'd had enough trouble keeping his hands off her before today, and hadn't done a very good job at all of preventing his hands from grabbing for her every time she got within reaching distance.

Now, with a love potion working on him, the best thing he could do was keep as far away from her as possible. She hadn't swallowed as much of the dosage as he had, and it would be easier for her to resist him. He'd just have to overcome the potion's power.

10

SOON AFTER REVEREND Jackson's arrival, the people gathered around the front porch of the general store. Sarah stood back on the edge of the crowd, hoping no one noticed her red-rimmed eyes and wishing she could have stayed at her cabin. It wouldn't do, however, not to attend the wake for Mairi's parents.

Someone slipped a hand through her arm and patted her on the shoulder. "It's all right to cry even if you didn't know Cal and Selene," Mandy said, making Sarah aware her red-rimmed eyes had been noticed. She didn't correct Mandy as she went on, "Feelings like that—a person crying—are a sign of sympathy for all the ones missing the two of them after they're gone."

Mairi pushed through the crowd and took Sarah's free hand. She was a much quieter little girl than she'd been when she was introducing Sarah around earlier.

"Would you come sit with me, Miss Sarah?" she asked softly. "Reverend Jackson said the family oughtta sit up on the chairs on the porch. There's way too many people here for the schoolhouse he uses for a church other times, so he's gonna hold the service right here."

She glanced up at Mandy. "And you, too, Miz Tuttle, if you don't mind. I think Uncle Dan might like to have you beside him."

Sarah glanced at Mandy in surprise, seeing a flush steal over the older woman's face. *Dan and Mandy?* she wondered.

Her hand tightening on Sarah's arm, Mandy said, "I'm sort of considered one of the family, since we live so close."

There was no time for further conversation as Mairi tugged Sarah's hand and they made their way through the crowd. Granny Clayborne still had the place on one side of Dan, and Dan motioned for Mandy to sit in the empty chair on his other side. Mairi led Sarah to two chairs between Wyn and Pris. She took the one beside her favorite cousin, and Sarah was left with the one next to Wyn.

Before long, Sarah's eyes teared again, and she didn't have to worry about explaining her red eyes. Reverend Jackson evidently knew Cal and Selene MacIntyre well, and before he was finished, Sarah wished she had been lucky enough to meet them. She pulled her handkerchief from her dress sleeve and wiped a tear tumbling free of her lower lashes.

"Had they been able," Reverend Jackson was saying, "Cal and Selene MacIntyre would have returned to these mountains. They were both born here, and they had mountain air in their lungs, mountain soil in their blood. They left only to seek what they thought would be a more prosperous life for their child and found instead the path back to their ultimate home with our Lord."

He turned to smile at Mairi. "And the Lord never judged them for their decision, made with the free will He Himself afforded them at their birth. In fact, He watched over their child, leading Mairi to safety and to a wonderful woman named Sarah Channing, who brought her home to her family."

His eyes touched on Sarah, and she felt the warmth of his gaze throughout her entire being. Another tear trembled, then fell, and she thought how truly blessed the mountain people were to have as wonderful a preacher as Reverend Jackson.

She heard a muffled sniff beside her. Instinctively she glanced at Mairi, prepared to offer the little girl the use of her handkerchief. But Mairi appeared to be holding up well, her small hands clasped with Pris's. Hearing the sniff again, she turned to look at Wyn in time to see him wipe his shirt cuff beneath his nose.

"Here," she said softly, pushing the handkerchief into his hand.

He shook his head, then shifted to reach into his back pocket. He pulled out a bright red bandanna, and despite the seriousness of the occasion, Sarah had to bite back a smile as he wiped his eyes and blew his nose with the brilliant cloth. It was a minute or so later before Sarah realized she'd slipped one hand beneath his arm and was patting the top of his forearm with her other hand in a comforting gesture.

As soon as she became aware of what she was doing, she furtively wiggled her hand free, with no resistance from Wyn. Reverend Jackson concluded the first part of the service and opened it up to eulogies from the departed couple's family and friends. Wyn rose and helped his pa roll his chair over to the middle of the porch where Reverend Jackson had been standing, and remained behind the wheelchair while Dan spoke.

The mountain people told stories of Cal and Selene, some heartrending and some humorous. When Reverend Jackson rose to say a final prayer, Sarah was surprised that the service was over, and that quite a long while had passed. Shadows had lengthened and the temperature was slightly cooler, but not one person had moved to leave.

Wyn stood beside her, and Sarah realized the reverend had asked everyone to rise to their feet. When she stood, her leg muscles stiff and cramped from sitting so long, she stumbled slightly. Wyn reached out to steady her, but when she looked up to thank him, he kept his head bowed. For an instant, his fingers tightened on her waist, then he dropped his arm and clasped his hands in front of him as Reverend Jackson began to pray.

The final amen had barely left everyone's mouth before the crowd began breaking up. Reverend Jackson walked over to Dan and shook his hand.

"Right nice service, Reverend," Dan said. "Sure wish you'd make it round here on Sundays more often. Your preachin' is exactly what a man needs after a week's work."

"I'll come as often as I can," the reverend said. "But there's other places in the mountains where I'm needed, too."

"We understand." Dan turned to Sarah. "I told you the name of the lady who brought Mairi back to us, but I don't think you've actually met her, Reverend. Miss Sarah Channing, Reverend Kyle Jackson."

Sarah held out her hand. "A wonderful service, Reverend."

In keeping with the solemn occasion, Kyle Jackson wore a black suit jacket and white shirt, with what looked like a thin black string tie around his collar. Sarah had never seen that style of tie before today, but she'd noticed a variation of it on several of the other men.

The minister had the whitest smile Sarah had ever seen. His full head of black hair curled over his forehead, looking as silky as one of her ball gowns. Warm brown eyes were set in a rugged face, and his entire attitude made her trust him on sight. He seemed much too young to be so popular a minister in these out-of-the-way mountains, as Sarah would have imagined it took a much older man to gain these people's respect. But the mountain people had surprised her more than once since she arrived.

"You are to be commended for bringing Mairi home," Kyle told her, still holding her hand. "I remember you from when you first entered society at your coming-out ball, but I left for the seminary that same season."

"You're from New York?" Sarah asked. "For goodness sakes, you must be Loretta Jackson's son."

He finally released her hand. "Yes, and I've been here in the mountains since I graduated from the seminary. I was rather astounded when I heard that a young lady had traveled alone from New York with Mairi, even when I realized who it was and that you must be at least twenty-five by now."

He shook his head slightly. "Darn it, forgive me. I've been out of polite society for so long I've forgotten it doesn't do to mention a lady's age. I guess it slipped out because while I was thinking of you, I realized that when I left New York, I was your same age now. It's been seven years since I was back there."

"Not much has changed," Sarah told him. "Of course, you know all of your sisters are married now. And your mother is as beautiful as ever."

"My sister Carol wrote me of your father's death. You have my condolences."

Sarah couldn't keep from thinning her lips. But her years of training in manners and hiding her emotions allowed her to catch the action, she hoped, before it became too noticeable.

"Thank you."

"If you're not already committed," Kyle said, "I'd like to have supper with you today. The letters I get from my sisters are wonderful, but they write only infrequently. It's been a long while since I've been back home, and you can give me a more recent update. I admit to wanting to go back and see everyone again, but my duties here keep me fairly busy."

"I'd be delighted, Reverend."

"Then please call me Kyle," he said. "And we might even get a chance for a dance. I've heard Tater play, and he is actually quite good. The mountain people believe in doing things at a wake that the departed would have done had they been there themselves. And Cal and Selene did truly love to dance."

He centered his attention on Mairi, and Sarah felt a prickle on the back of her neck. Swiftly turning, she saw Wyn at the general store door. He shuttered his eyes quickly, but she could have sworn the dark thunderstorm color was back. However, the lengthening shadows under the overhanging porch roof made it difficult to be certain, and he walked on through the doorway without a word.

When Kyle Jackson moved away from Mairi, the young

girl attached herself to Sarah again, apparently needing a woman's comfort after the reminders of her departed parents. Sarah gladly complied, holding hands with Mairi on one side of her and Pris on the other as they strolled around the area.

At first, Mairi talked about her parents, but by the time they had wandered over to the schoolhouse and sat down on the steps Jute kept cleanly swept, Mairi was telling Pris about her beautiful room at Channing Place.

"Miss Sarah said I could come back and visit whenever Uncle Dan would let me, Pris," she said. "Maybe you could come with me. It's a real pretty room, but I still like livin' in the mountains lots better."

"Pris will be more than welcome, if it's all right with her father," Sarah agreed. Not for the first time since her arrival, a stab of reluctance to return to Channing Place went through her. But it would be Stephen's and her home after they married, since she had no desire to live in the dreary VanderDyke mausoleum, which had grown even worse given Stephen's family's lack of funds for repairs.

She supposed Stephen would correct that after their marriage, and since she did feel rather sorry for the widowed Mrs. VanderDyke, she had no objection to that.

With the huge fortune Father left me in charge of, I could even do that for them if Stephen and I weren't married.

Sarah stifled a gasp as that thought flew through her head. What on earth had brought something like that on? She'd thought out her plans ever so carefully over the last two years, and she had chosen Stephen after a prudent study of his faults and failings, as well as his few commendable attributes.

She had also chosen him when her father had been in fairly good health, with no thought that she might soon find herself in an independent state, free from his control. With the matters of her father's estate to handle, as well as her desire to take Mairi to her family, she hadn't taken time to check with her attorney as to what sort of power Stephen would have over her financial state after their marriage. She assumed he would have quite a bit, given what she'd seen of her friends' marriages. Had she not wanted children of her own so desperately, she might think a lot harder about placing herself back under a man's dominion again.

But even though they aren't my own, I've got lots of children right here, she thought.

"I didn't never know how old you were, Miss Sarah," Mairi said, breaking into her thoughts. For some reason, her statement puzzled Sarah.

"As I told Kyle, I'm twenty-five," Sarah said.

"Cousin Wyn's only twenty-two," Mairi told her, an even more out-of-the-blue statement in Sarah's mind.

"Ummmm," she responded.

"Wonder if that matters?"

"Matters for what?" Sarah asked.

Mairi gave a start, then shook her head. "Oh, nothin' really. Wonder if we're 'bout ready to eat. My belly's a-fixin' to rub my backbone."

A dinner bell clamored through the pure air, and Sarah stood, reaching out a hand to each girl. "Guess that answers your question, huh? And I'll have to admit, my stomach—my *belly*—is wondering when I'm going to feed it again, too."

Kyle Jackson met her at the edge of the crowd, easily agreeing when Mairi and Pris asked if they could eat with them also. After joining the line at a series of long tables groaning with food and filling their plates, they went back over to the schoolhouse steps. Balancing laden plates on their laps, the two girls chattered while she and Kyle reminisced about mutual acquaintances in New York.

A couple times Sarah felt that prickle on the back of her neck, but when she shifted to scan the crowd, she didn't notice anyone watching her. Each time she shrugged and went back to her conversation with Kyle.

Soon a lively fiddle trill split the air, and Kyle surged to his feet. "Whoops," he said. "I need to say something more before Tater gets into his tunes. Shall I take your plate?"

Instead, Sarah reached for his. "I'll take care of these. You go on."

"Don't forget our dance."

He left, and Sarah and the girls followed more slowly.

She realized another reason for the placement of Granny's wagon when she spied Tater in the bed of it, with a couple other men joining him. Kyle leaped up with the players for his announcement.

"Cal and Selene would have wanted us to remember them with joy," Kyle said. "And I haven't found anything more joyous in these mountains than Tater's fiddle, Casper's jute harp, and Elias's banjo. So everybody grab a partner and dance."

The next thing Sarah knew, someone reached around her and took the plates from her, handing them to Mairi. She was swept out into the forming circle of couples before she could even determine her partner's identity. Lonnie Fraiser's older brother, Jedediah, had a strong hold on her. He swung her around, skirts flying, as Tater's fiddle belted out a lively tune she recognized from hearing one of the children sing it—"Sourwood Mountain."

She had no idea what type of dance steps fit "Sourwood Mountain," since her wallflower status hadn't given her that much experience dancing back in New York. But one of the band members called out some type of directions interspersed with the song's regular words, and the men evidently knew exactly what the caller meant for them to do. They passed her and the other three women in the square of four couples from one strong pair of arms to another, and before the song was even halfway through, Sarah was gasping for breath, her head whirling from dizziness.

But she'd never had so much fun in her life!

A couple hours later, her toes were sore from being stomped on by the clumsy boots worn by mountain men with more enthusiasm than dexterity, and her head still spun. But when she tried to slip off to rest for a while, someone always caught her. The only respite she got was when the musicians would take pity on the dancers and play a slow ballad, which called for a waltz to which even Sarah knew the steps. Too bad some of the men had their own version, however. She quickly learned not to anticipate the men's steps, since pinched and bruised toes again resulted from that mistake.

Kyle caught up to her as one of the slow ballads began, barely managing to grab her one second ahead of another man. As the beautiful strains of "Bonny Barbara Allen" floated from Tater's fiddle, Sarah relaxed in Kyle's arms. Surely a man from the social strata of New York would manage a dance similar to what she was used to.

He did, and she relaxed even more with not having to endure the strain of trying to outguess the next move of his feet. He smoothly waltzed her to the edge of the crowd.

Leaning close to her ear, he asked, "Do you need to sit down for a minute? You're as flushed as though you've been running."

"I almost have been in trying to keep up with these lively dancers," she said with a breathless laugh. "What on earth are the names of those dances?"

"They're variations of different types of quadrilles and square dances," Kyle said. "You didn't get much of a chance to watch, but even the children were dancing in their own area. That's why all of them know the steps so well—they start out dancing as soon as they can walk."

"Well, they're wonderful dances, but since I don't know the steps that well and haven't developed an ear for that patter the caller uses yet, my feet got in the way of more than one set of hobnail boots. So yes, I would like to sit down, if you can find somewhere I'll be hidden from the men who keep insisting their name is next on my nonexistent dance card!"

With a naughty grin, Kyle took her hand and pulled her with him around the side of the store.

11

"*THANK YOU!*" SAID Sarah as she stopped at the edge of a circle of light beside the side of the store. Someone had hung lanterns around the porch, and the one on the side where they stood gave a welcome light in the evening shadows.

She waved a hand in front of her face. "Whew! I didn't realize how warm I'd gotten or that night had fallen. I should be cooler, but I guess the exercise of dancing kept me from feeling the chill."

"It'll get to you now that you've stopped moving so fast," Kyle assured her. "And you don't want to come down with something, so maybe we should fetch you a shawl. I heard yesterday that Doc MacKenzie left for Nashville to attend his yearly medical convention. He won't be back for a couple weeks, so it's just Leery to handle things while he's gone."

"I probably should get a wrap," Sarah agreed. "I—"

"Miss Channing," a voice called from around the edge of the store. "Where'd you get to, Teacher? I git the next dance!"

"Oh, mercy," Sarah said in exasperation.

Kyle grabbed her again and pulled her out of the light, deeper into the shadows. She held a hand over her mouth to still her giggles, and he didn't stop until they were at the back of the store. Shushing her, he pushed her around by the back porch, then stuck his head back around the corner. She could barely restrain the giddiness bubbling in her, making her feel as carefree as a child playing hide-and-seek.

Kyle pulled his head back, and she managed to see him nod in the darkness.

"Nobody followed us," he said in a low voice. "But they'll be looking all over for you. A pretty new woman on the mountain will have every unattached man within fifty miles beating a path to her door. But if we wait a minute, maybe we can sneak down to your cabin and get your wrap without anyone seeing us. The moon's not due up for another half hour, and it's getting darker by the minute."

"Well, if it's a pretty woman these men want," Sarah said softly, "I don't understand why they're bothering with me."

"You obviously haven't paid much attention to mirrors lately, have you, Sarah Channing?"

When Sarah didn't answer, Kyle went on, "I'll admit, you were a skinny, gawky child your coming-out season. But if I hadn't known your name, I wouldn't have recognized you today. You're one of those late bloomers, Sarah, and you'll carry your age well until the day you die. Lots of other women will lose their looks by the time they're thirty, but you'll put them to shame."

"Pooh," was all Sarah could think of to say.

Kyle chuckled, then took her arm and led her back to the edge of the building. After a quick check for any observers, he hurried down the path toward her cabin. She opened the door and both of them rushed inside.

Sarah left the door ajar until she located the matches in a drawer in one of the end tables. Within a few seconds, she had the lantern on the table lit, and Kyle closed the door.

"You needn't worry that I'll make improper advances to you, Sarah," he said as the light glowed bright. "As soon as Fairilee MacIver's mourning period is over next month, she and I will be married. There's even talk of having a permanent church over in Baker's Valley, although I'll still do some circuit riding to the areas that don't have a preacher of their own."

"That's wonderful, Kyle. Congratulations. And no, I wasn't worried about you. Sometimes you meet a person and know right away that they are fine and upstanding. I felt that way when I met you today. And although I don't remember you, I do know your mother and sisters. You have a very nice family. "

"Well, maybe I shouldn't have mentioned how different you look now, but I have a confession to make, Sarah. I knew something of your situation back in New York City and that you were overshadowed by the season's other debutantes. When I saw you today, I realized how much you'd changed, but you still appear a little unsure of yourself. I just wanted you to know that you have proven the truth of that fairy tale about the ugly duckling turning into a swan."

"Oh, I wouldn't go quite that far, Kyle," Sarah said with a tolerant laugh.

Kyle cocked his head and studied her. "To the right man, it would be true. Don't sell yourself short, Sarah Channing."

At that moment the lantern sputtered and died.

"Oh, land sakes," Sarah muttered. "I meant to replenish that kerosene this morning, when I saw how low it had gotten. Let me try to remember where I stored the can of extra fuel."

The moment the light went out in the Sarah's cabin, Wyn gritted his teeth and stepped over to the porch post. He'd been standing in the darkness on the rear porch for at least a half an hour, uninterested in rejoining the dancers out front. He'd watched fully half of the men present swing Sarah around until her petticoat showed during a square dance or hold her close when a soft ballad flowed from Tater's fiddle. Some of them had managed more than one dance, and he hadn't even gotten to her once. He'd tried distracting himself with a couple of different women, but all he could think of while he danced with them was how different Sarah felt in his arms.

He'd fought his attraction to her, feeling sure the love potion had something to do with it. Still, he spent most of his time trying to anticipate where each of her partners would end up, so he could be there and claim the next dance. Each time, he miscalculated and someone else shouldered in front of him to collect her only seconds before him. Finally he gave up and came to the back porch.

He'd kept in the shadows, since his sisters would probably accuse him of moping if they found him here while the dancing was still going on. Then they'd dig at him until they thought they'd figured out what his problem was. There were few secrets in the MacIntyre family.

But dash nab it, he *wasn't* moping.

Drawing back his fist, he thudded it into the porch post. Pain streaked through his knuckles and up his arm, giving him a strange satisfaction, as though he'd landed the blow on Kyle Jackson's face.

Damn it to hell! How could Sarah fall for that line Kyle fed her, yet turn a completely deaf, or at least disbelieving, ear to his compliments? Shaking his hand against the pain, he barely kept himself from coldcocking the post again. Hell, it wouldn't bother the post none!

Why the hell should it be bothering him anyway? He'd felt as though a cage were closing around him when he heard Mairi and Leery talking about that love potion. Even his mother had believed in a lot of old superstitions handed down through the years. They had come with the families who settled the mountains—much like extra baggage on the ships carrying the displaced people from Scotland who had settled the mountains.

Ma had planted her garden in accordance with each phase of the moon, as did every other family. Over each door in the store and their living quarters, Ma had hung horseshoes for good luck. She also believed that a bird flying into the house foretold of a death within a fortnight, and indeed she'd received word of her sister's death barely two weeks after the sparrow had flown in an open upstairs window.

There were numerous beliefs regarding love and marriage in the mountains, which Ma had known and Leery preached as gospel truth to young and old alike. He'd recalled the one about violets only a little while ago, when Sarah handed him the purple violet. Leery would have told him to gather purple violet buds, as well as white ones, and toss them haphazardly in the wind. If the purple buds fell into a clear pattern suggesting a name or initials, the marriage with that suggested person would be passionate. If the white buds fell clearer, the mate suggested for that marriage would always remain faithful. He couldn't believe how tempted he'd been to return to the patch of violets and try the divination, in hopes that Sarah's name would show up.

He didn't know for sure which herb Mairi had baked into the muffins, but he supposed she had used myrtle or rosemary. Both were well known for use in love divinations.

The pain in his hand intensified, and he ran a finger over his knuckles, feeling a sharp piece of wood snag his finger pad. Damn, he'd gotten a splinter.

Stomping across the porch, he entered the storeroom and headed for the stairs to the living quarters. He'd have to find Sissy's sewing basket, get a needle to pry the splinter free, and then put some salve on the wound. He'd learned long ago not to let a wound fester in the mountains, after watching them bury his friend, Husky Hamilton, when he was ten. All Husky had done was leave a fishhook wound unattended, a wound that he'd gotten a few days earlier. The blood poisoning had sent red streaks up Husky's arm the last time Wyn had gone to see him before he died.

Finding Sissy finishing up nursing baby Sarah, he waited until she put the babe in the cradle that had held dozens of MacIntyre children over the years. When he told Sissy about the splinter, she ordered him to sit at the table and brought her sewing basket. After holding the needle over a candle flame for a second, she took his hand.

"Lordy, Wyn, how'd you do this?" she asked.

"On the back porch post."

"Looks like you deliberately punched it."

Sissy lifted an eyebrow, but Wyn didn't answer, so she bent over his hand again. Sissy had too much on her own mind right now to dig into Wyn's business. After diligently removing the splinter, Sissy bathed his knuckles with some antiseptic and rubbed some pungent-smelling salve on them.

"Dang, Sissy," Wyn grumbled. "I'll smell like a dead fish."

"Better smelling dead than actually being dead."

"Yeah, I was remembering Husky a few minutes ago. If he'd have told his mother about that fishhook wound, he might still be alive."

"Maybe and maybe not, Wyn. If it was his time, he would have gone one way or another. Leastwise, that's what Ma always said."

Wyn watched her gather the things up from her sewing box and medicine kit. As he had known she would, Sissy took the sewing box into her room and returned to place the medicine kit back on a kitchen shelf. With so many people living in the area over the store, their ma had drilled into them never to leave even one thing out of place. She believed in cleanliness and neatness, not messiness and chaos. Since her death, Sissy had managed fairly well to keep that rule in place.

"Sissy," he said, "if Robert did get a job somewhere outside Sawback Mountain, I don't know what we'd do without you. I doubt very much Carrie will stay unwed too much longer, and I don't know much about raising girls. Pris and Mairi are getting into that part of their lives where they need a woman around even more than they have so far."

Sissy shrugged. "You'd do what you had to do, Wyn." She sat back down at the table with him. "I suppose you heard some of what Robert and I were talkin' about earlier today, you being in the storage room."

"I made myself known as soon as I found you two," Wyn denied. "But I figure you were talking about Robert's 'shine business. Sis, Robert makes the best 'shine this side of Lynchburg, where Jack Daniels has his distillery. Shoot, Robert doesn't even drink the stuff himself, but he makes it pure and no one's ever been poisoned by it. I've seen him even boil his Mason jars, like Ma did when she canned garden stuff."

"But it's illegal, Wyn. Ain't been no revenuers round the last few years, but that don't mean they won't come again. It wouldn't bother me none if Robert would get a job at that place in Lynchburg, but I suppose they've got all the help they need and their own recipe. And besides, Robert doesn't really want to leave the mountains. He only went to West Virginie to look at the mines because he figured the living there would be something like it is here, with the mountains and all."

"From what I hear, he wouldn't get to spend much time anywhere except deep inside those mountains, Sis. Look, you're gonna have to trust Robert to take care of you and the young'uns. He's a proud man and he won't let you down. We all approved of him when he first started courting you."

"I love him, I do, Wyn. I just hope I don't have to keep our love alive by writing him letters in prison."

Not knowing what else to do, Wyn patted her hand. "Why don't you get down there and take advantage of being able to show Robert you love him by dancing with him right now? I'll stay up here a while and keep an eye on baby Sarah. I'll come down and get you in an hour or so, when it's time to put the twins to bed, and help you do that, too."

"That would be nice. Bobbie's asleep, too, in his trundle bed. Is that all right?"

"Go."

She gave him a radiant smile. "Let me check my hair first."

A few minutes later, with another thank-you to Wyn, Sissy headed down to the party. Wyn stirred up the fire, and after checking on baby Sarah, he sat down in the rocking chair in front of the fireplace. He kept one ear cocked for baby Sarah, jumpy as a cat on a summer-hot roof over being left in charge of that tiny being. He'd no sooner settled in the chair than she snuffled and gave a little squeak. He immediately leaped to his feet to rush into the bedroom.

Sissy had turned the lantern low, but he could see baby

Sarah on her stomach in the cradle. Her little rosebud lips were pursed and making a sucking motion. Lordy, maybe she was hungry again already! But he didn't want to drag Sissy up here to feed her this soon unless it was necessary.

He held his breath and watched her. She curled one tiny hand into a fist and stuck it in her mouth. After a couple slurps, she relaxed completely, her breathing evening into sleep again. He tucked the blanket up around her shoulders and went back to the fireplace.

He wanted children of his own someday—children like his brothers and sisters. Well, maybe not exactly like the terrible twins, he considered with a smile. But he wanted children. And he wanted a mountain woman to have them with—a woman who understood his love of the mountains and lack of desire to live anywhere else.

Hell, the time he'd spent in Washington, D.C., had shown him nothing could compare to Sawback Mountain. Mind you, he wouldn't object to going back there and visiting now and then. His young'uns should have their own options as to whether to stay here or roam the rest of the world and look it over before they decided where they wanted to spend their lives. He'd taken several trips with the senator during those two years, but he hadn't even had to think twice about where he wanted to be when he'd received word of his ma's death and his pa's paralysis.

Sawback Mountain was home. Always had been and always would be.

The pitch of the background noise to his thoughts changed, and Wyn frowned. Rising from the chair, he went over to the window at the front of the living area and looked out. The porch overhang blocked most of his view, although he could see a few people running toward the store. Then he heard a woman scream.

With only a quick glance at the bedroom, he raced over to the stairwell and pounded down the steps. Rushing through the store as much by instinct as sight in the darkness, he careened out the front door. He found Mairi and Pris huddled behind his pa's wheelchair and grabbed Pris by the arm.

"Get upstairs and watch baby Sarah," he ordered sternly.

She nodded and took off, with Mairi following her.

"What the hell's going on, Pa?" he asked.

"A fight," Dan said in a grim voice. "Someone went against my orders and snuck some 'shine in. The two are out there on the edge of the crowd somewhere."

"You know who they are?"

"Jedediah and Elias. Elias put his banjo down for a couple songs and figgered he'd dance with Sarah. Jedediah figgered it was his dance."

Wyn shook his head in wonder. Dang, that woman got around. "She was in her cabin with Kyle Jackson a few minutes ago!"

He didn't even realize he'd spoken aloud until his pa answered him.

"She's been back here long enough for this to happen. You better get out there and keep an eye on things afore someone gets hurt bad."

"Hell, if they're both drunk, they won't be hurtin' until tomorrow."

But Wyn stepped down from the porch and headed across the yard. The people had formed a circle just outside the area of light cast by the lanterns, and he shouldered his way through, knowing what he'd find in the middle. For a moment he stood there and watched Jedediah and Elias circle each other. Elias made a wobbly right jab at Jedediah, and Jedediah stumbled backward, barely keeping from falling on his ass.

The two of them were fairly evenly matched, both in their early twenties and both around the same weight. And from what Wyn could tell, both were on about the same level of drunkenness. No wonder Elias had laid down his banjo. He probably couldn't remember which chords to pluck.

Someone shoved through the crowd and shook his arm.

"Stop them!" Sarah said. "They'll get hurt!"

He glanced at her, then back at the fighters. "Maybe. But I doubt it."

"They're fighting!" she cried.

"They're trying to," Wyn said. "But I haven't seen any blows landed yet."

Jedediah lowered his head, let out a roar, and charged Elias. Elias tried to jump aside, but his foot slipped in the grass and he went down. Unable to stop his forward impetus, Jedediah crashed into a couple of other men on the edge of the circle.

"Uh-oh," Wyn said, tensing in anticipation of a free-for-all if the men Jedediah ran into took offense.

But the men only grabbed Jedediah by the arms and shoved him back inside the circle. By then, Elias was back on his feet. He curled his fists and held them up in front of his face, shaking them at Jedediah.

"Come on, Mr. Casanova!" Elias yelled. "I'm a-gonna beat your face in, then I'm a-gonna dance the rest of the night with Miss Sarah! Come on!"

Sarah gasped and hung her head. Wyn noticed several people look over at her, and he'd have been willing to bet her cheeks were flushed in that high color that made the gold dust in her eyes glow brighter.

"Maybe you ought to get back on the porch with Pa," he muttered.

Her head came up. "No! Since you won't, I'm going to put a stop to this foolishness."

He barely caught her arm before she surged out at the fighters. "Whoa! I told you to get back on the porch."

"You *suggested* I get back on the porch," she said, jerking at her arm to try to free it. "And I'm refusing."

The crowd let out a roar, and Wyn looked at the fighters. Jedediah had Elias in a bear hug, but the banjo player was beating on Jedediah's head. Elias finally landed a hard enough punch that Jedediah released him, backing away and shaking his head like a plow horse fighting flies. Elias pulled back an arm and landed a haymaker to Jedediah's jaw, and Jedediah crumpled to the ground.

Elias stood there swaying, with blood dripping from his nose. Wyn guessed he must have missed a punch somewhere, since he hadn't seen the one that landed on Elias's nose.

"There, you sorry SOB," Elias said. Then he raised his head. "Where's Miss Sarah?"

Sarah turned away from Wyn, this time heading in the opposite direction, back through the crowd. Elias must have caught a glimpse of her, because he came toward Wyn on wobbly legs. Wyn stepped out to meet him, grabbing him by the collar.

"You and Jedediah are done dancing for the night," he said. "Both of you are gonna get on your horses and head home. And if either one of you bring 'shine around my family again, you're gonna have a headache and sore body a lot worse than the one you're gonna have tomorrow, after I get done with you."

"Didn't bring it," Elias denied. "Got it here."

"From who?" Wyn snarled.

"Hell, I got mine from Jedediah," Elias said, wiping a shirt cuff at the blood beneath his nose. "You know him and me's friends. Jedediah didn't tell me where he got it, but it didn't taste like Robert's."

The crowd was breaking up around him, most of them realizing the party was over for the night. Wyn didn't worry, anyway, about what Elias had said. Everyone in the mountains knew Robert made and sold 'shine, and they'd sooner drown one of their prize coonhounds than turn Robert in to the authorities. The 'shine must have initially been made by Cabbage Carter, the other local moonshiner, but he hadn't seen Cabbage at the wake.

The person he wanted was the one who had brought the 'shine to a gathering where they knew the family had strict prohibitions against drink being consumed. When she was alive, his ma had made it known she wouldn't tolerate drinking in front of her children, although she didn't mind the adults having a few drinks later on in the evening, after the children were in bed.

The rule was as much for the protection of the children as anything else. The fight just now had been more or less of a farce, with Elias and Jedediah too drunk to do much damage to each other. But now and then a more deadly confrontation took place, fueled by a belly too full of 'shine.

Last summer, they'd buried Heddy MacPeters when her husband, Mack, had shot and killed her. The neighbor who'd heard the shot had run over to find Mack passed out, with his finger still on the trigger of the empty double-barrel shotgun. He'd also found Heddy's six-month-old little girl lying beneath her mother unscathed.

As soon as Mack woke up, they'd brought him in front of Pa. At Pa's direction, they'd sent Mack down to Razor Gully to wait for the circuit judge, and Wyn had heard later that Mack's only defense was that he didn't remember a thing.

He sighed as he scanned the crowd. The trouble was, the same loyalty that protected Robert from someone ratting on him about his 'shine making would protect the person he was looking for now. Elias hadn't had any problem telling Wyn that Jedediah had given him the 'shine he'd consumed, because Elias knew danged good and well, even in his drunken state, that Wyn wouldn't blame either one for sharing what they'd already found on the premises. Both his and Jedediah's butts were in trouble for the fight, not drinking the 'shine.

And with Jedediah passed out right now more from the drink than the slight beating Elias had given him, Wyn probably couldn't question him until the next day. All he'd have to do then was say he didn't remember who he got the booze from.

First things first, though. Wyn walked over to Jedediah and managed to get him over his shoulder. He carried him along the line of horses and buggies at the side of the road until he found Jedediah's gray mare. When he flung him over the saddle, he could have sworn the mare gave a long-suffering sigh. Maybe she did, because Wyn had heard of Jedediah going home more than once he same way he was fixing to go home right now.

He untied the mare's reins and looped them around the saddle horn. Leading her out onto the trail and heading her up the mountain, Wyn turned her loose. She plodded along slowly, not even jostling Jedediah. Had it been winter, Wyn would have followed to make sure Jedediah got home all right. But it hadn't been cold enough these past few days to bother Jedediah if he ended up sleeping outside his door rather than inside his cabin. Especially with a belly full of 'shine to keep him warm.

As he walked back toward the store, he looked toward Sarah's cabin. A light glowed in the window, and he thought about going down there to make sure she was all right after her embarrassment. But that would have to wait until he said good-bye to all his neighbors and thanked them for coming. While he was doing that, he'd also keep in mind that one of them had brought in the 'shine that had started the trouble. But he had little hope he'd find out who it was.

A family with the mother and father each carrying a child in their arms paused to say good-bye, and Wyn politely chatted with them for a moment. It was a full half hour before he finally made it to the porch, since he helped a few of the families lug their sleeping children out to the wagons and buggies. By then Sarah's windows were dark.

12

*ε*ARLY THE NEXT morning, hands sweaty and stomach jittery, Sarah was nevertheless determined to accept her punishment from Dan for being the cause of the altercation at the wake. He surprised her when he only waved her away when she went to see him at the store.

"Weren't your fault," Dan said. "I'd blame it on both Elias and Jedediah being young pups, but at times I've seen grown men act just like male dogs a-growlin' at each other, same as those two did. Don't you worry none about it. Some of the folks will be back this mornin' for church, since Kyle's here. You watch. Won't none of them care a whit about what happened. If anything, they'll let those two young whippersnappers know they was the ones in the wrong if either of them is able to come today."

He proved right when soon the trail was filled again with wagons and buggies, this time with people attending the church service. In fact, she realized, some of the wagons had spent the night on the trail in front of the store, and the people began waking up and cooking breakfast over fires they built. She took her courage in her hands and walked out among them, offering them the use of her cabin to wash up before church. Many of them took her up on it, as well as the offer of use of the outhouse behind her little cabin when the line in front of the one Dan and his family used grew overlong.

Kyle conducted another service, this time at the school-house, and after that the day flew by. When the sun was halfway through its afternoon path, people began leaving. Sarah was waving at the wagon carrying Carrie's friend, Patty, and her family when she heard someone clear a throat behind her and turned to see Kyle Jackson.

"Haven't had even a chance to talk to you today, Sarah," he said. "And I've got to get on the way myself now if I want to make it to Baker's Valley tonight. As it is, I'll be traveling until well after dark."

"I sincerely enjoyed chatting with you, Kyle," she said, offering him her hand. "Please say hello to your sisters and mother for me when you write."

"I will. Uh . . . Sarah, I may be out of line here, but . . . well, how long do you intend to stay here and teach?"

"I don't know why you'd think you were out of line, Kyle. But truly, I only agreed to stay until Dan can find another teacher. I'm sure he'll be getting some letters back in answer to the inquiries he sent out soon, but no one will want to come out here until the fall term starts. I assume I'll be leaving at the end of April, when this term is over. That's what . . . about five weeks from now?"

"Yeah, on my calender it is," he said with a laugh. "I suppose everything will be all right."

"Am I doing something wrong, Kyle?" Her brow fur-rowed and she felt a stab of uneasiness. "Dan said no one would think the fight that happened last night was my fault."

"They won't," Kyle assured her. "It's just that . . . well, I noticed you had a lot of drawings up in the classroom, and they were on a better-quality paper than Miss Elliot had for the children to use."

"Oh, I bought Mairi some drawing pads in New York, to keep her busy while she was recovering. She brought them with her, and I asked her if I could borrow them for the children. I have some more pads coming that I ordered to replace Mairi's. They'll probably arrive on Jeeter's next load."

"I see. Well, I'm sure the children enjoy having that nicer paper to work on. Supplies are pretty scarce here, but the people do the best they can for the school, Sarah. Each family will give Dan as much as they can spare after the fall crops are in, so he can get a few things for the new school term."

Something about Kyle's demeanor kept Sarah from telling him what she'd done. Surely the mountain families wouldn't mind a little help for their school, especially from people who wouldn't miss it at all. But she sensed a warning in Kyle's voice, which he didn't expand upon.

She gave him a brilliant smile, ignoring the jittery feeling in her stomach when she remembered how politely the mothers had declined her offer of the use of her tub and rose-scented soap for their children that morning before church. Those who had used her cabin to wash up used their own scratchy lye soap, and their own flour-sack towels. The only thing they had accepted from Sarah was warm water from her stove, and then they made sure they carried enough water from the creek to replenish her water barrel out back before they left.

Kyle mounted a huge black stallion, then tipped his hat to Sarah. "I'll try to make sure I see you again before you leave, Sarah," he said. "I try to have church over here at least once a month when the weather permits."

He urged his horse forward, and she waved at him until he disappeared, then started back to the store. He was the last person to leave, and she really wanted to get back to her cabin and rest. She felt as though she'd been on display for two days, which in a sense she had been, and even her mouth ached from smiling. But she saw Wyn on the porch, and he beckoned to her.

Then he must have decided he could talk to her as well out in the yard, because he walked down the porch steps and met her halfway across the yard.

"The families will expect you to start making your calls

to them this coming week," he said without preamble. "Do you think you can be ready to go as soon as school is out each day?"

"I'll be ready," she assured him. "Should I bring a gift for each family, or anything like that?"

"No!" Wyn said in what she considered a voice louder than necessary. "All you're doing is making a duty call to them, to show them you aren't above them. Even Miss Elliot managed to keep her nose from turning up on her calls to each family."

"Are you insinuating that I'd consider myself too good to associate with these families?" Sarah asked with a gasp of indignation.

"I'm not making any judgments—at least, not until after we visit a few places around here. Just remember, right now you're not a New York City debutante. Instead, you're working for a salary that these people are paying you. Whether or not you need the money, it's still coming out of the pockets of the people who live here, and every penny is hard earned."

She started to tell him what she thought of his lecture, but Wyn changed the subject.

"Kyle get off all right? Seemed like you and he had a lot to talk about."

"We knew some of the same people back in New York," Sarah said without much thought to her words. Continuing to fume over what she considered Wyn's high-handed censure, when she only wanted to help the mountain people, she said, "I better get a head start on my lesson plans for next week, since I won't have the evenings to work on them."

She strode away without another word, not stopping until she reached her little cabin. Completely uncharacteristically, she slammed the door behind her. Then, instead of going to her desk and opening her lesson book, she sat down on the tiny settee and crossed her arms, patting her foot on the floor. When she became aware that her bottom lip was sticking out mutinously, she jumped to her feet and circled the room.

"Who on earth do you think you are, Wyn MacIntyre?" she grumbled. "I'm doing everything I can to help these children find a better life, and *you* tell me you're not making any judgments yet. What even gives you the right to *make* judgments about me?"

She stopped in front of one of the small cabin windows and stared outside. The sun shone beautifully in the clear air, making her wish she was out there enjoying it instead of in here with a pile of work facing her.

Well, why not? She didn't necessarily have to do her lesson plans right now. Maybe she would go over and talk to Mandy.

The next afternoon, Sarah's respect for the mountain families grew with each minute of her trip to the first family on her list of parents. The parents of Carrie's friend, Patty, and her younger brother, Pete, were the only children who didn't ride to school on a mule, and she could only imagine how hard it was for them to make the trip twice a day on foot. But they both declined Wyn's and her offer to ride with them and made just as good a time as the horses.

She shifted on the saddle now and then, glad none of her New York friends could see her actually riding astride! If she'd had any inkling the MacIntyre family didn't own a sidesaddle, she'd have added one of those to the lists she sent back to her attorney. And after lambasting Wyn's ears over the lack of an appropriate seat for her on that huge animal he'd led over to her house a while ago, she wasn't about to tell him that she actually thought this might be a more comfortable and safer way to ride.

It took them at least a half hour to reach Patty's small cabin, and the length of time the trip took reconfirmed Sarah's awe of the children who lived farther away. How on earth did they make it to school without having some limbs frozen, given the shabby coats and footwear she saw hanging in the cloakroom? But they came—came every day the school was open. Perhaps the parents' dreams for their children kept them coming.

She scanned the cabin they were approaching right now

and revised her opinion of that premise. Perhaps it was Patty's mother, not both her parents, who kept those children in school. The man on the porch wore a pair of faded overalls, stretched tight over his huge stomach. He lounged in a broken-down chair with stuffing falling out of the armrests, thumbs cocked into his shoulder straps. He didn't appear to be the sort who cared about anything except not moving any more than necessary.

If he had, he would have cleaned up a few of the things in the yard and done some repairs. He surely didn't need to spend any time mowing down grass in that muddy expanse. A broken-down wagon with only three wheels sat off to one side. There were several rusty barrels here and there, as well as what looked like three separate burning piles with tin cans in them. On the right was what was evidently a chicken coop, since several hens and a rooster pecked around it. But the fence was useless for keeping the chickens penned up, and one entire coop wall lay in splintered boards on the ground.

Two washtubs lay over by the porch, and one pole holding up the clothesline had broken off and been propped against the cabin wall. There was only one window in the front of the place, made from eight smaller panes of glass. Four of those had rags stuffed in them rather than having the broken glass panes replaced.

A mangy brown-and-white hound crawled out from under the porch, but it must have taken its cue from its owner, since it didn't bother to bark at the strangers. Instead, it sat down and lifted a leg to scratch its ear.

Patty and Pete ran on ahead and both of them disappeared inside the cabin without saying anything to the man on the porch. Pete must have gone straight through the house and out the back door, because a couple seconds later, Sarah saw him racing up the mountainside behind the cabin, with a rifle in his hand.

The man on the porch spit a brown stream over the side of the flooring, then called, "'Afternoon, Wyn. Hey, Nettie! Get out h'yar! Teacher's come to call!"

The skinniest woman Sarah had ever seen came out the

door, wiping her hands on a rag—except she wasn't skinny in her stomach. Having recently seen Sissy prior to the birth of baby Sarah, Sarah imagined the woman in front of her was also on the verge of giving birth. And no wonder Pete never smelled very clean and had matted hair. Nettie looked as if she hadn't had a bath all winter, so how could she expect her children to learn cleanliness?

Making a mental note to start focusing on the effects of being unsanitary to her class, Sarah pulled her horse to a stop and then debated how she was supposed to dismount. Fortunately, Wyn swung down and came over to her. He took her reins from her hands and looped them on his forearm, then held his arms up to her.

"Swing your right leg over the back, and I'll help you down," he said.

Surprisingly to Sarah, it worked well. He caught her waist and lifted her to the ground as though she weighed no more than baby Sarah. She turned and smiled straight into his face, forgetting immediately what she was going to say. His blue eyes were only a couple inches from her own gaze, and her lips so close she could feel his breath on her face—only for a split second, though. He jerked as though someone had shot him and released her so quickly she bumped back against the horse.

The horse snorted and sidled away, and when she staggered, she felt her foot slip on something. She got her balance, then lifted her skirt aside to examine her shoe. The ripe odor told her immediately that she'd stepped in some animal's waste—probably that flea-bitten hound over there.

Gritting her teeth, she glanced at Wyn to see a warning in the set of his face. She briefly closed her eyes, then, holding her skirt up far enough to avoid the mess on her shoe, she hobbled toward the steps.

"Hello," she said, as nonchalantly as she could while using the porch step to clean her shoe.

"Howdy," Nettie replied. "Come on in and set a spell, an' we kin wipe you off."

"Thank you," Sarah said in relief. Now that Nettie had

spoken of the mess, surely it would be all right for Sarah to say something. "I really would appreciate it."

She came on up the steps and stopped beside the chair where Nettie's husband sat, but he didn't rise.

"This here's Clem," Nettie said.

Sarah politely extended her hand, but Clem only gave her a rotten-toothed smile, never removing his thumbs from his shoulder straps. "Been tellin' that ol' hound he oughtta do his bizness somewhere else, but he don't lissen none. Just like this h'yar pack of young'uns."

Biting back the retort she really wanted to give, Sarah dropped her hand to her side and said, "Patty and Pete are both doing very well in school. Pete got a hundred on his arithmetic test the other day."

"Good." Clem spat over the side of the porch again, then continued, "He kin make sure ole Dan ain't a-mischargin' me on my store bill, he keeps that up."

Sarah flashed Wyn a look, but he appeared to be ignoring Clem's comment. "I'll wait out here for you," he said. "Take as long as you want, but remember we have to get back home down that trail tonight, and it's easier with some daylight left."

Nodding, Sarah followed Nettie inside. In this, the woman of the family's domain, she found some neatness, although the smell didn't bear this out. In a private moment on the way here, Wyn had told her they could avoid eating with this family, since they were close enough to get back to their own places for a late supper. But at the other homes, she would be expected to share a meal before the longer return trip.

The grimy pot hanging in the fireplace made her very grateful for Wyn's advice, and the smell of boiling cabbage heightened her gratitude.

The dimness inside the cabin was so deep she missed seeing the other occupant, only noticing when she heard a clatter in the corner. She glanced over at another child, this one probably half Pete's age of ten. The little girl stood up and Sarah saw another child behind her.

"That there's Minnie," Nettie said. "Say howdy, Minnie."

"Howdy," the child said. She took the other child by the hand and pulled her forward a step. "This here's Janie, but she cain't talk yit."

"Well, hello to both of you," Sarah managed. The second child still wore diapers, and the one she had on sagged as though it desperately needed changing. Probably that was where some of the smell came from, but again, it could have been from Sarah's shoe.

"Sure hope this'uns a boy," Nettie said in an aside. "Mebbe I kin rest in between it an' the next one." She gave a tired sigh. "Let's git you cleaned up."

After her shoe was clean, Nettie waved Sarah to the rickety table and placed a chipped cup in front of her. It looked clean, as far as she could tell in the light coming in through the open back door. After Nettie poured them both a cup of thick coffee, they discussed Patty and Pete's schoolwork for a few minutes, then the wake and Kyle's sermon at church.

Sarah was running out of polite conversation by the time Pete returned. He raced in the back door and threw three dead squirrels on the table, then headed over to the fireplace and put his rifle on the pegs overhead. One squirrel slid across the table at Sarah, landing with its dead eyes staring up at her. Sarah's gorge rose, but she managed to keep the coffee down, although she did leap to her feet.

Pete came back over to the table, pulling a penknife from his trouser pocket.

"Are you leaving, Teacher?" he asked. "Well, you jist give me a jiffy shake and I'll fix these here squirrels for you to take back with you. Ain't nothin' better'n fried squirrels and biscuit gravy. Iffen you don't know how to fry 'em, why, me and Patty kin stay over tomorrow evenin' long 'nuf to do that for you."

Something told Sarah not to refuse the boy's offer, and she managed a thank-you. "I've been taking most of my meals with Mandy Tuttle, though, Pete. I'll give her the squirrels to fix for both of us."

"That'll work," Pete said. He picked up one of the squirrels and made a cut across its back. When he worked a finger inside the skin and started tearing one portion of the fur toward the squirrel's head, the other one toward the rear of it, Sarah's eyes flew to Nettie, begging for help.

Although she stifled a chuckle, Nettie seemed to understand, and rose from her chair. "You wash them squirrels off afore you wrap them up for Miss Channing," she told her son. "And bring 'em on outside when you get done. We'll wait out there."

On the porch, Sarah took a deep breath of air. Clem wasn't in his chair, and she saw him and Wyn over by the broken-down wagon, both leaning on it and discussing something. Wyn had tied their horses to the wagon. As Sarah watched, Clem picked up a clay jug from the wagon bed and swung it into the crook of his elbow. He took a long swallow, then offered it to Wyn, who shook his head.

Over by the dilapidated chicken coop, Patty was throwing feed to the chickens, and Sarah noticed a young man she'd seen at the dance and church following her around.

"That there's Sam Carter," Nettie said to Sarah. "Cabbage Carter's boy. I ain't sure he's who I'd pick out for Patty, but Clem ain't run him off, so I cain't say nothin.'"

Sarah only nodded, staring out over the junk-filled yard. Beyond the cabin, the mountains stretched out in a heart-stopping vista, their beauty making a sharp contrast to the tiny piece of earth where the cabin sat. She thought of her own existence back in New York and the household budget she was given before her father died. Why, she allowed the cook more funds for a week than Patty's family probably had for a year.

On past the wagon, she noticed a plot of weed-choked land where someone had started digging up new earth. A few days ago, she'd seen Wyn out with one of the horses plowing up a piece of ground on the opposite side of the store from the schoolhouse. Mairi had told her that as soon as the moon was right, they'd begin planting their garden in that spot.

She'd asked Mairi why they planted at night during the moon, and the child had broken into peals of laughter. At last she'd managed to tell Sarah the planting was actually done in the daytime, but the determination of *what* it was time to plant was made by whatever phase the moon was in the previous night.

"I see your husband is getting your garden ready," she said to Nettie when she realized the silence was stretching out to the point of rudeness.

"Naw," Nettie denied. "Me and the little'uns are doin' that when we kin, a little at a time."

Shocked, Sarah looked at Nettie's protruding stomach before she could stop herself. Nettie laid a grubby hand on the bulge.

"My babe ain't due for 'nother month yit. I figger we kin leastwise git our 'maters set out and the corn planted afore then."

To Sarah's utter relief, Pete came out. Despite knowing that there were three bodies that probably looked like naked rats inside the brown paper he handed her, Sarah took it from him gratefully.

"Wyn said he wanted to get back before dark," she said hurriedly. "I don't want to upset him by overstaying. You know how men can be."

Nettie rubbed her upper arm. "Yeah, I do know that," she mused, then seemed to catch herself. "Thankee for comin', Miss Channing. And you come back anytime, you hear?"

"Thank you for the coffee," Sarah said in response. She walked down the porch steps and carefully picked her way across the muddy yard. She handed the brown-paper–wrapped bundle of squirrels to Wyn, telling him what it was, and he placed it in the saddlebag on his horse. Then with Wyn's help, she mounted her own horse and said good-bye to Clem.

13

$\mathcal{I}$T WAS A silent ride back to Sawback Mountain. As he had on the way there, Wyn led the way. Sarah's horse needed little guidance, plodding along with its nose close to the tail of the horse Wyn rode. Patty and Pete had chattered on the previous trip, and they hadn't seen any animals, although birds filled the trees. On the return trip, she spotted a deer watching them at one point, and a red fox ran across the trail at another. The birds were still singing, but now she heard an owl hoot a few times.

After about fifteen minutes, Wyn stopped his horse and silently pointed up the side of the mountain. Quite a ways above them, she could see a cave. A tiny dark shape flew out of the cave mouth, then several more. Suddenly a huge cloud of black shapes poured out of the cave, rising into the sky and scattering like smoke.

"Bats," she said in an apprehensive voice.

"They won't bother you," Wyn assured her. "They're only after bugs and mosquitoes."

He urged his horse forward again, and she followed. Her scalp prickled and she glanced behind her a couple times. However, the cloud of bats had dispersed into the air.

Though the days were lengthening, the horses threw long shadows against the setting sun by the time they passed the stone chimney left from a previous cabin. Sarah recognized that as a landmark from the trip up the mountain. Just past the chimney, the trail widened a little, and Sarah urged her horse up beside Wyn's.

"Are all the places like that one?" she asked.

He didn't appear to need further explanation that she was talking about Patty and Pete's home.

"No, that's really one of the worst," he said. "Except for Cabbage Carter's place. Although there are a few just as bad. Clem's none too ambitious, and if it wasn't for Nettie working herself all the time and Pete's ability with that gun, those young'uns would starve."

"Why does she stay with him?" Sarah asked in disgust.

Wyn turned to stare at her for a moment before he answered. "What else would she do? She's usually carrying a babe. She's got the four of them, but she's lost at least that many more. And she never got to school a day in her own life. Guess that's why she's so adamant about her young'uns getting as much education as they can. She has hopes for Patty, but I saw Sam Carter hanging around. Sam will never amount to any more than his old man."

"Well, there *should be* an option for her!" Sarah tightened her lips. "Good heavens, she could at least insist that man leave here alone so she doesn't have a babe every year."

Wyn swung his horse across the trail, blocking her way. On past him, she could barely see the buildings of Sawback Mountain. Beyond them was a sky filled with the violent but stunning colors left behind from the sun, which had already set below the mountain peaks. Wyn stood out against that background like a satyr from Greek mythology.

"I'll throw your own words right back at you," he almost snarled. "What right do you have to make any judgment about Nettie? And Clem, for that matter? Maybe they're doing the best they can. For one thing, Clem could just up and say that the young'uns couldn't go to school at all anymore, and Nettie would have to abide by that. But he always manages to come up with his share of the teacher's salary every fall. And as far as her having a baby each year, maybe she gets as much pleasure out of making those babies as Clem does!"

"Ohhhh!" Sarah felt her cheeks burn. "How . . . how dare you talk about that in front of me!"

"About what? Lovemaking? Let me tell you what, Sarah. You were getting a hell of a lot of enjoyment out of just the preliminaries to actual lovemaking with me the other night. I'll bet you'd be a writhing ball of flames during the actual act."

The heat spread over Sarah's entire face, even down her chest and across her breasts, with her nipples crinkling into hard nubs. Her horse shifted under her, and the movement rubbed her nether portion against the hard saddle. Immediately the answer to why women rode sidesaddle flashed into her mind. All the feelings goosebumping over her skin cascaded down there, and centered between her legs.

She might have managed to maintain control, but she couldn't pull her focus away from Wyn's face. His eyelids lowered partly, and in the dimness the color of his eyes appeared a smoky blue. The ball of fire he'd said she might turn into would probably give off the exact same color smoke while it burned her to pieces.

"I wonder if that idiot who let you leave New York without him right there to keep an eye on you ever felt you turn into flames in his arms?" Wyn mused.

Then he seemed to realize what he'd said and dropped his head for an instant, shaking it from side to side. Looking at her again, he lifted his reins, moving his horse back beside her.

He reached out a hand. "Look, Sarah, I apologize, but—"

She kicked her horse in the sides, and it gave a startled neigh as it leaped forward. She raced down the trail, and when the horse tried to swerve beside the store and head for the barn, she held it onto the path to her cabin. When she reached her haven, she jerked the horse to a stop and slid to the ground in a flurry of skirts. Uncaring as to whether Wyn would have to chase the horse, she tossed the reins aside and rushed into her cabin.

She slammed the door behind her and leaned on it, gasping for breath. Heavens, the horse should have been winded, not her, but she couldn't seem to breathe deeply enough to calm herself. She heard the plop of horse's hooves outside and realized Wyn had followed her more slowly. Although she'd never worried about locking her door before, now she grabbed the heavy board propped in the corner and laid it in the iron hasps. After a few seconds' silence, she heard a bootstep outside just before a rap on the door.

"Sarah," Wyn called. "Are you all right?"

"Go away," she ordered. "I'm fine."

She thought she heard a chuckle, but she didn't notice any laughter in his voice when he spoke next.

"We're going a little deeper into the mountains tomorrow. Be sure and bring a cloak."

Clenching her hands at her sides, she fought the urge to tell him that she wouldn't be going anywhere with him ever again. She had no choice. She had to visit the families. Dan had also mentioned it would be expected of her.

Just as she thought perhaps he'd left, Wyn said, "I can leave the squirrels here on your porch."

"No! Uh . . . take them over to Mandy."

"Well, now, I might consider doing that for you if you asked me real nice." This time there was no mistake as to the laughter in his voice.

"Ohhhhh," she fumed quietly, so the sound wouldn't carry through the door to him. After a long, telling silence, she gritted out, "Would you *please* take the squirrels over to Mandy? I told Pete I'd have her cook them for me tomorrow night."

"We won't be back in time for supper tomorrow," Wyn reminded her. "But I'll ask Mandy to fix them so we can take them with us for a snack on the trail. You know, Sarah, we could talk a lot easier if you'd open this door."

"I'm going to bed," she said. "Mandy said she'd leave me a plate over here." She turned to stare across the room at the stove, but it was really too dark for her to tell much. "I'm sure she did. Good night."

She waited another long minute before she finally heard the horses leaving. Slipping over to the window, she cautiously pulled back the curtain and peered out. The horses were indeed headed toward the barn, but she didn't see Wyn leading them. Suddenly his head popped into view right in front of her face.

"Boo!"

She screamed. He was still on the porch, and he'd leaned over to stick his head in front of the window, knowing she'd be peeking out!

Dropping the curtain, she glared at the window, listening to the gales of laughter on the other side of her door. All at once she thinned her lips and nodded her head in satisfaction. She moved back over in front of the door and drew back her leg. She gave the door a good, hard kick, then stomped on the floor, hoping it sounded like she'd fallen.

Wyn's laughter immediately stilled. "Sarah?" he called.

"Ohhhhh," she groaned. "Ohhhhh!"

He pounded on the door. "Sarah! What's wrong? Open this door!"

"I c-ca-can't," she called back. "Ohhhhh! It hurts! Ohh-hhh!"

"What happened?"

She didn't answer him, and after a second, something thudded against the outside of the door—probably his shoulder, she guessed. She gave another convincing groan before she burst into silent laughter. He thudded against the door again, and she heard him give a yelp of pain, followed by a round curse.

"Sarah!" The next thuds—a rapid tempo of them—appeared to come from his fist. "Sarah, answer me!"

Holding her hands over her mouth and snorting in a most unladylike manner, Sarah backed away from the door. Any minute the sound of her laughter would break the bonds of her control, and she wanted to be at the other end of the room when it happened.

Suddenly the pane of glass in the window beside the door crashed in and broken pieces rained into the room. Her laughter died as a hand reached inside the window and flipped the board free of the hasps. Then the door was thrown open so hard it banged against the wall.

Sarah's legs encountered her bed, and she sat down on the very edge, hoping the springs wouldn't squeal and give her away. They didn't.

"Uh-oh," she breathed almost soundlessly, then fell silent.

"Sarah!" Wyn dropped to his knees and his head swiveled from side to side as he searched for her.

Sarah thought there was quite enough light coming in through the door behind him to show him that she wasn't lying there on the floor. She froze on the bed, waiting to see how long it would take him to find out where she really was. The cabin wasn't that big, after all.

He lunged to his feet just as she realized she'd worn a pale blue dress today. It probably stood out like a beacon in the dim room, especially given the multicolored quilt behind her on the bed. But he appeared to be too upset to notice her.

Instead, he bent over the end table beside the settee and pulled open the drawer holding the matches. A lot faster than Sarah ever managed, he had the lantern lit. When he held it aloft, the light illuminated the entire cabin, and also Wyn's face.

Her trepidation had barely commenced before she realized the look on his face was the complete opposite of worry for her. He must have realized as soon as he got inside that she'd been playing him false, because his blue eyes were alight with mirth, his mouth open in a wide smile. He reached up easily and slipped the lantern handle over a hook on a crossbeam, then took a step and shoved the door shut. Sticking his fingertips in his back pockets, he advanced on her.

"Why, Teacher," he murmured. "I do believe you played quite a prank. Guess that's what being around a passel of young'uns all day long will do to you."

Hardly realizing what she was doing, Sarah scooted back on the bed, holding out a hand in a useless gesture for him to halt.

"Stay away," she said. "You started it. You . . . you tricked me into thinking you were leaving with the horses."

He nodded in agreement, and a blond lock of hair fell across his forehead. "That I did. I'll admit to that. But I would've never thought Miss Sarah Channing, the New York City debutante, would retaliate by tricking me in return. You do a very convincing fake groan of pain, Miss Debutante."

"All I had to do was imagine one of those men at the dance stepping on my toes in those hobnail boots," Sarah blurted.

Oh, my God! she thought, when his mention of her former status sank in. She'd never done anything like this in her life, even when she was a child herself! What if some of her friends back in New York *had* seen her? She was acting like a scandalous lady of pleasure toying with her partner—just like the one she'd read about in the book her father would have burned if he'd found it under her mattress. She had to stop this.

She tensed her muscles to get off the bed. But Wyn took another step closer, and she dropped her hand. Pushing both hands into the bed, she scooted away another six inches. Her back came up against the cabin wall.

Suddenly realizing how ridiculous she must look, she bit the inside of her mouth to hold her laughter. Her legs stuck straight out on the bed, and considering how tall she was, there was plenty of leg to stick out. Wyn, on the other hand, still kept his fingertips in his back pockets, his stance stretching his blue workshirt tight across his wide chest. His eyes began a slow scan of her, and she could feel the heat trailing in the wake of his gaze.

"What did you do with the squirrels?" she asked in an attempt to turn his attention to something else before he proved for a fact that he could turn her into a writhing ball of flames—without even coming close to the "act."

"Hmm?" he said as though he hadn't understood a word she said.

"The squirrels!" she repeated louder. "One of the barn

cats might get them if you've left them on the front step.
Then how would I explain to Pete . . ."

In one fluid motion, he removed his hands from his back
pockets and lay down beside her on the bed. Bending his
elbow, he propped his head on his palm and gazed up at her.
She froze like a mouse in a snake's stare for a long, exciting
moment. Then she gave a squeal and lunged toward the
bottom of the bed. She managed to throw one leg over the
footboard before Wyn jerked her backward and loomed over
her.

"Now what are you gonna do, my lady Debutante?" Wyn
asked.

The word, close to the forefront of her mind ever since
Wyn had uttered it a while ago, popped out of Sarah's mouth
before she could stop it.

"Writhe?"

A white-hot flush of heat stole over her, and she caught
her breath in horror. How could she have said such a thing?

Wyn looked at her for a moment, biting his lips together,
the blueness in his eyes filled with dancing merriment. He
took a short breath, opened his mouth and said, "You aren't
even close to the point where you should . . . wri . . .
writhe . . . *writhe* yet!" he managed before he lost control
and fell on his back beside her.

His snorts of laughter and guffaws invaded the room, and
he rolled back and forth on the bed. She sat upright to watch
him, covering her mouth with one hand when her humiliation changed to amusement. He looked like a huge blond
child himself with the tears of laughter leaking from beneath
those long golden lashes.

After a while, Wyn clasped his arms across his stomach
and seemed to make an enormous effort to pull himself
together. His guffaws died to chuckles, and he raised one
hand to wipe his fingertips beneath his eyes.

But he looked over at her, and she raised her eyebrows
and dropped her hand from her mouth. She barely got her
mouth pursed for the *W* in *writhe* before Wyn doubled up
his knees and started cackling once more.

"Stop!" he said once, then managed to say it a couple

more times. "Stop. Please, stop it, Sarah! Oh, Lordy, my stomach's aching!"

"Why, I'm not doing a thing except sit here and watch you roll around like a dory on the ocean in the wind."

Taking advantage of his hilarity and weakened state, she scooted from the bed. She waited as calmly as she could for him to settle down, although it took every bit of effort she could muster not to break down and join his merriment. When he gained enough composure to look at her again, she propped her hands on her hips and gave him her sternest glare.

"Harumph! I can see my purity is in no danger from you, Mr. MacIntyre, since it seems I tickle your funny bone rather than tempt you. Now, if you'll be so kind as to leave my bed, I do have some chores to finish before I can rest."

"Aw, Sarah," Wyn said, tucking one hand beneath his cheek and staring at her. "Honey, you tickle a hell of a lot more than my funny bone. You just ought to be glad that it was my funny bone that reacted first to me being in bed with you. Otherwise, your purity would have definitely been in a hell of a lot of danger."

Her legs wobbled so badly she thought for a minute he would notice, even with her long skirts hiding the trembling. Though it meant moving closer to him, she toddled over to the bed and grabbed hold of a bedpost to steady herself. His blue eyes followed her every move, and he flicked his tongue out, wiping it across his top lip then drawing it back into his mouth.

"I . . . you . . . one of us needs to go," she sputtered inanely, hardly realizing what she had said.

He kept her captured in his gaze for a long ten seconds, then surged to his feet.

"I guess I should be the one to leave, since this is your home," he said.

Reaching up, he threaded the fingers of both hands through his blond hair to tame it into place. It didn't work, and her own fingers tingled with the desire to give it a try. She clamped them tighter on the bedpost.

"G-good night," she managed.

"Good night, Sarah."

He strode to the door, but drew back his hand before he touched the doorknob. He stood without turning for a few seconds, then said, "Sarah, can I ask you something?"

"I guess," she said, still gripping the bedpost tightly. "What is it?"

Without turning, he said, "Why were you here in the cabin with Kyle during the dance? With the light out?"

"What?" she asked, truly puzzled. Then she remembered. "Oh. The lantern was on at first."

"Yeah," he agreed, turning cautiously.

"The kerosene ran out just after we got inside. I couldn't remember where I'd seen the extra fuel, and it took me a few minutes to find it. If you were watching, surely you saw the light from the match Kyle had to strike to help me search for the kerosene can. We found it on a shelf outside the back door. I assume it's kept there to be safe—away from the stove, you know."

"I didn't watch very long. Not long enough, I guess. Can I asked you something else?"

"I believe you've had your quota of questions for one night. You've just reminded me that my cabin is visible to everyone who lives here. And that door's been closed for an awful long time, with only the two of us in here. I think you better go."

He nodded so slightly she could hardly see the movement. But his next movement came without doubt of his intention, and too quickly for her to avoid it. He strode back to the bed and circled a hand behind her neck. Then he kissed her.

He kissed her firmly at first, leaving her no doubt his mouth on hers was enjoying every second of the contact. He nibbled her mouth next, taking tiny little nips with his lips at her bottom lip, her top lip, each corner of her mouth, then claiming another full kiss. His tongue swept the crease between her lips this time, inching inside to smooth across her teeth. Helplessly, she opened her mouth and allowed him full entrance, letting go of the useless bedpost and grabbing his neck to keep herself from wilting to the floor.

Or worse, the last infinitesimal portion of her rational mind told her, to the bed behind her.

He withdrew before she had more than instinctively returned his brief tongue caress with her own, nibbling across her jaw and downward to her neck. He licked her once and then again, centering his attention for an all-too-brief period at the hollow in her throat. She became aware of his fingers moving in her hair, pulling pins free. The heavy tresses dropped from the neat coil, slithering silkily across her shoulders and down her back.

He moved his mouth toward the side of her neck, his breath beginning to sound harsher and his chest rising and falling against her breasts. She felt a slight, pleasant sting when he sucked one spot, but he nuzzled onward, and she felt his tongue caress the side of her neck in a place she hadn't even realized had such sensitive nerve endings.

Her rational mind blinked out at the same moment her legs gave up the battle and she slowly sank down. The bed caught her, and Wyn gently pushed her back on the mattress, then lay down on top of her. Balancing his weight on one elbow, he brushed back a tress of hair from her cheek and wrapped it around his fingers. Pulling it toward him, he caressed it across his mouth.

"I knew your hair would be beautiful," he murmured. "It's like silk, and so heavy and thick I don't see how you manage it on your head."

"It's so plain."

"Where'd you ever get that idea?"

"My father. He made the nurses, and later my maid, wash it every other day. He said it was such a lackluster color, but at least it had a shine when I kept it washed."

"He was wrong. It's the color of light brown sugar with a sprinkle of gold dusting it."

The compliment curled through her with a different warmth than she was feeling from the close proximity of his body. She dared to reach for the lock of hair always falling over his forehead.

"Yours is soft, such a pretty color and exactly what I think of when I think of blond. I'd always thought men's hair would be coarse and rough, like their whiskers looked. And all the men I've ever known used oily stuff on their hair. I like the way you allow yours to be free—to blow in the wind or curl where it will."

"I've never thought of my hair as being an attraction," he teased. "Maybe I should let it grow even longer."

"Maybe you should," she agreed.

"Can I tell you how beautiful your eyes are now? Or will you get such a swelled head that you won't be able to walk without wobbling?"

She couldn't believe she was actually lying here with this terribly handsome man, having this teasing give-and-take conversation. It was highly improper, but she couldn't for the life of her push him away, despite the chastisement the voice of her conscious tried to shout at her. He was so close, yet she didn't feel uncomfortable with him as she usually felt around a man; and she mentally locked her conscience away in a dark room—just for a few more minutes. Perhaps her enjoyment burgeoned because she didn't perceive Wyn judging her and finding her lacking. In fact, quite the opposite was happening.

"Maybe you could tell me just enough to make my head wobble the tiniest little bit," she said, venturing to trail a finger down his cheek.

"Well."

He quickly turned his head and caught her fingertip in his mouth when it got close to his lips. She gasped in surprise, but could no more muster the energy to free herself than she could have flown to the moon right then. He closed his teeth firmly but gently, then laved her finger with his tongue. Round and round and round.

"Ohhhhh," she whispered.

He pulled away from her finger, but only far enough to run his tongue across her palm, then swipe it back and forth on her wrist. She held her hand in the exact position he needed to continue his ministrations, not even moving when he shifted his weight and unbuttoned her dress cuff. Rolling the sleeve back, he followed with his tongue, sliding it all the way to the tender skin inside the bend of her elbow.

When she turned her head, her cheek landed on his hair. She closed her eyes and snuggled closer, pressing her cheek into the silkiness and gently moving it back and forth.

"W-Wyn," she said. "I think you better get back to talking about my eyes. I think I'm going to start writhing if you don't."

He gave her skin a gentle nip, then lifted his head. "Your eyes have the same gold in them that your hair does," he murmured. "Only this time it's scattered across a deep brown velvet that a man could imagine surrounding him like your soft body does."

"Ohhhh." She thought that about the most inane comment she'd ever made in her entire twenty-five years, but she couldn't think of anything better to say. She did concentrate on trying to think of something better; it was either that or start writhing just from his words.

Thought became impossible, though, as he kissed her once more, gently, longingly, before drawing away with a deep sigh and standing. Grabbing her hands, he pulled her up to sit on the edge of the bed in front of him, then cupped her chin in his palm to keep her eyes on him while he spoke.

"And if I was the man who had the right to do it, I wouldn't be stopping now. I *would* show you exactly what writhing means."

He dropped her chin, and started to turn away. Without even taking one step, he turned back. Bending down, he kissed her lightly once more. "Good night, Sarah," he said as he straightened. "I've had one of the best days of my life today. I've got a hell of a lot of thinking to do now."

He blew out a breath, jamming his hands into his back pockets, as though to keep from touching her again. "I haven't forgotten that you told me you were betrothed. I haven't even forgotten his name—Stephen. But you can't love him. You can't, and still act like this with me. There's something between us that's so damned good it's scary. I've never, ever sensed such a powerful ecstasy waiting for me when I've held any other woman before. I want you so bad it's tearing me apart. But I want a chance to see if this can be forever between us, not just for one time."

He walked over to the door, opened it, and spoke one last time. "I think it's the same for you. To be this good, the feelings have to be on both sides. But there are an awful lot of other things that are against us. Your betrothal is the least of it, far as I'm concerned. If I was sure we could make it together—sure you at least wanted to explore this thing between us as badly as me—I wouldn't stop until I'd given us at least a chance to see what can happen."

As though he knew she couldn't think of a word to say, he continued, "Someone may have already told you that I was keeping company with a debutante once. I'd even considered asking for her hand. But that was nothing at all compared to what I'm feeling now. Not even close. Good night, Sarah."

He slipped through the door and closed it softly behind him.

14

STEPHEN. I'M PROMISED *to Stephen.*

Sarah lay back on the bed, feeling the emptiness beside her as she'd never done before in her life. But overriding the emptiness came the guilt, breaking free of her attempts to hold it at bay at last.

She'd spent a lot of time thinking about what it would be like to have Stephen in her bed. What woman who was a virgin wouldn't wonder for hours on end what that part of her coming marriage would be like? She'd already begun redecorating her father's quarters for Stephen, and since her own bedroom was at the other end of the hall from the side-by-side master and mistress suites, she'd reluctantly begun eyeing the room her mother had used. Hardly any of her friends shared a bedroom with their husbands, although she'd heard whispers that Camellia and Jake Anderson spent their nights in the same bed.

The Anderson marriage was a love match, though, as anyone who spent more than five minutes in their presence knew. For the most part in other marriages, she supposed, the husband only spent a few minutes now and then in the wife's bed, or perhaps vice versa. She'd never had the courage to ask any of her married friends how that worked, or how long the husbands stayed or how often.

She'd be willing to bet her bloomers that Wyn MacIntyre would sleep all night long with his wife, if the length of time he'd spent just kissing and fondling her this evening were any indication! And she could probably safely add her chemise to the bet that his wife wouldn't mind sharing his bed a bit!

Another flush crawled over her cheeks—she'd lost count of how many times that had happened this evening. Land sakes, she had never had such indecent thoughts back in New York! Bet her bloomers and chemise, indeed!

She sat up so quickly her head spun, and she had to wait a few seconds before she got to her feet and went over to the stove. In the oven she found a plate Mandy had left, still a tad warm. Placing it on her tiny table, she unwrapped the towel from around it and sat in one of the two chairs.

A good fifteen minutes later, she came to herself and looked at her plate. The food was completely cold and unappetizing now, and her stomach gave a complaining growl.

Shoving the plate aside, she pulled the butter dish to her. On a corner of the table, Mandy had also left some fresh-baked bread to go along with her meal. She unwrapped that and buttered a slice. Her stomach subsided as she bit off a large chunk and chewed.

Wyn MacIntyre had absolutely no idea how much different their backgrounds were, she contemplated. She knew exactly what size fortune Rose Collingsworth came from and the probable amount of the dowry she had brought to the Hardesty son. Though not considered completely proper drawing room conversation, dollar amounts of fortunes served as prevalent gossip in her society.

The Collingsworths, Rose's parents, were what was considered comfortably rich if they didn't overspend. But as Petula Hardesty had correctly stated at the opera the night Sarah found Mairi, the Channing fortune could be frittered with for quite some time without making a dent in it. Even her attorney had told her not to worry one whit about the size of any bills she ran up with the various vendors—that the fortune was secure in investments and would fund lives for as many as a dozen of her great-great-grandchildren with no problem.

So much good could be done with that money, Sarah thought. Today she had found a situation even worse than the orphanage Mairi had been sent to. But she couldn't imagine the money not causing problems between her and Wyn, given the man's overabundance of masculinity and his probable lavish share of pride.

She'd had an inkling of the MacIntyre pride as soon as she arrived, when Dan informed her that he would repay her for the grave marker for his brother and sister-in-law. And he'd handed over the exact amount of bills to her right before supper that first night.

Not that there was really any reason for her even to be considering these matters, she halfheartedly assured herself. She was betrothed to Stephen. And until this evening, she had thought her attraction to Wyn MacIntyre was just an interlude—part of this time she'd decided to take for herself before she donned the shackles of marriage.

Of course, the thoughts about how much she was enjoying her freedom since her father's death had grown from tiny niggles to a full-blown yearning to hold on to that feeling for a while yet. Not that she was truly contemplating such an idea, but she supposed Wyn would be just as domineering as her friends' husbands, should he be someone's husband. He had all the other male attributes, including a self-confident demeanor that had people showing him a high level of respect.

The children didn't let that respect include fear, she thought with a smile as she recalled Jute telling her about Wyn's own run-in with a skunk. She couldn't seem to keep from thinking what would have happened had Stephen overheard even a young child cast aspersions on his pride. She could imagine that sneer on Stephen's lips and probably a snarl of outrage at the offender.

Wyn had no small amount of pride himself, but he handled it differently. Today he had bristled when she

dropped her guard and allowed her aversion to the way
Patty and Pete's parents lived to show. She had no doubt he
felt these were his people and no outsider had a right to
judge them. In fact, he'd indicated emphatically that she had
no right to do that. But he'd handled his disagreement with
her without the simpering or pouting she would have
expected from Stephen.

Stephen could very well change once they were wed,
however. And she could only assume at this point how much
worse the differences of opinions with Wyn might get the
longer they were around each other.

What if she did fall in love with Wyn MacIntyre, and he
fell in love with her in return? She had to be realistic,
because Wyn had made it clear that what he was beginning
to feel was a possible forever-type feeling. Could she be
happy married to Wyn?

She had no doubt she *could* be—at first. But what about
later? What about the "forever" part?

For one thing, how could she raise her children here,
where there was so much poverty? They'd have so much
better lives back in New York, wouldn't they? She sure as
heck hadn't had that good a life back there, though. The
twins had more fun in one day than she'd ever had—except
for today, with her teasing, fighting, and . . . kissing with
Wyn.

Could she give up the chance to have that be a part of the
rest of her life? Give up the chance to get to know Wyn
better? He was the first man who'd ever made her feel
feminine, even a little bit pretty. The first man who had ever
teased her and made her feel like teasing him in return. The
first man who had ever kissed her and curled her toes in her
shoes—made her long to learn exactly what he meant when
he assured her that he could make her writhe in ecstasy.

Like Wyn, she had some very heavy thinking to do.
Breaking her betrothal to Stephen would be a major step,
and not something to be taken lightly. In fact, she supposed
it would cause quite a scandal. She'd spent months on end
considering how to go about finding a husband. Once the
initial decision had been made, more months passed before

selecting Stephen. Did her choice between which way to go now deserve any less consideration?

Besides, she couldn't forget the fact that Wyn was probably much too young for her! Why, when she was fifty and over the hill, he'd still be in his forties, barely past prime for a man.

You're going to be fifty someday anyway, her mind insisted, *whoever you spend the intervening years with.*

She waved a hand as though chasing away a buzzing fly, but her mind refused to be intimidated by the threatening gesture.

Wyn rode up to Leery's cabin the next day around noon. He halted his horse at the edge of her neat, flower-strewn yard, leaning on the saddle horn and wondering if he looked a tenth as foolish as he felt. All morning, he'd been like one of the barn cats prowling around just before it goes into labor, until his pa had told him to get out for a while. As soon as he'd hit the saddle, he'd known where he had to go.

"Go on in," a voice said from behind him.

Somehow he kept himself from jerking the reins and startling the horse into rearing. He heaved a sigh, then stared down at the gnarled mountain healer.

"Dang it, Leery. You could have warned me you were around."

"You'da heered me if you'da been payin' attention. But you got that there schoolteacher on your mind, and ain't nothin' else managin' to get through."

He didn't *really* believe she could read his mind, but Wyn let his chin fall to his chest and shook his head. "I . . ."

"I said go on in," Leery interrupted him.

She walked by him and headed to her little cabin, passing on through the open door and leaving him to follow. Wyn urged his horse forward and dismounted at the front steps. Tying the horse to a hitching post, he studied the cabin for a minute.

Even this early in the growing season, Leery already had dozens of plants blooming and hanging around her porch eaves. If he hadn't known better, he'd have thought her supposed mystical powers allowed her to have flowers when the rest of the mountain people were still planting seedlings. But he knew about the small glass hut behind her cabin, where she nurtured her plants and grew various herbs. In the winter she moved everything onto her enclosed back porch, but usually by early February, she began receiving packages of seeds when Jeeter brought the mail.

He clearly recalled the time several years ago that Jeeter had begun bringing panes of glass up the mountain two at a time for her building. They were a birthday present for his mother, Jeeter had informed anyone who would listen. He'd read about something called a greenhouse in a book, and he was determined to build one for Leery. That way she wouldn't run out of the herbs she needed for her medicines over the winter.

And Jeeter hadn't had to build it all by himself. Until the greenhouse was complete, the services of the mountain healer could be had for the price of a couple hours' work on her birthday present. Wyn had even gone up there and done his own stint when his ma had an upset stomach and had been out of both chamomile and peppermint.

Leery came back out onto the porch holding two glasses. She set one on her porch railing, then sat in a white cane rocking chair, taking a sip of whatever was in the glass and pointedly waiting for Wyn to say something. He walked up the porch steps and picked up his glass. It looked like some sort of tea, and he took a hesitant sip, then sat down on the top step and leaned against the post.

"Good," he said, holding the glass out in a gesture to Leery. "Tastes like it has some sassafras in it."

"Little of that, little of some other things," Leery said. "But ain't none of the love potion ingredients in that. That's what you came to talk 'bout, ain't it? I knowed you was back behind that there barn door when little Mairi and me was a-talkin' the other night."

The side of Wyn's mouth twitched wryly, and he took a larger swallow from his glass. "I always thought one of the actual people wanting to pair up had to ask for that potion." He fixed Leery with a stern look. "That's what Ma always said, anyway, when she talked about that part of your ways. She said that the feelings between two people had as much to do with a potion like that working as any of the stuff you mixed in it did. That if one of the two didn't have some love to build on, the potion was worthless."

"Your ma was right," Leery said with a huge smile. "One of the two people involved *does* have to ask for the potion for it to work."

"So you mean . . ."

"Yep. Every one of them there feelin's you been havin' for Sarah is all your own. Ain't no help comin' from anywhere 'cept in your own heart. Scares you, huh?"

Wyn ignored that comment. "Then why did you allow Mairi to think she was using the potion to get us together?"

Leery grinned crookedly at him. "Little Mairi was real worried 'bout Miss Sarah leavin' at first, 'cause she was a-lovin' on Miss Sarah so much. What with her ma and pa only bein' dead such a short while, little Mairi wasn't up to facin' another loss right then. All I did with that potion was give Mairi some comfort and ease her mind."

"But what happens when Sarah does leave?"

"*If* that happens, little Mairi will be able to handle it better. Be some more time between her losses, so they don't hit her so hard."

"If?"

Leery laughed and wagged a finger at Wyn. "No, you don't, my boy! I ain't seen what the future's gonna bring for you and Sarah. You're gonna have to live out them days yourself and see what happens. But I will tell you this much."

"What?"

"I saw two white doves fly over your house the last time I was there. You know that's a surefire omen two people in your family will be married within a year's time. And I don't feel one of them is Carrie just yet."

That only left him and his pa, Wyn realized, but he listened closely as Leery went on.

"I'll even tell you this much. Love that's built slowly lasts

forever." Then she gave him a wink. "But then, I've also
seen love at first sight last forever, too."

She rose and reached for his glass. As soon as he handed
it to her, Leery went into her cabin. Knowing her habits
from the past, Wyn got up and went to his horse. Leery had
other things to do now, and he had been dismissed.
Mounting, he turned his horse toward home.

He had felt a bit of relief when Leery first agreed with
him about the love potions—that the spell didn't work
unless one of the actual participants in the potential match
asked for the potion. But his stomach began tightening ever
so gradually the farther he rode. If it wasn't the potion
working, that meant Leery was right. That everything he'd
said to Sarah Channing last night had come straight and true
from his own deep, growing feelings for her.

And Leery was right about another thing. That scared the
shit out of him lots more than it did when he thought he had
the excuse of some supernatural help on which to blame
those feelings!

Sarah remembered to bring her cloak when Wyn called for
her after school. Land sakes, she remembered every word
he'd spoken the previous night, so it wasn't any surprise that
she recalled his directive about the cloak. She should recall
every word, since she'd played each one of them over and
over in her mind until well after midnight.

She also recalled that Wyn had said he had a lot of
thinking to do, and he evidently did some of it while they
rode in silence. The cabin they visited was, as he had
warned her, deeper in the mountains than Patty and Pete's
home. Lonnie Fraiser rode with them, but he was as quiet as
Wyn, the same as he was in school. She wondered how
Carrie would even get enough words out of Lonnie to know
he returned her feelings, but she had seen the two of them
talking together. Well, mostly Carrie chatted away while
Lonnie blushed and listened.

When she met Lonnie's mother and father, she realized
the boy's reserved nature came from his father, because his

mother was more bubbly and vivacious than anyone Sarah had ever met.

"Come in, come in," Pearl Fraiser insisted, and Sarah complied as Wyn and Lonnie walked off with Lonnie's father.

The cabin was as neat as a pin, and a lot better furnished than the one she'd visited last night. It was much larger, too, although she knew from her chats with Mandy that Pearl only had one child, Lonnie.

A corner of the living room was taken up by a huge loom, and Pearl picked up a brilliant green shawl lying across the chair beside the loom.

"Granny Clayborne said to give this to you," Pearl said. "She's my great-granny, and she said I was also to tell you that there'd be a blanket waitin' for you at the MacHoolihans when you go there to visit."

"How beautiful!" Sarah enthused. "But I didn't bring my reticule to pay you for it."

"Ain't one penny owed," Pearl admonished. "My boy Lonnie is enjoyin' learnin' for the first time in his life. And I 'spect you'll find the same thing at the MacHoolihans, you try to give them anything for the blanket. She's my sister-in-law, and we been a-talkin' 'bout how my Lonnie and her Chester don't even need to be reminded to read a verse from the Bible every night afore bed. They's enjoyin' readin' so much, I had to holler at Lonnie to get on to sleep and not waste the candle the other night."

By the time Sarah left the Fraiser cabin an hour later, by all rights she should have felt that she was the best teacher this side of heaven. Instead, she found herself worrying about living up to the expectations of the mountain people. True, her charges had soaked up knowledge the past couple weeks like thirsty sponges, but there was so much yet to teach them. At least with the joy of reading she was instilling in them, they could continue their education on their own time, given the availability of books to read. And soon that should be a lot more convenient.

As on the trip out, Wyn was mostly silent on the return trip. The trail tonight was even narrower than the other one,

and they couldn't even think of riding side by side until
nearly back at the store. Wyn led the way directly to her
cabin again and dismounted, holding up his arms to assist
her.

As soon as he put her on the ground, he dropped his hands
from her waist. Someone had lit a lantern and left it in the
window beside her door—Mandy probably—and she could
easily see his face. He bent down and kissed her gently, then
whispered a good night, turned, and led the horses away
without another word. She had to make a distinct effort to
unclench her fist and open her door.

Inside the cabin, she closed the door and leaned back
against it. She knew she should feel guilty over Wyn's kiss.
Her betrothal committed her to Stephen, and she was
betraying her sacred word. Yet the strength of will and
determination she had built up over the years deserted her in
the face of her growing feelings for Wyn.

In an effort to prove herself undeserving of her father's
verbal denigration of her looks, she'd always adhered
scrupulously to the various rules and restrictions of her
society. Still, she had never received one voluntary touch or
even a nod of approval from her father. Stephen's touches
and brief kisses, too, were consistently more dutiful than
spontaneous.

Wyn freely gave his caresses, his touches, his kisses. As
hard as she tried to doubt the apparent honesty of his
actions, she couldn't dredge up the words to tell him never
to touch her again. She sighed deeply. Since she couldn't
find the gumption to fight against the pleasure Wyn gave
her, she would just have to continue to enjoy it, at least for
the time she had left in the mountains.

The next few evenings passed in much the same way, and
Sarah finally made the last visit to a student's parents. She
returned with the blanket from Pearl's sister-in-law. After
Wyn had kissed her and left as usual, she entered the cabin
and smoothed the blanket over her bed before she took her
supper out of the oven. The blanket she would keep, but the
shawl was already in the package over at the store, along

with the letter she'd written to her attorney. Tomorrow Jeeter was due, and the package would be on its way to New York.

It was a long letter, and she'd concentrated on it for several evenings after returning from her visits. Preparing it, both the instructions and the questions, had kept her mind too busy to pick apart her feelings for Wyn MacIntyre. But after lights out, it was a different tale.

Even with her disturbed sleep pattern, Sarah was up at dawn the next morning. It was Saturday, so she didn't have to teach, but she would probably still see several of her students and their parents. Today Jeeter was scheduled to arrive, and she felt confident there had been enough time since her first letters to New York for at least a few things to start arriving. She couldn't put off talking to Mandy any longer.

She hurried over to the boardinghouse and arrived just as Mandy was taking the coffeepot off the stove.

"Sarah!" Mandy said. "Goodness, you're early. I haven't even baked the biscuits yet."

"I'll help you, Mandy. But can I talk to you about something first?"

"Of course, but let me pour our coffee. I'm not worth a thing in the mornings until after a couple cups of coffee."

A few minutes later, Mandy appeared wide awake, despite only having drunk half a cup of coffee. She leaned her elbows on the table and looked at Sarah warily. She'd been hoping for a completely different reaction from Mandy, but at least she had her attention.

"Let me get this straight, Sarah." Mandy took another sip of coffee and kept her cup close to her lips. "You've written to your friends and pastor back in New York and asked them about sending books here. And you thought perhaps one of my extra rooms would make a nice lending library for the families to use?"

"I'll be happy to pay you your normal rate for the room, Mandy," Sarah said enthusiastically. "These books will be extras that would have gone into boxes to be stored in attics or just tossed in the trash. I've seen lots of people do that when their personal libraries get too full, and the children here can get lots of use out of those books. I'll even pay you a salary as the librarian, so you'll have a steady income and not have to depend on hit-and-miss business from your boardinghouse."

Mandy finished her coffee and rose to get another cup. When she returned to the table, she carried the pot and offered to refill Sarah's cup.

Sarah chuckled. "My cup's still full, Mandy. I've been so busy talking I haven't touched a drop of coffee."

Giving a sigh, Mandy set the pot down and reclaimed her chair. "Sarah, I think you have a wonderful idea, but I wish you'd checked with me before you went barreling ahead and having those books sent. Did you say Jeeter would probably start delivering them today?"

Sarah's stomach clenched at Mandy's attitude. "Well, yes," she forced out. "Please tell me what I've done wrong, Mandy. Why, most of these families only have a Bible to read, and those books my friends have would just go to waste otherwise. Channing Place has several boxes in its attic alone!"

"Let's don't get too worried yet." Mandy rose and, carrying her coffee with her, started for the kitchen door. "You said you'd help with breakfast, so why don't you start the biscuits while I go over and see Dan for a minute. I should be back before the biscuits are done, but if not, feel free to help yourself. There's fresh butter and persimmon jelly on the shelf right inside the pantry door."

Start the biscuits? Sarah thought about calling after Mandy to tell her she had no earthly idea what the biscuit recipe consisted of, but the other woman was already down the hallway and out the front door. She couldn't decide for several minutes if she should be more worried about not baking the biscuits or whatever it was that Mandy had to consult with Dan about.

Her growling stomach decided for her, and she saw the bowl in which Mandy always prepared the biscuit dough on the counter, a towel draped across the top of it. Hesitantly, she approached the bowl and lifted a corner of the towel.

Thank goodness. The dough was ready. All she had to do was dust the flour over the counter and roll the dough out. Then cut out the biscuits with the mouth of a fruit jar and place them on the baking sheet to stick in the oven. She'd watched Mandy do that many times. It couldn't be that hard.

15

$\mathcal{A}$LL THOUGHTS OF whether or not Sarah had brought on some trouble for herself fled when Mandy paused at the door to Dan's bedroom. She knew from discussions with Wyn that Dan tried to be as independent as possible. He washed and dressed himself, shaved himself, and only tolerated anyone else moving the wheelchair if he was totally exhausted. But she hadn't known Dan was trying to learn to transfer himself from his bed to his wheelchair on his own.

She clapped her fingertips over her lips to hold back her cry of astonishment and froze on the threshold of the partially open door. He stood—yes, *stood*—there between the bed and wheelchair, then slowly swiveled and collapsed in the chair. The chair flew backward several feet, but Dan caught the wheels and halted it before it hit the wall.

He glanced up and saw her. Placing an index finger to his lips, he whispered, "Shhhhh. It's a surprise for Wyn. This is the first morning I've been able to do it alone."

Mandy couldn't keep from rushing to his side. She laid a hand on his shoulder, blinking against the tears misting her eyes.

"Oh, Dan! How long have you been trying to do this?"

"Seems like all my life," Dan said with a chuckle. "But I reckon it's just been the last six months or so. Doc MacKenzie said it wouldn't hurt me none to try. And I'm dadblasted sick and tried of having Wyn take me to the outhouse."

Mandy felt her cheeks flush at his frankness, but she patted him on the shoulder. "I can imagine. How far do you think you'll be able to go? Maybe even walk someday?"

He shrugged, his firm muscles shifting beneath her palm. He had lost none of the hardness of his upper body, what with using his arms to move about in the wheelchair. He also helped Wyn unpack supplies and stock the shelves, because she'd seen him do it. He'd had Wyn make him a box to put on his lap, and he filled it with goods. He couldn't reach the higher shelves, but he kept the lower ones stocked.

Yes, the exercise kept his upper body trim, even developed. His shoulder was quite solid beneath her touch.

Dan cleared his throat, and Mandy jumped, pulling her hand back. Land o'Goshen, she'd been standing there actually rubbing her palm across his shoulder! And now she became aware that Dan had said something else. Blushing furiously instead of faintly this time, she backed away.

"Uh . . . I'm sorry. I . . . didn't hear what you said."

"Now, Mandy," he said in a teasing tone. "You were standing there with your ear right beside my mouth. And I know for a fact you're not nearly old enough to start losing your hearing. You're forty-six, the same age as me, and my hearing's as sharp as it ever was."

"I . . . was distracted." She nodded her head emphatically. "I came to talk to you about something Sarah has done, and I had that on my mind."

"Maybe when you first came over here that's what you were thinking about, Mandy," Dan said in quiet voice. "But I'd be willin' to bet you were thinkin' about somethin' else just a second ago—when you were touching me like a woman touches a man. Maybe the same thing I've been thinkin' about for a while now. Maybe the same thing that's another reason I've been trying to get back a measure of my independence."

A glimmer of hope flickered and grew in Mandy. She and Dan's wife, Maria, had been best friends while Maria lived. Both had been fairly new to the mountains as young brides. Maria had given Dan children, but Mandy hadn't begrudged Maria her happiness. Oh, she had been a tiny bit jealous, since her own womb remained barren, but she enjoyed Maria and Dan's children almost as much as she would have her own.

She'd had an otherwise wonderful life with Calvin. They had been as much in love the day he died at the young age of forty as the day they married. He and Dan were as good a friends as she and Maria, and when possible, the four of them played whist or cribbage in the evenings after the children were abed.

They always celebrated the holidays together, and once, before Maria had the twins, they'd even managed to get another woman friend to stay with Maria's children while they took a trip together to Lynchburg. That had been the trip that resulted in the friendship between Dan and the senator, which allowed Wyn his chance to see a few things beyond Sawback Mountain.

"Mandy." Dan rolled his chair closer and picked up her hand. "We've had a lot of years to get to know each other, haven't we? Were you remembering all the good times we had with Calvin and Maria?"

"Yes," she whispered.

"And a minute ago, were you starting to realize that I'm also a man and not just the widower of your friend?"

"I've been aware of that for quite a while now, Dan." She whispered again, unable for some reason to talk any louder.

"Maria and Calvin are dead," Dan mused, rubbing his thumb back and forth across the back of her hand. "We were two lucky couples, because we loved our mates real and true. But we're still alive, and I've been noticin' for a while now just how very much alive you are."

She stared helplessly into his blue eyes. "It could be just the convenience of living so close together. Just habit."

"And it could be friendship that's blossomed into something deeper. Don't you think we oughtta give ourselves a chance to find out? We've both mature enough to decide somethin' like that for ourselves, don't you think?"

"I'm . . . I'm sure old enough." She grimaced. "Way too old to be thinking that another man might be interested in this old body."

Then she gasped in dismay and tried to jerk her hand free from Dan's hold. "I . . . oh, I'm sorry, Dan. I know . . . I mean, I suppose you . . . not having any feeling and all down—"

With one swift effort, he pulled her onto his lap. She gasped again and tried to free herself, but Dan only wrapped his arms around her and laughed at her useless struggle. The developed body she'd been admiring had absolutely no problem holding her captive.

"You are a definite lapful, Mandy Tuttle," he said with a chuckle. "Perfect for a man to get a good hold on and enjoy every inch of that hold. And if you don't quit squirmin' around like that, you're gonna find out just exactly how much feeling I do have left down there."

"Ohhhh—!"

Dan's lips cut off her astonished cry.

Wyn stood stunned in the doorway of his pa's bedroom. That danged sure *looked* like Mandy Tuttle on his pa's lap. And it danged sure *looked* like his pa was kissing her. What's more, it *looked* like Mandy was kissing his pa back, what with her not struggling any longer to get off his pa's lap and having her fingers wrapped across the back of his head.

A huge grin spread over Wyn's face, and he leaned against the doorjamb, slipping the tips of his thumbs into his belt. Looked like Leery might be right about at least one marriage in his family.

After an extraordinary long time, the two people sharing the wheelchair broke the kiss.

"Oh, Dan!" Mandy said.

"Oh, Mandy," his pa said with a chuckle in his voice.

But when Dan trailed a finger down Mandy's neck and it *looked* like he might be heading toward the full breast touching his chest, Wyn harrumped to get their attention.

Mandy's eyes flew to the doorway, and she blushed as red as a summer cherry tomato. She wiggled on his pa's lap as though she wanted to get up, but his pa held her in place with hardly any trouble. Either that, or Mandy wasn't really trying that hard to escape.

"'Member what I said about what I can feel, Mandy," Dan said.

Her eyes widened, and Mandy stilled on his lap.

"What do you want, son?" Dan asked in a mild voice.

"Well, same thing I always want about this time of a morning," Wyn replied. "To help you into your chair. But looks to me like you've already done that."

"Sure have, son." Dan winked at him. "And I'm a-hopin' I'll be able to do lots more than that pretty soon. Soon as Doc MacKenzie gets back, I'm gonna have another talk with him. But in the meantime, I figger to keep working like I have been on doing a little bit more each day for myself. Don't figger on settin' out the rest of my days on the porch with a blanket over my knees."

"I'm sorry, Pa. I know you get agitated with me when I won't let you do stuff yourself. I just want to take the best care of you that I can."

"You've been taking darned fine care of me and everyone else in this family, Wyn. But from now on, I want you to wait till I ask you for help. That all right with you?"

"I think that's a great idea. Now, I'll leave you two—"

"No!" Mandy evaded his pa's hold this time and jumped to her feet. She gave Dan a teasingly triumphant look, and Wyn had to suppress a chuckle.

"You might want to hear this, too," she told Wyn after she focused her attention on him. "I'm not real sure what to say to Sarah about it, so that's why I came over here to speak to you and Dan first."

Wyn frowned and walked into the room. "What's wrong with Sarah?"

"Nothing's wrong with her," Mandy denied. "It's just that

she's come up with what she thinks is a wonderful idea, and she told it to me a few minutes ago when she came over before I even had breakfast started. But I'm not sure what folks around here will think about it."

"What is it?" Dan asked.

"She wants to start a library, and she's already sent back to where she's from and asked for a bunch of books. She seems to think some of them will start arriving as soon as today."

"Damn it," Wyn said, then, "Aw, shoot, I apologize for cursing in front of you, Mandy." He sat down on the side of his pa's bed. "But I was hoping that when Pa paid Sarah for that grave marker and from what she's seen around here so far, she'd know she can't go tossing her money around. Folks here don't take to charity. You know that as well as I do."

"Well, the way she explained it to me," Mandy told him, "these aren't books she's actually bought. They're books from her attic and also books her friends would have thrown away anyway. She's even got her pastor involved, collecting books at the church. When Sarah put it that way, I didn't see much to object to. But the rest of her plan won't sit real well."

"And what *is* the rest of the plan?" Dan asked.

"She wants to rent one of my rooms—with her paying for it, of course. She wants to hire me as the librarian and pay me a salary, too. Now, folks around here will avoid that place like the plague if they think it's her paying for stuff like that, and you know there are a few of them like Leery and Granny Clayborne who will want to know how this is being paid for. If the people don't use the libraries, those books will be just as useless again as they were sitting in those boxes in people's attics."

Wyn shook his head. "We can't let her pay like that, because this is a good idea if we could work things out. I guess we could sort of fudge the truth a little bit about the books. Tell people she discussed it with the three of us and we thought it was a good idea. We just wouldn't tell them that she only discussed it with us a few hours before everything started arriving."

Dan ran a hand across his mouth in a contemplative manner, and Wyn waited respectfully for his decision. After all, Pa headed the school board. All he could do was offer suggestions. And, of course, have a chat with Miss Debutante about her bulling ahead and thinking that the money she had plenty of gave her the right to overlook people's pride.

She was a darned good teacher. He had heard too many people praise her and thank her for their young'uns' new interest in learning not to give Sarah that credit. Shoot, even Luke and Jute didn't complain about homework any longer. The evenings when he took Sarah out to make her visits and she couldn't help them as she normally did, his Pa had told him all Sissy had to do was mention lesson time and all the children obeyed. Jute was so proud when he got an A on the spelling test, he had told every customer in the store that evening.

It was one thing to encourage people to improve on their own. That built self-confidence and assurance in people. It was another thing to give people charity and take away their right to make their own way in life, for themselves and their children.

"Well," Dan said at last. "I guess I can go along with the idea that we can use those books as well as anyone else could. But we need to set up some way the library can sorta fund itself, far as paying anyone to take care of those books and payin' for somewhere to set it up at."

"Dan," Mandy said. "The people will accept it if I donate a room for the library. I'm one of them, and I'd be proud to do that. I never have all those rooms full, and land o'Goshen, I've got two parlor rooms. Calvin built that house when he thought we were going to have a bunch of young'uns like you and Maria had. And I'd be the librarian for free, too, if I thought I could get by with it. That's probably going too far, though."

"How 'bout we charge something for renting the books?" Dan suggested. "Say, five books for a penny or somethin'.

If folks didn't want all five books at once, they can run an account and pay after that fifth book. In the meantime, we can look into how the other libraries work. Probably there's some sort of funding available from the government, and if we figger out what all the rules and regulations are, maybe we can get some help."

"Sounds perfect to me." Mandy nodded. "I'll go over and tell Sarah."

Dan grabbed her before she could take more than one step. "No, you don't, Mandy. We've got a couple of things to talk about, you and me. Wyn can go talk to Sarah."

Wyn heeded his pa's broad hint immediately. Rising from the bed, he left the room. Behind him, he heard that spring creak on the bottom of the wheelchair, as though Dan had shifted—or pulled Mandy Tuttle back down on his lap. He'd have laid his bets on the latter, but he didn't turn to confirm whether or not he would have won the bet with himself.

His pa and Mandy. Huh. Who would have thought? But then, if anyone had thought about it, it would seem perfect—as perfect as the plans for the library—the revised plans, anyway. Now all he had to do was get Sarah's agreement.

Assuming Sarah was still at the boardinghouse, since that was where Mandy had been talking to her, he loped across the yard. When he started in the boardinghouse door, he sniffed the air. Surely Mandy hadn't left something on the stove to burn while she came over to talk to his pa. Suddenly something crashed to the floor down the hallway, and a woman screamed.

He raced down the hallway and into the kitchen.

Sarah was flapping a burning towel around as though trying to put out the flames. He grabbed it from her and tossed it into the sink, where it sizzled out in a pan of water. Then he turned back to Sarah, his heart in his throat.

"Are you burned?"

She shook her head, tears standing in her brown eyes. He didn't believe her. Gently he led her over to the table and pulled out a chair, shifting it around so she would face him when he pushed her into it. Picking up her hands, he examined them, turning them over to check both the palms and the tops.

"I don't see any blisters. What happened?"

She choked on a sob. "I . . . got them cut out all right—the biscuits. Well, they were sort of messy—just a little bit—so maybe I didn't put down enough flour when I rolled them out. But I got them on the pan and put them in the oven. I didn't know how long they were supposed to cook, but I remembered hearing the cook say once that her cake fell when someone opened the oven. So I didn't want to look at them too soon."

Wyn pulled another chair close and sat down beside her. "Biscuits don't fall like cakes do, sweetheart. But go on. Tell me what happened."

She sniffed and rubbed her dress cuff beneath one eye, where a tear crawled down her cheek.

"Well, I didn't know that biscuits didn't fall like cakes," Sarah said in a forlorn voice laced with just a mite of stubbornness. "So I thought since Mandy's biscuits are even fluffier and lighter than Cook's, they might fall if I looked in before it was time. But when I smelled them burning, I knew . . . well, I knew they were burning! All Mandy had asked me to do was make the biscuits, and I burned them!"

Wyn reached out and brushed a dusting of flour from her forehead. "They don't look *that* burned, Sarah. But how did you catch the towel on fire?"

"I don't know," she choked out. "I didn't see an oven mitt, so I grabbed the first thing I could. I think it touched the side of the stove and the heat ignited it. I . . . I . . . what do you mean, 'the biscuits don't look *that* burned'?"

She scanned the floor and saw the biscuits lying scattered in front of the stove, with the iron pan lying in their midst. Suddenly she let out a wail and threw herself into Wyn's arms.

She was an armful, and Wyn braced himself and managed to keep his chair from tumbling backward. She was so distraught, she didn't protest when he snuggled her onto his lap and pressed her head against his neck. He stroked her back soothingly, murmuring nonsense to her, recalling seeing his mother get upset a couple of times over a burned dish or one that didn't come out exactly as she thought it should. His pa had held his mother like this on those occasions, and she'd quieted fairly soon.

But Sarah's cries continued for a long moment. Glad he'd remembered to put a clean handkerchief in his back pocket that morning, he retrieved it and stuffed it into her hand.

She drew back at last and pressed his hanky to her face. "I can't do anything right anymore!"

"What's that supposed to mean?" He waited until she dropped her hands, wringing the hanky in her fingers and staring at the floor. Picking up her chin, he said, "Seems to me you've done an awful lot right since you got here."

She shook her head and politely blew her nose. He'd never seen a woman manage to blow her nose in a mannerly way, but she did. However, he didn't think now was the time to comment on that.

"I have trouble with the stove at my cabin," she said. "It's not so bad now because it's warmer, but when I wouldn't wake up at night to feed the fire, it would be completely out in the morning. I'd have a devil of a time getting it going again."

"You're supposed to bank the fire at night." He immediately realized he'd said the wrong thing when her eyes again filled.

"See?" she said around a sob. "And I don't even know what you mean by *banking* a fire! And sometimes I don't have any water in the mornings to bathe with, both because I've forgotten to get any from the well the night before and because I don't have any way to heat it."

Wyn bit back the thought that flew into his head, but it was as though she'd read his mind.

"Oh, all right," she grumbled. "I guess I still haven't broken the habit of my maid having a hot basin of water waiting for me in the mornings!"

"Sarah, Sarah . . ."

Suddenly she gasped and leaped from his lap. "Oh, my!

What if Mandy had come back in and seen me sitting on your lap? Teachers are supposed to be the soul of propriety. Why, Dan would probably send me packing in a minute."

"I doubt that," Wyn said with a chuckle. "But sit down on your own chair again and let me see what I can do about the biscuits. Mandy's floors are so clean I doubt there's a speck of dirt on any of them, but we'll bake some more if there is."

He waited until she complied, then went to the stove and poured her a cup of coffee. After setting it in front of her, he walked over to examine the biscuits. As he expected, there was just the beginning of a burned crust on them, and he placed them on the pan, then found a hot pad in one of Mandy's kitchen drawers and put the pan on the countertop.

"I think they're fine," he said. "Shoot, half of them didn't even fall off the pan."

When Sarah didn't answer him, he looked at her to see her wiping her eyes with his handkerchief once more. She sniffled, then gave him a woebegone look.

"It's not just the biscuits," she said. "I mentioned something to Mandy a while ago, and she acted very strange. She left in rather a hurry to go talk to Dan about it. I thought I'd had a marvelous idea, but I guess I put my foot in it one more time."

"If you mean the library, she's already talked to both Pa and me," Wyn informed her. He poured himself some coffee and sat back down at the table. "And with a couple changes, we both think it will work fine."

"See?" Sarah jumped to her feet. "You have to make changes in what I came up with! I can't do *anything* right!"

Shaking his head, Wyn searched for something to say. This was a side of Sarah he hadn't seen before. Ever since her arrival, she had been poised and confident. Even when they argued, she held her own. Now she was restless and insecure.

Could this be a side of her that she didn't allow to show except to a few certain people? Could she be letting down her guard because she cared for him, trusted him? Those thoughts deserved a lot more time to pick apart than he had right now.

He watched her walk over to the counter to make her own examination of the biscuits. She halted in a position that left her profile clear to him. Her dark blue dress covered the long length of her, the white cuffs and collar a nice feminine touch to the garment. It fit her a little bit snugger in the bodice than some of her other dresses, showing off the rounded breasts that were the exact right size for his palm. He felt a surge in his groin, but he controlled himself. There were still way too many things left unsettled between him and Sarah Channing.

But when his perusal of her caught on the protrusion of her bottom lip, his heart ached for her discouragement. His control shattered as though he'd pushed it away with the coffee cup he shoved across the table. Surging to his feet, he was at the counter beside her before he'd much more than realized he'd left his chair. She looked up at him, her eyes still moist and the gold dust in them soggy with unshed tears. That enticing bottom lip jutted out a hair's breadth more. He bent his head and kissed it back into place.

She wrapped her arm around his neck and kissed him in return. He leaned back against the counter and pulled her between his legs, never once losing the delicious contact with her mouth. She fit just as she should down his body, curves contrasting with his solidness in the right places. She would fit like that in bed, too, as he'd come extremely close to finding out the other night. He'd bet her hair was long enough to wrap around both of their bare bodies.

He'd pulled only one hairpin free when she jerked away. "Oh, don't! I . . . Mandy. Mandy will be back. And . . ." She grabbed the hairpin from him and dropped her head, her fingers working to push it into place. "And I have no right to kiss you like that. Not with Stephen in the picture."

Wyn tilted her face up. "That statement sounds suspiciously like maybe you're having second thoughts."

"Yes. No! I . . . I don't know, Wyn. This entire situation is so . . . so scary to me. I . . ."

He led her to the table and made her sit again, scooting his own chair even closer and taking her hand. "Tell me about it," he pleaded. "Please."

She nibbled that tantalizing lip for a few seconds, and he forced himself to remember she had said she was scared—not remember how that lip tasted intermingled with the flavor of coffee.

"I don't fit in here, Wyn," Sarah murmured. "But then, I never fit in back in New York, either. But back there all I had to do was as I was told—conform to the mold and follow the rules of accepted behavior that had been drilled into me all my life. Here I'm not even sure what accepted behavior consists of."

She threw him a plea for understanding. "On the other hand, Father's only been dead a little over two months, and I've had a taste of freedom from his constrictions at last. I think part of my confusion is that I'm not sure whether I'm using my attraction to you to end my engagement to Stephen or not."

A light of comprehension dawned in Wyn, sparking the beginning of anger. "So you think you'd rather be completely free, from both your betrothal and from my attention."

"For a while," she admitted. "I'd sort of like to see what I could accomplish on my own, without having to take some man's dictates into consideration. But . . ." She tentatively cupped her hand on his cheek. "But I wouldn't want to lose the chance to see whether or not you were right the other night. Whether what's happening between us is a forever kind of happening. I just want . . . time, I guess."

He leaned into her hand, knowing she was right and allowing the anger to die a natural death. Hadn't he said the same thing the night they'd ended up on her bed? That there was a lot of thinking to do? Could he fault her for agreeing with him on that?

16

"WYN! YOO-HOO, WYN!"

Mandy's voice came down the hallway, and Wyn reluctantly rose to his feet. "I better go see what she wants."

"Wyn, I need you to come out here and bring Dan up the steps!" Mandy called.

"Uh-oh." Wyn ran a finger across Sarah's chin. "I was supposed to talk to you about some changes Pa and Mandy came up with in your library plans. They'll wonder why we haven't discussed that, since I've been over here so long. And I forgot to tell you that Pa's been exercising, and it looks like his legs might just have some feeling in them. He's been standing, and this morning I found him already in his chair. He also had Mandy on his lap, kissing her."

"Oh, all that's wonderful news!" she told him with a smile. "And we can blame the biscuits for not having time to talk about all this. Now, you better go get your pa before Mandy tries to do it herself."

"We're going to have to build a ramp on the boarding-house porch, so Pa can do his courtin' without help." He tossed her an enigmatic grin and strode to the kitchen door.

"Courting?" she said.

He turned and gave her a wink. "Yep. And just so you don't have to wonder about it, there's gonna be another MacIntyre man doing some courting. Slow and easy, like you want, but courting all the same. Far as I'm concerned, we can't figure out whether or not this is a forever thing without working on it."

"Wyn!" Mandy called again.

"You might want to wash your face a little, sweetheart. You look like you've been crying. I don't think there's much you can do about looking like you've been kissed, though."

"Wyn!"

Footsteps sounded in the hallway and Wyn left to head Mandy off. All the while savoring Wyn's endearment, she managed to pump some water onto a clean dishcloth and lay it on her face briefly before she heard Wyn returning with Dan and Mandy.

For a brief instant, she let herself wish she could get pumped-in water into her little cabin, but she supposed there was no sense doing that. Not until she knew who would be in the cabin next year.

Wyn must have explained what he'd had time to talk to her about and what not, and about the burned biscuits, because Dan rolled his chair up to the table and began discussing the library with her. By the time Mandy had fixed them each a quick breakfast of oatmeal, Sarah was nodding at Dan's suggestions. Too, she knew beyond a shadow of a doubt she had overstepped her bounds by not letting Dan in on her plans right from their inception.

Oh, Lord! What was going to happen when Dan found out what else she'd done? Wyn, too, given his actions and chastisement of her on the way home from Patty and Pete's cabin the other night. But it was too late now to do anything about it.

Their discussion ended, she glanced at the kitchen clock. Even with no school today, she had lots to do—lesson plans and some correspondence to take care of. Jumping to her feet, she made a hasty apology and hurried to her cabin.

Hours later, Jeeter arrived. Lost in thought over her letter, she decided to finish it first, then put it in an envelope. She hadn't realized how much time had passed, and she barely caught Jeeter as he passed the schoolhouse on his way back down the mountain. After handing him her letters, she straightened her shoulders and headed over to the store.

Dan was on the porch. "I've been waiting for you," he said. "The books are in the storeroom, and if this is only the beginning of them, we're going to have the best library in Tennessee. Jeeter says he's going to have to come back again tomorrow with the rest of the boxes, even though it's Sunday. He has other deliveries to make the rest of the week."

"I'll pay him extra for the additional time," Sarah hastily assured him.

"Yes, you will," Dan said, his smile making his statement less stern. "Jeeter already mentioned that, and I told him to let me know how much and I'd pass that on to you."

Despite her concern over whether Dan was still perturbed at her, Sarah was eager to see the books. An avid reader herself, she could imagine the delight on the faces of the children—and the adults—when they realized what wonders awaited them between so many different covers.

"Can we go see them now?" she asked.

"Sure. Wyn's back there prying open the crates. Let's go see what your friends have sent."

She hurried ahead of him, through the goods lining the aisles and on into the storeroom. Then she stopped abruptly. Wyn had what looked like a very expensive volume in his hand, leafing through the gold-edged pages. She recognized it as one of the books that had been boxed up and put in the attic when her father had acted on one of his whims to change the Channing Place library. She hadn't thought to ask her attorney to have someone go through the boxes to check them first.

When he looked at her, Wyn's frown told her that he wasn't pleased with what he held.

"I can assure you," she hastened to say, "that there's probably another edition of that same book still in the Channing Place library. Father probably found the spine broken on that one and decided to replace it. Or the author went out of style and Father didn't want his books in our library."

The thundercloud on his face deepened, and she realized immediately that she'd said the wrong thing.

"This is gold on the edge of the pages," he growled.

"Just a little gilt," she assured him. "And . . . I mean . . . well, I know it does mean the volume cost a little more. And I realize it seems truly wasteful to just keep books around for show, but at least *I* read a lot of the books in our library."

He continued to scowl, and she wrung her hands together in front of her skirt. "Please don't send them back just because they're expensive, Wyn. The children won't care whether there's gilt on the pages or not. They'll read them anyway."

"He's not sending them back."

Dan laid a hand on her arm, and Sarah moved aside so he could push inside the storeroom. "We've already made our plans for the library, and Sarah's right. A gilt-edged book will read just as well as a plain-paged one."

"Some of these don't even have the pages cut," Wyn told him.

"Probably the mysteries or detective stories," Sarah said. "I've never cared much for reading those."

"Well, I like them." Dan reached for the book Wyn held. "Hey, this is a Sherlock Holmes story! I've been wanting to read another one of those ever since *A Study in Scarlet*. This one's *The Adventures of Sherlock Holmes*. Cutting these pages will give me something to do while Mandy arranges the library."

"And while you're helping Mandy set up the library and cutting pages, who's going to help me in the store?" Wyn grumbled. "Robert's—" He suddenly appeared to remember Sarah and slid a glance at her. "Uh . . . Robert's busy and this time of year there's a lot of stocking to do. Customers come in to replenish their own supplies and buy seeds for planting."

"Well," Dan mused, still with his main attention on the prize in his hand, "I've been thinking the twins oughtta start helping out a half hour or so after school each day. And

Lonnie Fraiser's 'bout ready for a job. We might's well get some use out of him, with him a-hangin' round here after Carrie. And we can see if he's good enough for her a couple years down the road."

Sarah unfortunately said the thoughts flashing through her head aloud. "Carrie's only fourteen! Why, she doesn't need to get married yet."

"She's almost fifteen," Dan corrected her. "And reckon that's going to be up to Carrie. She wants to go away for more schooling after she gets what's available here, I'll see she does it. But she's the one who has to decide."

Another idea Sarah had had clamored for vocalization, but she wisely resisted the temptation to bring it up right now. Maybe later, after she found out how much hot water she got into over that other load of stuff Jeeter would surely be bringing before long. Perhaps there was a more subtle way to provide scholarships to the children who appeared promising and who showed an interest in further education. Right now, at least she'd managed to avoid being given her walking papers over the books.

When she heard Jeeter's wagon fairly early the next day, Sarah left her cabin and waved him down. She hastily explained the situation to him, begging him not to spoil her surprise. The freighter agreed, promising he would check her orders from now on and make sure he unloaded that particular one directly at her cabin. He also assured her this load only consisted of books.

Filled with relief but still aware that the entire problem hadn't been solved, she walked beside the wagon to the store to help sort the books after they were unloaded.

The day flew by, and she bid Mandy and Dan good-bye at last. When she came out the front door of the store, pounding coming from the direction of the boardinghouse drew her attention. Wyn was building a ramp up to Mandy's porch, so his pa could go "courting," she remembered him saying. She smiled, then recalled his promise to do the same with her as she continued on home.

Sarah realized Wyn hadn't forgotten his promise when

she found a bouquet of wildflowers in a vase on her table. They were arranged far too well to have come from the twins, as her other bouquets had. Sissy could have brought them over, but something told her they'd come from Wyn. She knew she'd guessed right when he stopped by her cabin.

"Thank you for the flowers," she told him after she walked outside onto her top step in response to his call.

"I'm glad you like them," he said. "Sissy put them in the vase for me. I'm pretty much all thumbs when it comes to something like that."

"Is this part of your courting?" she dared to ask.

"Yep," he said emphatically. "And I'd like to take you for a walk this evening, but it would have to be later on. I need to put one last coat of paint on the ramp at the boarding-house yet."

"I do enjoy a stroll in the evening air before bed."

He tucked his thumbs in his belt and grinned at her. "The bed part sounds just as interesting as the stroll, to my mind."

She attempted to give him a huffy glower, but it died in the face of her laughter. She did feel a faint heat steal over her cheeks, but for the most part she had an urge to think of a rather provocative comeback, something she never would have even thought of back in New York.

"Being in bed with you is definitely interesting, Wyn," she blurted, a gay laugh cascading from her when his mouth dropped open and *his* cheeks flamed.

He bent his head and shook it slowly back and forth, blond curls falling over his forehead to hide his expression. When he looked up at her, the blueness in his eyes sparkled like sunlight dappling a lake surface in the summer.

"Uncle," he said. "I'll be back over around seven. Will that suit? You eat at Mandy's at six, don't you?"

"Well, yes," she agreed. "But I think I'm going to have to start learning how to cook on my own. I'm sure Mandy would like to have Dan over for a private supper once in a while. I'd hate to be the reason she can't do that."

"Mairi's been learning to cook from Sissy. Maybe she'd give you a few pointers in the evenings. But don't let her stick any more of that love potion she got from Leery in—"

Wyn clamped his mouth shut, then turned away. "I just remembered something I forgot to do at the store."

Sarah flew from the step and raced after him. She caught him before he'd gone more than a half dozen strides, grabbing his arm and digging in her heels to pull him to a halt. He lifted an eyebrow in an imitation of innocent inquiry when she sidled around in front of him and put a detaining hand on his chest.

"Why, Miss Debutante," he said. "I'd be willing to bet a cord of cut and stacked firewood that you haven't skedaddled that fast since you started having a decorum coach teach you how a real lady walks. I'd also bet you even flashed a glimpse of ankle when you came tearing after me."

"You'd win both of those bets," Sarah said grimly. "What's this about a love potion that Mairi got from Leery?"

"Um . . . well . . . I . . ."

"Hey, Wyn!"

Sarah glanced over her shoulder to see Lonnie Fraiser waving frantically from the general store porch.

"Wyn, Tater got his shirt sleeve caught in the coffee grinder!" Lonnie yelled. "He was trying to grind his own beans. And now he says he don't have to pay for them 'cause there's shirt sleeve ground up in them!"

"I gotta go," Wyn said, with a whole lot more than a tinge of relief in his voice. "We don't normally open on Sunday, but Lonnie came in to talk to Pa about the job. And Tater came by 'cause he forgot coffee yesterday."

Sidestepping her arm, he took off at a trot. She whirled to watch him go, hands on hips and a glower on her face she was sure her *decorum coach* would inform her in no uncertain terms would result in a multitude of wrinkles. Gently bred ladies didn't glower—or frown, for that matter.

Well, gently bred ladies didn't curse, either, but right then every one of the words exploding in her mind had four letters, some formed into words she didn't even realize she knew. She had no doubt she had played some part in this scheme. Otherwise Wyn wouldn't have been so nervous over what he had obviously let blunder from his mouth.

How dare he leave her hanging after that inadvertent slip of possibly volatile information? Had he had anything to do with this love potion? Or had it been completely Mairi's idea?

She didn't give a diddly darn whether Tater wanted to pay for his coffee beans or not. Or whether Wyn was busy mediating the disagreement. If he thought he wasn't going to explain what he'd said to her fully, he had another think coming.

Gently bred ladies had tempers just like mountain bred ladies did!

She lifted her skirts and stomped toward the store, climbed the steps, and strode on inside. Wyn glanced up at her as he handed a small burlap bag to Tater, his expression turning wary. She paced over to stand beside Tater, responding with a nod with he greeted her. Crossing her arms, she patted her toe on the floor and waited for Wyn to total up Tater's order.

Tater appeared to sense the animosity Sarah was holding in check.

"Jist put that there on my bill, Wyn," he said, grabbing up the brown-paper–wrapped bundle lying on the counter. "I know you won't cheat me."

"Tater, you can wait a minute," Wyn insisted.

"Huh-uh." Tater shook his head. "I done had two wives and I know when a woman's got somethin' on her mind to talk to her man about. I'll see you next time."

Tater scurried out the door, and Sarah didn't even bother to call after him and correct his misbegotten impression that Wyn was her man. She continued to pat her foot and stare at Wyn. Was that a bead of sweat on his forehead? Why, could it possibly have been him that put Mairi up to getting something as crazy as a love potion from the old mountain healer?

He backed away from the counter, but he couldn't go far. The shelf behind him brought him up short, and she stood between him and escape into the storeroom. He took a quick glance at the front door, but she harrumphed warningly.

"You were saying something about a love potion," she said.

He rubbed a hand across his mouth, not once but three times. She waited impatiently, the rhythm of her toe-tapping escalating. From the corner of her eye she saw Lonnie come out of the storeroom, and she spoke to him without turning her head.

"Lonnie, you go on upstairs and ask Sissy if she and Mairi have any of the cookies left they baked yesterday."

Used to obeying her in school, Lonnie didn't think to check with Wyn first. "Yes, ma'am, Miss Channing."

His boots clumped up the stairwell, and Sarah continued waiting.

"Can't we talk about this when we go for a walk this evening?" Wyn pleaded. "There's really not that much to it."

"Then it won't take you but a few seconds to explain it to me now, will it?" Yes, she did believe that was a bead of sweat on his forehead. One lock of blond hair looked damp, and . . . why, yes, indeed, that was a drop of sweat curling down his cheek.

"The love potion," she reminded him.

"Look, Sarah." He stepped forward and propped one hip on the countertop, attempting a negligent wave of his hand. "It's really nothing, like I said. I overheard Mairi talking to Leery about a l-love potion that Mairi baked into those blueberry muffins she made. But I rode out there and asked Leery about it, and she confirmed that one of the pair the potion was intended to bring together had to ask for it. Otherwise, it didn't work. So, see, there's not a thing to worry about."

She tilted her head and studied him. "Were you that worried? About the potion working? So worried that you made a special trip out to Leery's to ask her whether or not it was Mairi—or possibly me—who'd asked for that potion?"

"Not worried exactly," Wyn denied. "Those l-love potions are just a bunch of hooey, I'm sure."

"You seem to have quite a bit of trouble saying that word," Sarah mused. "You said it fine a few minutes ago."

"What word?"

If he hadn't shifted his eyes, Sarah might have believed the puzzlement in his voice.

"Love," she said smoothly.

His hand slipped from under his chin and thumped on the counter. His elbow hit a jar of jawbreakers beside him, sending it crashing to the floor, the lid flying off. Somehow the glass remained unbroken, but the bright balls scattered across the floor.

Just then, Luke and Jute raced in, their eyes widening when they saw the jawbreakers rolling hither and yon.

"We'll pick 'em up for you, Wyn!" Jute shouted. With a yell of glee, Luke hit the floor along with his twin and they scrambled around on all fours.

Sarah calmly dropped her arms and gave Wyn a cool look. "You're right. That explanation didn't take long."

She moved toward the front door, dodging the twins with no problem. Their voices were steadily rising as they captured more and more of the elusive jawbreakers.

"Hey," she heard Jute shout as she went through the door. "Wyn can't sell these now. They're dirty from bein' on the floor. We'll have to eat 'em ourselves!"

"Yes!" Luke yelled in return as she swept down the steps.

All the way home to the cozy little cabin, she wondered if Wyn would show up for their walk that evening.

17

$\mathscr{A}$T SIX O'CLOCK, Sarah headed over to Mandy's. Seeing Gray Boy on the boardinghouse porch, she wasn't surprised to find Mairi inside with Mandy, as well as Pris. All three of them were digging through the crates of books scattered around the floor, and Dan was working with a crowbar to open a crate that was still nailed shut.

The room was a large one Sarah hadn't seen yet, across from the parlor where she and Mandy visited when they didn't sit in the kitchen. Mandy had the windows open, and a breeze fluttered the curtains, intermingling the odors of lemony furniture polish with the smell of the dusty tomes in the crates. A large cherrywood table sat against the far wall, now covered with stacks of books, and a few other pieces of furniture had been pushed back into corners of the room. Sarah could already imagine the huge room filled with shelves and the table portioned off halfway into a nice desk for Mandy.

"Oh, my," Mandy said as she caught sight of Sarah and stood. A smear of dirt marred her cheek and nose, almost as though a man's finger had trailed across her face. "Is it that late? I haven't even thought about dishing up supper, Sarah.

I'm sorry. I was so busy, I lost track of time. The girls and
I finished cleaning this parlor and decided on the spur of the
moment to start bringing books over here."

"There's no hurry on supper, Mandy," Sarah assured her.
Land sakes, she wasn't even sure Wyn would show up later,
so there was no sense rushing Mandy. And besides, she
wasn't real sure she even wanted to go with him, if he did
show up.

Liar, her mind accused her. She ignored that traitorous
piece of her body.

"Look, I'll help you with supper. What can I do?"

"Oh, I didn't totally forget to prepare the meal, just what
time it was," Mandy said. "I've got a stew on the stove. I'll
go slice some bread and butter it, then we can eat."

She left the room, and Dan spoke up quietly. "Mairi, you
and Pris better get on over to the house. I'm staying here to
eat with Mandy, but I've already told Sissy that."

"All right, Uncle Dan," Mairi agreed. When she started
past Sarah, she cocked her head and looked at her. "Thanks
so much for having your friends get all these books for us,
Miss Sarah. This is soooo wonderful."

"I'm glad you will enjoy them, Mairi."

The two girls skipped from the room, and Sarah caught
sight of Dan's face, creasing from a smile into a frown.

"Sarah," he said. "Reckon I need to speak to you."

"Oh, no," she couldn't keep from saying. "Now what did
I do wrong?"

Dan pulled his pipe from his pocket and nodded at a chair
near him. While he filled his pipe, she crossed to the chair
and sat, giving a huge sigh of apprehension.

"It's probably nothing," Dan said after he got his pipe
going. A thin stream of smoke exited his mouth with his
words. "But I need to ask you. Did you list anything special
when you asked for book donations?"

She bowed her head. "I told my attorney the school was
a poor one. I suggested he tell the people he chatted with
that they should send any old textbooks they ran across that
they didn't want."

Dan puffed on his pipe for a few seconds. "Sarah," he

said at last. "That crate of books I just opened is new textbooks, not used ones."

"Oh!" Her head flew up. "Well, that's wonderful for the children, Dan, and you can't possibly be thinking of sending the books back, just because they're new. Can you?"

Dan's scowl reminded her very much of the same disapproving glare she got from Wyn when he didn't agree with her about something. She truly didn't understand why he was upset over having brand-new textbooks instead of old ones, but she supposed he was going to tell her. The MacIntyre men were blunt and to the point, if nothing else.

"It's like this," Dan began.

His stern voice confirmed her fear, and Sarah curled her hands, her nails digging into her palms.

"This school is somethin' we have always supported ourselves," Dan went on. "We're proud of the fact that we've always managed to have a teacher here for every term, and always had enough money to pay her. Maybe our books and supplies ain't like a teacher would find in a large town, but they're the best we can do. The absolute best."

Sarah leaned forward. "But don't you see, Dan? If you had better books and supplies here, you'd attract better teachers. I'm sorry, but that Miss Elliot was incompetent. She—"

Quickly interpreting the look growing on Dan's face, Sarah leaned back and shut her mouth. Now she'd done it. Not only had she denigrated the precious books probably every mountain family had helped gather up, she'd also maligned their choice of teacher. Prudence Elliot was probably the only teacher they could afford, or at least the best of a poor bunch. She hung her head in shame.

"I'm sorry, Dan. I didn't think."

"I wish I could say it was all right, Sarah, but it ain't. You have to understand that you can't just come in here and decide you know better for these people than they do themselves. These people don't have much, but what they do have, they've earned all theirselves. They figger charity is for those who don't have any gumption or who don't have friends and neighbors to help them out. We all work together here."

"Dan," Sarah said earnestly. "I truly didn't ask for new books. I think I know what might have happened. The church I attend supports a couple mission schools, and perhaps these books were initially targeted for those schools. But when Pastor Pollywig got the notification from my attorney, he probably diverted the books here. I admit, I . . . the Channing family has always made consistent and large contributions to our church, so Pastor Pollywig was probably showing his appreciation by giving the books to a school I'd brought to his attention. Please, Dan. Don't deprive the children of the benefit of those books. I'll write to the pastor and ask him if that's what happened."

Brow furrowed in concentration, Dan puffed on his pipe. "Well," he finally said. "I supposed if they came from a church it's a little different. Even if they probably were bought with money that came from your own funds."

"Oh, Dan. All the money Pastor Pollywig collects goes into one big account. There's no way to tell whose money bought what."

Suddenly Dan broke up into laughter, shaking his head. "Paster Pollywig?" he finally choked out. "Where on earth did he get a name like that?"

Relieved at the break in tension, Sarah giggled back at hin. "Oh. I didn't realize that's what I was calling him. His real name is Pastor Paulmeister, but as children we always called him Pastor Pollywig. It's sort of a play on the word 'polliwog.' He always dresses in black and he sits a lot, so he's rather broad across the hips. When he walks, he's got a little sway to him, like a polliwog does when it swims. Sort of a wiggle."

Dan continued to chuckle. "Sure hope I don't get like that from sittin' in this chair all the time."

Sarah rose, hoping their discussion was ended on this more pleasant note. "I better go see if Mandy needs any help."

"I'll be there in a minute."

Sarah hurried from the room, but outside in the hallway,

she leaned against the wall, closing her eyes briefly. Taking a deep breath, she reopened them and carefully checked to make sure Mandy wasn't coming to call them in to supper. She needed a minute to get her legs steady.

Given his lecture on the schoolbooks, what on earth was Dan going to do when her other order arrived? She probably should just cancel it, but it was probably too late. It ought to arrive any day now.

Intermingled with her feeling of chastisement, however, Sarah felt a tiny bit of anger. Why on earth should every attempt she made to help these people be resisted? Couldn't they see she had the means to do things for them and just accept that?

Evidently they couldn't, and it made her realize more and more that she would never fit in here. These people would never accept her. They would always turn every attempt she made to give them a better life over and over in their minds, suspicious that she was undermining their pride. How could she make them understand she only wanted to help the children?

Wyn would side with Dan every time something like this came up, she realized. No matter how much they were attracted to each other, it could never be a long-term thing. Given all the thinking Wyn had said he would be doing, she supposed he was probably already coming to that same conclusion. After all, it wasn't as if they were two youngsters like Lonnie and Carrie.

Still, she mused, maybe Wyn was enough younger than her not to have the maturity to see the bigger picture. She would have to be the sensible one, although being a woman, she would be expected to bow to whatever male directives were passed out to her.

She straightened and tightened her lips. Well, she would see about that. As long as she didn't have a father to order her around and control her by managing her funds, as well as not having a husband, she didn't have to bow to a man. If only there was some way to have a child without having to have a domineering man as part of the bargain. . . .

Huh, her mind told her. *You weren't being dominated on*

the bed the other night. You were a full partner there, Miss Debutante.

"Hush up, mind!" she whispered sternly. "And quit calling me that name!"

"Sarah?" Mandy called. "Are you talking to Dan? If so, tell him to come on into the kitchen and eat."

"Uh . . . we'll be right there, Mandy," she replied, avoiding admitting to Mandy she was talking to herself.

She started back for Dan, only to find him already at the door of the room.

"I heard her," he said. "I'm on my way."

Sarah stepped aside and let him roll by. After he'd gone partway down the hall, she touched her cheek, confirming the rising heat there. Land sakes, if Mandy had heard her muttering to her mind all the way in the kitchen, Dan probably had heard it from only a few feet away. It certainly wasn't proper for a schoolteacher to go around talking to herself. Hopefully, Dan wouldn't add that to her growing list of sins.

She followed him into the kitchen, and they ate a leisurely meal, with Sarah letting Dan and Mandy carry the bulk of the conversation. Distracted as she was with her own thoughts, she still couldn't avoid being aware of the changed atmosphere between Dan and Mandy. They sat across from her at the table, touching now and then when they felt like it and teasing back and forth at other times.

After a delicious piece of apple pie, which Sarah could only eat a couple bites of, Mandy shooed her from the table.

"I could help you with the dishes," Sarah offered. Anything would be better than sitting around her cabin for the next twenty minutes, wondering whether or not Wyn would show up.

"Dan will help," Mandy told her. "And let me wrap up that pie for you to take with you. Maybe you'll get hungry for a snack a little later. Why, you barely even touched your stew."

As Mandy carried the pie to the counter, Dan gave her a pondering look.

"Mandy's right, Sarah. You didn't eat much at all. I hope you're not upset over the talk we had."

"Oh, oh, no," she assured him. Although if she'd been totally honest, that had started her upsetting train of thought. "I just need to remember—"

The scream came from outside, faint with distance but leaving no doubt in Sarah's mind of the panic interlacing it. Mandy dropped the pie and saucer she was carrying, and the saucer shattered on the floor. Both women froze, eyeing each other in dread.

Dan didn't hesitate. He was halfway down the hallway in his wheelchair before he called over his shoulder, "That's Sissy! Come on!"

His order thawed both her and Mandy, and they picked up their skirts and raced after him. She knew with certainty that whatever had caused the panic was serious. The scream had been bloodcurdling, and she could only hope that nothing had happened to either Bobbie or baby Sarah.

Dan barely paused at the newly constructed ramp, but it was long enough for Sarah to bypass him and race toward the store, leaving Mandy to follow with Dan. A strange horse stood at the hitching post, along with a horse she thought she recognized from Dan's stable. Both saddles were empty, and the people on the porch were gathered around something.

As Sarah pounded up the steps, Wyn turned as though in response to the noise her feet made. Past him, inside the circle of people, she saw a body lying on the floor. Sissy knelt beside it, sobbing and reaching out a hand, then drawing it back.

Wyn caught Sarah and pulled her to one side. "I don't think you better look at this. It's Robert, and he's burned pretty bad."

"Burned?" Sarah asked, horrified. "How? Is he—?"

"He's hurt seriously, but he's still alive. Look, the best thing you can do is keep the children occupied and out of our hair right now. Can you help Mandy do that?"

"Of course."

Dan yelled from the bottom of the steps, "Damn it, Wyn! Get me up there! What's happened?"

Wyn left her and leaped down beside Dan's chair. As he turned it backward to pull it up the steps, he shot orders over his shoulder.

"You young'uns go on over to Sarah's cabin and wait. Carrie, you stay here to help Sissy and Mandy out." He pushed Dan's chair up beside the figure on the porch and left him, gently taking hold of the arms of the younger children and urging them down the steps. "Go on, now. Sarah will take care of you."

She followed them down the steps, nearly stumbling when she heard Dan breathe, "Goddamn that still! I've told that boy to make sure his connections are always tight."

"Hold on, Pa," Wyn soothed. "Cabbage said he'd already sent one of his boys after Leery. We'll get Robert inside and wait for her."

This time when Sarah glanced back, without the crowd around the figure blocking her view of the porch, she could see Robert. His upper body was wet, but what drew her horrified gaze was the side of his face. It looked as raw and red as a piece of uncooked beefsteak. Covering her mouth to hold back the rising bile, she hurried toward her cabin with a pack of sobbing children following her.

As soon as she got into the cabin, she wished she'd gone to the schoolhouse instead. Her place was far too small for all the children, especially when she noticed Pris carrying baby Sarah and Bobbie tugging on Mairi's hand. But she would make do the best she could. In fact, the closeness necessitated inside the cabin might even be better for the scared children.

She lit a lantern and hung it on the hook on the ceiling beam. "Put the baby on the bed," she directed Pris. "And I'll spread one of the extra blankets on the floor for the rest of you. We can tell stories to each other."

Jute stuck out his lip and screwed his hands down further into his denim overall pockets. "Don't want to tell no stories," he muttered. "Want to go out there with an ax and chop up that stupid still, so Robert don't get hurt again."

"Won't do no good," Luke assured him. "Robert'd just build 'nother one."

"A still?" Sarah asked, recalling that Dan had mentioned the same word. "What is a still?"

"Makes white lightnin'. Moonsh—" Jute began, then hollered, "Ow! What'd you kick me for, Pris? That hurt!"

Pris ignored him and scooted up onto the bed beside the baby. When Sarah glanced at Mairi, the other young girl also avoided her gaze. Lifting Bobbie, she laid him on the bed and, following Pris's example, stretched out beside her charge.

"Oh," Jute said next, as though something had suddenly dawned on him. He sidled a quick glance at Sarah, then asked his twin, "Uh . . . did you bring Swishy with you, Luke?"

"Swishy?" Sarah demanded, immediately distracted. "Look, I've told you before that I don't care for snakes. Where is he?"

Luke gave a heavy sigh and reached into the front flap of his overalls. When he pulled his hand back out, Swishy dangled from his grasp.

"He won't hurt you none, Miss Sarah," Luke pleaded. "I'll make sure he don't get loose."

"I'll bet," Sarah said grimly. "There's all sorts of ways he can crawl out of that flap on your overalls."

"I gots a pocket sewed inside for him," Luke said. "Sissy sewed it for me. She—" Suddenly a sob escaped him and a tear tumbled down his already streaked cheeks. "Robert ain't gonna die, is he? Sissy won't be able to stand it iffen he does. She loves him an awful lot."

Wanting nothing more than to rush forward and hold the twin, Sarah nevertheless eyed the snake uneasily. "Put Swishy back in his pocket, and we'll talk about it, Luke."

"Awright," he said with a sniff.

As soon as he complied, Sarah knelt and held out her arms. Both he and Jute rushed to her and buried their faces on her shoulders.

"Robert's nice to us," Jute said. "We missed him when he went to West Virginie to look for a job. And if he d-dies, he'll be gone forever, like Ma."

Luke spoke up next. "We already don't even 'member what Ma looks like that well, Miss Sarah. But Pa gave us each a picture of her. And I don't think Sissy's even got a picture of Robert. She was gonna have that travelin' picture taker take one for her, but Robert'd already gone to West Virginie when the picture taker came back through."

Sarah knew they were babbling because of their worry over their sister and her husband, and she couldn't for the life of her think of anything to ease their fear. The sight of Robert's face lingered in her mind, and the twins had seen it, too. She had no idea how badly Robert was injured, either. He'd appeared to be unconscious, but that could also have resulted from the horrible pain he must be feeling.

She held them a little tighter, but loosened her hold when she felt something wiggling against her breast on the side where Luke clung—the snake, she was sure.

"I'll tell you what," she said, awkwardly leaning back on her heels. "Let's pray for Robert. We can tell God how much we love him and that we'd like him to stay with us down here for a while, not go up to heaven."

"But you hardly even knows Robert," Jute said logically. "Won't you be a tellin' God a lie if you say you love him?"

Despite her worry, Sarah had to smile at the child. Jute would probably never learn tact, and his habit of speaking his honest mind was endearing, rather than troublesome.

"I'll tell God that I love Robert as a fellow man, Jute. That will work, won't it?"

He studied the question for a minute, then nodded his head. "Reverend Jackson says we's s'posed to love our fellow man, so that should do it." He pulled away from her and grabbed Luke's hand to lead him over to the bed.

"Come on, Luke. And you and Mairi get down on the floor and kneel with us, Pris," he ordered. "We wants to be real respectful to God, so he knows how important Robert is to us."

Sarah joined them in kneeling beside the bed, folding her hands and bending her head over them. She allowed Jute to take the lead, and he poured out his little heart in his prayer, telling God how Robert had showed him the secret place where the fish always bit and where the wild strawberries his pa loved grew the sweetest.

Luke added that Robert had spent all day once searching the woods after a spring rain because Sissy had mentioned she was hungry for mushrooms. "That's when baby Sarah was still in her belly, God," Luke told him. "Pa says that sometimes women gets powerful hungry for certain stuff when they're carrying a baby in their belly. Sissy, she cried when Robert come in with that sack of mushrooms that evenin'. Pa says women cry lots easier, too, when they gots a baby in their belly."

By the time Pris and Mairi had told their own stories of Robert's kindnesses to them, Sarah was teary-eyed. She clenched her fingers even tighter, choosing her words carefully.

"Even though I don't know Robert that well, God, I love him as a fellow man. And part of the reason I'm sure he's a fine man is what these children say about him. Also, I've seen him and Sissy together, and I know there's a powerful love there. For Sissy's sake and the sake of their children, as well as the other people who love him, please heal Robert, God."

The amens echoed from five throats together, and Jute sniffed, wiping at his nose with his shirtsleeves

"Let me get you a hanky, Jute," Sarah said, rising to her feet. "Anyone else need one?"

Three other heads nodded, so she grabbed several hankies from her bureau drawer. After Pris blew her nose, she sat back on the bed, scrunching up her face when baby Sarah whimpered a bit.

"Uh-oh, she's waking up, Miss Sarah," Pris said. "And she always wakes up hungry. What's we gonna do?"

"Feed her, I guess," Sarah said with a shrug. "I'll run over and get a bottle for her, if you children will wait here and be good."

"Ain't got no bottles," Jute said, frowning at her. "Sissy allus feeds her from her breast. Guess that's what you'll have to do, Miss Sarah. You's the only one here with breasts."

"What? Oh, Jute . . . uh . . . I can't feed baby Sarah. I . . . I'm not . . . " She gazed into the expectant, innocent blue eyes beneath that mop of reddish hair, floundering for an explanation that wouldn't humiliate both her and the child.

"Miss Sarah can't do that," Mairi said in a superior voice, which nonetheless relieved Sarah's stupefaction. "She's not a mama, and only mamas have milk for babies. She'll have to take baby Sarah over to Sissy."

Nodding agreement, Pris picked up the baby and held her out to Sarah. "We'uns will be all right, Miss Sarah," she assured her. "We'll just sit right here and be good till you come back."

"I can read everyone a story now that we feel better after our prayers," Mairi put in. "If you've got any book here that's got words in it I know."

After shifting the precious bundle Pris handed her into the safety of her hold, Sarah said, "As a matter of fact, I brought *The Adventures of Huckleberry Finn* home this afternoon to paste some of the pages back in. It's probably dry by how, if you want to try that."

"Yeah!" both Jute and Luke yelled, with Jute as usual getting the floor for what came next. "Mairi knows lots of the words and we can all help her if she comes across one she can't read. We'll get to hear the next chapter afore the rest of the class, but it won't matter if we hear it again tomorrow."

Retrieving the book from her tiny desk, Sarah handed it to Mairi. "The place where I stopped is marked with the bookmark."

"Thanks!" Mairi scurried back to the bed and sat down on the edge with a plop.

"Let me hang the lantern a little closer so you can see better, Mairi."

As she moved the lantern to hang on a hook directly over the bed, Bobbie stirred, but he only turned to his other side.

"You might want to bring back an oilcloth for Bobbie to lie on, Miss Sarah," Mairi said in a frank voice. "He don't have accidents much, but every once in a while he'll wet the bed."

"I'll remember, Mairi. And you children remember that you've promised to be good now. If anything happens, Pris or Mairi can run over and get me. All right?"

"We'uns will be good," Pris said again.

Mairi opened the book and the children completely lost interest in Sarah. The twins plopped on the floor and crossed their legs, propping their elbows on their knees and chins on their palms. Pris sat down beside Mairi, and they all waited for her first words.

"'It must 'a' been close on to one o'clock when we got below the island at last, and the raft did seem to go mighty slow,'" Mairi read. Jute and Luke both sighed with pleasure as Sarah went out the door.

She wished she had the resiliency of the children and the ability to lose herself in a good book, but her own worry heightened with each step toward the store. Baby Sarah began whimpering and nuzzling at her, and Sarah felt her heart squeeze. How wonderful it would be to have a child of her own nuzzle her like that one day. Right now she needed to get the child to its mother, however, so she could nurse.

18

SARAH HURRIED HER steps until she was almost running by the time she got inside the store. At the top of the stairwell, she didn't bother to knock on the door before she went into the living area. Dan was sitting outside the bedroom Sarah had come to know was Sissy and Robert's, and Wyn stood beside his father. He glanced up as she came in.

Just then, Sarah heard a loud cry of pain. She clutched baby Sarah tighter when the baby reacted with a wail of its own.

"Leery's here," Wyn told her as she approached. He had to raise his voice somewhat to be heard over the baby. "What's wrong with baby Sarah?"

"She's hungry," Sarah explained. "Oh, Wyn, I hate to bother Sissy, but Jute said there aren't any bottles available for baby Sarah. So Sissy will have to feed her."

"Good." When Sarah looked at him in surprise, he continued, "We've been trying to get her out of that bedroom so Leery can work on Robert without worrying about Sissy passing out. She's in almost as much pain with her worry over Robert as Robert is from his burns. The baby will distract her."

He went in the bedroom and emerged in a few seconds with Sissy. With a moan of part motherly concern and part misery, Sissy reached for her baby. As soon as Sarah handed her over, Sissy cuddled her close and walked over to the rocking chair by the fireplace. She shifted the chair with one hand, then sat down with her back to the rest of the room. Sarah's cries, which had lessened the moment she was put into her mother's arms, died into stillness, replaced by the faint sounds of her suckling her mother's breast.

Sarah took this opportunity to ask about Robert.

"It's bad," Wyn told her without cushioning his words. "Leery doesn't think he'll die, but he'll be disfigured for the rest of his life. And if infection sets in the burns, he still might not pull through."

"My God. How Sissy must be suffering."

"Yes, she is."

"What's Leery using to treat him? Is there anything I can do?"

He answered her second question first. "Taking care of the children is the biggest help you can offer right now. How are they?"

"Mairi's reading to them. But I need to get right back."

"I'll let you know if Leery needs anything from you. Right now she's sent Cabbage out to her cabin to get another container of comfrey salve. She said she'd forgotten that the one in her satchel was almost empty after she treated a child who tripped and landed with his hand in the fireplace."

Sarah's stomach churned, but she managed to control herself. Right now everyone's attention needed to be focused on Robert, not her if she swooned.

"How horrible," she said faintly. "Should I wait for baby Sarah?"

"I'll bring her back over in a while," Wyn offered. "And I'll walk you home."

Mandy stuck her head out the bedroom door, glancing around until she saw Sissy over by the fireplace. "Wyn," she said quietly when she was sure Sissy was out of hearing distance. "Can you come in here? Carrie and I will probably need help to hold Robert down while Leery treats his face."

Wyn's mouth tightened, a whiteness appearing at the edges of his lips. But he gave a firm nod and went into the room, closing the door firmly behind him. Sarah moved over to stand beside Dan, and they both kept their eyes trained on the door, forgetting for the moment about Sissy. The scream tore through the door, though, and Sarah whirled toward the fireplace.

Sissy was bent over, and the chair was wobbling back and forth frantically.

"Go to her, please," Dan requested.

Sarah complied, hurrying over to kneel beside the rocking chair and slipping her arm around Sissy's shoulders. Baby Sarah began to whimper again, and Sarah cupped Sissy's other cheek, turning her to face her.

"It's going to be all right," she promised. "What they're doing has to be done, despite the pain."

"Goddamn that moonshine!" Sissy whispered harshly, her curse shocking Sarah into senselessness. "If this were about another woman, I could fight it. But it's Robert's damned pride and the market for that devil's brew that keeps him makin' and sellin' it."

All at once she appeared to realize who she was talking to. Fear replaced the anguish in her eyes, and she grabbed Sarah's arm.

"Please!" she begged. "Please forget I said that. Oh, Sarah, you don't understand what could happen if you told someone about this."

"I think I do," Sarah said quietly. "And please don't worry. I realize the authorities would probably arrest Robert for making illegal whiskey and not paying the governmental tax on it before he sells it. I wouldn't want your husband taken away from you for that—not when he makes such a wonderful-tasting whiskey."

Sissy gave her a tentative smile. "You've tasted Robert's whiskey?"

The answering smile on Sarah's face felt rather dreamy to her, especially since she recalled exactly what else had happened that night she'd tasted what Jute called moonshine. "The night baby Sarah was born," was the only explanation she gave Sissy.

"They say it's very good." Sissy sniffed back a sob. "But Robert doesn't drink it himself."

Another horrible scream came from the bedroom, and Sissy dissolved into wrenching sobs and shaking shoulders. When baby Sarah let out a wail, Sissy sat straight and tried to control herself.

"I . . . can you take baby Sarah back to your cabin for a little while?" Sissy asked. "Please, Sarah? I can come get her in a little bit."

"Of course I will. And Wyn already said he'd come after her." Sarah took the baby from Sissy's arms and stood. "But maybe you should come with me, too, just until they get done in the bedroom."

Wyn spoke from behind her. "Leery's done and, thankfully, Robert's passed out again. It'll be all right if Sissy wants to go back in and sit with him, although he probably won't wake up for a while. We gave him a pretty healthy dose of whiskey to help knock him out."

Sissy was halfway across the room before Wyn finished speaking. Sarah held the baby close, marveling at the power of love she sensed Sissy bore for Robert. It made her feel rather cheap and shamed to have in effect bought her relationship with Stephen, instead of holding out for true love. At the same time, she had a deep and abiding yearning inside, touched with a tiny bit of jealousy. She had searched for true love for years, though, and it had evaded her. Few men wanted a gawky wallflower for a wife, no matter how much money came with her.

"I'll walk you to your cabin," Wyn said.

His voice and his closeness made her realize she'd been fighting the desire to lean on him ever since she had heard that first scream this evening. Although it wasn't her husband or even a man she loved lying there fighting for his life, the tension, pain, and raw emotions hanging in the air had left her wrung out. It would be so nice to have Wyn's strong arms around her for a moment, and to steal some of his strength.

Mandy came out of the bedroom and put an arm around Dan's shoulder. She leaned down and whispered something in his ear, and Dan kissed her cheek.

Dan and Mandy. Sissy and Robert. For some reason those names spoken in pairs in her mind sounded much better than Sarah and Stephen. *Sarah and Wyn sounds perfect.*

She took hold of her thoughts and told Wyn, "Mairi said I should bring back an oilcloth for Bobbie to sleep on. Being so young, I doubt he wakes up before morning now."

"There's one downstairs on a shelf. We'll pick it up on the way by. I'll be bringing Bobbie back over here later, but I would like to leave the children with you for a while longer."

"That's fine. Really. If they don't mind sleeping on pallets on the floor, they could even spend the night."

"I might let them do that." Placing a hand to her back, he steered her to the door. "Except for Bobbie, of course. Sissy will want both her young'uns near for comfort."

"I understand."

Wyn stopped beside a closet near the stairwell door and opened it. He took out an armful of blankets, then nodded for Sarah to go on down the stairs. In the store, he added an oilcloth to his stack, and they headed for the cabin.

Outside, the night air carried a touch of chill, but she thought it always did in the mountains, even in the summertime. At this altitude, she didn't imagine there were many truly hot days. She recalled the humid stickiness of August in New York, with the sun beating down on all the bricks and stone, reflecting back to make a woman wish whoever had invented petticoats had never been born. Surely it must have been a male inventor. She also remembered that no matter how hard she would beg her father, he would never permit her to go to the Catskills with one of the families that invited her during the hot weather. Soon the invitations had dwindled to none.

The baby had fallen asleep on her shoulder, her breath barely discernible on Sarah's neck, and the broad-shouldered man beside her seemed made to walk there. Total darkness had fallen by now, with a rising moon in the distance only a hint of radiance on the horizon. The walk from the store to the cabin had never seemed so short. But the need to check on the children deterred her from prolonging it.

Her lips curved as soon as they entered the cabin. The twins were sprawled on the floor, identical snores coming from their mouths. Pris had cuddled up to Bobbie, and Mairi lay on her back with the book lying open on her chest.

"The sleep of the innocents," she murmured to Wyn.

"Yeah," he quietly returned. "Unless you're tired and ready to rest yourself, how about I shift them around and let them sleep for a while?"

"I'm far too wide awake to sleep yet."

Wyn nodded and went about rearranging the children. He placed the pile of blankets on a corner of the bed, then laid the oilcloth down and put a blanket over it. After lifting Bobbie onto it, he scooted Pris over to lie beside the little boy. Mairi followed, after he handed Sarah the book.

She turned from laying the book on her desk to see Wyn lifting the twins onto a pallet of blankets on the floor. He puzzled her when he walked over and pulled open her bottom bureau drawer. But she saw immediately what his idea was when he took the petticoats out and tossed them over a chair by the table, then lined the drawer with the last blanket. Reaching for baby Sarah, he laid her in the drawer.

After moving the lantern over to another hook, so the light wouldn't wake the children, Wyn whispered, "Let's go out and sit on the step."

Agreeable, she led the way. She kept the step swept, but it wouldn't have mattered if he'd asked her to sit down in a mud pile with him. She wanted to be with him—needed his presence beside her for a little longer. The maelstrom of emotions from the evening swirled in discord yet, and for once it was terribly nice to have a man beside her, even one telling her what to do. But it dawned on her that Wyn hadn't actually ordered her around. Instead, he'd suggested things to which she'd agreed. What a difference an attitude like that made in not giving rise to the resentment she had swallowed for so many years.

Perhaps, she thought as she sat on the top step, it would

have been as comforting to have a woman friend beside her—one who would share her confidences and soothe her troubled emotions—something else she'd never had. Somehow, though, she didn't think so. And somehow, she knew the comfort would have been lacking if it weren't this special man sitting down beside her. Mandy and Sissy had already learned that beautiful secret of love, although Sissy was experiencing the painful side of the secret right now.

Love? The word climbed out of her subconscious and invaded her entire mind. She couldn't be falling in *love* with Wyn. They were complete opposites! But something told her she was entirely too late to attempt any rational judgments on whether or not she would actually fall in love with Wyn MacIntyre. The fall had become a tumble, then a wild downhill slide, and she'd already reached the bottom of the hill. She already loved him.

Wyn intertwined his fingers with hers and raised her hand to his mouth. He gently kissed the back of it before laying both their hands on his knee and cupping his other hand over hers. The desire to break his hold was nonexistent.

"You all right now?" he asked

"Better," she admitted. "Poor Sissy."

"Robert's the one you should be worried about. Sissy will love that man whatever happens, but Robert's going to have a big adjustment to make after he first sees himself in the mirror."

Her shoulders heaved and she nodded her head. "I know what it's like not to care for your looks. And I suppose Robert will feel worse even, because he'll think what happened was partly his own fault. The guilt won't be easy to come to terms with."

"I wish you'd quit talking like that!"

"Like what?" She frowned into the night. "I don't feel guilty over my plainness. My father—"

"Your father should have been shot—or covered with honey and staked naked to a red anthill!"

"Wyn!"

He ignored her astonishment at his crassness. "Tell me this, Sarah. Why do you think yourself plain?"

Thinking she had long ago come to terms with this exact thing, Sarah stifled a stab of surprise at her reluctance now to talk about it to Wyn. She recalled Kyle's pleasant observation—pleasant to her, anyway—that she'd changed. However, she'd had to consider Kyle's background as a gentleman along with deciding how much credence to give his words. Like other men of his breeding, he'd been weaned on how to sweet-talk the fair sex.

"As I started to say, my father made sure I fostered no delusions about my looks. One day I even found him in our portrait gallery with my sixteenth birthday portrait propped below my great-aunt Hagatha's portrait. The word in the Channing family was that every time a woman found herself with child, she prayed very hard not to have a daughter who was a throwback to ugly Hagatha. I guess my mother's prayers went unanswered."

Wyn made a sound of disgust. "So you let your father convince you that you had inherited your aunt's lack of beauty. From what you've told me about that son of a—" He clamped his mouth shut, then shrugged as though he'd decided to finish what he'd started to say. "That son of a *bitch,* he probably set the entire scene up, knowing you would see him making that comparison."

"He . . . did call me into the gallery," she said hesitantly. "Oh, but he wasn't the only reason, Wyn. Why, I can't tell you at how many balls I was labeled the wallflower. I would much rather have stayed home and read, but Father always made me attend. He said it was the only way the men would know I intended to wed someday, and that he'd be willing to bestow a large dowry on me to make up for my plainness. If I'd stayed home, everyone would have thought I'd accepted that I'd live my life as an old maid. And I did so want to have children someday. Marriage is a necessary part of that, as I'm sure you'll agree."

"Your father was a bastard!" Wyn snarled.

"Yes, I agree with you there. But he was also right. The men avoided me, except for the ones who were deeply in debt. To my father's credit, even he supported me in turning down some of them. But I finally became so very lonesome that I decided I really needed to get married and have a family."

Dropping his chin to his chest, Wyn sat for a long moment without saying anything else. The lantern inside the cabin window cast a glow out into the velvet darkness where they sat, with a ring of light high above Sarah's left shoulder on the second floor of the store much brighter. She smiled wryly as the melodramatic thought went through her mind that the light in the living quarters above the store was holding back death for Robert.

The schoolhouse cut off her view of the boardinghouse across the way, but she'd noticed when they came back to the cabin that Mandy hadn't been home yet. No lights glowed in her windows, and she supposed the books were still strewn around the library room. After school tomorrow, she would see where her energies could best be used— either helping Mandy with the books, or leaving that to Dan while she did what she could to assist Sissy with her children and husband.

Far up on the mountain, she heard an animal scream. Wyn's head came up.

"Mountain cat," he growled.

"Mandy told me that Dan thought that's what spooked the horses the day of the accident."

"Yeah."

He tightened his fingers around hers. When he spoke again, she knew he didn't want to discuss the day his mother had been killed, but she didn't much care for his return to their former subject.

"Have you ever thought, Sarah, that it wasn't that you were plain, but that you were too much for these men who left you decorating the wall? Or at the very least, so smart you scared them? That you were way too much woman for a weak-kneed man?"

"Sure," she scoffed. "I—"

He turned swiftly and put a finger on her lips to still her words. "When I first saw you riding up to the store in Jeeter's wagon, I had a fleeting thought that you were a somewhat plain woman. That lasted about ten seconds, until

I looked into your eyes. And it scared me how I immediately felt about you."

"You'd already had one failed relationship with a debutante." When Wyn tightened his fingers as though in surprise, she continued, "Rose Collingsworth is married now, you know."

"No, I didn't know, but I wish her happiness. She was a nice young woman, although we weren't right for each other. And I'm afraid the same thing is true here. We're worlds apart, Sarah. I've had no business kissing you or . . ." He tried to pull his hand free, but she clung tightly. "Or," he continued in a wry voice, "even holding your hand."

"Tell me about yourself, Wyn."

"You've already been here several weeks. You already know me."

"No, tell me your hopes and dreams. What you want out of life."

"Everything like that centers around Sawback Mountain," he said, a warning tone clear in his voice.

"Tell me," she repeated.

19

*F*OR THE NEXT two weeks, Sarah barely had time to breathe, let alone worry about the fact that she'd fallen desperately in love with a man with whom she had absolutely nothing in common—except . . . Well, he felt like the other half of the whole she hadn't even realized was missing in her life. And they both loved the mountain people, wanting to do the best they could for them. And she loved his brothers and sisters nearly as much as he did. And they both reveled in the wondrous mountain air and scenery. And when Wyn dropped in at Mandy's library to help shelve books, they found out they both had read a lot of the same ones and enjoyed them, and started several others but never finished them due to boredom.

Plus there was that feeling she had in his arms, as though her world was only right or complete when he was holding her.

But Wyn didn't make her world right or complete even once during that next two weeks. He didn't avoid her, but he didn't seek her out privately, either. Gosh darn it, she mused while brushing her hair one morning, using the mountain vernacular she was picking up, he hadn't even kissed her that last time they'd been alone together on the front step!

And gosh darn it! She *did* have time to worry about it! She woke up worrying about it in the mornings, then tossed and turned each evening, her exhausted body refusing to drop off into sleep until she'd gone over—and over again—each and every word she'd exchanged with Wyn that day.

She couldn't talk to Mandy, because she and Dan were together every single time she saw the other woman. She would never burden Sissy with her problems now, with all the worry she had over Robert. Even though Leery had assured everyone there wasn't any danger of Robert becoming infected any longer, Sissy still had another problem.

She'd found Sissy weeping out on the back porch one recent evening and hesitantly approached the upset woman. Sissy had confided that Robert was already talking about repairing his still. The young wife had everything she could handle right now, and Sarah couldn't even ease her mind until she heard back from her attorney. No sense raising anyone's hopes and then dashing them.

But despite everything, she felt more at home here in these mountains—more needed—than she'd ever felt in her life back in New York. She didn't feel accepted yet, although she was coming to think the only way ever to be accepted here was to be born and raised in the mountains.

Chewing her bottom lip, she glanced over at the two boxes in the corner of her room. She didn't know how Jeeter had managed to leave those boxes the day before without everyone knowing about them, but no one had mentioned them to her. She supposed everyone was just busy when Jeeter showed up on his unscheduled trip, bringing a half dozen more boxes of books. Or maybe they had just thought Sarah had ordered some personal stuff.

Whatever the explanation, she'd also found the letter from her attorney she'd been expecting propped up on her writing desk when she came in after school. Now all she had to do was discuss a couple things with Dan and write back to Mr. Caruthers.

She glanced at those boxes again. She'd been worried

about them ever since her debacle with the books, but surely it wasn't the same thing. Surely she'd figure out a way to get the people to accept these. Why, every child she knew in New York celebrated their birthday with a party and received gifts. There wasn't a reason on earth she couldn't have a single birthday party for all her students as a once-a-year event. Was there?

Sarah contained her excitement until a half hour before the school day ended. Then Mandy brought over the cake Sarah had asked her to make, declining Sarah's invitation to stay and have a piece with the children on the excuse she and Dan were cataloging the newly arrived books. And Mandy hadn't mentioned one negative thought about Sarah planning a group birthday celebration for all the children, which she surely would have done had Mandy thought anything wrong with it. So everything was fine. Wasn't it?

After the cake, which disappeared down to the last crumb, Sarah asked Lonnie to accompany her to her cabin and help carry back the boxes. She had only thought the thrill of the cake and a celebration joyful for the children. Now they truly showed their excitement as they opened the boxes. She was afraid that shouts and exhilaration would draw the rest of the adults to the schoolhouse, but no one showed up. Then she wondered why she even cared and forgot the stab of guilt. She carried the remembrance of the delighted faces of the children to bed with her that night.

Her first substantiation of her gross error in judgment came the next morning, soon after she got dressed and prior to starting over to Mandy's for breakfast. Someone tapped on the door, and she opened it to see Jute and Luke standing there. The twins held a pair of shoes in each hand, one pair of boy's and one pair of girl's.

"Pa says he's sorry," Jute told her, "but we can't keep 'em. He said iffen you gots some chores you need done that we can help you with, might be different if we earned the shoes ourselves. Same with Mairi and Pris. Carrie will bring hers with her to school."

He set the shoes inside the door, and Luke followed suit.

"I sure hopes you does got some work me and Luke can do to earn them there shoes," Jute said hopefully. "They's sure are nice shoes."

"They were a birthday present!" Sarah insisted.

"Don't matter none, 'cording to Pa." Jute shook his head sadly. "Still smacks of charity, and he says we can't keep 'em."

After one last, longing look at the highly polished set of brown high-topped children's shoes, Jute and Luke leaped from the step.

"'Bye!" Jute called. "See you in school in a little bit."

Sarah suddenly realized she had no appetite for breakfast. The sick feeling in the pit of her stomach would probably have her heaving if she even tried to drink a cup of coffee. She pushed the four pair of shoes aside with her toe in order to shut the door, wondering if Mandy would come looking for her if she ignored breakfast that morning.

She ignored breakfast anyway, and Mandy didn't show up to check on her. That made her even more ill, because she assumed the woman whom she'd started to think a friend was upset with her, also. She hid in her cabin until it was time to ring the school bell, then straightened her shoulders and went over to the schoolhouse. The children were uncommonly quiet this morning, and they filed almost silently into the schoolroom.

As she called the roll, each child stood instead of only answering "Here" as on a normal morning. Each one, except the twins, Mairi and Pris, came up to her desk and laid a pair of shoes on it. Without examining the shoes closely, Sarah could tell they hadn't even been worn back to school that morning. They were highly polished and clean, having only been tried on the day before for a fit and then carried home in each child's arms.

By the time the last child had filed up to her desk and then back to a seat, Sarah's vision was so clouded with tears she'd had to read the last two entries on the roll list from memory. These children hadn't even made the offer that Jute and Luke had of earning their shoes with chores. She had to turn her back on the room for a moment to get control of her emotions, but somehow she managed and finished the rest of the day—after she asked Lonnie and the twins to carry the shoes over to her cabin.

She didn't know what else to do, since she'd never have been able to handle her lessons if those shoes had stared her in the face all day. But they mocked her as soon as she entered her cabin door that evening.

Slamming the door behind her, Sarah raced across the room and flung herself on the bed. Grabbing the pillow, she buried her face and wailed.

She'd *never* fit in here! *Never!*

She pounded one fist on the mattress and stuffed the corner of the pillow into her mouth to muffle her cries. Those shoes were birthday presents, damn it! Not charity!

The curse word flashing through her mind, even though unspoken, shocked her. What on earth was she coming to, cursing like a man and worrying about fitting in with people who would never accept her? At least back in New York she knew the rules. Knew what was expected of her. Knew what she could and couldn't do or get away with. Knew what the penalties for disobedience of the rules were.

The penalties here were evidently much the same—being shunned and ignored—since no one had offered her a bit of sympathy today.

She'd been raised to fit into a certain type of life and the mold of society in New York, the same as the mountain people had been raised to fit the mold of their own very different community. She'd never be able to change now, no matter what the possible treasure beckoning her at the end if she were successful—the treasure of a life beside the man she loved.

Burying her face even deeper in the pillow, she kicked her legs up and down and wailed.

Not receiving an answer to his knock, Wyn opened the cabin door anyway. He'd seen Sarah go inside only moments ago, but she'd been in some sort of hurry, since she hadn't heard his call from the store porch. The door squeaked loudly— he'd been meaning to get over here and oil it—but the sound didn't gain the attention of the woman throwing what looked like a walleyed fit on the bed.

Despite his worry, Wyn hesitated. For one thing, if he approached too close, there was the danger of the heel of one of those hard leather shoes kicking him, maybe in a vulnerable spot, given the exact right height of the bed and the brutal cadence of the kicks. For another, he wasn't sure if Sarah was furious or upset.

From the corner of an eye, he saw something on the floor and turned to survey it. Shoes. There were neatly set pairs of various sizes of shoes lined up against the wall. Boys' shoes and girls' shoes. Shoes a little larger for young men, possibly about Lonnie's age. Another pair of shoes for a young woman Carrie's age, with another perhaps Patty's size.

There were a few boxes unopened yet, and he silently crossed the floor and opened one of them. Small shoes, Bobbie's size. Fluffy yarn booties for baby Sarah.

Uh-oh.

Needing to get away for one of his rare evenings of privacy yesterday, and after Robert begged him for three days in a row to go check on his still, he had shouldered his rifle and told Pa he was off to go hunting. Shucks, Pa knew this was the wrong time of year for hunting—that he could never shoot an animal when it probably had young in its den—but he didn't protest. He could get himself in and out of bed now, and Mandy was there for a lot of the things he had depended on Wyn for previously.

Everyone had been in bed by the time he got home last night, and this morning he was too busy watching for a private moment to report his suspicions to Robert to pay much attention to anything else. Now he recalled a sort of quiet uneasiness in the atmosphere.

He started realizing something was definitely wrong around noontime, when he didn't see Sarah go over to Mandy's for lunch. He hadn't ever realized he set his watch by her every day around that time until Sarah broke her pattern. But a customer kept him too busy for the moment to follow up on whether something was wrong or not.

There was no doubt right now. Something had broken

Sarah's spirit and demeanor, and he would bet it had something to do with the lonely line of shoes sitting against the baseboard. Surely she hadn't tried to give them to the children without checking with his pa first.

He thought he understood what the twins had meant when they asked him after school how many hours a body would have to work to earn a pair of shoes like in the Montgomery Ward catalogue. Maybe his pa offered to let them earn their shoes instead of accept them as a gift.

He heaved a sigh, tucking his fingers in his trouser pockets and glancing at the bed again. Knowing Sarah, she had probably thought of some shrewd idea of how to get the children to accept the shoes and not think of them as charity. She hadn't taken the parents into consideration, though.

Or perhaps she had and thought her way to trick them into accepting the shoes foolproof. He *was* coming to know Sarah very well. Although she would never deliberately hurt anyone's feelings, she was stubborn enough to want her own way.

As he cautiously approached the bed, Sarah's sobs slackened, and her legs stilled. He moved around to the foot of the bed, trying to catch a glimpse of her face. Her hand relaxed, those wondrously long and delicate fingers, which felt so pleasant in his hair, falling away from their clutch on the pillow. She hiccuped once, and he got ready to explain his presence in here. But she snuggled down into the pillow, and her breathing eased.

Her long, golden-brown lashes fluttered once, then stilled. Her cheek was flushed and wet with tears, and his heart gave a lurch of sorrow at the dejected picture she made. He wanted to lie down beside her and gather her in his arms, but she probably needed sleep and relief from the agony of the past few minutes more than any comfort he could give her.

Silently he walked away from the bed, stepping on the rag rugs scattered on the floor rather than bare floorboards. He looked at the line of shoes again, his stomach a hollow pit of sadness for the woman he'd realized he had fallen in love with. She must have been so excited when she got those shoes, and so devastated when they refused her gift.

In the same corner of her room sat the little writing desk one of the parents had donated when they built and furnished the cabin. Right smack dab in the middle was an overstuffed envelope, which must have several pages inside. The paper of the envelope was of extremely fine quality, with even an engraved name in the upper left corner— Charles Caruthers. Probably her attorney, Wyn mused.

He wouldn't have been human if he hadn't felt an urge to pick up the envelope and read the letter. But he resisted the temptation with very little willpower, settling for only running a fingertip across the envelope to confirm the linen-looking superiority of it. No one in the MacIntyre family would ever think of invading another's privacy—no mean feat with the crowded living quarters they shared. He didn't even enter the twin's room without a preliminary warning and a few seconds' wait.

He couldn't stop the other feeling invading his senses, however. The fine quality of the envelope was at the other end of the spectrum from the thin paper letters Jeeter brought for the mountain families. Rare and far between, the families would have to save up postage money to afford to reply to the relatives who had left Sawback Mountain.

Wyn saw several other envelopes stuck in the holes along the top of the desk. Sarah evidently kept in close contact with her friends back there. Probably each and every one of them knew her plans and when she would return to New York, to the life more suited to her.

He wondered how many of those letters had come from her fiancé, stifling that thought the best he could. Jeeter usually had at least one letter for Sarah on each mail run, but most of the time there were no return addresses—or at the best, only a last name. He didn't recall ever hearing her mention any name except Stephen.

He should leave. Another glance at the bed, though, told him that he could no more walk out of Sarah's cabin right now without finding out why she'd been crying than he could deny he'd fallen in love with her. Or than he could deny the hopelessness of that love.

He sat down at the tiny table, determined to wait until Sarah woke.

She began stirring only about fifteen minutes after he sat down, and he rose immediately. Moving over to the side of the bed, he waited patiently for her to wake completely.

She turned her head on the pillow, giving him a view of her other profile and her mottled cheek. Wisps of gold-brown hair scattered on her forehead and cheek, and her usually neat twist on the back of her head had pulled free. That glorious mane of heavy tresses covered her shoulder and upper arm. As heavy as water and as luxurious to his touch as the finest silk, it beckoned his fingers. That was one urge to which he could give free rein.

He reached out and tangled a finger in a curl. The feeling swelled his heart in the same way as when baby Sarah closed her tiny fist around one of his fingers. The only thing he could imagine giving him more heartfelt pleasure would be seeing Sarah hold a child the two of them had made together.

But that would never happen. She was probably already making plans to go back to New York.

Her eyelids fluttered and opened. He could tell she didn't see him yet, since she didn't react to his presence. Instead, she put a hand over her face, her breath catching on another sob.

He sat on the side of the bed, and she gasped, her eyes flying open.

"Sarah," he muttered. "Tell me what's wrong."

She shifted over onto her back, rubbing the heels of her palms beneath her eyes. "How . . . how long have you been here?"

"Long enough." He pulled his handkerchief from his back pocket and handed it to her. "Here. Wipe your eyes."

She sniffled, took the handkerchief, and complied. Without looking at him, she handed it back.

"I'm all right. You can go now."

"Huh-uh. I'm not in any hurry."

"Please go," she pleaded. Turning on her other side, her shoulders went rigid and she choked on another sob.

"Huh-uh," he repeated.

Smoothly he lay down beside her, ignoring her gasp of affront. She tried to scramble away from him, but he grabbed her around the waist, pulling her back against him and holding her to his length. Taking advantage of her struggle, he maneuvered an arm beneath her other shoulder and captured her.

As soon as she stilled, he laid his cheek against hers and whispered, "Tell me what's wrong, Sarah. I can't help you if I don't know for sure what's bothering you. And I can't rest easy knowing you're upset."

"Please," she said. "The door . . . anyone could come in. If they find us in b-bed together . . ."

He heaved a sigh of compliance. "Damn it," he grumbled, releasing her and rolling off the bed, "we should have built a separate bedroom on this cabin!"

She rolled over against the far wall, eyeing him warily. "Well, you didn't, and . . . Wyn! What are you doing?"

He laid the whole board across the hasps and turned, quirking a puzzled eyebrow. "Why, securing the door, of course. That's what you wanted before you'd tell me why you were upset, wasn't it?"

"Yes. No! But . . . but . . ."

He sauntered back over to the bed, lay down, and held out his arms to Sarah. "Now, where were we?"

20

SARAH STARED AT Wyn in horrified amazement, until a tear inched through her lashes and trickled down her cheek. Then, giving an agonized sob, she flung herself into his embrace. His arms closed so comfortingly around her, safe and secure. The sensations were illusions, she well knew, but she would foster the illusions as long as she could. Reality would intrude all too soon.

He didn't question her again, only held her. She choked on her sobs for a few brief seconds, then happened to open her eyes and catch sight of the shining row of shoes against the wall. Boys' shoes. Girls' shoes. Young children's shoes and, stuffed in one of the boxes, baby shoes.

Tears drowned her vision and she wailed, burying her face against Wyn's shoulder. Somehow she found his handkerchief in her fist again, and she pressed it against her nose. She couldn't breathe through the clogged stuffiness and opened her mouth to take a breath. Broken words tumbled out instead.

"Hate me . . . never work. So hard. Hurts. Oh, hurts bad! Only wanted . . . oh, their little feet, Wyn! Cold. The snow . . . Wyn. Oh, Wyn, make the hurt stop! Make it feel better!"

Vaguely she could hear his whispers—feel the stroking on her back.

"Shhhhh. Shhhhh, Sarah. Oh, God, Sarah, don't cry. It's killing me."

"Ca-can't stop!"

He gathered her even closer, and she threw her arms around his back, clasping him frantically. She'd never cried like this—never in her life. It hurt even worse than the times her father threw her tentative feelers of love back into her face.

She tried once again to stop, but still couldn't. The few times she *had* cried, in the privacy of her room, she'd never dared show her face until all traces of her breakdown had faded. If she thought she were plain at the best of times, tears left her totally ugly. Thinking of how she would look to Wyn as soon as he saw her now made her cry harder.

Finally, no matter what her thoughts, her sobs abated. She felt wrung out, exhausted, drained. She tried to keep her face buried, but he gently and firmly pulled away from her, scanning her face.

"There's so much hurt in your eyes it breaks my heart," he said. "Is it those damned shoes, Sarah?"

She nodded, crumpling the handkerchief in her fingers, then wiping her cheeks. "I'm sure I look horrible."

"You look sad. Hurt. There's a big difference."

"I should have known better." She pillowed her head on her bent arm and looked into his face, knowing how ghastly she must look but unable to refuse herself the soothing balm of his blue eyes.

"Tell me," he urged.

After a moment of gathering her thoughts, she briefly explained it to him. Dan had chastised her about the schoolbooks to the point where she knew she would be making a huge mistake to offer the children shoes. However, every time she remembered the rows of battered shoes and boots in the cloakroom during the deep snow, recalled the children's chattering teeth and how she would sit them beside the stove until their feet warmed each morning, she knew she had to figure out something.

The group birthday had seemed perfect. On birthdays, children received gifts. No one would be impolite enough to turn down a birthday gift.

But the mountain families had, including Dan. They had taken the shoes as charity instead of the heartfelt gifts she had meant them to be. After she stumbled through the tale of her suffering that morning, her complete agony, as the children carried their shoes up and dropped them on her desk, she brought her downcast gaze back to Wyn's face. The look he gave her in return was troubled rather than understanding.

She dropped her eyes again. "I know I was wrong. I'll . . . I'll send the shoes back on Jeeter's next load. The church can use them."

"Pa and I will buy the shoes off you if necessary."

She lifted her eyes hopefully. "If necessary?"

"I was recalling something the twins asked about this morning. How much the shoes cost, so they could figure out how they could earn them on their own. Perhaps the mountain families would accept some sort of compromise like that."

Her hope fled. "These people don't compromise. It's their way or none."

"Is that how you felt when Pa and Mandy came up with the compromise about the library?"

"Well, no. But that was different."

"How?"

She thought about it. "I don't know. But it has to be, doesn't it? They gave me credit for having a good idea, and came up with some way it could still work, without damaging those overflowing pockets full of pride these people have."

He tenderly touched her cheek. "I think there's a debutante within our midst that has a few full pockets of pride herself. And she's pretty smart. Bet she can come up with something to get her own way."

Sarah pursed her lips, studying him, but her mind drifted.

She started to speak, but Wyn broke in, "The only thing I ask is that you talk to me about whatever idea you come up with first. I'll be candid with you and tell you whether or not it will work, and you have to promise that you'll pay attention to me and realize that I'll only tell you the truth."

Excitedly she sat up on the bed. "I can come up with something. I know I can."

"I would hope so. You've been here among these people for several weeks now. I've met people who could live here all their lives and never be smart enough to understand this way of life, but you are. The reason you can is because you care. You honestly care, Sarah, not just for yourself but for the people."

She reached out a hand and cupped her palm on his cheek. "Thank you, Wyn. That means a lot to me."

"Enough that your thanks might include a kiss?" he asked hopefully.

"Maybe even more than one," she murmured.

When she attempted to lie down beside him again, he stopped her and sat up. Leaning forward, he stared at her for a long, silent moment, his eyes caressing her almost as though he were memorizing her features. Then he tilted his head and kissed her. Very, very gently. Very tenderly.

All too briefly.

When he ended the kiss, she followed his withdrawal yearningly. He tapped her on the lips with his fingertips.

"No. Only one, Sarah. Only one. And only that one because I can't bear to see you unhappy. We'll work this out, Sarah, sweetheart. Get your self-respect back, as well as the respect of the children's parents. Then you can go on back to New York with your pride and esteem intact."

Sarah stared at him with wide eyes. How could he do that? How could he call her sweetheart and in the same breath tell her to go home? But he was right about one thing. Pride filled her own pockets, too, and she would sooner die than ask Wyn why he wanted to get rid of her instead of seeing if they could make a relationship work.

He'd informed her days ago about some heavy thinking he needed to do. Evidently he had done that thinking and she had come up lacking. Or, more to the point, his feelings for her had come up lacking.

Her debacle with the shoes clinched things. He probably realized she would never fit in here without a lot of help and someone overseeing her actions at all times.

He only felt sorry for her right now because she was crying, as any decent gentleman would. He'd made his choice, although putting it that way wasn't exactly right, either. His choice had been made two years ago when he left Rose and returned to his family. Being with Rose would have meant a change in mind, not a choice. She would have meant expanding his life to perimeters he didn't feel necessary. He had his hands full caring for his family. He didn't need to take on a woman who would only cause him more worries and problems.

Until that moment, she didn't even realize she had done her own share of heavy thinking. That she had come to her own conclusions. Didn't even realize exactly what her own doubts were, what her downfalls would be.

His last, brief, final kiss had been an act of sympathy, not shared love. That hurt her more than anything. That pain was deadly—devastating. That pain would carry her away from here as soon as she could go, as soon as she could finish the last three weeks of the school year. That would also be enough time to at least write down all her ideas and the contacts needed to carry them out. The mountain people could either then follow through with her other offers of assistance on their own, which would suit their pride, or turn her down flat, which might suit them just as well.

"Wyn!" Someone pounded on the door. "Wyn, are you in there? Why's the door locked? Miss Sarah never locks the door."

Wyn rolled off the bed and reached down to pull her to her feet. The bedsprings protested the movements, and she realized they'd squealed more than once the last few minutes. She cast an alarmed look at the door.

Wyn gently shoved her toward the stove and washbasin in the other corner of the room. "Go wash your face," he said in a low voice. "The twins are probably here for their evening homework help. I'll tell them I'll help them at the store this evening."

"No!" She wiped her eyes yet again, then continued, "Please. I need to keep busy this evening. I'll go wash my face, but let them in. I'll work with them here."

"If you're sure."

She only nodded, but inside her mind she said, *Oh, I'm sure. Night will come soon enough with all my thoughts tumbling around inside me. I want to put it off as long as I can.*

She wondered if he realized she hadn't promised to check with him before she carried out any more of her ideas.

More than once the next few hours, Wyn wished Sarah had left that evening's tutoring of the twins to him. No customers showed up at the store, and Dan had already stocked the shelves with the latest load of supplies from Jeeter. Wyn wandered up and down the aisles, here straightening a can, there picking up a nail from the floor and tossing it back into its box.

Sarah, though, if she were as unnerved as he, probably welcomed the distraction of working with the twins. It would keep her from recalling her distress over the failed gift of shoes. It would also keep her from dwelling on his blundering attempt to let her know there could never be anything further between them.

He hadn't meant to tell her that way. But he hadn't expected it to come crashing down on him that suddenly, either. He hadn't expected to realize he had fallen deeply, irretrievably in love with Sarah Channing while he stood there and watched her tear-streaked face.

And he hadn't expected to realize how much his love would bring her down, make her suffer, put her through the same type of agony as the shoes had many more times over. Or how much Sarah would be giving up, if he were stupid enough to pursue his quest to make her love him in return.

The problem—the major problem, the one that broke his heart and made him aware of just what he would be giving up in return for his safeguarding of Sarah's heart—was that he was pretty darned sure he could make her love him in return. And he was damned sure he would never love another woman the way he loved Sarah. His feelings for Rose paled compared to the wrenching desire he felt to see Sarah happy and fulfilled in her life.

And that was another major problem. His love, should she return it, wouldn't make Sarah happy. It would make her suffer. His love would turn on him—on them—and he'd end up all too soon aware he was the one responsible for the gold dust fading from Sarah Channing's eyes, leaving them an ordinary, dull brown. The one who caused those firm, beautiful shoulders to bow. The one who stood by helplessly and watched her dwindle into nothingness—watched her love for him turn to resentment.

That happened to plenty of mountain women. Of course, it never happened to his mother, but she'd had his pa's love to lean on. And she was a mountain woman born and bred. She and Mandy, while not born in the Great Smokies, nonetheless came from Kentucky, meeting his pa and Calvin Tuttle when they forayed out from Razor Gully in search of an adventure before settling down for good.

He'd heard the story many times, how Mandy and Maria had left their homes in the Cumberland Mountains and found jobs clerking in a store in Lexington. How they all met, and how all four of them hated the city and came up with the idea of a store and boardinghouse in Sawback Mountain. Each new MacIntyre child had to hear the story as soon as he or she was old enough to understand it.

Near sundown, Wyn's only break in his troubled yet decisive thoughts came when Robert walked in as he was thinking of closing and washing up for supper. His brother-in-law settled on one of the cane-back chairs at the wood stove, which was cold this evening. During the warmer weather, like now, Wyn never lit the stove, but in the winter he and Dan kept the fire hot for the visitors and customers. The spit-cans scattered on the floor had brown stains on the floor around every one of them, but most of the men hit their mark. As well as not drinking, Robert didn't chew, and he nudged one spit-can aside to stretch out his long legs.

Wyn settled beside his brother-in-law, pleased with the

diversion. Sorrowfully, he noticed Robert sat with the scarred side of his face in the shadows.

"Glad to see you out and about," he told Robert. "You've been hiding in that room upstairs for the last two days, when it's been time for you to see people besides the family again. I'm not gonna say your face isn't bad, but hiding isn't gonna make it go away."

Robert raised an eyebrow and shook his head slightly. "I'm not the only one hidin' from myself. At least I've got an excuse. You never know when a customer who's got a young'un with her will show up here at the store. Right now I'd scare the bejesus out of a young'un who hadn't seen me before. Give the poor thing nightmares for months."

"And what the hell am I supposed to be hiding from?"

"Not what. Who. That pretty schoolteacher who's gotten to be Sissy's friend. You know, I never met that there Rose I heard you took up with while you were gone from Sawback Mountain. And since she never had no desire to come meet me, neither, I doubt I'm missin' much."

"Sarah's not really a schoolteacher. You weren't here when she arrived, but I would have thought Sissy would tell you. Sarah's a Channing from New York City. Her father died a couple weeks before she brought Mairi back here, and Sarah's an heiress with more money than every one of these families all put together will see in ten lifetimes. Maybe more even."

Robert let out a low whistle. "Why the hell's she hangin' around Sawback Mountain then?"

"Teaching school," Wyn told him succinctly.

"Well, she's doing a danged good job of that," Robert admitted. "Sissy's already worryin' that we won't have as good a teacher here when Bobbie gets ready for school. That we might get another one like that there Pruneface Elliot!"

"Ah, women always find something to worry about."

"Yeah." Robert gave a wry chuckle. "Trouble is, lots of times they come up with things damned important enough *to* worry about. Then we've got more things added onto our list of worries, too."

Wyn let the silence stretch out for a moment. Then he

said, "I ordered your copper tubing. And this time, make sure you check the connections closer."

Robert grunted, but something about the way he acted bothered Wyn. Everyone knew all along Robert would go back to making 'shine after he failed to find a job up in West Virginia. Robert enjoyed the process and having his whiskey praised by his customers. If Robert could have found a job in Lynchburg or one of the other distilleries, he could have lived his life the way a lot of men only dreamed of doing—making money and supporting their families at jobs they enjoyed.

Yet Wyn somehow sensed this long-standing ache in Robert's life wasn't what troubled him now.

"You been out to the still yet?" he asked.

Robert shook his head. "All I know's what you told me. But I'm going out tomorrow. And I'd like to take your rifle with me."

Wyn got the picture immediately. "I didn't see any sign of tampering at that still. Cabbage has never operated like that before."

"Well, maybe Cabbage thought I was leaving for sure and got a little upset when I showed up back home and opened my still again. But since Cabbage carried me here to the store, and even sent one of his boys after Leery 'cause he knew Doc MacKenzie was gone, I ain't really thinkin' he did anythin' out there."

"Hell, Robert. Just because those footprints I saw out there looked like they were made from newer boots doesn't mean revenuers are snooping around. Pa's sold several pair of new boots here recently. I asked him."

"Can I use the rifle or not? And you might's well go ahead and order me a rifle of my own, next order you send in."

"I'll do that, but you explain your need for a rifle to my sister."

"*No one* will explain anything to my wife," Robert growled. "I'll keep the gun somewhere she won't see it."

"You make damned sure you also keep it where no young'uns will run across it," Wyn snarled in defense of his censure of Robert. "One of them young'uns might be Bobbie. I've been thinking of starting to train the twins on gun safety—Pa always said each of us would learn in time, and Ma agreed with him. But I haven't done it yet, and I don't have time right now. I don't want them running across a rifle and trying to figure out how it works. You can't call a bullet back once it's fired."

Robert surged to his feet. "If I thought I was being stupid, I'd forget about this, Wyn! But the only thing I feel stupid about right now is the thought of going back out there without somethin' to protect myself. And it ain't bein' a coward! My family depends on me to take care of 'em, and I can't do it six feet under!"

"Damn it, Robert! A feud's awful easy to get started in these mountains! I could name you two of them not that far from here that have been going on for a hundred years!"

"Then we'll have to make sure one don't get started in our end of the mountains, won't we?"

Robert stomped off, his boot heels clumping furiously on the floorboards. Wyn had remained in his chair, in a hopeless attempt to defuse the situation instead of pushing Robert into a fight. Now he leaned back and dropped his head to his chest, shaking it back and forth in uneasiness.

21

SARAH WALLOWED IN self-pity for a week or so—
until she realized what she was doing. Then an emotion with
which she hadn't had much experience tentatively poked its
head up. It happened during a restless night, nagging at the
edge of her consciousness until she had no choice but to
examine the puzzle of it.

The closest thing she could ever remember to this
emotion was the way she'd felt when she stormed after Wyn
the day he mentioned the love potion. She had symbolically
left her etiquette book in her little cabin and dared either
Wyn or Tater to make her feel embarrassed over her lack of
manners. Come to think of it, she'd come out on top in that
confrontation, too!

Yes, that unfamiliar emotion was definitely anger. With it
identified to her satisfaction, she found she actually enjoyed
it.

It didn't bother her a bit when she only managed three
hours or so of sleep for the rest of that night. Morning found
her brighter and more chipper, as well as more determined,
than she had been in ages.

She put her plan into motion discreetly, mentally smiling

at one point and thinking maybe she might have made a tactical commander worthy of West Point, had she been of the opposite sex.

Funny, she couldn't even have formed a comment like that in her mind prior to dealing with the mountain people. And deal with them she would. Maybe she would go home with her tail tucked between her legs, as they would say here in the mountains, but it would be because the tail had been singed in the blaze of glory given by her last confrontation with the people of Sawback Mountain.

She didn't tell Mandy of her plan. She played the meek and chastised schoolteacher to the hilt. Perhaps she even overplayed it, because she noticed by the end of that first day, Dan and Mandy were giving her extremely strange looks.

Wyn didn't look at her much at all. Each time she drew near him, she could sense him mentally counting off the days until her school term was over. So be it. She wouldn't crawl to him. She'd crawled to far too many males in her life as it was. If Wyn didn't have the courage to face the problems they would have in a relationship, it definitely wouldn't work. She might as well admit to the failure now.

She sent word of her plan home with the children on that first day, asking them to invite their parents to a competition at the end of the following week. She assured them there would be a written invitation coming home with them the next day, and she made enough copies to send one home to each family and keep her promise. In them, she explained the competition would be much more than a spelling bee. She didn't mention prizes. In her mind, that would be making a tactical error.

On Saturday afternoon, Kyle Jackson arrived. At first, his visit surprised Sarah, since she didn't remember anyone mentioning that he was scheduled for services in Sawback Mountain that week. While she greeted him, she reviewed the cleanliness of the schoolhouse in her mind, but she knew the children had, as usual, left it orderly on Friday afternoon.

And she supposed it wasn't any wonder she hadn't

realized Kyle would be there that weekend. She'd been so busy with her plans she had barely remembered it was Mandy's birthday Saturday, and that she'd been invited to a more special dinner than usual.

Kyle showed up at her door about the time she was due over to Mandy's, offering to escort her.

"I've got a dual purpose for this, Sarah," he said after she asked him in until she fetched her present for Mandy. "This afternoon when I arrived, you seemed awfully distracted, like you had something bothering you. Is there anything you need to talk about?"

"Not of a religious nature," Sarah assured him with a small laugh. "But . . ."

She picked up the present and considered Kyle for a minute. "You're planning on staying here in Sawback Mountain even after you get married, aren't you, Kyle?"

"Definitely. Fairilee's like a rare mountain flower. She wouldn't be happy anywhere else. She'd wither up and die. I don't think my family has given up on me coming back to New York to live yet, but they're going to have to accept it."

"Then you'll have an interest in the schools in the mountains, as soon as you start having children of your own."

"I'm hoping we have lots of them," Kyle agreed. "And I truly have an interest already in the schools, given that they educate the children of my parishioners."

"I didn't think of that. I understand."

Taking the package with her, Sarah left the cabin and waited until Kyle closed the door behind them. On the way to Mandy's she went on, "Will you have time for us to talk a few minutes after supper? There are a couple things I'd like to tell you."

"Of course, Sarah. I'll come over to see you as soon as I can get away."

"Thank you."

They arrived at Mandy's and were engulfed in the huge MacIntyre family. Despite the cacophony, however, Sarah sensed something in the atmosphere. Inside the boarding-house, Kyle took her package from her and laid it on a table in the parlor, where some other wrapped presents lay. Sarah approached Mandy, who sat on one end of the settee, with Dan in his wheelchair beside her.

"Why, Mandy," she said, acquiescing when the older woman took her hand and urged her to sit beside her. "You look absolutely beautiful this evening. And I do indeed feel underdressed."

It didn't seem possible, but the color in Mandy's cheeks heightened. "I'm very happy this evening, dear," Mandy said. "As soon as Wyn gets back, we're going to make an announcement."

"We?" Sarah asked.

Mandy's look at Dan left no doubt in Sarah's mind what the announcement would be.

Dan winked at Sarah and reached over to take Mandy's hand. "You'll have to wait like everyone else," he teased.

Sarah laid a hand on Mandy's arm. "I'm extremely happy for you." She slipped a wink back at Dan. "Whatever the announcement is."

Just then, Wyn came back, with Robert and Sissy along. Robert carried baby Sarah, and Sarah had already recognized Bobbie's voice in the kitchen among the other MacIntyre children's loud noises. Sissy set about rounding everyone up, and Wyn glanced briefly at Sarah, his eyes traveling on to where Kyle stood behind her side of the settee. Then he carried a bottle over to the buffet in the parlor to set it down.

He ignored the two armchairs in the room, instead propping a shoulder against the cold fireplace and crossing his ankles. Robert evidently decided the other side of the fireplace needed his support, imitating Wyn and concealing the scarred side of his face with his stance.

As soon as the children were ushered in and tamed well enough to sit cross-legged on the floor, Dan cleared his throat.

"I guess most of you have probably figgered out already why Mandy and I asked you to all be here this evening."

"Yeah, so we can have some cake!" Jute called. Luke nudged him in the ribs, and Jute gave his twin a surprised look. Some silent message appeared to pass between them, and Jute's eyes grew wide and round, as did his mouth. He glanced back at his father in awe, but kept his thoughts to himself.

"If everyone is paying attention now," Dan said with a tolerant glance at Jute, "I want to make an announcement. Mandy Tuttle has made me a very happy man by agreeing to be my wife. We asked the reverend here to marry us tomorrow."

"Tomorrow!" Sarah shifted to face Mandy fully. "You can't possibly get ready for a wedding overnight!"

"You can for a mountain wedding," Mandy said placidly. "Lonnie's already ridden around putting the word out."

Suddenly Sissy rushed forward and threw her arms around Dan. "I'm so happy for you, Pa. And Mandy." She hugged Mandy and the rest of the MacIntyres finally realized what had happened. The buzz of excitement in the room rose to a crescendo.

Except for Wyn, Sarah noticed. He threaded through the crowd around the happy couple and gave each of them a hug, as well as a brief kiss on Mandy's cheek. Then he casually strolled out of the parlor. She thought to go after him, but Mandy grabbed her arm in a tight hold, eagerly explaining her plans for the next day to everyone.

Guess I could leave now if I wanted to.

Although he'd been trying to keep the darned thought buried, it finally broke into Wyn's conscious mind. It began rumbling around in his subconscious a few days ago, when he became fairly sure his father and Mandy would wed. He had no idea how they would split up the household, but it seemed plausible the girls and the twins would move into Mandy's house with their pa, leaving the living quarters over the store for Robert, Sissy and their young'uns.

Guess I could leave now if I wanted to.

Yeah, he could, *if he wanted to.* The responsibilities holding him here would soon be Mandy Tuttle's . . . no, Mandy MacIntyre's obligations. She'd be a good mother to the girls, and she'd always loved those twins to distraction. She didn't even flinch at Swishy the snake.

He didn't want to leave, however—at least, not permanently. Two years away had shown him his heart and his very soul lay in these mountains—with these people—with his family and friends. Nowhere else on earth could he find such peaceful satisfaction as he did the mornings he sat on the front porch before everyone else was up. Coffee cup in hand, he watched the sun slowly invade the misty distance, bringing to life the view he carried in his mind whenever he couldn't actually see it for real.

He wandered up the steps to the general store porch, then turned opposite the direction he gazed each morning. Sundown was a few minutes past, but the fiery streaks hadn't completely faded. If anything at all was more beautiful than sunrise, it was sunset. Darkening gray clouds interspersed the vermilion and magenta colors Granny Clayborne had somehow managed to capture in the colors of her wool, with the rolling mountain peaks in the foreground of the panorama. The briefness of the spectacle made it that much more special.

And the only thing that could make it even more special would be watching it with a woman he loved. No, with *the* woman he loved, he admitted once again. With the one woman he could never ask to give up her affluent life and live in the mountains with him. Days of wrestling with the problem had shown him there was no solution. No matter how much his heart wanted Sarah, his mind left him no doubt she would come to resent him over the years.

Rose, at least, had been honest enough to tell him she would never make a mountain wife. For her own good, Wyn would let Sarah go. She had another man waiting for her anyway, who was a man of her own social station. A man she had chosen herself, who would suit her much better than a man who had mountain water mixed in his blood.

He didn't know what he would do with his life now. He needed to step aside and let Robert and his father take care of the store. Sure, he enjoyed that, but his pa and Robert would do every bit as well. Pa enjoyed the bookwork and ordering. It would do Robert good to handle the clerking and get over being ashamed of his face. Meeting and dealing with people would help that along. Sissy would be ecstatic that Robert had a legal way to support her and the young'uns.

Finally even the faint tinge of pink in the west faded, and Wyn sauntered over to the far corner of the porch. Shoving his hands in his pockets, he leaned against a corner post. He could always go back to Washington, D.C., and find a job. Despite the near betrothal between him and Rose, the senator and he had parted on good terms. But it wasn't really what he wanted, since it would mean leaving the mountains.

"Meow."

Gray Boy curled around his ankles, coaxing to be picked up, and Wyn complied. The kitten cuddled against his chest, and he stroked the soft fur, wishing it was a heavy mass of gold-brown silkiness instead.

He couldn't decide which stabbed his heart deeper—the thought of some other man burying his face in Sarah's hair while he buried another part of himself inside her, or the thought of another man's child suckling Sarah's breast while she cuddled it as she did baby Sarah. Both of them ranked right up there with the deep agony he would feel every morning and evening for the rest of his life while he watched the sun rise and set without Sarah beside him to enjoy the wonderment.

And the worst agony would be knowing another man had the pleasure for himself. Were he a lesser man, he would accept the few years it would take Sarah to realize she should never have stayed in the mountains for his own. Store up the memories to savor during the bleak rest of his life after she left him.

"But that would be even worse," he told Gray Boy, laying his cheek against the soft fur. "I'd be selfishly ruining the life she already has planned for herself, for the sake of a little time with her of my own. And what if we had children, which is a definite possibility from how bad I want that

woman. It would tear me apart enough when I finally lose
Sarah. To lose our children, also . . ."

He definitely had to leave the mountain, too. With Pa and
Mandy married and taking care of the children, and with
Sissy and Robert a pair, he would be odd man out. His ache
of loss would intensify watching the happiness of the other
couples.

The beautiful day allowed the windows and door to be
opened on the schoolhouse, a good thing since the crowd
overflowed the confines of the building. The same people
who attended the wake came to the church and Kyle raised
his voice loud enough for those gathered outside to hear.
The sermon over, everyone adjourned to the yard in front of
the store. Even though Mandy and Dan sat together in
church, Wyn wheeled his father ahead to the porch to wait
for his bride. Sarah, the maid of honor to Wyn's best man,
accompanied Mandy through the crowd as Tater played a
very adequate wedding march on his fiddle.

Dan had only eyes for Mandy, and when Sarah stepped
aside, the look between the two of them sent a hush over the
crowd. Kyle opened his prayer book, but rather than starting
the ceremony immediately, he waited for something only he
appeared to realize was still to be played out before the first
words could be spoken. Even Mandy gave a slight gasp
when it happened.

Dan braced himself on the arms of the chair. Slowly and
firmly, he stood, all the while keeping his eyes on Mandy.
Sarah saw Mandy's eyes fill with tears, and a film misted
her own gaze. Only a little wobbly, Dan turned to face Kyle,
then reached and took Mandy's hand. Shoulders straight, he
stood there with his bride.

"Dearly beloved . . ." Kyle began.

Sarah glanced across at Wyn in time to see him swallow
and brush the back of his hand against the corner of one eye.
He wore a white shirt and a dark blue, almost black, suit
today, and perhaps one of his sisters had cut his hair. It
gleamed in the shadows beneath the overhang as though just
washed, but now lay smoothly on his neck rather than

curling around his collar. She had rather liked the longer length, but she supposed it only proper that he tame it for the wedding.

He looked at her, then immediately away. But as Kyle continued speaking, Wyn's eyes came back to hers. The blue color was deeper today, almost as though some sort of shadow had passed over the sun. When Kyle cleared his throat, Sarah realized he'd asked Wyn for the ring, and their gazes parted.

Dan's husky voice made Mandy his wife, and she joyfully repeated her own vows. After Dan kissed her and shook hands with Kyle, he carefully lowered himself back into his chair, then pulled Mandy onto his lap. She giggled in embarrassment, but Dan wrapped one arm across her waist to hold her to him and swung the chair around to face the crowd.

"I'm right proud to present to all of you Mrs. Mandy MacIntyre," he called. "Now, let's get some food in our bellies and then kick up our heels and celebrate."

Sarah gave Mandy a hug and Dan a kiss on the cheek, then stepped back to allow the rest of the people to offer their good wishes. She didn't even realize tears were streaming down her cheeks until Wyn silently offered her his handkerchief. She thanked him with a quiet, watery smile.

"Sorry we didn't get a chance to talk last night, Sarah," Kyle said from behind her. "Mandy kept us busy with wedding plans."

Patting her face dry, Sarah turned to face him. "We can talk today. It was a beautiful ceremony, Kyle."

"Thank you." He took her arm and led her toward the steps. "Tell you what. Let's get some food, and we can talk while we eat."

From the corner of her eye, she saw Wyn take a step toward them. However, instead of asking her to eat with him, as she admitted she'd had a faint hope he would do, he only stuck his hands in his pockets and slouched against the side of the store. Sighing in resignation, she went with Kyle, silently rehearsing the plans she needed to let him know about so she wouldn't forget anything. The people didn't want her here, and neither did Wyn, but she couldn't bring herself not to care about them.

It took them a while to get to the food tables, since several parents stopped Sarah to tell her they thought her competition for the end of the year was a good idea. She especially liked the gleam she saw in a parent's eye now and then that made her think the parent was sure their child would win whatever contest she came up with. Finally, though, they managed to fill their plates and find a somewhat private spot beneath a huge oak tree to eat.

"You know you're taking a chance, Sarah," Kyle told her after she'd explained her plans to him. "But I think you're right to at least give these people the opportunity to do these things, and I'll be glad to oversee the plans. It would be better if you stayed around yourself, though."

"I can't, Kyle. And I disagree that it would be better for me to be here. In fact, if there were any other way, I wouldn't even let the people know these were my ideas. I'd much rather they think they came through you, since you have your own contacts back in New York."

"Well, we've got a few days before you leave to work out the details," Kyle mused. "I'd planned on staying around this area for a while to visit some of my parishioners. I'll use Dan's room, since I don't want to intrude on the honeymoon at the boardinghouse."

"Then we can talk in the evenings."

"We'll do that."

Tater's fiddle spoke again, and Sarah glanced up. As at the wake, the dancing followed the meal. She saw Dan wheeling his chair with one arm and dragging Mandy out into the center of a cleared space in the yard. He stood once again and managed several slow, halting dance steps with Mandy, then collapsed laughing into his chair and held on to her hands. They stared into each other's eyes as the space around them filled with other dancing couples.

A mountain man headed for Sarah, and the first thing she looked at was his feet. Indeed, he wore heavy, hobnailed boots. She quickly tried to call up her previous experience and remember how she had learned to avoid those boots. Luckily, Kyle dragged her past the man for the first dance, so she had a little time to brush off that memory before she had to start the quickstepping for that day.

Nonetheless, she managed to laugh and enjoy herself for the rest of the day—on the surface anyway. Since Wyn didn't ask her to dance, at least he didn't ask any other women, either, except for Mandy.

22

$\mathcal{I}$T JUST DIDN'T make sense to her. Mairi turned over for the umpteenth time and scootched her cheek into her pillow another way. Instead of those neat feathers of sleep she always welcomed forming on the edge of her mind, she was as wide awake as when she had gone to bed.

When she flopped over onto her back for the gazillionth time, Pris, who shared the bed with her, grumbled, "Darn it, Mairi. Go to sleep. We've got school tomorrow."

"I can't sleep," she whispered back. "I'm gonna go talk to Miss Sarah, in case anyone wakes up and sees me gone."

"Go," Pris said grouchily. "Then maybe *I* can get to sleep. And don't wake me up when you come back to bed, all right?"

"I'll try not to."

Slipping out of bed, Mairi grabbed the soft housecoat Miss Sarah had bought her in that wondrous New York City store from the foot of the bed and put it on. She cautiously opened the bedroom door, but she'd heard everyone else go to bed a long time ago. 'Course Uncle Dan was staying over at Miss Mandy's tonight, and would be from now on, from what she gathered. Carrie said they were "honeymooning,"

but only snickered and got a sort of snotty look when Mairi
and Pris asked her to explain that.

Well, Mandy had already allowed her and Pris to choose
their own room over at the huge house, so they wouldn't
have to put up with Carrie making them feel dumb much
longer. Once school was out, they'd all move over there,
leaving the space in the store for Sissy's family and Wyn.

And that's what bothered her, she admitted as she made
her way down the stairs and through the store without even
once stubbing her toe in the dark. Out on the front porch,
she paused as Gray Boy meowed and ran to her. The kitten
had recently decided he enjoyed prowling around at night,
although Uncle Dan said he always left the back door ajar
for Gray Boy. Come to think of it, though, with Uncle Dan
over at Mandy's, no one had thought to crack open the back
door.

She picked Gray Boy up, realizing calling him a kitten
wasn't going to work much longer. He was almost as big as
the other barn cats and filled her arms. But he still
understood everything she said to him.

"Cousin Wyn's gonna be staying over here when the rest
of us move to Mandy's," she told the cat. "I asked him, and
he said he'd move into Uncle Dan's room. But then he said,
'just for a while,' and wouldn't answer me when I asked him
what that meant. I was hopin' it meant maybe him and Miss
Sarah would be the next two a-gettin' married, but I don't
think so. Cousin Wyn didn't even dance with Miss Sarah
today, did you notice?"

Gray Boy meowed in response, satisfying Mairi that the
cat was paying attention. Mairi walked out to the edge of the
porch and peered toward Sarah's cabin.

"Look. There's a light on, so she can't sleep, neither. And
when I snuck out of my bedroom, I saw a light under Cousin
Wyn's bedroom door. Let's go talk to Miss Sarah."

She scurried down the steps and ran toward the cabin—
not that she was afraid of the dark here in the mountains. In
New York, she'd never gone out after dark until she ran
away from that home after her parents died. Here the night

sounds were friends. She was only anxious to talk to Miss Sarah.

After tapping softly on the door, just in case Miss Sarah had gone to sleep with the lantern burning, she clutched Gray Boy tightly and waited. Almost as though Miss Sarah had been standing directly on the other side of the door, expecting someone, it opened immediately. Miss Sarah was still dressed, too, instead of ready for bed.

"Oh," she said. "Mairi."

Mairi cocked her head. "Was you expecting someone else, Miss Sarah?"

"No. No, of course not," Miss Sarah assured her. "But what on earth are you doing out of bed so late? Come on in."

Mairi carried Gray Boy inside and set on one edge of the little settee. She waited until Sarah sat beside her, then looked up at her, wondering how to say what she was thinking without hurting Miss Sarah's feelings. She loved this woman almost as much as her mother.

"I . . ." Mairi said the same instant Sarah spoke the same word. Sarah laughed softly and pointed to Mairi to speak first.

"Well, I'm not exactly sure . . . did you ever have a feeling things weren't right, but you just weren't sure what wasn't right 'bout them, Miss Sarah?"

While Sarah seemed to be pondering what she'd said, Mairi screwed up her forehead more, hoping maybe that would help her think and say what she was feeling so Miss Sarah could understand her.

"I mean . . . well, I mean, what I said's not really what I mean. *I* think *I* know what's not right, but it's what *I* think. That might not be what *you* think's not right, Miss Sarah. Is it?"

For a few silent seconds, Sarah looked completely puzzled by Mairi's words, and the little girl searched her thoughts for another way to get her worries across to Sarah. But then she looked away, and Mairi saw Miss Sarah's hands clenched awfully tightly in her lap.

"Things can't always *be* right, Mairi," she whispered. "Sometimes people have to live with their mistakes, as well as live with the reality that some problems are insurmountable."

Mairi kicked her legs back and forth. Gray Boy meowed loudly, and Sarah looked at the cat with a smile.

"I'm glad Gray Boy didn't give up finding someone to help me, even though that appeared to be one of those in-insurmountable problems for a while," Mairi mused. "I could hear mostly what was goin' on that night you found me, but I was too tired to move. I sorta knew I needed to try to find someone to help me, but I guess Gray Boy knew it, too. He meowed at lots of people, but they wouldn't pay him no attention. One man even kicked him. I guess that's why he stayed out of sight beneath the bush from then on. But he kept meowing, till you found me."

Sarah reached for her and pulled her into her arms. The cat gave a muffled meow of indignation and leaped to the floor, where he sat licking a front paw and looking at them as though they needed a good talking-to. Mairi giggled, then ignored Gray Boy and flung her arms around Sarah's neck.

"I'm very, very glad Gray Boy didn't quit trying to get someone to help you, too, Mairi," Sarah said, giving her a tight squeeze. "I love you an awful lot."

"And I love you, too, Miss Sarah. Mama told me once love keeps a-growin', and that the more you give away, the more comes back to you."

"That's true, darling. Your mother was very smart."

Letting go of Sarah's neck, Mairi sat back and pulled her knees up to her chest, wrapping her arms around them. She stuck her tongue between her teeth and the tip poked out her lips, but that didn't help her think much, either. She didn't want to hurt Miss Sarah, but they still hadn't talked about what had kept Mairi awake tonight.

"Cousin Wyn's not sleeping neither," she ventured.

Miss Sarah's pretty eyes clouded, and she dropped her head to look at her hands, which were twisting again in her lap.

"Can I ask you something, Miss Sarah? You don't have to answer iffen you don't want to."

Not looking at her, Sarah nodded that she could go ahead and ask.

"Well . . ." Mairi took a breath for courage. "Do you really wanna marry that Mr. Stephen and live with him for the rest of your life?" She heard Sarah gasp and saw her shoulders stiffen, but she went on. "I guess you might've been all right with doin' that afore you met Cousin Wyn. Mama said something once about people not knowing what they was missin' iffen they hadn't never known nothin' else. She was talkin' about how much she and Papa missed the mountains, and how those people in the city probably couldn't even understand what else was out there. It was right before they decided they was gonna come back here. But they got sick and died instead."

"Oh, Mairi!"

Sarah reached for her, and this time Mairi scrambled onto her lap, snuggling her head against Miss Sarah's shoulder.

"Is it that you gots too much money for Cousin Wyn to be happy with you, Miss Sarah?" she asked, then felt Miss Sarah nod against the top of her head.

"That's part of it," Miss Sarah said.

"That there don't seem a near bad enough problem for the two of you to live apart and lonesome for each other all your life."

"I've been thinking the same thing, Mairi. It doesn't seem proper to me, though, to give away the money. There's a lot of good that can be done with it, and I feel I could decide what good to do as well as anyone else."

"Then that's what you should do, Miss Sarah. And you know what else you should do?"

"What, darling?"

"Tell that there Mr. Stephen to go find someone else to marry who wants to live in that dirty old city with him. That you found you a new home in the mountains that you like better."

"I do believe you're right about that, Mairi."

"Good. Then maybe I can tell you, too, what you should do about Cousin Wyn."

"Do, darling."

"Tell him that you love him and that it's a-gonna be his own darned fault if he lives a lonesome life, when you're waiting with all this love ready to give him. Tell him you're not gonna give up till he stops being dumb and admits he loves you, too. And that the two of you oughtta get married."

Sarah turned her conversation with Mairi over and over in her mind the next few days. She only convened school for half days this last week, both because she needed time to work on her other plans during the day in order to discuss them with Kyle in the evenings, and because Dan had informed her that the children were needed at home now. She had come to some decisions, but for now she would keep them to herself.

Today Jeeter had made his mail run and delivered supplies, and he'd left her several letters. Since the children were already dismissed for the day, she settled at her writing desk to read them. The first couple were from friends, and she set them aside to enjoy later. The one from her attorney was the most important to give her attention to right now. She hoped she could later furnish Kyle with the answers to a couple questions he'd asked.

A moment later, Sarah stared at the letter from her attorney in horror. How could Stephen do something like this? But it sounded *exactly* like something Stephen would do—worm his way into the good graces of her attorney's clerk and ferret out confidential information. Being dismissed with no reference was far too good for the clerk. She dearly hoped the man was blackballed from ever holding another confidential position for the rest of his life!

But she had to decide what to do now—who to tell—who she could trust, even though it would probably mean her own banishment from Sawback Mountain. She would probably never see Mairi again, either, but if she didn't stop Robert's arrest, Mairi would never want to contact her anyway in the future. If she had learned one thing during her sojourn in Sawback Mountain, it was that family loyalty was treasured far above friendship with an outsider.

Kyle was gone, in his usual routine of visiting a parish-

ioner during the day and returning in the evening. Wyn. She
had to tell Wyn. No matter that it would ruin any chance of
even a friendship with the man she loved. She couldn't let
one of his family members, and possibly some of his
friends, go to prison.

Hoping desperately there would be no customers at the
store, Sarah hurried from her cabin, the letter Jeeter had
delivered an hour earlier clutched in her hand. At the
entrance to the store, she hesitated, anxiously scanning the
interior for customers. Instead she saw only Dan stocking a
nearby shelf with cans from the box in his lap.

"You lookin' for Wyn?" Dan asked.

"Uh . . . how did you know?"

"You didn't say howdy to me. Looked like you had
something or someone else on your mind. Wyn's out in the
barn. Alone. All the young'uns are upstairs studying for that
competition tomorrow."

"Thank you."

Sarah hurried on through the store and out the back way.
She rushed into the barn, pausing inside to let her eyes
adjust to the dimmer light. A horse stuck its head over a
nearby stall door, and she recognized the one she'd ridden
into the mountains on her trips to visit the families. It
nickered in greeting, and she instinctively moved over to pet
it.

It smelled like horse, and she identified other odors as her
breathing calmed from her harried rush to the barn. It was
cool in here, and the dirt floor gave off a damp odor similar
to what she'd smelled in the woods the day she and Jute ran
into the skunk. Hay particles floated around in a beam of
sunlight, and her nose itched in response to the sight.

She didn't hear any sound that could be Wyn working in
the barn and wished she'd thought to ask Dan where exactly
she would find him. Not having spent much time in a stable,
she had no idea where to look. She moved away from the
horse, which nickered again in loss, and cautiously walked
deeper into the gloom.

She found him at the back entrance, which opened into a
large corral. Shirtless, he was perched on the top gate

railing, preparing to jump to the ground inside the barn. Her breath caught and for an instant the only thought in her mind was how much he looked like one of the gods she had read about, perhaps the sun god. He completed his leap, then stepped back to put some space between them, reminding her of the much more than physical distance separating them.

"What's wrong, Sarah?"

"I don't know how you knew something was wrong, but it definitely is."

"I could tell by your face. And it looks serious."

"It is. I . . ." She held out the letter, then decided it would be faster to tell him the situation than to wait for him to read about it. "I wrote to my attorney a while back, asking him to let me know what it would take to set up a distillery here in the mountains. I thought it would be much better for the men to brew legal whiskey, the way it's done in Lynchburg, than the illegal moonshine they make now. I'll admit, I was going to finance the operation, but I felt it would be a good investment for me.

"Normally my correspondence with my attorney is completely confidential, and he would lose his license to practice law if he broke that confidence—even if I told him of an illegal situation. I believe it's called attorney-client privilege."

Wyn's face darkened, his eyes searing hers with beginning fury. She had no choice except to continue.

"Somehow my fiancé, Stephen VanderDyke, got the information out of Mr. Caruthers's clerk about some of the men here in Sawback Mountain making illegal whiskey. Stephen has been begging me to come back to New York so we can marry, and evidently he thought he could make me return faster if he sent the authorities in here to arrest the whiskey makers. Maybe he thought I wouldn't pursue the distillery idea if the men I needed to work it were in jail. Who knows?

"Anyway, Mr. Caruthers caught his clerk talking to Stephen outside the office one day and could tell by how furtive the conversation was that the clerk was up to no good. He forced the clerk to tell him what was going on. The revenuers are on their way here now, Wyn. Or they could already be here. Mr. Caruthers got tied up in a personal situation with his daughter, and it was several days before he sent this letter off to me—after he hired a new clerk."

Wyn grabbed her shoulders and shook her, firmly but not so hard it hurt. "Do you have any idea what you've done?" he snarled. "Making illegal whiskey is a federal offense! If Robert's caught, his children will have children of their own before he ever sees them again! And this will kill Sissy."

Sarah shoved his arms from her shoulders and glared at him. "Why do you think I'm telling you this? You can yell and scream at me all you want to after we make sure Robert's safe. And Cabbage Carter and whoever else the federal authorities will be after. Damn it, Wyn! I wrote to Mr. Caruthers weeks ago. They could have sent a spy in here and found out where the stills are and who's making the stuff by now. Or they could have even found out down in Razor Gully, I guess, if some of that illegal whiskey goes down there with Jeeter."

Wyn's guilty look told her she'd hit on a truth, although she had no idea what he could be thinking of. She shook her head.

"Don't these people know how word spreads?" she asked in frustration. "Gossips are all over, and secrets will get out. They have to expect to get caught sometime or another."

"Word only gets out through outsiders," Wyn said in a dead voice. "No one in the mountains would ever turn in one of their own."

Pain singed through her at his unspoken but clear accusation. She determinedly fought it back. "As I said, we can argue about whose fault this is later. Where's Robert?"

"Probably out at his still," Wyn admitted. "And . . . oh, my God!"

"What?"

"The young'uns are supposed to all be up there studying, but I saw Mairi heading off into the woods a few minutes ago. If she's going to see Leery, like I suspect, she won't go

anywhere near where Robert has his still. But if she hears
anything going on in the woods . . ."

"Let's go!"

Sarah picked up her skirts and turned, but Wyn grabbed
her arm. "Whoa! You're not going anywhere. I'll go find
Mairi and send her home. Then go warn Robert."

"The day Jute and I got sprayed, I saw the sun glint off
something way on up the mountain," Sarah told him.
"Copper shines like that, and Mr. Caruthers told me the
most expensive items I'd need in setting up a distillery were
the things made of copper. One way or another, I'll get a
saddle on that horse. I'm going with you to find Mairi, then
I'm going up there to that still!"

"And what if the authorities are already there? What if
you ride straight into a raid and get arrested? I'm sure your
fiancé would appreciate that!"

She shook off his hold. "I'm going, Wyn. If I have to
walk, I'm going. I won't wait here and worry about what's
happening—both to Mairi and Robert."

He stared at her in fury, then sighed in defeat. He whistled
shrilly, and a horse neighed, then Sarah heard pounding
hooves. Seconds later, the horse Wyn usually rode cantered
out of the pasture and into the corral. Wyn caught the halter
and led it toward her.

Less than five minutes later, the two horses were both
cantering up the trail she and the children had walked the
day of their field trip. She hadn't taken time to change, and
Wyn hadn't suggested she do so. That alone told her how
afraid he was that they might be too late. Whether too late
for either Mairi or Robert, she couldn't know for sure, but
perhaps there was no danger yet. Perhaps Mairi had indeed
taken the other fork in the trail, which Wyn had mentioned
while he saddled the horses, and which led to Leery's home
rather than to Robert's still. Perhaps the authorities hadn't
arrived yet, and they could warn Robert and Cabbage in
time for them to hide the evidence of their illegal activities.
Perhaps they would arrive before bullets began to fly.

Heart pounding, she made sure her horse kept pace with
Wyn's. Try desperately though she might, she couldn't keep

the fear from curdling her stomach. She would die herself if anything happened to Mairi, and Sissy would never forgive her if her inappropriate actions sent Robert to prison. None of the MacIntyres would, nor would anyone else in the mountains. She would worry about that later, though. Right now, there was still a chance nothing would happen.

At the split in the trail, Wyn quickly dismounted. He knelt, then pointed at a shoeprint in the dirt.

"She went toward Leery's," he said in a relieved voice.

But some sixth sense told Sarah he'd made a mistake. She looked down the other fork in the trail, pointing at what she saw. "Maybe she started that way, but she must have changed her mind and walked off the path on her way back to this fork. That's the same type footprint over there!"

Wyn stood and, looping his reins over his arm, hurried over to the other fork, the horse trailing behind him. When he straightened with a grim look on his face and sprang into the saddle, Sarah knew she'd deduced correctly.

A gunshot sounded, and Sarah cried out in dread. Wyn's horse was already in a gallop by the time she realized he was leaving her behind. Leaning down on her horse's neck, as she had seen some jockeys do, she hied it after him. She heard another shot as she rounded the bend in the trail where Wyn had disappeared a second ago and caught a brief glimpse of Wyn's riderless horse before her own horse slid to an abrupt halt. Then it reared, neighing shrilly. Sarah landed in a heap on the ground, the breath knocked out of her.

She fought the swirling blackness, struggling desperately to breathe. Interspersed with her ineffective heaves for breath was her terror over what had happened to Mairi and Wyn. But suddenly Wyn was beside her, lifting her into his arms and carrying her behind a barrier of rocks. He laid her down and she gratefully drew in a breath, her vision clearing as she saw Mairi crouched in the shelter. When she held out her arms, Mairi hurtled into them. Then her worried eyes centered on Wyn, crouched beside her, unerringly going to the blood on his forehead.

"My God! You've been shot!"

"No," he denied. "The bullet hit a rock, and a piece flew off and creased my face. Are you all right?"

"I'm fine. What are we going to do?"

"*You're* going to keep your head down and hold on to Mairi. And stay quiet."

Obviously certain she would obey him, Wyn turned from her and crawled to the edge of the pile of rocks. He eased his head around them, and Sarah held her breath, this time on purpose. She hadn't had more than a glimpse ahead of her before she lost her seat on the horse, but she remembered the area from her previous trip. They'd ridden further up the trail than she and the children had gone that day, but the surroundings were similar. Huge pines, oaks, and maples grew thick in places, yet every once in a while there would be an open space. Most of the high banks they rode beside were made of eroded rock, bare to the sunlight that managed to make its way through the trees.

All at once, Wyn scrambled to his feet. "Goddamn it, Cabbage!" he shouted. "It's me! Put that damned rifle away!"

Silence stretched out for several tense seconds, and finally Sarah heard someone return Wyn's shout. "Well, that might be you over there!" a voice yelled, which she recognized as belonging to the man who had brought Robert to the house the day he'd been burned. "But you better hide your ass before whoever's over on the far side of that mountain gets a good bead on you!"

Wyn dropped back behind the rocks a split instant before the next shot rang out. Sarah actually heard the bullet whiz by, sounding like an angry bee. It thudded into a tree behind them, splintering shards of bark over them, and she clutched Mairi tighter.

"My God," she breathed, forgetting for an instant that Mairi would hear her words. "They're trying to kill us."

"Why do they want to kills us, Miss Sarah?" Mairi whimpered.

"Shhhh, darling," Sarah soothed. "I didn't mean that. They're just trying to scare us off—make us go back down the mountain."

"I think we oughtta go, then," Mairi said. "They's got guns and we don't. I was going to see Miz Leery when I heard some people yelling up this way and came here instead. I wish I'd've went on to Miz Leery's."

"Wyn and I will protect you, Mairi. I promise."

"Give it up!" a voice yelled from the opposite side of the clearing from where Cabbage Carter had taken shelter. "We're with the Bureau! Everyone here is under arrest!"

"You heard him," yet another voice called. "Come out with your hands up, you damned hicks!"

Mairi pulled back and frowned at Sarah. "Isn't that your man from back in New York? What's his name?"

"Stephen! It is, Mairi!" Sarah shifted Mairi from her lap. Keeping one arm on the young girl to make sure she didn't move from behind the protection of the rock, she stuck her head up.

Wyn cursed and grabbed her, jerking her back immediately. But this time no one shot.

"Let go of me!" She caught Wyn off guard and pulled away from his grasp to stand up completely. When Wyn started to rise beside her, she gave him an unexpected push with both hands on his shoulders, which knocked him back down. "Stay with Mairi," she ordered, then raced out from the rocks into the clearing.

"Does anyone out there have the nerve to shoot a woman?" she yelled. "Stephen! I recognized your voice. Tell those men you were mistaken about what you thought was going on here. Tell them to leave!"

"Damn it, Sarah!" he screamed. "Get out of there!"

"No! If you know what's good for you, Stephen, you'll do as I say." She quickly scanned the open area in front of her, realizing whoever owned the still had managed to dismantle it and move it before the federal authorities arrived. All that remained was a dark spot where a fire had been built, and a few pieces of scrap wood.

"There's nothing here, Stephen! You were wrong!"

The voice evidently belonging to one of the federal authorities spoke next. "He has the information he learned that he can testify to! We'll call him into court, and that should be enough to send these men to prison."

"Not if he realizes he misunderstood that information!" Sarah told them. "Stephen, I think you better come down here and talk to me!"

"Jesus, Sarah," Wyn whispered loudly. "Get back here and get on your horse. Leave. They won't bother you, now that they know who you are. Your *fiancé* will tell them what could happen if they messed with someone of your social status."

"But they'll bother you," she replied. "And Robert and Cabbage."

"But—"

"Psst!"

Sarah stiffened and cautiously sidled her eyes to the right. Behind a huge tree, she saw Robert.

"Oh, God," Wyn said with a groan. "Get on your horse and get the hell out of here, Robert. They won't know who you are, if you duck down on your horse's neck."

"No," his brother-in-law said. "I won't let you get arrested in my place."

"Both of you shut the hell up!" Perhaps it was her swearing that shocked them, but both Wyn and Robert fell silent. Taking advantage of their surprise, she said, "Don't either of you move."

Mairi echoed her. "Shut up and let Miss Sarah take care of things. Leastwise, they aren't shootin' at *her!*"

Wyn's angry gasp made her smile a tiny bit, and a little of the fear left her as she realized Mairi was right. They weren't shooting at her. They weren't shooting at anyone now that she was standing in the clearing.

"Stephen!" she called once more. "Come down here and talk to me! Now! If you don't, consider our betrothal broken!"

For a long moment, she actually thought Stephen might ignore her. The other man's angry voice ordered Stephen to stay where he was. Finally, though, she saw Stephen for the first time since she'd left New York. He half stumbled, half slid down the side of the mountain across the clearing, at last making his way to the more level ground where the still had been built. She hurried over to meet him, in order to have at least a semblance of privacy for their talk. Wyn let her go without further protest.

Stephen's face was more haggard than she had ever seen it, and it grew even worse as she talked to him. He refused to meet her eyes, gazing past her shoulder and breathing hard, drops of sweat covering his forehead. Only when she got to what she considered the end of the conversation did he face her, a faint hopefulness in his eyes.

"That's all?" he asked. "That's all I need to do, and you'll do what you just said?"

"It's your only chance, Stephen," she told him. "A chance for a clean start. I won't do this again. It's time you grew up and became a man."

"I can, Sarah," he said earnestly. "You'll see."

"No, I won't see," she told him enigmatically. "But I'll do this for you once and once only. You need to accept this and do what I ask, not only for me, but for yourself, Stephen."

He stared at her for a long, heartfelt moment, then nodded and took her hands in his. After squeezing them firmly, he dropped them and called to the man up on this mountain side, "Miss Channing's right! There's nothing illegal going on here. I was wrong. You can go on back to Washington!"

"Damn it, VanderDyke—!" the federal authority began.

"I mean it!" Stephen yelled. "I won't testify against these people. If you try to force me, I'll say it was all a mistake! And Miss Channing and I have enough influential friends to see that you lose your job, if you don't do what I say!"

Sarah held her breath until the man on the mountainside stood. He shook his rifle angrily, then strode on up the mountain. A few seconds later, she heard horses' hooves and caught sight of the man riding away, leading another horse behind him.

"Looks like I need a ride off this mountain," Stephen mused wryly. "He took my horse."

"You can ride down with me," Sarah offered.

Robert stepped from behind the tree, a rifle polished to high perfection in his hands. Stephen gave a start, having caught sight of Robert's face, Sarah was sure. Then Cabbage Carter walked down the hillside toward them. When he reached them, he and Robert glared at one another, but they kept their guns pointed at the ground.

Sarah sensed rather than heard someone else move and saw only the back of Wyn as he left, holding Mairi by the hand. Without a word, he strode over to where his horse had waited nearby and swung Mairi into the saddle before he mounted behind her. Keeping his neck and back stiff, he rode away.

To distract herself from the pain in her heart, she turned to Robert. "How did you know you needed to move the still? That the men would be coming today?"

"We've been seeing some strange tracks in the mountains," Robert told her. "Wyn saw some first and told me about them, and Cabbage came to me last night, saying he had a feeling we oughtta both move our stills. We helped each other do it."

He held out his hand, and Cabbage reluctantly took it. "I still think my 'shine's better'n yours," Cabbage said.

Robert laughed and shook his head. "Looks like we'll both be around to let our customers decide for themselves."

Yes, Sarah thought, *but in another, safer, way.*

She longed to discuss her plans with Robert, but she and Kyle had both agreed it would be easier to talk the men into accepting her financial help if they first heard of the distillery from their minister. She held her peace and looked around for her horse. After she sent Stephen to capture the horse, he helped her mount and climbed on behind her to ride down the mountain. Robert and Cabbage followed, but Cabbage left them at the fork in the trail.

Back at the store, she found all the MacIntyres on the front porch. Dan had a forbidding look on his face, and Sarah gathered her courage again. Murmuring to Stephen to stay on the horse for his own safety, she slid to the ground after Robert dismounted and walked over to assist her.

"Wyn already told everyone what happened," Dan informed her as she approached him. "Then he took off for a ride somewhere. He wouldn't tell me where."

"I'm very sorry this happened, Dan—" she began.

He held up his hand. "It wasn't your fault. Wyn explained things, and it would be a sorry person who couldn't see that you were trying to help, not hurt anyone. 'Sides, Kyle's been tellin' me a little of what you have in mind, and I been agreein' with him. But we'll talk more about that later. Right now, we've gotta get that feller off the mountain afore more folks find out what happened. There's them that will shoot him without blinkin' an eye over what he did."

Sarah glanced back at Stephen, whose face was white with fear as he apparently digested Dan's words. "You're right. And he needs to go now."

Dan took charge, issuing orders in a voice expecting obeyance. "Robert, you get back on your horse and ride with him down to Razor Gully. See he gets on the evening train afore you come back. Best the both of you keep your mouths shut 'bout what happened till he's well gone. Them folks in Razor Gully ain't as quick with their trigger fingers as some of the men up here on our part of the mountain, but the sheriff down there won't appreciate your stirring things up if you let on as to what *he* done." Dan jerked his head at Stephen, an unpleasant sneer on his face.

"The rest of you just pretend we ain't never seen that city feller," he continued. "Word will get out soon enough, but it ain't worth the stir it will cause if he ends up dead. A story like that might hurt the sales of that there liquor we're gonna be famous for."

Dan wheeled his chair around, then disappeared inside the store. The rest of the children and adults followed him, leaving Sarah and Robert the only ones out there with Stephen. Sarah went back down the steps and over to Stephen.

"I hope you understand how much danger you're in until you get out of here, Stephen."

"I do," he said, his fright clear in his voice. "And believe me, I won't say anything, either. Just let me get out of here and I'll forget I even heard of a place called Sawback Mountain."

"Then you better get going." She nodded toward where

Robert now sat on his horse. "The sooner you get moving, the more chance you'll have of getting on the train before anything happens to you."

Stephen reined his horse around, then halted it. His eyes met Sarah's. "I want to say this before I leave, Sarah, even if it means I might be letting danger catch up to me. I always knew I wasn't worth your little finger, and never could see why I was lucky enough to have you choose me. I think what happened today—and seeing you again, knowing what I'm losing because I'm not man enough for you— might make me a better person. I hope so. But whatever happens, I wish you happiness, Sarah Channing. I've never met a woman who deserves it more."

Stephen lifted a finger to his forehead in a salute to her, then kicked his horse in the ribs. A few seconds later, he and Robert were out of sight.

23

"*E*-S-T-A-B-L-I-S . . . UM . . . H-M-E-N . . . T!
Establishment!"

A huge grin on his face, Jute whirled to face Sarah. "That
means a place where folks can buy stuff—like our store!"

"That's right, Jute," Sarah said. "And I do believe that
makes you the winner of this stage of the competition. In
fact, you spelled a word a couple years beyond your grade
level."

Jute grinned from ear to ear, then swaggered back to the
bench where the other students sat. Just before he took his
seat, he placed one hand across the front of his waist and
bent his other arm behind his back. Briefly, he bowed to his
audience. Then he scooted onto the bench and reached into
his lunch pail, pulling out Swishy, much to the dismay of
several young girls near him.

"Miss Sarah said if I made the finals," he told the
audience at large, "I could let Swishy watch me get my
prize!"

Sarah tolerantly nodded her head, then continued with her
competition. They'd moved the ceremony onto the porch of
the general store, since more than just her students' families

attended. She was beginning to realize the mountain people took advantage of anything at all to gather together and visit with each other—a wake, a wedding, or a school competition.

Mandy and Dan were on the porch with her, and Granny Clayborne's wagon, filled with various-aged folks watching the competition, was pulled up in the spot that appeared to be reserved for it. Later today she would tell the elderly woman about the enthusiasm the shawl had garnered among her New York friends, hoping to gain her backing for a mail-order wool business. Mandy had also agreed it was a wonderful idea for the mountain women. It would give them their own way to make spending money for their families, and might just prove more profitable than the distillery.

Wyn was back today, but he hadn't said a word to her. He lingered in the corner of the porch, watching everything that went on. The previous night she had waited until she could no longer keep her eyes open, hoping against hope he would return and come talk to her. But when she heard a horse come in and jumped out of bed to run to the window, it was only Robert. This morning she confirmed with Dan that Stephen had safely made the train.

Finally it was time to give out the prizes for the winners of the competition, and Sarah stepped to the edge of the porch to face the crowd. Sissy had already told her that the mountain people were very proud of what she'd done the previous day, protecting two of their own from the revenuers. For some reason, that didn't matter nearly as much to Sarah as how they were going to take what she did the next minute or two.

"I know you are all proud of your children," she began. "And I suppose just winning and having their names inscribed on the school rolls might be enough for the children. But I prefer for them each to have some tangible remembrance of their wins today."

"Tangible!" Jute hollered. "T-A-N-J-A-B-L-E! Tangible!"

Sarah shook her head and laughed. "Good thing you already won your prize. That's wrong."

Jute's face fell, but then he must have realized that

particular misspelling didn't count, because he immediately brightened. "I'll learn it for next time."

"You do that. Now, as I call each child's name, I want him or her to come up and accept his or her prize. First is Jute MacIntyre."

Jute leaped up again, wrapping Swishy around his neck. He swaggered up to Sarah, and she reached behind her, into a large box. Pulling out a smaller box, she handed it to Jute. He recognized it immediately.

"My shoes!" he chortled. "And I earned them all by myself by winning my spelling bee!"

Sarah's look dared anyone in the crowd to protest the award of the shoes, and for just a bit, her stomach heaved in apprehension. Then Granny Clayborne took her pipe from her mouth and laughed more loudly than it should have been possible for a woman a hundred years old.

"She done it!" Granny said around her cackles. She slapped a hand on one knee. "She outsmarted all of us. She figured out a way for the young'uns to earn them there shoes themselves. Ain't nobody got no right to take away somethin' a young'un earned for itself!"

Tolerant laughter spread through the crowd, and Sarah's heart lightened in the same proportion her stomach unclenched. She knew it was no surprise to the mountain people that each and every child in her class won a pair of shoes, but no one had the audacity to object. Soon each and every child clasped a box holding shoes to his or her chest.

Pride filled Sarah as she concluded the ceremony and tried to hurry from the porch. However Dan moved his wheelchair to block her way. When he nodded in a movement that left her no doubt she had to stand there and listen to him, she complied, though with reluctance.

Dan swiveled his wheelchair around to face the crowd, then stood with Mandy's help.

"I don't think there's anything I can say here that we haven't all thought about Miss Sarah Channing," he said. "She is the finest and most capable teacher it's ever been our pleasure to attract to Sawback Mountain. She's given our young'uns the desire to learn 'cause it makes them happy, not just 'cause they're afraid they'll get a ruler 'cross their fingers if they don't know their lessons."

He turned to face Sarah. "I wish she would take the job as teacher here in Sawback Mountain permanently, but I know—"

"I accept!" Sarah fairly shouted.

Dan's brows lifted, and he seemed at a loss for words.

"You can't withdraw the offer now," Sarah told him. "I accept. I want the job as teacher here permanently, not just on a temporary basis."

A sly grin crawled over Dan's face, and he winked at her. Had she been less observant—or less acutely aware of every faint motion Wyn had made ever since the beginning of the ceremony—she would have missed the faint flicker of Dan's eyes toward his eldest son.

"You're hired," Dan said, and the crowd broke into cheers. Her awareness of Wyn let her know he had thrown a leg over the side railing of the porch and leaped to the ground. He disappeared around the side of the store, and Dan said, "We'll discuss terms later. You go talk to Wyn."

She did. She took the shortcut through the store and caught him as he was passing the back porch. He glanced at her as she raced down the back steps, halting and sticking his fingertips into his back pockets as she approached. A warm glow filled her as she saw how provocative he looked in that stance, but she managed to maintain control of her urgent desire to throw herself into his arms.

"You don't have to worry," she said, thinking all the while she was going to be lying through her teeth with her next words. "I won't bother you. I won't embarrass you by following you around like a lovesick calf."

I will. I'll follow you around until you tell me to leave you alone—that you don't love me. And I don't think you can do that. I know you love me, too!

"I probably should go ahead and leave, but I just can't abandon the children. Since I'll never have any of my own now . . ."

They will be our children, not just mine. She bit back what she supposed the books called a secret smile.

Wyn took a furious step toward her. "What the hell does that mean? You're meant to be a mother, and your fiancé came after you all the way here from New York. He even brought the authorities with him to try to force a situation here and make you come back with him. I'm sure he's waiting for you right now!"

"You're not listening. I'm not leaving. You heard me take the job Dan offered me."

"You've got a fiancé." Wyn spread his hands in a helpless gesture.

Sarah shook her head tolerantly. "Stephen knows our relationship is over. And he didn't come after *me*. He came after my money. He got that, because I told him I'd pay his debts this one time, but after that he was on his own. I'll send my attorney a letter to that effect soon."

Wyn shook his head. "He's an asinine fool. Your damned money isn't nearly as valuable as you are, Sarah."

"Exactly," she said, her lips turning again in that secret smile—not so secretly this time. "And how valuable am I, Wyn? Valuable enough to love?"

"Oh, God, yes. There's no woman on earth I could love more than you."

"Then I lied to you, Wyn. Now that I know you care that much for me, I'm going to pursue you each and every minute I have free. If I thought it would work, I'd crawl in bed with you some night and seduce you to get you to marry me. I love you, Wyn MacIntyre. And you love me, too. Admit it."

He stared at her with so much yearning in his eyes she felt her knees wobble. But then he shrugged his shoulders. "It won't work. It can't."

"No, not if you're such a damned coward!" She plopped her hands on her hips and inched her nose to a hair's breadth from his. "I guess I was wrong! I guess you don't love me. I guess I've made a fool of myself."

Pulling back, she started to turn away to hide the secret smile again, and he did exactly what she hoped. She actually heard his fingertips pull free from his back pockets, and he grabbed her, jerking her into his arms and claiming her mouth before she could say another word.

Not that she wanted to speak. She had her confirmation.

She needed to hear him say it, though, and he complied as soon as he finished kissing her. "I love you, Sarah. We'll make it work. Marry me. Marry me and I'll spend the rest of my life showing you how much I truly love you."

"Yes."

She laughed into his surprised face. "Yes, I said. Did you truly think I'd say no?"

"Uh . . . well, I thought it would take longer to convince you. I thought I'd have to . . . ah, hell. We'll talk about that later. I love you, Sarah Channing."

He swept her into his arms and strode toward the little cabin. Laughing, she clung to his neck and said, "I'm too large for you to carry."

"The hell you are."

"Where are you going then?"

"I'm taking you into that cabin to seduce you. To start filling your belly with our children, although Pa will probably be ticked as hell that he has to look for a new schoolteacher in nine months. And I'm gonna make sure everyone sees us go inside alone, so Kyle will marry us before he leaves after church tomorrow."

"You don't have to blackmail me, Wyn. We'll get married before Kyle leaves."

He carried her up the cabin steps and pushed the door open with his back. "Yeah, I know we will. Because we're not going to come out of this cabin until time for church tomorrow."

He stepped inside and slammed the door with the swing of a hip. The crack of wood hitting wood was loud enough to draw the attention of everyone in front of the store, and Sarah felt her cheeks heat up.

A second later, her cheeks heated from a much more pleasant sensation, and she kissed Wyn back as frantically as he kissed her. She didn't realize they'd forgotten to place the bar across the door until she heard the giggles. Gasping in embarrassment, she sat up on the side of the bed, with

Wyn beside her. Numerous heads poked around the side of the doorjamb, but Kyle was the only one who had actually come inside. He carried his open prayer book in his hand.

"'Dearly beloved,'" Kyle began.